N.J. Fountain is an award-winning comedy writer, chiefly known for his work on the radio and television show *Dead Ringers*. He has also contributed to programmes such as *Have I Got News For You*, *2DTV* and the children's sitcom *Scoop*. He also writes for *Private Eye*.

PAIN
KILLER

N.J. FOUNTAIN

sphere

SPHERE

First published in Great Britain in 2016 by Sphere
This paperback published in 2016 by Sphere

1 3 5 7 9 10 8 6 4 2

ISBN 978-0-7515-6121-0

Typeset in Garamond by M Rules
Printed and bound in Great Britain by
Clays Ltd, St Ives plc

Papers used by Sphere are from well-managed forests
and other responsible sources.

MIX
Paper from
responsible sources
FSC
www.fsc.org   FSC® C104740

Sphere
An imprint of
Little, Brown Book Group
Carmelite House
50 Victoria Embankment
London EC4Y 0DZ

An Hachette UK Company
www.hachette.co.uk

www.littlebrown.co.uk

If you were a tree
I could put my arms around you
And you could not complain
If you were a tree
I could carve my name into your side
And you would not cry
Because trees don't cry.

NEIL HANNON

Monica

I wake up . . .

Monica

I am sleeping on my own tonight; my Angry Friend is awake. Dominic is asleep, and I had to go to the spare room.

I need something, anything, to concentrate on, because I know I will be awake with my Angry Friend all night. So I open drawers. I search through cards, papers, looking for old love letters to reread, and I find the letter at the bottom of a basket.

It is brittle to the touch, even though the date at the top suggests it is only four years old. It looks as though it has been folded and refolded until the paper wore out. It smells odd. A chemical odour.

The paper is decorated in autumn leaves, scattered around the edge. I recognise the pattern. I also recognise the handwriting. It says:

Dear Dominic

I am sorry I have to write this, but not as sorry as I feel that you have to read this. I cannot go on like this. I really do not wish to leave you, but my body is still lying at the bottom of a deep dark hole, and twelve months later, I can see no way of climbing out. When I wake every morning I know I should be thanking the world that I have your love and support, but instead I'm just counting the seconds until the drugs manage to take me back to sleep.

I feel such a burden to you. You are young and can start again. You deserve that chance.

2

By the time you read this I will be dead. Do not grieve for me, for I am now without pain. When we meet again it will be wondrous for both of us.

Yours truly for ever,

Monica

XXX

I don't remember writing the letter; but then, I don't remember lots of things. I just wonder why it's there. I put the basket back in the cupboard and lie back on the bed with the letter in my hand, and wait until morning. *Perhaps trying to focus on the letter will take my mind off my Angry Friend*, I think.

I am wrong, of course.

Dominic lowers his newspaper and smiles at me when I come down the stairs. He doesn't have to ask where I was when he'd woken up alone; he knows the ritual.

'Long night?' is all he says.

'Very,' I say.

He springs up. 'Breakfast?'

'I'll get it.'

'No, I'll do it. It's no trouble.'

'No really, I need to move about. I don't want to sit.'

He pops his bottom lip out. After all these years, he still isn't used to it; the rhythm of chivalry dies hard with him. He instinctively reached for me in the early days after the accident, to comfort me, and he couldn't bear it when I recoiled. His hand used to hover over the small of my back when we walked to the car, not knowing if his touch was a comforting presence or an agonising weapon.

I busy myself in the kitchen.

'Are you going to work today?' I call.

'Yes. I'm meeting with a client. Low-fat spread. They're

3

bored with it being seen as just healthy. They want fun and healthy.'

'Ah.'

'I think we want different things. He wants talking cows that talk like drug dealers and do that twerky dance. I want to punch him. I think we're going to have to meet in the middle on that score.'

Dominic works in advertising. I always think it sounds fun, but if I try talking to him about it for more than a minute he starts to froth around the mouth. I watch him through the door as I make my breakfast. He really is still a handsome man. I remember when I had friends, and we used to get invited to dinner parties, and I saw them with their husbands, and I was shocked by how quickly the men expanded like balloon animals from year to year, big round ugly things with huge bellies and no necks.

Sure, he's put on a bit of weight, I think, *that's to be expected. He spends a lot of time parked behind that computer.*

But his hair, even though grey, is still recognisable from our wedding photos. He hasn't lost a lot of it, from the front, anyway, and his face, though *very* round now, still has an impish, cheeky youthfulness.

I make my breakfast and lower myself into a high-backed chair, one of the ones we have bought since the accident.

'I was in the spare room, just going through things, trying to take my mind off, as I do . . .' I am trying to keep my voice casual. 'When I came across this . . .'

I put the letter on the table between us. He makes a big play of reapplying his reading glasses to his nose, and unfolds the frail piece of paper.

He takes a long time to read it; far longer than it should have taken. He eventually puts the letter down and removes his glasses, plopping one of the arms in his mouth, and he makes a quizzical expression.

4

'Yes?'

'Well, I just wondered if you could talk to me about it.'

'What would you like me to say?'

'Um ... Everything?'

'Oh.' He looks down at his crumb-laden plate, and then looks up again. 'It was about four years ago ... Before we got the drugs right.'

'OK.'

'... Well, you were lying on the floor all the time. You couldn't bear to be touched. You couldn't comb your hair. You couldn't take a bath ...'

'I remember all that, Dominic, tell me about the letter!'

My Angry Friend makes me speak sharply. He picks at the loose threads of my mind and unravels my patience. Dominic raises his eyebrows, but he doesn't comment on it.

'You hadn't slept in days, and it didn't look like things were ever going to get any better. I popped out for a few minutes, just to get a paper, and you'd written the note and left it on the table.'

'I'd tried to commit suicide?'

'You were going to try. You'd crawled to the cabinet and got the pills out; you said you were going to overdose but you must have passed out.'

'Jesus. I'm sorry you had to come home to that.'

He flinches when I say 'Jesus'.

'I was just glad I came home early, and found you when I did.'

I pick up the letter. 'I must have been in a very dark place.'

'Very. But you're not there now.'

He pushes his hand across the table, trying to reach my fingers, but I'm slightly too far away.

'It's just odd,' I continue.

'What's odd?'

5

'Well . . . What's it doing in the box?'

He returns to his newspaper. 'Why shouldn't it be in the box?'

'Keeping an old suicide letter. It just doesn't seem . . . well, it just doesn't seem right.'

Dominic looks like he's thinking.

'Why not?'

'It just doesn't. It feels freaky.'

'I think you wanted to keep it, because you wanted to know how far you'd fallen. You wanted to look back on it and say "at least I'm not there now".'

I think about this. 'That doesn't sound like something I'd do.'

He shrugs. 'Well, that's what you said, or something like that.' He goes on, 'I didn't think it a good idea at all. I said you should destroy it, but you didn't want to.'

I look at the letter. 'Well, I don't know what I said then, but I don't want it now. Frankly, it makes me feel ill.'

Dominic shrugs again and holds his hands up in surrender. 'Well, that's fine too. Shall I tear it up now?'

'Ah . . . Yes.'

'Sure?'

'Yes. Definitely.'

He reaches across and takes it, and tears it precisely in half, and then in half again, carrying on until there is a little pile of peach confetti on the table. Then he brushes the bits off the table into his palm, and walks to the downstairs office, and empties his hand into the waste-paper basket. Then he goes back to the paper, without a single word. I have been married to him for ten years now, and I know when he gets grumpy and he's not reading the paper. He's just staring at the black shapes of the words, waiting for his temper to subside.

So I eat my muesli, and he simmers down, and the pages of the

6

newspaper start to turn again, and we don't talk about the letter again that morning.

And that, I thought, was the end of the matter.

Monica

There are whole months that are a blur to me. That's the thing about my life. My pain consumes half of my mind, and the drugs that deal with the pain consume the other half.

Whole sections of my memory got shut off. I can't remember places I've been to and books I've read.

And – and this is the really tragic thing for me – I can't remember a life without pain.

I don't remember the tune Dominic and I listened to on our honeymoon in Egypt. I had signed my name 'Monica Wood' in the hotel register, still practising my signature, and we'd got room service to change the pillows because I'm allergic to feathers.

We had a meal by candlelight in the open air, and the stars were very clear and very close, and there was a dreadful violinist who moved between the tables of the restaurant and only played one tune and wouldn't leave us alone, and had us in stitches all night.

Dom laughed so much in the room afterwards he had a nose bleed.

When I realised I couldn't remember what tune the violinist played, even though we heard it dozens of times, I panicked and started crying uncontrollably. It was just like that

7

Christmas Eve when I was a little girl, tucked in my bed, and I couldn't remember the name I was going to call the rabbit I was getting from Father Christmas in the morning, and I cried because I thought I had lost the name for ever. My mother sat on my bed, and stroked my hair, and told me I was going to call it 'Jumpy'.

I was lying on the floor, a year after my accident, and I realised I couldn't remember the tune the violinist played, and I sobbed. I must have sobbed, or made some kind of noise, because Dom came rushing in from the kitchen, his hands still wet from washing up. He knelt on the floor, bending over me, asking me, 'What's wrong?' The silly things we say sometimes. Something is always wrong. We both know that. The question should have been 'What's *more* wrong?' but that just sounds silly. We both knew what he meant.

I told him about the violinist; and that I couldn't remember. He told me the tune was the theme music from *The Godfather*.

'That's why we were laughing so much,' said Dominic. 'He played it so many times, and it was meant to be romantic but it was so sinister. And I said he must have really done his research, because he knew it was your favourite film, and he was going to play the tune as many times as you'd watched it, and that ... that made us laugh even more. We shook the bed until two o'clock because we couldn't stop laughing.'

The Godfather.

I clutched at the piece of information like a drowning man clutching at a piece of driftwood. I was still thinking of *The Godfather* when the cocktail of painkillers started to send me to sleep.

Then I was crying again.

I realised I couldn't remember seeing *The Godfather*, or anything about it. Even though Dominic told me it was my favourite film.

Monica

Dominic has always been brilliant. He has treated my pain like a crusade. Like it was a mission from God. He would heal the sick.

He would make the lame walk.

He would cure me.

He scoured the websites and periodicals for new drugs, new treatments. It was Dominic who found out that Gabapentin was becoming Pregabalin, even before my pain specialist.

Gabapentin was this drug that I took at the beginning, before there were drugs for chronic pain. Gabapentin wasn't for pain relief; it was designed for epileptics. It was engineered to cut off certain signals to the brain, to stop sufferers flailing about.

In short: it kind of worked, but it made me imagine the wardrobes in my bedroom were trying to eat me, so it was counter-productive, to say the least.

But it was Dominic who found out that they were refining the part of the drug that dealt with the pain centres of the brain, and this meant, finally, that

a) I could speak, get out of bed, wipe my bottom, etc., and

b) I could go to the window without trying to jump out of it.

But no drugs are that specific; no drugs just do that single thing that they're supposed to do. There are always side effects, hallucinations, paranoia. The particular combination of drugs I'm on now have erased a huge chunk of my memory, from way way back at the start of the accident, when things were very very bad.

The mind – and the body – they both have ways of surviving. They shut down the horror and carry on.

It can be frustrating, sometimes. My mind is like the suicide note; folded and dog-eared until the words are hard to make out, and now ripped into shreds.

But there are still fragments.

Monica

I wake up . . .

. . . Not good today.

I open my eyes and my Angry Friend's sitting on my chest, gnawing at my innards with his incisors. My own teeth have been trying to grind together all night, and they've been mashing against my mouth guard.

This means the muscles in my neck have tightened into rock-like sculptures.

This means the blood to my head is constricted, and a searing headache is lancing into my right eye.

This means . . . It's an average day in the life of Mrs Monica Wood and her Angry Friend.

My phone beeps, and beeps again to remind me that it's just beeped. I moan as I know I have to move to reach it. Groaning. Gasping. My fingers fumble over the bedside table and the phone tumbles to the floor. Even the *flumph* as it hits the bedroom carpet sends shudders into my body.

Shit.

Straining. Stretching. Pushing the covers back. Sometimes they're too heavy for me to move and I stay there, entombed like a dead Pharaoh. Willing myself to stand up. Then willing myself to bend down.

11

It's another text from Niall. U ok? Niall xxx

It's his fifth U OK? text this month. I haven't replied to any of them yet, because they all arrived at bad times, when the tips of my fingers couldn't bear to make contact with the phone screen. And when the pain had not been so bad, my mind erased the memory that I got a text, and I only remembered again when the agony in my fingertips reminded me.

I think about just replying *No, that is y I'm not replying. Go away.* But he's a useful person to have around. I think about replying politely but I don't even have the energy to do that. I have to look after myself today.

So I send nothing at all, and concentrate on getting downstairs.

Men always find ways of not speaking, do you notice that? Anything to avoid words. It's like their mouths are permanently on low battery. For example, it would take words for Dominic to ask 'Is it OK to hug today?' Instead, he has developed a habit, call it more a *strategy*, so when he leaves for work he just plants a kiss on my forehead like I'm eight years old.

It really irritates me, but we've argued about so many little things in the last five years I let some of them go, which is bad, because when you've got chronic neuropathic pain, it's the little things that matter; like me being left to carry the towels downstairs to the washing machine, like him buying the big cartons of milk, the ones I find impossible to lift.

So he goes to work, and I'm left alone with my Angry Friend.

I don't know why I created a character for my pain. It's just another thing I can't remember. It doesn't sound like something I would come up with on my own. Perhaps it was Angelina's idea to humanise it, so I would have someone I could swear at, someone I could blame for all the shit I endure every day.

Perhaps it was Dr Kumar's suggestion, that it's an established medical thingummy that's been scientifically proven to ease the psychological pressure on blah blah blah. Whatever. Sometimes it works, and I can laugh in the face of my Angry Friend, and sometimes he's laughing in *my* face, and I wish he'd never been born.

Sometimes, like today, my Angry Friend has me by the throat.

It takes me a long time to get dressed. I'm hobbling about like an old woman because my toes have curled over, cowering under my feet, and I have to prise them free, one at a time.

I avoid a shower because I'm worried about slipping and hitting my head on the edge of the bath. It's happened before. The nights without sleep can take its toll, and this is definitely one of the woozy days.

I sit in the study, starting work with a cup of tea and my first collection of painkillers for the day.

I used to be a theatrical agent, an incredibly successful one. That's why I'm lurching around a very expensive house in North Kensington. I did flirt with becoming an actress once, and I went to drama school for a year, but I soon realised that sitting round waiting for things to happen and smiling prettily at idiotic leading men wasn't my style.

I set up a small office in Soho, and within five years you couldn't watch a drama or comedy on television without seeing one of my clients. I represented half of the cast of *Chucking Out Time*, the British romcom that stormed through multiplexes a decade ago.

Well, to quote a Coldplay song: 'That was when I ruled the world.'

I was invincible then, and producers and directors quaked and fawned in my presence. I earned much more than Dominic; it was incredible to think that he and I once talked about him escaping his miserable existence in advertising and becoming a house husband.

And then the accident came, and I couldn't walk, or stand up, or think, and I stopped being a theatrical agent very quickly.

And now Dominic is our sole breadwinner, and we can barely make ends meet. Scrub that: we *can't* make ends meet; his wage is pitiful, and the mortgage is being paid off with the interest from my savings account, which is getting smaller all the time. Less savings, less interest, no mortgage payments, and then ... What then?

So now, to stave off financial ruin and homelessness, I'm trying to be an agent again. It's early days (well, actually, two years) and it's a slow painful process (ha ha).

I only have two clients at the moment: a retired stuntwoman who is usually billed as 'Old Lady Who Falls Into Hedge' in the credits of sitcoms; and Larry, an extremely thuggish-looking man with a dubious past who makes a lot of money playing tough guys in films and detective series. They don't need an agent; they can make a good living without one. I need them more than they need me, but the one thing they have in common are hearts of pure gold. They know my situation and are very happy for me to take their calls and my 15 per cent commission.

I go into my side of the computer. My picture has a photo of a sunflower on it, and underneath there's a white box, waiting for my password. I type in 'Dominic'. *Peck peck peck peck peck peck peck.*

Soon I'm staring at my emails, waiting for one of them to make sense. I try to reply to one.

Deer Sir, I type.

Pleese find inclosed my cliant's invoice. Payment can be transferd directly to the company account via baCKS. If you wich to send a chek you may do so at the address below

Half of the words have little wiggly red lines under them. I know what I've written would make the eight-year-old version of me giggle, but I just can't form the correct spellings in my head any more; just like I sometimes can't form words when I speak.

I try to click on spellcheck, but my arm goes into spasm and I spill the tea all over my white T-shirt.

I strip off like a demented hooker, throw my shirt into the wash, and go and get paper towels. Thank God none of it went on the keyboard. I throw one of Dominic's baggy T-shirts on, then lower myself slowly onto my hands and knees, tears springing into my eyes, and try to wipe the floor around the desk. I'm on my hands and knees when I have another spasm, my arms go from under me, and I pass out, colliding with the floor.

I regain consciousness.

Ow. Ow ow ow.

I could have been out two minutes, or the whole morning. From the sunshine hitting the blinds, I'm guessing I wasn't out long. I realise I can't get up.

The tiniest movement makes my vision darken, the heat surges, and I start to fall down the rabbit hole again. I'm stuck down here for the duration.

I lie on the furry rug, placed here especially for days like these. After a while, the cold of the marble floor seeps through. I have nothing to do but wait. My eyes are pointing under the desk, fixed on the dormant radiator, the dust and the spiders.

I must get Agnieszka to hoover under here, I think.

Then the phone rings. And rings. And rings. Even noises are hurting me. I have to stop it. I pull an arm out from under my body, and tug at the telephone cord until it falls off the desk and hits me.

Ow.

That's so funny.

More pain.

15

I stretch out across the floor and I wrestle with the receiver.

'Hi, sis.' It's Jesse. Her dutiful, weekly call.

'Hi. Jesse. Good to hear from you.'

'You sound different.'

'I'm having a little lie-down.'

'Good for you.'

I have no wish to tell my sister what's happened. She never understands, she'll just freak out and send an ambulance or something.

'How's tricks?'

'Tricks are fine. How's yours? How's work?'

She goes into a ten-minute diatribe about the stupid owner of the restaurant and how she won't change Jesse's shift. Jesse is a chef, a good one, and having a job where she hides in a back room and shouts at people is a great fit for her, but it's not good for nurturing her minimal listening skills.

I'm just lying there, holding the phone to my ear. I can't move my head, so my vision is trained at the waste-paper basket. I can see the little bits of the letter through the wire mesh.

There, hanging on the edge of the basket, is a tiny fragment. The word 'burden' is intact, perfectly preserved on this little piece of paper. It dangles above me, twisting in the breeze from the open door.

Jesse gets to the climax of the story, where she threatens to leave and the manageress falls to her knees and begs her to stay, if only for the sake of the day's specials, and I'm watching the tiny piece of paper dance.

'How's your back?'

I fight the urge to sigh. 'There's nothing wrong with my back. As I keep saying. I have pain that originates from my damaged sciatic nerve.'

'The one in your back.'

16

'If you like, attached to somewhere near my back.'

'So I was right to ask you about your back. Because I just read an article on BBC online. They got this woman with a completely severed spine, like completely literally severed, literally, you know . . . '

Not again.

'Like there's not even bits of muscle holding it together, and she looked really awful in the photo, with the neck thing, like Christopher Reeve had, and guess what? They built her a new one, a metal one, more aluminium, really. She's windsurfing again. Her dog's really happy about it.'

'And how does that help me, actually?'

'Well, it just goes to show—'

'Yes, Jesse, it just goes to show how surgery to mend spines is coming on in leaps and bounds . . . '

'Exactly.'

' . . . But the accident injured my sciatic nerve. It's the place where all the tiny nerve endings join up, like a central processing unit in a computer.'

'I know what a computer is. Don't patronise me, Mon.'

'I'm not patronising you.'

'Mon, I'm a chef. I know what patronising sounds like. That's what I do.'

'All right, whatever. So my sciatic nerve got injured in the accident and it's gone a bit crazy, and even though the pain of the accident is gone, it doesn't know that. What it's doing now is randomly sending messages of pain to all parts of my body and there's not a damn thing any surgeon can do about it.'

'Yes, but . . . ' Jesse was like a dog with a bone. No one told her she was wrong; no one told her how to run her kitchen, or how to run her life, or how to run *my* life. 'It's all the same thing. Surgeons can do miracles now . . . '

How many times have we had this conversation? Who was the one with the memory lapses, my sister or me? The muscles in my neck are really bunching together now, they're squeezing tighter, and the headache is howling around my brain. *I need Niall. I need him right now.*

'They can't do miracles on me. Look, working on a spine is easy in comparison; like fixing the axle on a car. Fixing the nerves in the body is like trying to change the colour of a red car to blue by agitating the paint job with a blow torch.'

'Good image.'

'That's my pain specialist for you. On my first appointment, he quite cheerfully told me that they'll be happily mending spines and making the paralysed walk, decades before they even start to understand how the nervous system works.'

'Oh.'

'So he told me the chances that a new surgical procedure would come along and help me are minimal. So I'm really happy for the windsurfer, and I'm really happy for the dog, but—'

'Your pain specialist told you that on your *first* appointment?'

'Yes.'

'"Minimal"? he said that? "Minimal"? His exact word?'

'Oh yes. I remember that word. When I forget my own name, the word "minimal" will be burnt on my cerebral cortex.'

'That was a bit shitty.'

'Well, he believed in being upfront about these things.'

'I'd hate to be on a first date with him. God, can you imagine. "Jesse, I'm going to level with you, I'm a doctor, so even if you skip dessert, the chances of you losing weight in order to be sufficiently attractive for me to want sex with you are *minimal*..."'

I laugh, and it encourages her.

'"And to be utterly frank, Jesse, even if we do have sex, I have to tell you that my chances of making you come are not good. I'm sorry to inform you that my penis is completely *minimal* . . ." '

I'm laughing a lot now, and it's jolting me, but I don't mind. I'm glad she's phoned. It takes a while to get to that point, but I always end up glad.

Half an hour later, I hear the key in the door. Of course, it's Wednesday.

'Got to go now, sis, cleaner's here.'

High up on the window sill is a photo of Dominic and me, and I can just see it. There we are, perpetually dressed for our wedding in Dunfermline. Our sunny smiles are plastered on our faces, daring the cold and the wind to blow them both away.

With us is my mum (ten years dead) who is standing warily next to Dominic. I'm with his mum (six years gone) and his dad (still hanging in there, sulking in his decrepit cottage in the Highlands). Jesse is not there. She couldn't make it for some reason, lost in the mists of time.

Every time I look at that photo I hope to see Jesse in the background. Sometimes, I even see her paying a visit.

Like now.

She wanders into the photo holding a big hat on her head with an apologetic sorry-I'm-late expression on her face. She kisses Mum hello and takes her place next to me, throwing wary glances at my new husband.

She waves at me. Not the me in the picture wearing the wedding dress, but the me slumped on the floor.

'I can't wave back,' I find myself saying. 'My arms can't move.'
Damn! I thought I would be over this by now.

Monica

Agnieszka is, inevitably, from Poland. She is an excellent cleaner, young, bright, friendly and efficient. Thankfully, she is also very strong.

'Meeses Wood? Moaneeka?'

'In here, Agnieszka. I'm down here.'

She sees me, gasps, presses her hand comically to her mouth, and explodes with all manner of foreign oaths. She rushes towards me and her strong arms carefully lift me into a vertical position.

My nose is pressed into her large bosom and I smell lilac. I know she is being careful, so I try not to scream, but to my shame I fail, and the distress on Agnieszka's face at the noise is one more knife to add to the collection of daggers inserted into my body.

'Meeses Moneeka, you not good today! You go to bed, sleep, get rest!'

'No, Agnieszka, I fine.'

'You not fine! You on floor! Is not fine!'

'Just a silly fall. Pain not too bad. I not go to bed. I will be OK, no rest, really.'

It always amuses me that I fall into this silly cod foreign accent when I talk to Agnieszka. It doesn't belong to any particular country, and it probably makes it more difficult for her to understand me.

'I be in kitchen, now, I clean, if you need, I come, OK?'

'OK.'

'You promise now?'

'I promise.'

She won't leave me alone, even though I try to bat her away. In the end I assure her I'm absolutely fine now, and I allow her to make me a cup of tea I don't want, in exchange for some privacy.

I listen to her scuttle around the house, dusting and hoovering. I was hoping to go out today, but now I'm trapped in the office, the only place where she's not allowed to dust.

I want to go back to bed, but she'll be changing the sheets soon, so here I am, a prisoner, sitting alone in the office, teeth chattering with the pain.

I look back at the photo. Jesse is gone, of course.

I make a few calls, and then Agnieszka says goodbye, and my body tells me that's the end of the day. I realise I never showered this morning, but I don't have the energy to have one now, even though it would make me feel slightly better.

Then the day is over.

I'm lying on the bed in the spare room, and the room is nearly dark when Dominic comes home. Today I've swallowed a ton of Lyrica (which is the pretty corporate name for pregabalin. I guess someone in Marketing realised that a drug that sounds like it's the literal transcription of someone having a gibbering fit would be a hard sell, so it's 'Lyrica' now, which I think is something you might call a 'Hits of Vivaldi' CD) and it has side effects. Did I mention all my drugs have side effects? Yes, I think I did. Lyrica's little trick is that it enhances all my senses: sight, smell, taste and hearing. In my head everything sounds noisy, like I'm in a horror movie where they've turned up the sound effects. Every broken twig is a pistol shot; every ticking clock a klaxon of mortality.

From my room I can hear the rattle of Dominic's keys in the door, his feet huff-scuffing on the mat, the tired flap of the umbrella (has it been raining?) and the kitchen noises as he makes a cup of tea.

He used to look for me straight away if I wasn't there to greet him, running around thinking something awful might have happened, but now ... I suppose you get used to everything, even the most

21

gut-wrenching of fears. I remember when Jesse had her first baby. 'Those first few days I couldn't sleep, I didn't dare,' she laughed. 'I was listening for the breathing all the time, waiting for the noise to stop so I could leap into action and save my baby. Two weeks later and we're lying in bed, and we're praying for the little bastard to stop screaming and shut up.'

I wonder if that's what Dominic feels about me, sometimes.

Eventually, I hear the door creak open.

'You awake?'

'Yes.'

'Bad day?'

'Yes. I'm afraid so.'

'Sorry to hear that.'

'Thanks.'

'You want anything? Something to eat?'

'No.'

'Drink? Cup of tea?'

'No, thank you.'

'Have you taken your drugs for tonight?'

'Yes.'

'Do you want the telly on?'

'No, thanks. I think I'll try and get some sleep.'

'OK. Love you lots.'

'No, love *you* lots.'

'You hang up.'

'No *you* hang up.'

'No *you* hang up.'

'No you—'

'Brrrrrrrrr.'

Happy that he has left me smiling, he closes the door and goes downstairs. *Thud thud thud.*

Twenty-two *thuds.*

22

I know, because I count them every time. Then the television switches on and the microwave goes ping. I'm still awake when the twenty-two *thuds* go upstairs and our bedroom door opens and closes.

The hours pass, and I'm still lying awake. My super-hearing means I'm forced to listen to the clunks and gurgles the house makes at night, the scurrying animals in the garden and the cars on the road. The drugs designed to help my pain make it harder to sleep, and being sleep-deprived makes it much harder to combat the pain.

My life is built on solid irony. They are the foundations of my existence.

But finally, before I realise it, I have fallen asleep, a tiny fragment of orange paper nestled in my hand.

Monica

I wake up ...

... I feel much better today.

The sleep has done me the power of good. Dominic notices the change in me, and he looks (**relieved**) happy. He even gives me a tiny hug when he kisses my forehead goodbye.

The fragment of paper was still in my hand when I woke up. It never stood a chance to escape. The pain makes me clench my fists so tight during the night I sometimes end up with fingernail marks on my palms.

I leave the paper in a matchbox in the drawer. I don't know why. I keep sliding the box open and shut to see if it hasn't vanished like a magic trick.

Open ...

burden

... and close.

Open ...

burden

... and close.

I do it about twenty, thirty times, stuck in some kind of time loop. Something about the bit of paper bothers me. It smells funny. It looks wrong. But it could just be the drugs dancing around my brain, creating a distorted view of the world.

Enough now. I feel good enough to leave the house. I can't waste the day.

I'm *definitely* going to Westbourne Grove. That is my solemn pledge to myself.

Another text from Niall. This time the U OK? has three question marks and four kisses. This time I reply NO BUT GETTING THERE! Mx (thank the good Lord for predictive text) and I get a :) in return. I hate those upended smiley faces people put in text messages; they look like the lopsided, dead smile of someone who's fallen and broken their neck.

So after breakfast I'm in the car, driving, off to see one of my friends (**my only friend**). OK, I admit it, my only friend. Apart from my Angry Friend, of course. He always stays around.

Most of my friends have gone. Of course they have. Why would anyone be my friend? The only conversations are the ones that go nowhere; they used to talk to me about my nerve pain, as concerned friends, and they inevitably used to ask what it felt like, and I inevitably used to tell them it's like red hot needles under my toenails, or spears in my side, or like being kicked and punched all night, and they inevitably used to say something like:

'Oh well, at least it's not like you're *literally* getting needles under your toenails/spears in your side/kicked and punched.'

Then I inevitably used to say they were wrong, and talk about the physical effects of constant pain, and then their eyes used to glaze over, and then I stopped talking about it, and then I would pretend I'd stopped thinking about it.

I ended up pretending (**lying**) to everyone, all the time. Well that's bound to erode any friendships. I'm lying to myself too.

I have to.

I'm pain in pain the car, breathe, smile, relax, driving to Westpain Grove. I tell pain myself I am being painanoid. It's inevitable. Pain, breathe, relax.

There must be a simple expaination. Breathe, smile, relax. Pain consumes everypain, paincluding my pain mind smile, breathe and relax more often than pain I pain up alone inside my pain pain pain breathe, smile, relax . . .

I lie to myself that those things aren't in there.

I drive on to Westbourne Grove, street signs and cars flashing past me (**every obstacle is a way to end my life**) as I drive.

Angelina is different. She listens, and because conversation to her is like a fair exchange, I tell her about the gnawing pain in my face, and the crippling electrical shocks in my thighs, and she tells me about her night of disastrous sex with a t'ai chi instructor with mirrored ceilings, or her ex-boyfriend in the city who once suggested a threesome with his wife.

'Fair exchange is no robbery, sweetie,' she says, and I'm pitifully grateful she lets me speak of my life without feeling guilty.

When I text her to say I'm coming over she replies with OMG!!!! We haven't seen each other in a while, so I guess we're both excited. Westbourne Grove is only ten minutes in the car, but for me it might as well be in Japan. It's been months since I had the strength to come out this way.

My hands are almost shaking with the prospect of meeting actual people.

I park the car as near as possible to Angelina's art shop, and inch my way out of the driver's seat. There is a woman watching me, sitting on a bench. She is in her seventies, bundled up against the summer breeze, and using her *Daily Telegraph* as a windbreak. Her expensive coat and silk scarf cover most of her face, but her eyes are fixed on mine, and they are looking at me with unvarnished disgust.

I'm used to it by now. Old people glaring at me with righteous indignation. What they see is a very attractive middle-aged woman, dressed in expensive designer clothes, wearing stylish spectacles, driving a big glossy German car, parking in a disabled space.

That's what *they* see.

I see a woman who's driving a big German car because she can't cope with a car without cruise control. I see a woman wearing expensive clothes because cheaper clothes would be too rough on her body. I see a woman wearing stylish spectacles, because one of the many painkillers she takes (the little blue pills in her purse) dry out her eyes so much she can't wear contact lenses.

But I do look damn sexy, though I say so myself. I'm still youngish, forty-three, and even though I'm a bit short, I'm quite trim. I can eat most things and still stay thin because the pain burns up calories like a forest fire.

Lucky me.

Hey ho, I think, I know by now exactly what the old people are thinking, because some of them tell me. Some of them have no trouble unburdening their minds. As I'm not elderly, or doubled up with arthritis, or on a mobility scooter, I am not one of *them*, and I have no right to be there. They are trained like attack dogs by the *Daily Mail*, to salivate and growl at possible scroungers, cheats milking the system.

There was one time when Dominic and I parked in Sainsbury's one Sunday, for our weekly shop. I was driving. I had insisted that I drive. I hadn't driven for years, because the act of changing gear was not good for me. Little actions like that would send me back to bed for days. When we got an automatic it got easier, so I wanted to try and pull my weight by driving as much as I could. I had barely started to look for my little blue card to put it in the windscreen when a voice said:

'There's people who will need that space, you know.'

It was an old man standing there with his little dog. He had been watching us like a hawk, watching us park, waiting to see who was going to get out of the car that had so thoughtlessly parked in the precious space.

I didn't say anything, but Dominic was furious. I'd never seen him so angry, and it scared me a little. He'd seen the looks and the expressions too, but he'd never actually experienced an actual comment made by an actual person before. His face grew red and he slammed the car door with far too much force.

'*What* did you just say?'

'There are disabled people who need that, you know.'

'Well actually,' said Dominic, his voice quavering, 'actually, for your information, my wife happens to be disabled.'

The man was already walking away. He'd done his job. He'd given the scroungers What For. 'Oh yes,' he said with a sly wink to my husband. 'We're *all* disabled now, aren't we?'

And the old man walked into Sainsbury's, his dog trotting behind him. Dominic looked like he was going to follow him.

'Dom,' I called, using my most exhausted voice. 'Can we go and shop now?'

Dominic recovered himself, and brought out the bags from the boot. We went round the supermarket and when he thought I wasn't looking, he kept peering around, searching for the man, presumably to show the old sod how exhausted I was looking, using the trolley as a crutch to stay upright, but we didn't see him again. I guessed he'd just popped in for some fags and a lottery ticket.

So to sum up – I don't look ill. Not to the casual observer.

I used to look bad. I used to walk with a stick, and my hair went white at the roots, but once I found the better drugs, and started to manage the pain, and got some hair dye, I started to look better.

On the surface, on a good day, I look fine.

It's when you look close up you can see what's inside.

*

Angelina is ridiculously thin, pale, with wide olive eyes and tinted red hair, which falls to her shoulders and hangs in a fringe over her forehead. She is always draped with coloured bead necklaces and bracelets, comprising shiny stones and bits of silver. I always think of her like a sea nymph, decorating herself with jewels from Davey Jones' locker, emerging from the ocean all damp and alluring.

She looks artful and disinterested, but I know it's all an act, a character that fits her job running her own tiny art shop; literally a single room and a big window. One wall is covered with her paintings and sculptures; huge angry shapes in oils, sheep skeletons and human skulls and screaming mouths. She's got a grim style, but she's never ghoulish when it comes to me. She is one of the most sensitive, warmest people I know.

I once asked her about it, if she ever felt drawn to my condition because of her art.

'Jesus no, sweetie,' she said, tapping her cigarette into an ashtray. It was the nearest she ever sounded to being offended. She gestured round her studio. 'This is all work, yeah? It's what I do, not what I am. I don't sleep in a coffin. At five o'clock I go home and stroke my cat and watch *Masterchef*.'

We sit outside the trendy Eat Me café, sipping our coffee. We watch the bored yummy mummies turn up after dropping their little darlings off at their expensive schools.

'How's Brian?' I ask.

Angelina pulls a face, widening her mascara to form inkwell circles and contracting her bright red lips into a tiny budding rose. 'Brian? *Brian?* Oh, *Brian!* He's ancient history, sweetie. Long gone. Looooong gone. He decided to go back to his wife.'

I frown. 'I thought you said he was a widower.'

'Yes, darling, that's what *he* said. So, obviously . . .' she cocks an eyebrow and spins her eyeballs to the heavens, 'she got better . . .'

She dips her finger in the froth of her coffee and sucks it. 'I'm with Clyde now. He's a struggling artist. Which is about the same as having an extra cat, but the cat vomits less and shows slightly more affection. I think of him as an investment, yeah?' She winks. 'Which means he can go down as well as up ...'

It takes twenty seconds of coffee-blowing before Lena cuts to the chase. 'So, how's the pain?'

'Good at the moment. I'm dealing with it.'

'That's great. You look really well.'

'Thanks.'

'And how is Dominic?'

I was thinking about the suicide note. I was thinking about the expression on Dominic's face when he reached for the note and tore it up.

'He's ... OK.'

'You don't sound convinced.'

'Well ... work is a problem. There's never enough of it ... He's not really suited to his job. He struggles with it a lot ...'

'Tell me about it. 'Twas ever thus. We all have to struggle.'

Angelina doesn't struggle at all, but I know what she means.

'I know. But sometimes I feel I'm a bit of a burden ...'

'You should never think like that, sweetie. Dominic is with you because he wants to be with you. You know the statistics of guys who stay with their sick wives?'

'I don't want to know.'

But she's already scrabbling in her pocket. 'I put it in my phone. I thought it was really interesting.' She scrolled to the correct page. 'I think this might be just America, but I could be wrong ... Marriage break-ups, when the man gets sick ... Three per cent. Marriage break-ups when the woman gets sick ... Twenty-one per cent. Fuck. Men are such feckless bastards.'

I roll my eyes. 'Lena . . . that makes me feel *so* much better,' I say in a sarcastic drawl. 'Why did you read that out?'

'But don't you see, darling? How long is it since the accident?'

'Five years.'

'So there you—'

'Five years *this week*.'

'Jesus. Seriously?'

I nod.

'Five years this week since . . . ?'

I nod again. 'It's my anniversary. That's why I wanted to come out.' I shrug and give an embarrassed chuckle. 'That's why I needed to come out.'

'Jesus . . .' She stares, looking at nothing for slightly too long. Then she recovers.

'Well, there you go. Five years since the accident and Dominic's still here, still going strong. He's a diamond, darling. An absolutely twenty-six carat diamond. You could put him in the window at De Beers.'

'I know he's great,' I sigh. 'But that doesn't alter the fact that I feel a burden . . .'

The suicide letter flashes across my eyes.

. . . B-u-r-d-o-n. Is that how you spell it? No . . .

. . . Burden. I'm a B-u-r-d-e-n . . .

'. . . I can't do things that I could do before.'

'Like sex?'

'Lena! I was thinking about gardening.'

She lowered her coffee cup. 'Don't evade the question. Sex is still OK, yeah?'

'We manage,' I say evasively. 'It's not hanging from the chandeliers but we manage. I can't hold any positions any more.' I flick my eyes from side to side, watching for eavesdroppers, and lower my voice. 'I can't ride him, or anything like that.'

31

'So sex is basically you lying there doing nothing, thinking of England, and him running up the flag and doing a twenty-one gun salute over your tits?'

She says this in an incredibly loud voice, quite deliberately. A couple of starved Kensington housewives look up from their papaya salads, and I giggle with embarrassment, blowing bubbles into my coffee.

'Angelina!'

'But I'm right, yeah?'

'Pretty much.'

'Hey ho,' she drawls. 'It's still sex, even if you're lying there like a stranded fish. I had a boyfriend who was a bit of a closet necrophiliac. Had this thing about me playing dead during sex. I had to stay absolutely still while he did his business.'

My eyebrows catapult up my forehead in shock.

'My God. How horrible.'

'Not so bad, it was rather restful actually. Better than those "athletic" men who want you to turn cartwheels across the bedroom, but yes, playing dead can get a bit samey. One night I decided to make it more interesting. I became a zombie and bit him on the nipple. We split up a few minutes later.'

I give a full snort, throwing the froth from my cappuccino onto the saucer.

'Well we don't quite do that. We get by.'

'Good for you both. Seriously, girl, don't worry about Dominic. He's a keeper.'

'Angelina,' I say slowly, 'was I ... was I in a dark place when I ... just after the accident?'

She looks at me steadily, almost frozen. Her mascara-strewn eyes flicker, just the once.

'Yes, darling. You were in a very dark place.'

'Did I talk about ending it all?'

'With Dominic?'

'With everything.'

'Oh.'

'Did I?'

'Yes, you did.'

'Oh.'

She thinks for a while. (**For too long**)

'Are we talking about your suicide attempt?' she says at last.

'You knew about that?'

She sighs. 'Of course I knew about that.'

'And you didn't tell me?'

'Mon . . . It's really not important now.'

'But it's what I did . . .'

'Mon . . .'

'I did that thing – or I tried to. Even if I can't remember it now, it's still something I did. I have a right to know those things. I should know about all the things I did. You can't keep things from me . . . It's my own . . . history.'

'It's *ancient* history, darling. You were in a bad place. When I came to visit you in the first year, when you had to lie on your back and stare at the ceiling all day, you talked about ending it, yeah, so I came every day, just to make sure you were hanging on in there, but even though you talked about it, when Dominic told me what happened, I didn't believe it of you . . . You were too much of a fighter, girlie. That's who you are now. So forget about that other Monica. The one who tried to do that. She's long gone.'

'I can't believe you didn't tell me. And I can't believe Dominic—'

'Dominic loves you. And he knows you've got enough crap without shovelling more of it on your plate . . .'

She grabs my hand, very lightly.

'Darling. You once told me something that's always stayed with

33

me, something your doctor told you. You told me that the brain has a survival mechanism, it throws bad things in the rubbish, so it can carry on.'

'Yes, that's right. The brain does that. It takes the horror away. That's why women are stupid enough to have that second baby, because they can't remember the screaming agony of childbirth. And why torture victims stay sane after the experience, they can't remember the intensity of the pain they suffered...' I blink away a tear. 'Unless they're tortured every day, all the time. Like me.'

The pressure on my hand intensifies, but not too much.

'So maybe you forgot about that moment of madness for a reason. Do me a favour, Mon. A favour for your best friend. Promise you'll put the memory of it back in the box, and forget about it again. Just live your life, move on, and pretend it never happened.'

I think about it.

'I suppose you're right...'

'Promise you'll forget?'

'Promise.'

I leave her after an hour; I'd like to stay longer but the chair is (**killing me**), and I have a place to go.

As I climb back into my car and scoop my blue disabled card off the dashboard, the old woman lowers her *Telegraph* and glares at me, a look that says nothing, just to say *I'm looking at you*.

If she had sunglasses, she would have pulled them down her nose to demonstrate how much she was looking at me.

I give her a big, charming (**dead**) lopsided smile and drive off.

Monica

I wake up . . .

. . . And the pain hits me like a wall.
   God's punishment for my happy moment with Angelina.
   I stare at the ceiling, and I scream. I count the seconds, trying to leave a whole minute before I allow myself to scream again.

And I do that until the room goes dark and I hear his footsteps.

Monica

I wake up . . .

. . . And the pain is slightly less.

And I still feel like screaming, but only every ten minutes or so.

Sometimes having slightly less pain is worse. Because it allows the tiniest window for the mind to think; to appreciate the glacial passage of time, stretching out the day. For me, the past is a discoloured bruise and the future is an unspoken nightmare, so to stay sane, I try to only live in the present tense.

Take your mind somewhere else.

Anywhere else.

Please.

My hand reaches for my book of Keats' sonnets on the bedside table.

I can't read novels any more, because I get so far into a book, and the pages I read fade from my mind, and I lose the thread of the story. So I read poems instead. The Romantic poets.

When I'm trapped in bed, pale and fading away, I sometimes fancy myself as a romantic poet. There are little notes in the margins of my book, stray rhyming couplets, thoughts, notions, foundations that I might build upon, for a larger work. I fantasise about channelling my pain into something creative, like Keats. But my pain doesn't work like that. Not quite.

For example, this is Keats' last sonnet. His very last sonnet.

Bright star, would I were steadfast as thou art—
Not in lone splendour hung aloft the night,
And watching, with eternal lids apart,
Like nature's patient sleepless Eremite . . .

I suppose it should make me sad, but most of the time it makes me giggle like a mad thing. I think he's pleading that he can be constant and awake, and that is what I have already achieved, though the constant is pain. Living for ever is the ideal, which I can only contemplate as a horrific nightmare.

I could never use the word 'eternal' in a poem. Even thinking about the word makes me shudder. Perhaps I'll never be a poet because I cannot face words like that. Being creative adds to the experience of life, and everything in my life is designed to take that away.

I do hope to cry at Keats's poems, one day. I know they should make me sad. But the only time I cried is when Dominic gave me a book on Keats's life, and I found he died far, far away from home, in Rome. I found out that in the weeks before his death from tuberculosis, his friends kept his laudanum from him, because they were worried that he would use it to commit suicide.

So for the sake of a few more miserable weeks of existence, he died in agony, without his painkillers.

That was when I cried. For him. And for the fact that he could write a poem about life and even use the word 'eternal' when he was in such pain; well it gave me some kind of hope. Not a lot, but some.

I look at the notes I made in the margins. I give out a croaking laugh. This is another reason why I can't be a poet. The pencil squiggles are crude, unintelligible: like a drunken spider has staggered across the poems. I can't read any of it. I think I can make out the word 'rose', and perhaps, yes . . .

There is the word 'burden'.

But it looks like 'bourbon', or 'boden' or 'bidden', but I'm guessing it's 'burden'.

I open my bedside drawer and find the matchbox. There is the fragment of letter still inside, with

burden

written on it.

I look at it.

I realise something. There is definitely something wrong with the bit of paper. With the whole note.

I can barely write words, even now, with the new combination of painkillers. I can't write legible notes in my book of poems, and I can't type a letter without misspelling half of the words.

I experiment in the margin of my book of Keats. I put the fragment of paper back in the matchbox, and try to write the word 'burden' in the margin of one of the pages with a pencil.

It comes out as a shaky scrawl.

And I've spelt it 'burdon'.

How did I write it then? How? Back then, when things were so very bad? How could I have written such a perfect note, with perfect spelling, and beautiful handwriting?

Monica

Perhaps I took a lot of time over the note. Perhaps I planned it one letter at a time. I wrote it very slowly.

That makes sense.

But if I was in such great pain, so much so, that I made the decision there and then . . .

. . . Dominic said he'd just popped out for a paper, just for a few minutes. How did I have time to plan it?

I try to think about it, but I can't concentrate on anything; nothing but the way I'm feeling. I was hoping the poems would distract me, but distraction doesn't always work.

Things bleed in.

I'm powerless to stop my mind spinning to the past. About last week. All I can think is why couldn't the man from Atos have come today, and not last week? It would have been much easier if he'd seen me like this.

He came round to see if I deserved my disabled blue badge and couple of quid a week from the government. He came to see if I *looked* like an invalid. Just like what the little old man with his dog was expecting to see. He had to know if I looked the part.

His boxes on his questionnaire, the ones he had to tick, they were always about surface. His questions were: 'Can you walk thirty feet?' or 'Can you dress yourself?' Not 'What kind of hellish conversations do you have over the breakfast table, and just how much did you scream with rage when your husband got his sleeve in his scrambled eggs?'

So Dom and I dressed up, and got our props out; the old walking sticks I used to use, we even got out Dominic's mum's old wheelchair and left it in the hall. I'd not washed my hair, and I combed olive oil through it to make it look lank. I wore my rattiest cardigan and put a blanket over my knees.

Dressing the set.

I wondered if the Atos man would turn up in the same sick-brown suit as he did last year. And he did. The very same one with the stains around the crotch, and the shoulders speckled with dandruff, and he carried a very old briefcase. He mumbled, very quietly, as if he was ashamed at the words that were coming out of his mouth.

He did seem like a pretend doctor, as though we were all playing parts, including him. I wondered if he used to be a proper doctor, and he'd had a nervous breakdown, or got struck off, and this was the only work he could get.

So in he came and Dominic showed him into the living room, and I gave him the feeblest of handshakes, and he settled down and he went through his questions:

Him: 'Do you have a dog?'

Me: 'No.'

Him: 'Do you ever use public transport?'

Me: 'No.'

Him: 'Do you own a car?'

Me: 'Yes . . .'

That was the prelude to the killer question. That was followed up by: 'Do you drive?'

I knew this question would come up: this was the logic of the bureaucratically challenged. If you can drive yourself, then you don't need to be classified as disabled. If you're not classified disabled then you don't need a disabled badge. Why they even bother to make blue disabled badges for cars, I haven't the foggiest, but I was ready for him.

'Yes . . . But I rarely drive the car, because it causes me too much pain. My husband drives me most of the time. I keep my licence going, in case there's a cure, but I can't go for more than a mile before I turn back.'

Lies. Dominic hates it so much. He's got that Catholic thing about not bearing false witness. But I point out it's for the greater good. And if Dominic grumbles some more I point out that if he felt so strongly about it, he shouldn't have taken a job in fucking advertising.

Him: 'Do you go to the hairdresser's?'

Me: 'Yes, but my husband drives me, and I can't bend my head back at the sink so they never wash my hair.'

And on it went.

Then he came up with a question I hadn't heard before. I hadn't heard it myself, but I'd read about it on the internet, where other people who suffer chronic pain and are on disability benefit get together and reminisce about their horror stories at the hands of Atos.

'How much pain relief do your drugs give you? Would you say ten per cent? Twenty per cent?'

Another trick question. If you give a percentage, then Atos conclude that the drugs are working; ergo they enable you to function. If you're able to function then you are not disabled. No disability, no disability benefits. Several people had been caught out this way already.

'It's not like that,' I said. 'It's not a question of how much pain relief I get.'

'I see. But how much relief would you say you do get? Forty per cent?'

His pencil was hovering over a collection of boxes.

'No.'

'Thirty per cent?'

'No!'

'Twenty-five per cent?'

'Listen to me, "doctor",' I said. My anger was rising and stabbing me in the legs. 'It's not a question of percentage. It's not twenty or thirty per cent. My drugs don't take the pain away. There's no actual relief.'

'Shall we say fifty per cent?' he mumbled.

'No! I will not say a percentage.'

'Have a think.'

'I will not "have a think"! Look – I want you to write this down. Write this: "The drugs bring down the levels of pain so that Monica Wood doesn't actually kill herself." Can you write that down?'

He looked at me. He showed no sign of writing anything.

'Dominic!' I shouted. 'Dominic! Come in here!'

Dominic rushed in, glaring at the Atos man. 'What? What's up?'

'I want you here. I want you to witness this. This man is not listening to my answers. He's refusing to do as I ask. He's not listening to me.'

Slowly, remorselessly, we forced him to put down, word for word, what I wanted him to write, in the margins of the page. The man didn't look very happy, but he did it, and after he'd finished, Dominic read what he'd written, like a teacher marking homework.

And then we went on with the tests. Dominic didn't leave.

The Atos man then took out a plastic tube and asked me to blow into it, as if I was a drunk at the side of the road. It looked like something that kids use to inflate balloons with, and it had been inside his briefcase; not in a plastic bag or anything, not sterilised.

Dominic erupted. 'What are you doing?'

The mumbling doctor looked at Dominic in surprise.

'She's not a horse. That's not sterilised. It's just been rattling around in your case.'

'I'm sorry,' he said. 'I'm sure this must be disturbing for you.'

'But it's not clean. And why are you asking her to blow into anything? She's got neuropathic pain. You know she's got asthma. It's in her notes. You should have her notes. Why are you getting her to blow into a filthy piece of plastic? What's the point of it? You're just risking giving her a lung infection.'

'I'm sorry,' he said. 'This must be very distressing for you.'

This was not the time. Dominic was talking to a script, and not a person. I made a tiny movement of my head, warning him. *Back off.*

Answer one of the questions wrong, and you were branded an evil state sponger, chucked off the disability register and drowned in red tape. The joke is this: this whole miserable circus is about saving the government money – well, I never wanted the disabled allowance in the first place. I didn't want their bloody charity. What I needed was the blue disabled badge to put in my car windscreen. I was desperate to keep the badge because, on my bad days, that lack of fuss when parking, the few extra couple of feet nearer to the supermarket, they made all the difference to me.

On the bad days.

But as you can guess, the Atos form doesn't have a box that says 'good days' and 'bad days'. It just has boxes that say, 'Can you walk unaided?' And if you're truthful, and you say, 'Yes, sometimes, on a good day', it just goes down on the form as 'yes' and there go your benefits and your badge, and there's nothing left to do but put in endless appeals and allow the bureaucracy to swallow you whole.

As soon as he left I sagged onto the sofa, unable to hold myself up. Dominic lunged forward to catch me, and we gripped each other, listening to each other breathing, holding each other like we were lovers.

It's only now that I realise how silly that thought was: we *are* lovers. Sometimes, it just doesn't feel that way any more.

'God,' I said. 'What an ordeal.'

I felt Dominic's shoulders tighten. He doesn't like me using religious swear words, but at that moment, I didn't have the energy to apologise.

'My pain levels are through the roof. You'd have thought they'd want me functioning so they could take their money away. What kind of sadistic country does this to its disabled citizens? Poke them with a stick, make them dance, drive them into a wheel-chair or an early grave – just to make sure they're getting value for money.'

'It's not fair,' said Dominic.

'You're telling me. Christ . . . '

'*It's not fair*,' he repeated. 'It's . . . just . . . not fair.'

At that moment, I realised that Dominic wasn't talking to me any more. His anger was rising, and like a lot of men, he was turning it in on himself. I used to see it in a few of my old boyfriends. Rage rising at the world became rage at themselves, and then it all collapses in a soufflé of self-pity. It's not pretty.

'Hey, handsome,' I said pressing my forehead to his. 'Why not make us a cup of tea?'

He came to his senses, shaking his head like a dog coming out of a pond. 'Yes of course. Earl Grey? Decaf?'

'That would be lovely.'

He smiled again. 'Coming right up.'

So he left, and I pushed my pain back into myself, in case it further inflamed his anger.

It's all very well him having qualms about bearing false witness, I thought. *But he doesn't mind it when I lie to him.*

Every single day.

Monica

I wake up . . .

. . . Not too bad today.

It's taken three days but I think I can get out of bed. Maybe even out of the house.

Breakfast. OK. Fine. Dressing myself. A bit of a struggle, but yes I get everything on. Tights. Skirt. The works.

So now I'm up.

What do I do?

I'm tired of thinking about the letter. Thoughts affect my emotions, and emotions affect my pain. I'm sure the mere fact the letter troubled me, and it prowled around my brain like an angry tiger, helped to keep me in bed for three days.

Perhaps I should do something positive. Get out of the house. Perhaps I should keep that appointment with my pain specialist. His secretary has been leaving me messages for weeks, reminding me that I'd been booked in for a consultation today.

I ease the car into the hospital car park, and soon I am in the tiny pine-themed reception area, barely big enough for four people. I am greeted with a smile from the overly tanned pine-themed receptionist. It's not long before she tells me, in words so soft that I can barely hear what she's saying, that Dr Kumar is ready to see me now.

He welcomes me warmly, gestures to a seat, but does not shake my hand. Inadvertently causing his patients to scream by touching them is an occupational hazard.

His office is pristine; a smooth desk, devoid of clutter, an anaemic watercolour of some forget-me-knots on the far wall. On one of my better days we got to chatting, and he happily took me through the decor in his office.

'When I started,' he explained, his voice swooping and rising like a flock of swallows, 'my office was very cluttered. I had a big clock on that wall over there, and family pictures covering the back wall, and a bird who took drinks from a glass on the desk, a present from my daughter when she went to Mallorca. Then I realised after some weeks many of my patients had little tolerance for such things. The ticking of the clock, the reminders of a carefree family life, the repetitive movement of the ornament ... Because of their condition they fixated on these things and it made them quite agitated. Now, as you can see, I keep things very clean, very tidy, no distractions ...'

I listened and I sympathised and I pitied those people, because it was one of my good days.

On another day I knew I would be imagining myself (**tearing the clock off the wall and stuffing his bloody drinking bird down his throat**)

Now, when I'm on a bad day, I fixate on the forget-me-knots, wondering if the painting is designed to provoke me. Forget-me-knot. *As if I could.* Sometimes I even look at the places where the clicking clock and the dipping bird used to be, imagining the bobbing movements and hearing the tock-tock-tock.

I wish he hadn't told me.

Today, like every day I see him, he is in good humour. On my better days I admire him for that; his job – dealing with poor wretches like me, day in, day out – must be very difficult, and he has cultivated a crusty shell of bonhomie to keep him sane.

On my bad days I would like to (**take him by the throat and crush his bonhomie out of him**)

'So, five years. Is it really five years now?'

'Yes, five years.' I don't know what else to say, so I just say 'yes' again.

'Goodness.'

'Five years.' I don't know why, but I repeat myself.

He knows better than to supply the automatic response: 'Doesn't time fly?' Because he knows it doesn't. Instead he grins his big sunny smile and says, 'Well perhaps this will be an auspicious day, a new chapter of your life. How are the combinations working these days?'

'Fine ...'

'Good.'

'Well ... OK. Well, I say fine, I mean, not fine, exactly.'

'I see. You still have the usual symptoms.'

'Oh yes. My spatial awareness is still wonky, and I still have incredibly weird dreams ...'

'Yes, yes ... yes ... right ...' He is making notes.

'My sense of time is shot to hell – I lost three days this week.'

'Oh dear oh dear ...'

'Like that old Tommy Cooper joke ...'

'Hmmm?' Smiling bemusement.

'You know. "I've been on the whisky diet".'

More mystified beaming.

'"I've lost three days".'

'Ah,' he says. 'Ah! Very good! Ahahah! I will remember that one. Whisky diet. Yes. Well. Oh dear. A lot of this to be expected, I am regretful to say.'

'Oh, of course. I know it's because of all the drugs, but the pain levels ... I need to take bigger doses. I take more so I can get to sleep ...'

'I see . . .'

'. . . but even before that, I knew I was taking enough to put a bull elephant into a coma.'

He knits his fingers together and gives a dazzling smile. 'Well yes, we have discussed this . . .'

But even though we *have* discussed this, he continues anyway. Same words. Same everything.

'Most drugs — and I am including nicotine, alcohol, heroin in that category — are alien substances that we put into the body. In most cases our bodies build up an immunity to these alien invaders, and we have to take greater doses to create the same effects.'

'Only I can't, can I?' I finished his lecture for him. 'I'm probably harming my kidneys by taking this amount as it is . . .'

He pulls a sad, helpless face. I continue.

'. . . You did tell me I'm ruining my health by keeping some of the pain at bay.'

'In some ways.'

'But even at those health-ruining doses they won't work for me soon.'

'That is only a possibility.'

'Irony of ironies.'

'. . . But there are always options.'

'Not from where I'm sitting.'

'Have you considered moving onto morphine? I know we have talked about this before.'

My eyes grow cold. 'I did. I tried morphine at the start. Look at your notes. According to my husband I was incomprehensible; practically a vegetable. I kept asking him to change the channels so I could watch a different ceiling.'

'Oh dear, yes. Ah, but there are combinations. The prescribing of morphine is a much more sophisticated process now. It is not what it was.'

'And you said there was a possibility I could get addicted.'

'Well, yes, that is the case, but . . .'

'But?'

He spreads his hands again, and I realise what the gesture means.

'Ah.' I nod. 'I see. I get you. I see what you're saying. What's wrong with me getting addicted to something I could never be able to stop using anyway?'

'Actually, it is more controllable these days . . .'

'No thanks,' I say firmly. 'I haven't come to that yet. The drugs work. Most of the time. And not totally. But they sort of work. They get me out of the house. Sometimes.'

'Well, maybe drugs will no longer be needed. At least for some periods of time . . . Because I may have some auspicious news for you!'

This has been on the tip of his tongue since I entered the room. He has been waiting for this; he has been waiting for me to turn down the offer of morphine again, so he can tell me something. I've told you the drugs make me so very sensitive to everything; smells, noises, moods. I sensed his excitement the moment I came in, a hum of anticipation coming from his body.

'There has been some new research. They are conducting trials, and they are asking for suitable subjects. They are very interested in you, Monica. They think you might be an excellent subject.'

'Gosh.'

'Indeed, and furthermore, they would like to include you in the trials as soon as possible.'

I sit up straighter, trying to make myself comfortable. 'So what is it? Don't tell me. Amputation?'

'No, it is not amputation.' I can hear a grin in his voice but his medical precision compels him to take my question seriously. 'This is quite a different principle. Amputation is designed to trick the nerves into forgetting about the pain. The process of applying capsaicin patches to the body is to block the signal of the nerves that transmit pain to the brain.'

'Capsaicin what?'

'Patches. Yes.'

'Which is . . . ?'

'Oh. Please excuse me. Capsaicin is a compound extracted from very powerful chilli peppers. Very hot. It is commonly used in pepper sprays and to repel rodents and insects.'

'You're not really selling this to me, doctor.'

'It has been proving very successful with arthritic pain and post-cancer care, and they are expanding trials to look at how it can deal with chronic pain management. To use an analogy . . .'

I smile.

' . . . it is like a farmer burning the stubble from his field, so that nothing may grow back.'

'So you're going to burn me so I don't care about the pain any more.'

There goes his funny little laugh again. 'You are making light of this, Monica, and I think you are right to make light of it. I do not wish to get your hopes up. It is an experimental trial, yes,' he continues, 'and there may be unpleasantness. I am not telling you to do this, but if you do agree, I would do all I can to ensure you make an informed choice before you say yes.'

'I'll do it,' I say.

Monica

Of course I said yes. I was hooked the moment he said 'new treatment'.

I go home and celebrate. I celebrate by going to the toilet.

One of the side effects of the pain is constipation. The muscles contract with the pain; shoulders, neck and ... down below. Things don't work as well as they should, and I do get backed up, and I have to deal with it.

My body leads me upstairs, into the bathroom, and the unwelcome form of a pale blue ring of porcelain. I squirm on the seat, staring at the puddle of knickers around my ankles, staring at my forehead reflected in the bottom of the mirror. I count the agonising bullets as they splash into the water. Sometimes I lunge forward and I see my whole face, stretching and wincing, grinning savagely (**like a mad woman**).

I stand, wobbling uncertainly, clutching at the towel rail, and I scuttle crab-like around in a circle and look down at the result.

Two tiny little pellets are bobbing in the pan. Little rabbit pellets.

I remember my rabbit Jumpy, and crying when I couldn't remember his name, crying when he died, watching my father going up the path to the back of the garden, the soft flap-flap of the tops of his wellingtons.

I can remember Mum shouting at Dad for emerging with the red-tipped spade. *How could you be so stupid, Adrian?*

Not now. Don't think of that. Back on the pan.

The front door bangs, and I can hear movement downstairs. Sure enough ...

'Monica?'

I can't answer back. Not now. I can hear him moving about,

the *thud* of his briefcase on the kitchen top, and the slow, laborious twenty-two *thuds* on the stairs.

'Monica?'

'In here! In the bathroom.'

His footsteps come into the hallway. I can see a dark form take shape in the pebbled glass. A huge fuzzy, dark mound.

'Hello?'

'Won't be a minute. On the toilet.'

'Take as long as you want.'

'Don't worry I will.'

'I'll be down in the kitchen.'

'Wait . . . I've got something to tell you.'

'Oh. Right.'

'Guess what? Dr Kumar has found something that might help me!'

The fuzzy mound in the glass takes a different shape, bigger, as he comes closer to the bathroom door.

'Oh really? Great. You mean an operation?'

'Not quite. They put patches on your body and burn you with this super-jalapeno. It's meant to stun, or kill off the nerves under the skin.'

'Which is it? Stun or kill off?'

'I'm not sure. Why?'

'Well, killing all the nerves? Won't that mean you won't be able to feel anything?'

'Fine by me.'

'You know what I mean.'

'I don't think it's like that. I think they kill off some. The burning process just knocks out some. It reduces the pain more than anything.'

He frowns. 'Doesn't sound very pleasant. Do you want to try it?'

I'm surprised by the question. 'What have I got to lose?'

'Your skin, by the sound of it.'

'It won't scar. It'll just *feel* like I'm being boiled in oil.'

'Right.'

'I've got info. I'll show you what it's all about.'

He backs away, dutifully; he knows I hate him listening to my bathroom sound effects.

He's sitting waiting in the kitchen, tapping idly on the table. I show him the information Dr Kumar has given me – the photocopied sheets, and the doctor's own handwritten notes which he has thoughtfully scanned for me – and I tell Dominic I have a website he can look at.

We go to the study. He's on his side of the computer, and the little square box for his password is sitting in the middle of the screen; there's a picture of a tiger next to it.

I sit down and he leans over the desk, masking the screen with his back, and pointing his bottom in my direction. He's changed into casual clothes, and I can see his boxers through the worn patches of his jeans.

Yes, he's put on weight a bit, I think. *But he's over forty now. He's allowed.*

He puts in his password – *peck, peck, peck, peck* – and sits back heavily on the chair. 'OK . . .'

I give him the URL and he finds the site, studying slowly. I peer over his shoulder, not reading, just staring at the pictures and wondering what he's thinking.

'Very interesting.'

'It looks promising, doesn't it?'

He nods, but says nothing.

'The whole process lasts less than a day. I don't even have to stay in overnight.'

He's still reading, eyes darting up and down the screen. 'It says here that the results are partially successful . . .'

'Yes.'

'And even if the results are successful, most – if not all – of the pain returns eventually.'

'Well, you know Dr Kumar. He's always keen for me to try things, even when they're at a very experimental stage. They're still investigating what happens when they repeat the treatment. If they do it enough ... the results could be permanent.'

'But they don't say that, do they?'

'No. That's just me saying that,' I say reluctantly. 'But it stands to reason, doesn't it? When you pluck your eyebrows, it doesn't hurt so much after you do it for years and years. That's my logic and I'm sticking to it.'

'Hmmm. Right.'

'If I get some relief, even if it's only temporary, I might be able to come off the drugs for a month or two. And I'll be helping their research. That's a good thing, surely.'

'Yes, it would be a good thing.'

He just says it as a fact; *helping people is a good thing, that is certainly true*. Not approving or disapproving.

'Well well,' he says at last. 'Very interesting.' And then he says 'well well' again.

Then he closes down the computer and leaves. I'm still sitting there, slightly underwhelmed, humming from the anticlimax, when his words float from the kitchen.

'Fancy a cup of tea ...?'

It's later, and I want to talk more, but when I emerge he is already parked in front of the television, hand poised on the remote. He's not inviting discussion.

I make and drink my laxative and I sit with him, and we watch together. We exhaust everything the television has to offer and go to bed. As I'm not too bad today we end up in the same bedroom.

He gets undressed as I watch, coyly taking off his shirt behind the wardrobe door before emerging in his long T-shirt, shorts and tiger slippers. The effect is comical.

He's very careful not to jiggle the bed as his (**vast**) bottom descends on the edge of the mattress. He's very good like that. We sleep a respectful foot apart on the huge orthopaedic bed.

Once he gets in and the light goes off, his hand snakes over to my side, and rests gently on my belly. Then it starts gliding up and down in a stroking motion; up to the bottom of my breasts, and down to my abdomen. Up and down. Up and down.

I rest my hand on his, and I bring it up, kiss it. And put it back on my belly, holding it motionless.

'Good night, darling.'

'Good night.'

I hate myself.

One of the few nights I'm capable of making love, I just don't feel like it.

That journey to Doctor Kumar drained my batteries. These days I'm like an iPhone with too many apps left open; if I want to do anything that requires energy, I have to do it quickly before I go completely dead.

After a few minutes the hand snakes away and he rolls onto his side, his breathing slow and regular and gentle. He's not (**bloody**) snoring tonight, but the noise is enough.

Those sodding drugs.

My senses are too acute.

Everything is noisy.

Everything is unfiltered.

I'm thinking about noises, and I can't get to sleep.

I'm thinking about the *peck peck peck peck* as Dominic typed in his password.

Peck peck peck peck.

I count the *pecks* in the study just like I count the *thuds* going up the stairs.

Peck peck peck peck.

That can't be right.

Peck peck peck p . . .

Monica

I wake up ...

... Not too bad today.

So I decide to go and see Niall; can't put it off any more. I need him.

Niall can be annoying; he's a bit needy, as some men can be, as you can probably gather from the texts with too many kisses and the lopsided smiley faces, but I can't deny that he is one of the few good things in my life. Literally a godsend.

He dropped from heaven one day, about two years ago, when I was trying to get my life back.

I'd gone to the gym to get a massage, trying to ease the headache that had been squeezed into my brain. The massage was very thorough, but it didn't seem to do anything. I was walking through the gym, watching the people on the treadmills, legs lifting up and down, arms pummelling the air, bodies gliding back on forth on the rowing machines—

I used to do that, I thought, with naked envy. *I used to do that every day. I'd spend half an hour on the treadmill and think nothing of it. Now I can't twist a doorknob without crippling myself.*

—and I was suddenly taken by a roar of agony, the heat rushed up, the inkwell beckoned, and I knew I was going to faint. I cringed at the embarrassment of doing it there. I lay on a bench, flat on my back, and pretended I was stretching my arms, waiting for the shimmering on the edge of my vision to stop.

There was a pair of well-toned calves by my head.

'Hello.' A male voice.

Through the haze I could see chunky sports socks hugging thick ankles. It looked like his shins were wearing roll-neck sweaters.

He continued. 'Don't we know each other?'

A pathetic chat-up line. I'm sure I should have come up with a hundred withering put-downs. All I managed at that point was an 'I don't think so'.

'I'm sure we do.'

'We'll have to agree to differ on that.'

'How's the pain?' He dropped his voice to a whisper. 'Is it bad today?'

'I'm sorry?'

'You're in a lot of pain.'

'Go away.'

'It's all right, Monica. I understand. Your secret is safe with me.'

'Fuck off.'

He turned and left. I could see more of him – well, the back of him. I watched his shiny blue buttocks oscillate away, taking it in turns to wobble as he moved to another part of the gym. He pulled weights, shimmering and flickering gently as my Angry Friend fluttered his fingers in my eye-line. It almost felt like my Angry Friend was trying to distract me from this mysterious man.

He was saying (**Move away! Nothing to see here! Gosh, Monica! Look at those expensive trainers! Look at that man reading the news on that television on the wall! Look at that fat man! Look over there! And there! Look at anything else but that guy!**)

But I refused to be distracted. My Angry Friend was doing this for some evil purpose of his own. I knew then that this man with his shiny blue buttocks was the key to something important.

'Screw you,' I said under my breath to my Angry Friend. 'I'm going to talk to him.'

Of course I had to talk to him. It felt like this stranger had just scanned me like a barcode and, somewhere far away, the word 'cripple' had lit up on the screen of an omnipresent machine in a dusty government building.

I pulled myself up and walked over.

'OK ...'

'What?'

'How did you know my name?'

'I'm a mind reader.'

'Don't be an arsehole.'

He smiled, and held his hand against his forehead theatrically. 'I knew you were going to say that.'

'Are you following me?'

'I come here all the time. It's my local.'

'So you say.'

He smiled helplessly. 'I haven't seen you here before.' He stroked his tidy beard suspiciously. 'Hmmm. Perhaps *you're* following *me*.'

My Angry Friend was dragging me away by the arm, pulling me to the exit. It was just a matter of time before I fell down the rabbit hole, so I spoke quickly.

'I haven't got time for this bollocks.' I wanted to turn abruptly and stalk away, but of course there was no chance of that. I pirouetted awkwardly on my right leg, and tried to drag my carcass to the exit.

I only got a few feet when he took pity on me and said: 'I'm sorry. I'm being a prick. You used to be my agent. When I was an actor.'

'I did? Really?'

'Yes.'

'I don't remember you.'

'Oh. Well . . . '

I filled the embarrassing moment. 'I'm sorry I don't remember you. A lot's happened to me since I was an agent. What's your name?'

He grinned shyly. 'Niall Stewart.'

Niall Stewart. The only face that came into my mind was round and chubby. John Lennon glasses. An untidy beard at the front, and a scrappy ponytail bringing up the rear. It didn't resemble the man squatting in front of me. The face of the Niall Stewart I knew was what I – and casting directors – would call a 'type'. To my mind, Niall was 'Disgruntled hippy'. 'Ugly friend'. 'Annoying computer nerd'.

I remembered that the Niall Stewart I knew got a slow and steady trickle of work on the strength of his general slobbyness.

But this man could not, in any way, in any form, in any universe, be cast as a slob. He looked like a personal trainer or cycle courier. He was very aerodynamic; short stubbly haircut and trimmed beard, and was obviously very fit, but he wasn't one of those men that didn't know when to stop exercising and end up looking like an inflatable doll. I read a book once that described someone as having a 'tidy physique'. Now I knew what the writer was thinking of.

'You're Niall Stewart?'

'Yes.'

Disbelief must have been scribbled all over my face.

'I am. Honest.'

He sat up and unzipped the bulge below his waist. I wondered what the hell he was doing, and then I realised he was opening a bum bag. He proffered his driver's licence. Leaning forward as far as I dared – which was not a lot – I took it, and there were the words 'Niall Stewart' and a photo of the rugged-looking man who lay before me.

'Fine. You're Niall Stewart. I believe you.'

'Lucky me.' He smiled. 'It's good to see you again.'

'I'm sure it is. Now explain how you know I've got pain.'

Niall's eyes darted around him. I suddenly became aware of how noisy it was. The air was filled with grunting and pounding and thumping music.

'I don't want to shout about how I know,' he said. 'And I guess you don't want me to shout it either. Let's go somewhere more private.'

Of course I was intrigued. I had to find out how he knew. What he could see in me. Foolishly, I thought once I had dyed my white roots and stopped walking with the stick, I was able to hide the pain from the world.

I was even foolish enough to think I could hide it from my husband. One day, on a good day, I decided to think positive, look the world in the eye, rise above my condition and do something outrageous. I went to a professional photographer, and had glamorous photos done. I was stark naked, sitting coyly in a wooden chair draped with a sheepskin rug, and though I say so myself, I thought I looked bloody hot.

The photographer thought so too, because even when she didn't have to look at me through her lens, she still kept looking at me. I could see that easily, even though I wasn't wearing my glasses.

I got one framed for Dominic, and gave it to him for his birthday.

'Ooh, I say!' he said suggestively as I struggled to get this huge package out of the wardrobe. 'Is it socks?'

He wanted to help me, I could see he was straining to take a corner, because he knew the act of lifting it was sending searing tendrils of hot lava pouring into my arms and legs, but he also knew that I wanted to – that I had to – do this myself. So he waited patiently for an age as I inched his birthday present to where he lay under the duvet.

I leaned over him and nibbled his ear – just the way he likes it – and I watched with almost carnivorous interest as his hands slipped in the seam of the wrapping paper and glided along the edge, separating the tape from the paper.

He pulled it back to reveal me, cross-legged on the chair, one arm up, clutching the sheepskin blanket over my shoulder, the other arm down, elbow bent low, pushing my breast into my body and half-concealing a cheeky nipple.

There you go, tiger, I thought. *That's me, baby. Your hot-to-trot girl. Come and get me.*

But he looked up, smiled, and thanked me, and when he guided me down and planted a kiss on my forehead, he let me go almost immediately.

He kept his smile fixed on his face as he opened the rest of his cards, like he'd bought the grin from a joke shop. I didn't know what I'd done wrong. He looked disappointed somehow and it broke my heart. He certainly didn't mind me being slutty in the past . . .

Had I been reclassified as an invalid, in his eyes? Was I not supposed to wave my bits in his face like I used to? Was I just supposed to become a smiling sexless creature, and sit, and take it easy, and have cups of tea made for me for the rest of my life?

He opened his cards and his other presents, but his eyes didn't rest on the picture again.

It was only after he'd gone to the bathroom, and I was left alone with the picture, that I realised. It was sitting on the floor, leaning against the wardrobe, aimed in my direction. It was like a magic picture, the ones where you stare at lots of coloured blobs, and suddenly you see a leaping dolphin.

I saw what Dominic saw. I saw me, in my nudity. I saw my legs, my breasts, my thighs, but most of all I saw the pain in my face, the unnaturally dark crow's feet from the sleepless nights showing through too much make-up. The eyes open slightly too wide, fighting the weariness, fighting to look like I'm really enjoying sitting in this awkward position, fighting not to show the agony it was causing me.

I felt sick.

It looked like an ugly photo in some paedophile's collection; where the provocative nakedness of the body was juxtaposed with a face that looked like it didn't want to be there.

The following morning, when he went to work, I got Agnieszka to put it in the attic. It's stayed there ever since, and Dominic has never asked about it.

It's always been our little secret.

So I was intrigued enough to allow Niall to drive me to a pub, The Westbourne, and let him buy me a drink. He plonked down a sparkling water and a tomato juice on our table.

'Thanks.'

I appraised him out of the corner of my eye. Men think they're the only ones who do that. They're wrong, of course. He was still wearing a lot of lycra, shorts and top, but not in a look-at-me kind of a way. But even though his expression was modest and self-effacing, his body could not stop showing off. He sat down on a stool, and his chunky thighs forced him to sit with his legs wide apart, with his huge glory on display.

I felt quite odd sitting there; like my body was going on an adventure and had assumed my mind would tag along for the ride.

I could tell my Angry Friend was furious at this turn of events, because he had sunk his teeth into my legs, and stabbed me in both thighs. (**You shouldn't be here**), he said.

'You don't look like the Niall Stewart I remember. You were . . .'

'What?'

'Different.'

He gave a short, brittle laugh. 'Well you look exactly the same. Unmistakable.' He laughed. 'Unique.'

'I'll take that as a compliment.'

'You should.' He swigged his water. 'You were a great agent. One of a kind. Well, I thought so. You were the best agent I had.'

'Are you still acting?'

'No, not since after the accident. I got injured during a theatre tour a few years back. I was in some rubbish play about the sixties, playing some grungy hippy ...'

Of course you were.

'... and I tripped over a scatter cushion in the wings and hurt my back. I was laid up for months – God, the pain was indescribable! And when I managed to finally walk upright I was a martyr to sciatica.'

My mind was hot. *He had an accident. I had an accident. He has sciatica. I am sandblasted by my sciatic nerve. I think I've found my soulmate. Someone who might have some inkling of what I've been going through. No wonder my Angry Friend is furious.*

Niall continued. 'We, well, that is, me and Equity, we started to sue the theatre company for hundreds of thousands, but Equity got scared ...'

I nodded, understanding. I knew the actor's union very well.

'... and they settled, and I ended up with peanuts, barely enough to live on. So I had no money, nobody would employ me as thanks to the court case I was now unofficially labelled as a troublemaker, so I decided to take control and do something about the bits of my life I could do something about. I took up physiotherapy, to get my body in shape ...' he waggled his fingers vaguely in the direction of his gluteus maximus, 'hence the difference in how I look. And now I'm an osteopath. That's how I knew you had pain.'

'Just because you're an osteopath.'

'Because I could see you were in pain.'

'But I don't look like I'm in pain.'

'Ah. OK, you don't.'

He let the silence fester between us.

'Well I don't!' I sipped my tomato juice intensely, glaring through the bottom of the glass at him. 'OK? What?'

'What?'

'What was it that gave it away?'

'It was the way you walked.'

'I walk fine.'

'Of course you do.'

'I do.'

'Go on then,' he said nonchalantly. 'If you walk fine, go and walk up and down this pub.'

'What?'

'Go on. Just to that Trivial Pursuit game and back.'

'No.'

'If you're scared ...'

'I'll look stupid.'

'If you're scared of looking stupid ...' He caught my eye. 'Just walk into the toilets, then. Wait a minute, then come out again.'

I looked at the toilet door. It suddenly shrank into the distance, as though I was staring at it through the wrong end of a telescope.

'OK fine,' I said. 'If it makes you happy ...'

I stood up, glowering at him, and strode purposefully across the room. I made sure I walked like a god. One foot confidently in front of the other, arms held firmly at my sides. I strode like a superhero past the Trivial Pursuit machine. I turned heads with my determined, masculine stride. I barged into the Ladies, thrust the door aside, and nearly crushed a girl against the hand-dryer in the process.

Then I sagged, holding onto a basin, gasping and scrabbling for purchase on the damp porcelain, and sobbing with the effort. Thank God for ladies' pub toilets. There are a million reasons to cry in them, so you can honk as hard and as noisily as you like. No one freaked out, and I got sympathetic *I've-been-there* glances from women as they left and entered the cubicles.

They didn't want to intrude. *It's not as bad as it seems. You'll get over him.* That's what they were thinking.

But it *was* as bad as it seems, and 'him' was my Angry Friend, so they were so very (**wrong wrong wrong**).

Five minutes later I emerged and strode out, doing my superhero walk, as if I was Wonder Woman, and I sat down on my stool and took a big manly swig, finishing my filthy horrible tomato juice, and said, 'You see?'

Niall sighed. 'Sorry. It's more obvious now.'

'Get lost! What's more obvious?'

'You favour your right side. Your shoulders are an inch higher than they should be. Nerve pain begets muscle pain. Muscle pain distorts the body. You carry on ignoring it and you're going to spend the next decade curled up like a woodlouse.'

'Charming.'

'Sorry to be blunt. Seriously. I see people with bad posture due to pain all the time.'

'I thought I was able to hide it.'

'Maybe you thought that. Trouble was, all that effort and you were doomed to fail, because the body you're working on is already twisted out of shape,' he said. 'That's how chronic neuropathic pain cripples so many people, and it doesn't have to happen. If you get a sharp pain, like a burn or a punch in the head, the muscles react.

You tense up. If you suffer from pain twenty-four-seven, they're tensing up all the time.' He held his big hands apart and pushed them together until they locked around each other. 'They contract, and when they do that, they twist you out of shape.'

'Oh great,' I said, gloomily. 'It's bad enough feeling like this, but now I'm going to end up like some scrunched up mutant, limping along the pavements with my head tucked under my arm.'

Niall laughed. 'No, you won't end up like that. You don't seem like the kind of woman to let that happen.'

I blushed. *This well-toned version of Niall Stewart is young enough to be my son*, I thought.

'You need a good massage.'

'I've just had a massage.'

'Not the ones they give at the gym. That's just tickling the muscles. You need a good deep-tissue massage,' he said.

'Really?' I smiled, and this time it was his turn to blush.

'Seriously, I can do a lot for you. Just say yes, twenty minutes on a table with me, and you will feel the difference.'

'That's what's all the boys say,' I said. And this time we both blushed together.

What have I got to lose? I thought.

Twenty minutes later, and Niall was driving me to a swanky hotel in Holland Park. He explained it had a huge well-equipped spa centre, and – it just so happened – he worked there at weekends as a trainer and masseur. There were rooms we could use, if we picked the right time of day. And – it also just so happened – after lunch was one of those right times.

We went into the foyer and I sat on big ugly chairs while Niall went to reception. He explained he had to get them to ring downstairs and check if any rooms were available. There were, and soon we were in a dimly lit chamber dominated by a long

67

low table, fuzzy with steam and filled with the heady smell of lavender.

This has got to be the most elaborate chat-up line in history, I thought.

I emerged from the changing rooms, hugging a thick fluffy dressing gown against my body. Niall was standing by the table, and he gestured me over.

'Step into my office,' he grinned.

I carefully pressed the gown against my private bits.

'Now, I have to examine you. I need you to remove the dressing gown.'

'Yeah, right.'

'Seriously, I do.'

'Seriously ... you don't.'

'I need to have a proper look at your posture, so I know where to concentrate.'

'I'm sure you'll need no help knowing where to concentrate.'

'Fine.' He threw his hands up in surrender. 'If you can't take this seriously ...'

I dropped the dressing gown to the floor and stood there, defiantly, in my not-bad-for-a-forty-three-year-old nakedness. 'This seriously enough?'

He choked and cast his eyes to the ceiling. 'You are supposed to keep your underwear on.'

'Oh.'

I jumped back into the changing room and struggled with my knickers and bra. 'That wasn't embarrassing in the slightest,' I shouted.

'I did say. Just now. Five minutes ago.'

'I'm sure you did.'

'It wasn't a ... I did say.'

'I'm sure you did. I'm sorry. I find it difficult to concentrate on what people say. The pain gets in the way.'

'Of course.'

'So what did you think?'

'Fantastic. Just fantastic.'

'I meant about my posture.'

'Ah. Of course. Well, before my brain shut down from overheating, I noticed that my initial diagnosis was correct. Your shoulders are a mess, and the muscles in your left side have contracted.'

I re-emerged, and at his gesture I positioned myself face down and exposed my back and bum to the elements. He positioned the flat of his hands either side of my spine.

'Hands not too cold?'

'No, it's fine.'

He's not going to rape me. He's gone to far too much trouble, I thought.

He can't rape me, anyway, there's people walking in and out of that steam room every other minute, I thought.

Please, God, don't let me get moist while I'm lying here, I thought.

It wasn't erotic in the slightest. *Hellfire!* Even to a hardened pain-junkie like me, it was fucking agony. He buried his elbow in my shoulder, making me want to scream. He worked his way up my back, stretching the spine, pushing at my hip.

'As I thought,' he said grimly, 'the muscles have really pulled you out of shape.'

As he pummelled my body I stared fixedly through the hole in the table, eyes wandering over the shapes in the marble floor. There was a very round whorl in the pattern, and I imagined it was a huge clock, and imagined the second hand of the huge clock lurching its way around the dial slowly, slowly. *Don't think 'agonising slowness', don't think 'painfully slow', just think ... Just don't think. Thunk. Thunk. Thunk. There goes the second hand, away from the four ... Thunk. Thunk. Thunk. Thunk. Over the five Thunk. Thunk. Thunk. Towards the six ... Just twenty more times around the dial ...*

And then he said, 'I'm done.'

I got up off the table and stood, and walked around the room, afraid I might break into little bits. I caught my reflection in a shiny wall, and saw I had grown bright red goggles, where the hole in the table had left a mark around my face.

My hip was sore, but felt wonderful. Every limb felt lighter. My Angry Friend was still with me, of course, but the other pains, the muscular ones I had taken for granted as part of the general shitness of the way I felt, had eased considerably. The dull headache, the one I'd had since March, had gone.

'That's amazing,' I said, balancing myself on the balls of my feet. 'I feel like I've grown another three inches.'

'You're standing taller, I can see it from here. And your shoulders have dropped.'

I moved my head, and the action was glorious and uneventful. No cracks, no twinges, no stabbing feeling between the eyes.

'My God. My doctor told me not to expect any miracles. This comes close to a miracle in my book.'

Niall was getting embarrassed again. He coughed. 'It's nothing really. You just need to release the muscles, keep them from seizing up. They will start to bunch up again with the pain, almost straight away, so it's a never-ending process, I'm afraid.'

I nipped back into the dressing room and grabbed my jeans. 'Don't worry about that. My life is filled with never-ending processes. I take my drugs three times a day. I attach electrodes to my body to try and hold back the pain. I put my mouth guard in every night to stop myself grinding my teeth to a fine powder ... One more never-ending process I can deal with, especially if it produces results like this. How much do I owe you?'

'Call it a free sample.'

'Well, thank you. You don't know how much this means. I am so grateful.'

Of course I burst into tears. The release. The kindness. It was

70

impossible not to. He cautiously entered the changing rooms and held me, patting my shoulder very gently like my mum used to.

'I would advise you to let me do this to you regularly. My rates are very reasonable.'

And so I let him do it to me regularly.

I took his mobile number, he took mine, and we met up every two to three weeks. He put me through the blissful agonies of deep-tissue massage, then his 'payment' was to let me buy him a sparkling water in the hotel bar afterwards.

I got to know a bit about Niall. He liked extreme sports like rock climbing and paragliding. He was single. When he said that, a spasm hit me, as if my entire body tensed up for battle, and a klaxon in my chest sounded. I told myself it was just another pain spasm.

He enjoyed acting, but he never thought he was quite good enough at it. He said it to provoke a reaction, and when I said nothing, he caught my eye. 'I take it from your silence you agree.'

'Sorry,' I said. 'My silence means I can't remember a great deal. I remember you got a lot of work. You were always working . . .'

'Not really the same thing.'

'If it's any consolation, if I was your agent you were probably a very good actor. I never took on rubbish.'

'Yes, that's what you used to say to me. "I never take on rubbish." You use to say it all the time — well, whenever you saw me. That was your motto.'

'Did I say that? I suppose I must have done. I can't remember that either.'

He snorted. 'That was your catchphrase! You can't even remember your catchphrase? Weird . . .'

He was starting to irritate, acting like I was a curiosity. Like some of the friends I used to have, who used to poke me with their words, hoping to see me wince.

He continued. 'The last time you said it to me, I was really down. I didn't get a part, and I thought I'd done very well in the auditions, and you emailed me and told me that to keep my pecker up, that I was really good, and you didn't take on rubbish, and to keep trying, no matter what obstacles were thrown in my way, and it really made an impression. I even printed the email out and . . . I . . . well . . . '

'What?'

'I framed it.'

'You framed it?'

'Ah. Yes.'

'Did you hang it up?'

'Um. Yes.'

I was enjoying myself now. 'You're kidding. Please tell me you put it in your toilet.'

'You're embarrassing me. Let's talk about something else.'

'Like what?'

'Like . . . How did you get this way? How did all this . . . ' he gestured at my body, like I was a prize in a quiz show, 'how did this happen to you?'

'I had an accident.'

'Yes.'

He waited. He had a big 'and . . . ?' expression on his face.

I thought about it. I was in such joy from the easing of the pain, I didn't feel like dwelling on it here. It felt so . . . negative. Backward-looking. I didn't want to talk about it. Not in this place of miracles.

'No,' I said at last. 'Not here. I don't really want to talk about it. I hope you understand. It doesn't matter any more.'

'OK. I'll not mention it again.'

'Good.'

He didn't pursue it but just said, 'So you didn't have a kid, then.'

Wow, I thought. *This was pain. An old kind of pain. Nothing to do with nerve pain. A good old-fashioned emotional punch-in-the-gut.*

Oblivious, he continued, 'I just heard you were going on maternity leave, that's all. That's why I thought you disappeared from the agency. I must have got the wrong end of the stick. Do you have children?'

'No,' I said, too quickly. 'So let's talk about something else. Please.'

He pulled a face like a slapped puppy and fell silent. We sat there, trying to think of something else to talk about. Eventually, we groped to a few subjects, and the conversation spluttered back to life.

We met more times, and chatted amiably like old friends. I was relieved that Niall obediently dropped it, but I felt that he was always hovering over the subject of my accident, like a drowsy bee near a flower, waiting until it was safe to land.

I just couldn't face it.

Monica

Back to today. I park in the hotel car park, and walk into the reception area.

It's been months since I last met Niall here. The hotel has had a facelift, like hotels do, because, like women, they can never decide if the world wants them to be practical or decorative.

This particular hotel was moving from functional brown to stylish cream. Gone were the thick chairs with the dark wipe-clean panels; now there are curved taupe sofas with pale leather cushions.

Next year, after those pretty cream cushions become filthy grey, I guarantee it'll probably go back to functional.

I can't make up my mind whether I'm hard-wearing or decorative, because I feel the accident split me in two and made me into both; like a tiny doll with pink accessories and gorgeous hair discovered in the wreckage of a plane crash. As my weary and confused husband knows, there's just no way to talk, to relate to, to just *be* with me, nothing that encompasses both facets of who or what I am. I'm very vulnerable and yet life has proved me invulnerable; an elegant vase that falls and smashes into a million pieces and yet stays whole, all at that same moment.

Niall is sitting uncomfortably on one of the new, impractical sofas, and he springs up to meet me, lunging to carry my bag.

'You're here. Great. Finally,' he says, unnecessarily.

He's got a look on his face. I've seen that look before. He looks like a wounded date, left waiting for hours in a restaurant, drinking water and chewing the flowers, hoping she turns up before the kitchens close.

I know I hadn't seen him in months but I do have a habit of not showing up. My condition often derails my day. Niall's making me feel guilty. He has no *right* to make me feel guilty. I feel tension gathering in my shoulders.

'I've already got the room downstairs,' he says, gesturing to the lifts. 'Shall we go?'

Back in the steamy atmosphere of the massage room, I manage to relax a little. I dip into the changing rooms and shrug off my shirt and skirt. The hotel dressing gown is there waiting for me, soft and freshly laundered.

I lie on the table, and brace myself. Niall is too eager to get started, and his hands are still cold. I suck in a sharp breath. He doesn't notice.

'Where have you been? I haven't seen you for months.'

'The usual. Pain. It's been rough. I haven't been up to visiting.'

'You didn't reply to my texts.'

'No I didn't. The pain stops me doing little things too. I have told you that. Oww. I guess you weren't listening.'

'I thought you'd disappeared again. Forgotten about me.'

'It's been rough. I haven't been up to coming out.'

His knuckles press into the small of my back and drag ever so slowly up my spine. The agony is immediate and profound.

'Fuck . . .'

Niall ignores my expletive.

'If you can't come out, then I should come to see you.'

'I've told you that as well. I'm a private person. I don't want you coming to my house. I don't want therapy at home.'

'I'm not anyone.' He sounds hurt.

'Sorry, Niall. I've got nothing against you, but my home is my sanctuary. It's my personal place where I try to conduct a normal life, as wife and human being and normal member of the human race—'

I gasp at the sudden pressure.

'—Mr Atos comes into my home every six months and I feel I have to fumigate the place. I don't want therapists and consultants in my house, sitting on my sofa and turning my house into a surrogate clinic. Meeting here with you works for me fine.'

The reason I don't want him in the house is because this feels too much like I'm having an affair.

That's what I'm really thinking.

'Well it's not working is it, because this . . .'

His hands find a knobbly bit of muscle, and I howl.

'. . . is not good. Not good at all. You've left it far too long.'

'I can't help it, if I haven't been up to it. As I said, it's been rough.'

'If it's rough, then that's more reason than ever for me to come over.'

'Yes, Mum.'

'I'm serious.'

'So am I. I have days, really bad days.'

'We all have bad days.'

'Oh God, you're not going to try the tough-love thing, like my sister? You'd better not tell me to pull myself together, or I will bite your bollocks off.'

He's not ready for my anger, and it unbalances him. How ironic, as he was the one who saw how unbalanced I was in the beginning. 'I'm just saying we all have bad days. It's how we deal with them—'

'Oh fuck off,' I snap.

'That's not a positive attitude. I'm trying to help.'

'Oh, fuck off some more. And when you've finished fucking off, fuck off some more. And then come back and fuck off again.'

My pain is rising now. It roars around my body like a forest fire.

'No one has bad days like me,' I say eventually. 'I have days when I can do nothing, absolutely nothing.'

'Well of course we—'

'Don't interrupt. Sometimes I am a living, breathing dead body, lying in state. Sometimes I open my eyes in the morning and pray for the day to end. Don't be one of those stupid people, who think because I've got a head on my shoulders and legs under my body that I can text and answer the door and make you a cup of tea and sit and talk and think like a normal human being. Because I can't.'

'I know, but a lot of it is state of mind.'

'Are you trying to raise my pain levels? Because that's what you're doing right now.'

76

I can't take any more.

'Stop it,' I say, and get up off the table. 'I can't do this now. You've upset me. And when I get upset it exacerbates the nerve pain. I've told you this a dozen times but I guess you didn't listen. No one really listens when I talk about my pain.'

I stumble back into the changing room and put my clothes on. Niall doesn't know what to say.

'I'm sorry,' he says eventually, through the partition.

'It's a bit late for that.'

'I shouldn't have said those things.'

'. . . Is the correct answer,' I say bitterly. 'You win a food mixer.'

'Let me take you to the hotel restaurant for lunch. On me.'

'What? You are priceless.'

'Please, so I can say sorry.'

'So you can feel better about yourself? No thank you. I would like to concentrate on me feeling better, thank you very much.'

'You need to calm down, and you need to stay inside, in the warmth, and you need a full stomach. Let me help you recover enough to drive home.'

He's right. So against my best wishes, I'm in the restaurant. The big stodgy lunch has been very naughty, but it was very badly needed. The restaurant has a fire, and I'm feeling warm inside and out. The pickaxe in my head is now just a toothpick, I still feel like shit, but I'm feeling more relaxed. Not the way everyone else understands the English word 'relaxed' but how the little country that is Greater Monikastan understands it. In Greater Monikastan 'relaxed' means 'slightly less pain'.

Niall apologised profusely for the first five minutes, but he had the good sense to sense that even that irritates me, and he now makes light, bright conversation about politics, television, music . . . Anything but talk about my pain. I appreciate that.

But this situation, this is the reason why I'm never giving Niall my address. I have visions of him gripped by a zeal to cure me, like Dominic had in the old days. I have nightmares of him turning up uninvited on my doorstep, a sloppy lopsided stupid grin on his face like one of his cheery text messages, and putting me through pain, shame and agony on the spot, whether I want it or not. I can't cope with that. This has to be on my terms. I have to control this thing or the walls will crumble, and my life will be invaded by Niall and people like Niall, and I will be a full-time patient and plaything for people with creams and pills and massage tables.

I don't know how to explain this to him without hurting him. So I don't try. I just try to communicate what it's like to be me, and hope he gets the message.

Niall wants to be a good boy again; he wants to examine what he has done like a knotty muscle, and give it a thorough massage. 'I shouldn't have talked like that, but I was anxious. I hadn't seen you in a long while, and I thought you had . . . forgotten about me.'

'Well I'm here.' I waggle a finger at my face. 'Almost alive and almost kicking.'

'I couldn't stop myself.' He was getting angry with himself. 'I know all about how your pain works, how stress makes it worse, but I still carried on.'

'I laughed when Dr Kumar explained it to me,' I say. '"You should avoid stress, Monica," he said. "The nerves will turn that fight-or-flight response into more pain." God how I laughed when he said that. The irony.'

Niall is starting to mope now, like he is the victim in all this. 'I knew all that. I turned a good day into a bad day.'

'Niall, don't worry. I know your chronic condition.'

'My *condition*?'

'Your life is afflicted by a bad case of being a bloke.'

I say it lightly, and he purses his lips, trying to take the joke in good part. *He wants to be different from the rest*, I think. *I can see it. He wants to be the confidant, the one who can hold my hand, the one who understands.*

'OK,' I say. 'Let me tell you about a *bad* day. A day when I was suspended over hot needles, when the pills didn't do anything but turn my brain upside down; when the shapes in the wallpaper were laughing at me and the pavement outside looked so inviting to splat against. I developed a theory; I reasoned that if there was less of my body to feel pain, then it would be bearable.

'I went to my doctor and talked seriously about the possibility of getting my arms and legs amputated. I would have rather lived the rest of my life as a paperweight than endure my life as it was. Dr Kumar entertained my theory. I was sweating buckets in his office, trying not to end up as a pool of insensible offal under his chair, and he was seriously talking about amputation, and I was seriously listening.'

'What did he say?'

'He said, and I quote . . . ' I put on my best Dr Kumar voice, ' "It is not that ridiculous. It is actually a method they use with wounded soldiers." He said it in that lovely way of his, the way he avoids all contractions, like a robot. There's no "it's", no "she's". I love it.'

People who hail from the Indian subcontinent have such a beautiful precise way of speaking, I think, it's as though they're still in love with the English language. It's why I've kept Dr Kumar longer than the others.

'Anyway, he told me that the soldiers that lose limbs sometimes get a variation on phantom-limb syndrome. They're feeling that limbs are still present when they're gone. Sometimes arms and legs that are causing pain get blown off in action, but it happens so abruptly that their nervous system doesn't realise they're missing.

Dr Kumar said it was "like a magician whipping away a tablecloth and leaving all the plates on the table . . ."'

I smile at Niall. 'Even though I love his speech patterns, I'm *less* keen on Dr Kumar's analogies. So they're still feeling searing agony from limbs that just are not there any more. Kumar said it was a terrible disorientating condition to endure, but I couldn't muster up much sympathy, obviously. Well, to cut a long story very short, very very short, they found that by taking an extra inch or two off the stump, a body would "get the message", sometimes, so to speak, and stop sending pain signals into the brain.'

Niall speaks at last. 'So what did you say?'

'What did you think I said? "Then let's do it. Take the fuckers off. Take my arms and legs off. All of them. Right now."'

Niall looks shocked. I go into my Dr Kumar voice. ' "Wait a moment, Monica. Hold those horses. This is the problem we will be having with that approach; your pains in your arms and legs do not start there, they start in your sciatic nerve, and we cannot remove that. Once again we come up against the mystery that is the nervous system. No matter what extremities of your body we remove, there is no possibility that your pain will cease." And I said, "There will be if you remove my head."'

Niall laughs at last. I laugh too.

'So he strongly advised me not to pursue this course of action. So I admitted defeat, and took my horribly intact body back home.'

He digests this.

'What I'm trying to say, I'm sorry I snapped at you. I say things that I know I don't mean. It's the pain talking. Or rather it's a different me.'

'That's OK.'

'No, it's not. So enough with the "that's OK" stuff. Let me

explain.' I speak slowly, choosing my words carefully. 'So many things have happened to my body over the last five years, and most of the time my mind has been dragged screaming along behind, like a man with his coat caught in the doors of an underground train. I've just found out I tried to commit suicide, four years ago, and I can't even remember . . .'

His eyes widen.

' . . . so what with the pain and the drugs doing things to my brain, sometimes I feel I've lost sight of the real me. I don't know which me is here on which day. I'm not even sure which me is sitting here now . . . That's not very clear, is it?'

'No, it sounds perfectly clear,' he says calmly.

'It's like . . . Take last month. I'm in the kitchen, and I'm screaming at Dominic, like *really* screaming at him, for forgetting to unload the dishwasher . . .'

He listens very intently. All men are wolves, deep down, and wolves sense weakness. They always listen intently to attractive women talking about marital strife at home.

'Would the painless me have ever done that? No. Would the painless me look at the pain-racked me screaming about a fucking dishwasher, and be horrified at what I was doing? Would the pain-racked me kill someone, cut off her legs, have an affair, or would she not? I don't honestly know. I know the pain-free me would be horrified if I did any of those things, but I couldn't say honestly, hand on heart, that a pain-racked me wouldn't just say, "Fuck it, life's too short."'

He nods vigorously.

'It's like there's lots of me, like loads of Monicas from alternative dimensions. Sometimes I'm a bad Monica with evil thoughts in my head, like I've been driven insane by the pain. Sometimes I'm a good Monica, who has been made a better person *because* of the pain. But *both* of those Monicas come from the pain, so perhaps there's *another* Monica, the real one that I've completely lost track of.'

Niall drinks his sparkling water. Finally he says, 'Would you like me to drive you home?'

'That's very sweet of you, Niall, but there would be no point. My car would still be here.'

'I could drive you there, drive back, drive your car to your house, and take a taxi back.'

'Don't be stupid.'

'It's no bother.'

I'm too tired to argue, so I just have to be rude. Close it down.

'And I'm not an invalid, Niall. I'm just in a fucking world of pain.'

That ends my confession.

Dominic

Monica was out today, so Dominic took the opportunity to phone in sick and go 'home'.

He went 'home' every six months or so, so he and his dad could sit in the front room together and not talk to each other, but nowadays he felt like he was coming to a foreign country.

Of course, he knew very well that Scotland *was* a foreign country, but it never quite felt like that before; not when he first moved down south in the nineties and started travelling 'home' to his parents. He put this 'other country' feeling down to the journey rather than any shifts towards nationalism in the political landscape. Trains were more like planes these days, with their comfy seats and smart waistcoated stewards, their wi-fi, and their singsong bing-bong announcements. Every effort was made to fool the commuter into thinking they were embarking on an international flight to somewhere exotic.

So when the eye-watering flatness of Peterborough and the undulating landscape of Yorkshire gave way to rocks and crags, he imagined the undercarriage wheels unfolding, and the train gliding down to land in Edinburgh.

It felt odd, not going to see his dad, but it couldn't be helped. He really didn't have time. Not this time. Once he got to Dunfermline he power-walked along the quiet, tree-lined street, watching the cross appear amongst the chimney pots, like a satellite dish calibrated to pick up signals from heaven. It grew fatter and blacker, and soon, beneath it, there it was; the church, *his* church, just as he remembered it. Old and shabby, coated with soot and exhaust fumes, squashed between two gleaming office buildings like a rotten tooth interrupting a dazzling smile.

The interior hadn't changed much. Not in years. There were collages on the wall, trees with leaves fashioned using the paint-smeared hands of Sunday school infants, and there was a brightly coloured crèche decorated with fat cushions and a wooden Noah's ark, complete with smiling animals. *A crèche!* When he came here as a boy they didn't even have hassocks. Father Jerome had a thing against them. Father Jerome had a thing against everything.

Truth to tell, he still hated the place, and almost gave an involuntary gag as he stood in the vestibule.

He focused on the confessional. God's photo-booth. That's what he and the other choir boys called it. There was a photo-booth in Woolworths in Dunfermline high street, just the same shape and size, and he and his mates crammed into it. They used to put 50p in the slot and tried to confess all their sins before the machine stopped flashing. Their faces and mouths were a crazed blur on the strip of photos that dropped, wet and glistening, into the little cage at the front. That was a very long time ago. He wondered where the photos were now. He wondered fleetingly where James Rennie and Spud Ferguson were now. Working in whatever shop replaced Woolworths, if he knew them.

He'd rung ahead, as was proper, and when he entered the booth, heavy with the smell of beeswax and damp, there was the extra, sandalwood odour of Father Hancock's hastily shaved chin.

'Long time no see, Dominic,' the priest's voice rumbled through the screen. 'Not that I can see you through this bloody thing, but I'm guessing you're somewhere in there.'

'Hello, Father.'

'I was surprised to get your call for confession. I must make a little confession myself. I never thought I'd see you back here again. I thought you'd gone off to London.'

'I live in London, Father. I'm just in the area today.'

He was 'just in the area today'. That was funny. An eleven hour train journey, five and a half hours here, and five and a half hours back again.

'And you came to see me? I'm flattered, my son.'

Dominic said nothing.

'Well ... OK then ... I suppose we should ...?'

'Bless me, Father, for I have sinned,' Dominic said, low and urgent. 'It's been three months since my last confession.'

'So ... What can I do for you, my son?'

'I have had thoughts. Bad thoughts. I've had ... urges ... In my head. Terrible thoughts.'

'We've all had those thoughts, my son. There's nothing to be ashamed of.'

'I've been thinking that ... I ... I want to kill my wife.'

Dominic

Father Hancock's breathing spluttered to a halt. A low wheeze sounded from the grille as he let out a lungful of air. 'Now why would you want to think such a terrible thing, my son?'

'Lots of reasons.'

'Marriage is a very hard road. Love is a delicate thing, but even when it fades, it can endure. You just need to—'

'Don't misunderstand me, I do love my wife.'

'I see?'

'Yes, Father. With all my heart.'

'Well, then, you have to help me, Dominic. I have to say I'm a little confused here. I do recall I conducted the ceremony. And ... I do believe that was the last time I saw you. Yes. Yes, I do I believe it was. The last time I saw you, you were sitting on a gravestone in a force nine gale, raindrops being snatched off your nose in the wind, and you were telling me that you loved your new wife, and you wanted to protect her from the evils of this world. And I thought, "My experience tells me that here is a bond that will last." And here you are telling me you love her. Why on earth would you ever think of harming her?'

'It's not that simple, Father.'

'It never is.'

'She has pain. Deep chronic pain.'

'I see.'

'She's had it five years. It's tough. For me. It's not easy, living with the pain.'

'You aren't living with the pain, my son. Your wife is living with the pain.'

'That's just it. I do live with the pain. All the time. The pain makes her impossible. Sometimes ...'

'That's why she needs you, my son.'

'I know that, Father. But sometimes it feels like I'm not living with my wife any more, just the pain. Sometimes, maybe most times, I'm on my own, just as my dad was on his own when Mum was near the end of her life, when the cancer had completely devoured her. He was just living with a piece of meat that happened to have the same name as the woman he'd once married.'

'Very sad and tragic, Dominic, but that's not quite the same.'

'It is, Father. Sometimes it feels like Monica disappears, that all trace of her gets wiped from existence, and all that remains is pain, a crying, screeching, bitching, nagging, physical representation of pain. And I live with this Thing That Is Not My Wife, day in, day out, day in, day out.'

'It's still not the same. You can talk with your wife. She still knows she loves you.'

'But at least my dad got peace sometimes, at least Mum was passive when she was on the morphine, and he could read a book or listen to the radio. Not with Monica. When someone is in that much pain, then the Rest of the World is always wrong, and in Monica's case, the Rest of the World is me.'

'But you are so lucky, my son. I've had strong men and women in here, weeping for their husbands and wives, taken by Alzheimer's. It's the living death, the silence that they can't stand.'

'I live for silence. I *dream* for silence sometimes. I fantasise about it.'

'Dominic ... You and your wife, you still love each other, and she still knows she loves you. You know you can talk things through.'

'You don't get it. You don't understand.'

'I'm trying, my son.'

'I can't talk things through. Not at all.'

'You can. Of course you can.'

'I can't. Monica complains about me not speaking, but how can I? When every word I say is a step, and every step is part of a journey across a live minefield, where every step might blow up in my face ... Well, I err on the side of not speaking. Wouldn't you?

'You see, Father, everybody talks about how the accident, the pain, how it changed Monica ...'

'Well ...'

'No one ever noticed that it changed me, too.'

Dominic

'You must put these dark thoughts out of your mind, my son.'

'I'll try, Father.'

'You of all people know that the flesh can be weak. But that was why God made the soul within you unchanging and everlasting. You might think yourself changed, but you are the same loving husband you always were. Call upon God for strength, and He will answer.'

'I will, Father.'

'Go in peace, my son.'

Dominic's fingers were drumming on the wall of the confessional. Father Hancock sensed his impatience and gabbled through the sacrament. He assured the Father of his contrition and was assigned penance for his shameful thoughts. The moment Father Hancock struggled out of his side of the booth, Dominic dashed out of the church and practically ran back to the train station. He had to get his connection to Edinburgh, and then he'd be back home by seven at the latest.

Monica

They say that truth is stranger than fiction; that our lives are far more improbable than stories.

From my experience, I am the best person in the world to say that observation is completely and utterly true. My life is one fat collection of ironies; and coincidence is the handmaiden of irony.

We leave the hotel restaurant, and there is a little boy playing on the table in front of the reception. He's about four years old, and he's arranging the magazines in some order that I can't quite discern. He has a mop of tousled brown hair and he's wearing a Thomas the Tank Engine jumper which is slightly too small for him. I notice with some satisfaction that his grimy fingers have already marked the white leather cushions.

Niall tenses. His eyes dart around, sensing danger. He thinks I don't notice, but I do.

The drugs make me notice everything, whether I want to or not.

Niall keeps walking to the boy, who looks up from his monumental task and smiles at him. 'Hello, Daddy,' he says to Niall. 'Look what I'm doing.'

'That's lovely, Peter,' says Niall, 'very pretty. Where's Mummy?'

'She's gone for a wee-wee,' says Peter. He points to the ladies' toilet. 'Over there.'

'I see,' mutters Niall. 'So . . . She's left you on your own.'

'She's only gone for a wee-wee.' Peter is exasperated. 'The lady behind the desk is watching me.'

The lady behind the reception desk gives Peter (and us) a fluttery little wave. Peter waves back. Stupidly, I give the same wave to the receptionist.

Niall doesn't know what to do. He wanders around the perimeter of the reception like he's in a cage, stalking in a wide circle until he comes back to me. Then he's staring at me as if he wishes I would evaporate, but I'm not going anywhere.

'Oh, OK. Right. I'm going to . . . You should . . . '

'I didn't know you had a wife.'

'I don't. Ex-wife.'

'Or a child.'

89

'Well . . .'

'I thought you'd have mentioned it. You told me you liked to do paragliding, and rock climbing, and you told me your favourite actor was Peter O'Toole, and you were thrilled to meet him when he did *Jeffery Bernard is Unwell* in the West End, when you sold ice creams at the Apollo—'

'I didn't want to,' he snaps.

'—and you told me you were a fan of Sting, and had seen him eighteen times in concert, but you've never mentioned—'

'Let's make a deal, OK?' He looks at me with sudden, quiet anger. 'I don't bring up your accident, do I? You don't bring up my ex-wife and son.'

I blink. 'OK.'

'Good.'

The next thing I see is a woman walking from the toilets. She doesn't look happy. She is pretty, with large hazel eyes, dazzling cheekbones and immaculate teeth. I am quite struck by her elegant long coat, and her shiny black hair.

I'm also struck by how like me she looks.

'Well, well, fancy meeting you here.' Her eyes flick from Niall to me, and scans me with unvarnished disgust. 'Is this the new one?'

He steps in front of me. 'She's a friend.'

'Of course she is,' she sneers.

'What are you doing here, Lorraine? Are you following me?'

'I come here all the time,' she laughs, echoing Niall's words to me when we met in the gym. She pulls a sour smile. 'I didn't have to follow you, Niall. Claudia uses this place all the time. She saw you two lovebirds come in and she phoned me. Why? Is it a problem? Goodness, you haven't been avoiding me, have you? By any chance?'

Niall looks at me with a pain-stricken face. 'I'm so sorry. I can't tell you how sorry I am about this. I hope this confrontation hasn't elevated your pain levels.'

Lorraine demands his attention. 'Never mind about her pain levels, worry about your own.'

'I have nothing to say to you.'

'Well I've got a lot to say to you.'

Niall and Lorraine are edging slowly away from me, towards the back of the hotel, so they can swear at each other without upsetting their son. Lorraine flings herself on a couch near the restaurant, and Niall paces angrily in front of her, back and forth. I can guess their conversation is about money or, specifically, maintenance, but in case there's any doubt, Lorraine leans forward, puts her hand up to Niall's face and rubs her thumb and first finger together.

I suddenly realise I'm left alone with Peter. I sit down, not too close, but not too near. You hear stories of adults being accused of all sorts of things. But Peter has no such reservations. He trots over to me. 'Do you like tigers?' he says.

'Oh I love—'

'Rarr!' he says abruptly, before I have a chance to finish, curling his tiny hands into talons. He finds this very funny. He tells me it's a joke he's learned from Kevin in playschool.

'They can kill you.'

'Oh, certainly.'

'I think tigers are awesome. Kevin likes them too.'

He advances on me, holding a big squishy book with a tiger on it. 'Here you go.' He puts the book on my lap, then clambers up to join it.

Oh Christ fuck fuck fuck fuck. My body screams. *I can't take this. I can't take this. This is too much for me.*

But I don't put Peter on the floor. I can no more put the child down than I can wish away my pain. I read him the story about

91

the tiger, twice, while the pain paces around my hips in a wide circle and snarls to the world. I look nervously across to the receptionist, but she just smiles back at us. Obviously she saw Niall with me, Peter with his mummy, Niall with Peter, and she's assumed I'm some friend of the family or a child-minding aunt.

I can hear the conversation between Niall and Lorraine, even though it is being exchanged in snarled whispers. It's the drugs. I just can't help it.

Niall's been a naughty boy about child support, says Lorraine. Niall counters by saying he knows damn well she's seeing someone, so why can't he dip into his pocket? Why can't he make an honest woman out of her, and pay for Peter's clothes and shoes? She says it's none of his damn business, and Niall should man up, take responsibility for his child, and stop whining.

After ten minutes, Lorraine notices Peter is on my lap, and her face contorts into maternal outrage. She struggles to her feet and totters towards me as fast as her Manolo Blahniks will allow.

'I have to go,' I say to Peter.

'OK,' says Peter, not that bothered.

'See you.' I smile, and I pat Peter on the head. 'Thanks for sharing your book, Peter.'

'It's not my book,' he says pityingly. 'I found it on the table. They have it for the babies to read.'

'Well, thank you for sharing the hotel's book,' I say. 'It's just a big shame that you don't like tigers.'

'But I do like—'

'Rarr!' I say, curling my fingers into talons before he finishes. And he giggles hysterically. He is still giggling when his mother gets to him, and I'm on the other side of the hotel's revolving door.

Monica

I'm sitting back, keeping my breathing steady, mustering up the strength to drive home.

Thank God for automatic cars.

I'm thinking about little Peter; about his tiny fat fingers turning the quilted pages, the smell of his thick mousy hair. When my arms circled him to keep him safe, I felt the tiny rise-and-fall breathing of his chest, and the comforting prickle of his jumper on the palms of my hands.

I can still feel the weight of his little bottom on my lap. This time the pain is a reminder of my time with him, so I embrace it.

I would have been a good mother.

I don't drive home. Even in my desperate state, when I turn the key and pull out of my parking space, I don't drive home. Just like when I went to the pub with Niall, my body is taking me on an adventure and my mind is tagging along for a ride.

I find myself in the multi-storey car park belonging to the hospital, driving round and round to get up to the roof. Not to get treatment, of course. What I have is beyond the abilities of anything Casualty can give me.

This is where I had my 'accident'.

Monica

I reach the top of the multi-storey, and the world explodes with light. Gravel crunches under the weight of my driving shoes as I walk from the middle to the tarmac around the edge.

I gaze out over Kensington High Street, and beyond. You can see the whole of west London from here; so many cranes in the air, building the future. It's cold and blustery. The wind plucks at my clothing. This kind of view deserves a poem. Perhaps I should try to write one. The sky is glorious, a beautiful pale blue, so very pale blue, almost white, like ...

Like the colour of my amitriptyline pills.

No, it's like a sparrow's egg. Like the paint job on my first car. Like our bathroom. Like the romper suit I bought for Jesse's little boy ...

Like the colour of my amitriptyline pills.

Shit!

My mind struggles to kid itself that it thought of all those glorious things first, but it's fooling nobody. I know the first thing that popped into my head.

(**amitriptyline pills**)

Shit!

Shit shit shit!

My Angry Friend has robbed me of my body, my career, my friends, my hopes for motherhood, and he's bloody near taken my sanity. And now he's poisoned my imagination. Some hope for me becoming a poet.

I turn round and look at the stairwell from where I emerged. This is where my Angry Friend took all those things from me.

This time, I count the steps. There were twenty-two. *Of course. There had to be twenty-two.*

94

Thud thud thud.

This is where I fell, just there, and everyone was so relieved that it had not been worse, that I had not broken my spine.

(**Ha ha ha**)

Minor surgery, nothing more.

When the pain stayed, they said it was just residual effects from the surgery. When the pain got worse they said it was a side effect of the injury healing itself. When it got unbearable, they admitted that my acute neuropathic pain had been replaced by chronic neuropathic pain, and that it might be here to stay . . .

That whole first year I can't remember, but I was dimly aware of a blur of plot twists, each one bringing fresh hell into my life. I felt like a teenager in a horror film; where every revelation took me deeper and deeper into a nightmare. I often think, if those luckless teenagers were blessed with self-awareness, they would review their situation. An hour ago, they were packing for a nice summer vacation, now their friends are dead and a zombie with a chainsaw is chasing them in the wood.

And they would ask themselves, 'How exactly did I get from there to here?'

Because I can't quite work it out. My mind can't fit it all in my head. I try to work it out but I can't, and no one can quite explain the whole thing to me.

I knew I was at the hospital because Dominic and I had been trying for a baby. He told me that. We'd been trying to conceive for some time. We had both been getting tested to see if the problem was at my end, or his, and that had also been another long period of discovery, full of twists and shocks, but finally, success. Wouldn't you know it, my lady parts were perfectly functional, and we discovered that Dominic's sperm was rather lazy and lackadaisical, lacking 'get up and go'.

But things had been done, plastic tubes had been inserted, and then we were told there was a life growing inside me. I'm sorry to say that I can't remember that moment either, but Dominic used to describe it to me. He used to do it so well, exaggerating the significance of that fateful moment every time he told it, until there was a star hovering above the ultrasound machine, and three wise men waiting in the hospital's Costa Coffee.

Then he started to sound like he didn't want to describe it any more, and so I stopped asking.

I had come up to the roof to get the car, to drive it down to Dominic who was buying a newspaper in the hospital shop. The morning was very busy, and we had to park on the top floor. I reached the roof of the hospital, up the steps, coming out into the morning daylight. I must have looked at the skyline of London, this view, the one I'm looking at again, which I guess would have been the last thing I would have seen as a woman without pain. Then someone found me at the bottom of the stairwell, and I couldn't move, and there was something sticking in the small of my back: my stiletto heel. Lying there, wounded and helpless, about forty feet above the Casualty department.

How ironic.

Two lives had been extinguished that day; the tiny blob of orange growing inside me, and the life of Monica Wood, agent, sister, wife, prospective mother.

And no matter how much of a blur my life has become, no matter how many chunks of my memory float away, I remember the flat of the hand against my back. The hand that propelled me into the stairwell.

They all say that I imagined it.

I didn't.

Because that hand pushed me, and the owner of that hand left me for dead.

Monica

I've not come up here since ...

Well, not since the accident.

I mean, why would I? What would be the point? To investigate the scene of the crime, find some hitherto undiscovered vital piece of evidence that would be left miraculously intact after five years exposed to the elements?

Evidence that would lead me to the door of my mystery assailant?

Even as I'm laughing at myself for even thinking about the idea, I find myself looking around, looking for footprints, or patches of blood, or bits of cloth torn from my attacker's clothes, fluttering in the breeze.

Nothing. (**Of course not. Stupid, stupid woman**)

Maybe that's why I'm obsessing about my suicide letter. It just *feels* like a piece of evidence, an item discovered in the first act of a creaky old whodunnit play, or placed in a bag in the first minutes of a TV thriller.

Perhaps the letter is exactly what it seems to be; a letter written by a woman in pain who wanted to die. Perhaps it's just me, trying to find some drama in the discovery. Perhaps I've worked in the entertainment industry for far too long.

As my head swivels from right to left and back again, shapes appear on the edge of my peripheral vision, fat black blobs appear in front of me, floating around like airborne slugs. I'm used to these things; they appear from time to time when I'm exhausted by the pain.

But these weren't slugs. They were three figures, floating, hovering over the edge of the concrete wall and the black metal fence. Three smiling, elderly figures: my parents and Dominic's mother.

Sometimes, in my head, in my muffled, fuzzy, drug-soaked brain, reality leaks into my dreams; visions of pain and torture that are carried into my slumber as a hangover from the day's suffering.

And sometimes, even more frighteningly, dreams leak into my reality.

Shit!

I can't stay up here, not this far off the ground! I can see myself happily walking off the edge of the building trying to shake hands with the dead.

I walk back to the steps, shielding my head from the visions that float on the horizon, fearing that they, like sirens, will lure me to my doom. I go to the top of the stairwell, and I nearly miss my footing and fall down the steps.

As I said. Irony.

I don't stop walking until I'm leaning on my car door, fighting to retrieve the keys from my pocket, then I hoist myself into the car seat with a grateful sigh.

Monica

I go home and I can hear Dominic busying himself in the kitchen, clattering and clanging and hurting my ears.

'Hello!' I call.

'In the kitchen!' he calls back.

The pain levels are making me lose control of my thoughts. My Angry Friend is laughing, and my brain is hot and rebellious.

Of course you're in the kitchen. I can hear that.

Why

did you say that?

Why

did you have to say that? You could have just said 'hello' back, but that was too simple for you, you had to say you were in the kitchen when I can bloody well hear you're in the kitchen!

Why

would you need to say you're in the kitchen? It's not a big house. Are you saying I can't manage to find you in the house without you helping me?

Am I that helpless? Is that how I appear to you?

There's a beige square lying in the hallway. A letter – and it's addressed to me. A white-hot spear of rage pierces my belly.

He must have come in from work and ignored it.

How

could he have done that?

He knows how I feel. He knows how much effort it takes for me sometimes, to reach down. You knew that and you came in and you

just walked past it.

'Oh, that's all right, I can see from here it's Monica's letter, she can pick it up. I'll go and get myself a drink and potter around in the kitchen. I did my bit this morning, when I brought her up a cup of tea. She can pick up her damn stupid letter. She can do that. She can pick it up.'

Yes,

I'm not doing anything at the moment. I can pick up my own damn letter.

I bend over as far as I dare, holding my breath so I can release it when the pain comes. My fingertips scrabble for the edge of the envelope. I tickle it into my grasp, breathe out, pick it up and open it.

God, that was quick! Dr Kumar must have been on to the clinic the second I had left, and they must have made the appointment there and then.

Surgical Admissions Department
369 Fulham Road
London
SW10 9NH

Application of Capsaicin Patch for Pain

Dear Mrs Wood

I am pleased to inform you that arrangements have been made for you to attend the Treatment Centre at Chelsea and Westminster Hospital.

On: **Monday 7th July at 9 a.m.** for your treatment with 8% capsaicin patch under the care of Dr Martin or one of his team.

On receipt of this letter, please phone the confirmation line to confirm that this date is convenient. Please note it is not our policy to call you back once you have confirmed your admission.

If you do not confirm your attendance two weeks before your admission date, your appointment will be cancelled and you will be discharged back to the care of your GP. Please note that even if you have spoken to an Admissions Scheduler on a previous occasion regarding your admission, you must call the above number to confirm.

Please read enclosed additional information that we have supplied to help keep you informed about your admission and procedure.

<u>Information about your admission for this procedure</u>

You should arrange for someone to escort you home after your procedure in the Treatment Centre/Clinic.

Please take all your medications as normal on the morning

of the procedure, including your painkillers. You may take blood thinning medication as normal.

You can eat and drink as normal before this procedure.

Please bring all your regular medicines into hospital with you and ensure that they are in their original containers. Please inform the nurse who is looking after you exactly what medication you have brought with you and anything you have taken on the morning of your admission.

If your procedure is going to take place in the Treatment Centre please note that the Treatment Centre reception serves as a drop-off and collection point for patients. On admittance all companions should supply a contact telephone number on which Treatment Centre staff can contact them with an approximate time for collection.

Please be aware that in order to comply with new guidelines for same accommodation we restrict accompanying partners in the clinical environment.

If you have any questions which are not answered by the information we have already sent you please contact us.

That was all on the first page. I make a quick mental calculation. Seventh of July. Nearly two weeks' time. I'd better ring them as soon as possible before it slips my mind.

I go into the study, put the envelope in the shredder, and read on to page two.

You will be admitted for application of capsaicin 8% patch to help with your pain. The capsaicin patch contains a form of chilli and when applied to the painful area it is hoped that it will make the nerves in this area less sensitive to pain.

Before the procedure, we will apply local anaesthetic cream to the painful area and leave it there for 60 minutes. This cream should make your skin feel numb so that when we apply the capsaicin patch it is more comfortable for you.

The patch will then be applied to the painful area and left there for 30–60 minutes depending on the location of your pain. During this time you may experience heat and burning in this area and you may need extra pain relief to help this settle down. You should let staff know if this heat and burning becomes difficult to tolerate. Your blood pressure may go up as a result of this and we will monitor your blood pressure during the treatment.

We will then remove the patch and apply some cooling gel to help with the burning sensation. The skin may look red. You may leave the hospital approximately thirty minutes after we have finished the procedure, and you must have someone to take you home.

Monica

The letter lifts my mood, and my mood lifts some of my pain. I'm always amazed how emotions – anxiety, happiness, anger, joy – all either feed or starve my Angry Friend, if only for a short time. I even give Dominic a sunny smile when I sit down to the dinner table.

Dominic has decided to cook. He sits me down and brings in prawns in avocado, with rocket salad and tomatoes. One of the simple, healthy meals that he's mastered to spare me lifting pots and pans.

'OK, this is your starter . . .'

It's only after he is sitting down that I realise. 'Did you say "starter"?'

'*Mais oui, mademoiselle*. Did you sink ah would be starving you tonight? Zis is merely the first course in ma leetle *déjeuner*. Not a *petit déjeuner*, mark you; zat would be breakfast. Zis is merely ma leetle *déjeuner*. 'Ow are you off for waine?'

I notice he has a tea towel draped over his arm, like he's pretending to be a head waiter. I smile and get into the act. I waggle the stem of my glass. 'Are you sure this is wine in my glass? It looks like cranberry juice to me.'

'*Non*. It iz zee finest waine, made with ze finest grapes squashed wiz ma finest feet.'

I sip from my glass, and yes, it's wine. It's deep and makes my lips feel warm and fuzzy. It tastes expensive.

He turns the lights down and I look around the darkness in wonder. 'Is this romance?'

He sipped his wine. 'Could be.'

'Oh.'

'If that's all right,' he says, suddenly cautious.

'It might be, only ...'

'Only ...?'

'If this is romance then I have to have a candle. It's the law.'

'Right, you asked for a candle, zen Madame gets a candle.' He springs up again and I hear rummaging in the kitchen drawers.

'Your avocado is getting cold.'

'Don't worry. Carry on eating. I'll be there in a minute.'

And then he's back, and he sticks a birthday candle on the table with a blob of Blu Tack. He takes out a box of matches and a tiny pathetic flame rises out of the candle.

'*Voilà*.'

I smile. 'So you remembered.'

His smile freezes. 'Remembered? Remembered what? Nowhere

103

near our wedding anniversary. Not your birthday. Definitely not your birthday. Phew. Safe there.'

'It's an anniversary. Of sorts.'

'It is?'

'It's five years this week, since I had my accident.'

His eyes go cold. 'I didn't know that.'

'I do. It's in my calendar on my laptop.'

'Well, OK. Hm. Let's get this straight. I just want to say. All this . . .' he gestures to the food and the candle, 'this was not to celebrate five years.'

'I thought you were being positive. You know what the websites say: embrace it. Celebrate it.'

'Sod that.'

'I'm joking, darling. Of course this isn't to celebrate. You were just being romantic. I know that.'

We carry on eating in silence.

'I got my appointment today for my treatment. The one where they cover you in chilli oil and fry you over a naked flame.'

'Right.'

'Here's the letter.'

I offer it to him. He doesn't look like he wants to take it, like he wants to carry on eating, but he does, and flips the stapled pages back and forth. It doesn't look as if he's reading very carefully.

I chunter on. 'It's looks like it's quite a major treatment. They do say that someone has to be with me afterwards. I can't drive home or anything like that.'

'Have you finished?'

'No, I really want to talk about it now.'

He smiles. 'I mean, have you finished your starter?'

I laugh. 'Yes, I'm finished.'

He takes up the plates and comes back with two plates of chilli con carne.

I look at my food. 'This is lovely, darling.'

'Thanks. I wish I had picked a better day.'

'You picked a perfect day.'

We eat for about a minute before he says: 'Monica, I'm not sure this is a good idea.'

'No, it's a lovely gesture. Really.'

'Not the meal. The treatment.'

I look at him, astonished. *Did I hear right?*

'I don't understand.'

'Did you read this?'

'Of course I have.'

He holds it up and reads it anyway, out loud. ' "During this time you may experience heat and burning in this area and you may need extra pain relief to help this settle down . . ." '

He stares at me and shakes the letter, so it flaps like a wounded bird.

'Extra pain relief? Extra pain relief on top of all the other pain relief you're taking? What kind of treatment asks you, of all people, to take *extra pain relief*?'

'It's a different kind of pain. It's on the surface.'

'It's a lot of extra pain, and for what? And I did some more reading on their website.'

'Bully for you.'

'Don't be like that,' he sighs. 'You know in the past I've always taken a huge interest in how to help your condition. I've put in hours on the internet finding out new treatments for you. The thing is, this capsaicin trial . . . Yes, they've had results, but the actual treatment might be as nasty as the pain, and all the results they've had are temporary.'

'Yes, but the trial is in its early days, they're still finding out what the effects are on people like me.'

'You don't have to be their guinea pig. There are other people

105

out there, with less pain, people they can experiment with to their heart's content and it won't be such a big thing to them.'

We eat in silence. Somewhere, somewhen, the evening has taken a wrong turn, as it so often does these days. The atmosphere has cooled, and I know that both of us regret it, but neither of us has the energy or the temperament to turn it around.

Finally, I say: 'I'm a big girl, Dominic. I can take it.'

'No you can't. I know you.'

'I think *I* know *me* a lot better.'

'You might get a month or so of pain relief, and then it's back to normal ...'

'Isn't that good enough? Isn't a month of *not* feeling like this good enough for me?'

'Not enough. Not nearly enough.'

'Dominic ... I can't believe you. I can't believe your attitude.'

'Don't you understand? What if you do get, what, a bit of time with a bit less pain, what then?'

'What then???!'

He sighs.

I hate that sigh, because he's let slip he's weary of me, weary of something I've become, something that I have no control over. There's such a thing as 'compassion fatigue'. Everyone gets it. My friends got it long ago, that's why I don't see them any more, because no one can be sympathetic for ever.

Dominic gets compassion fatigue too. He says he doesn't, but he lies. *We both lie.*

'What if they stop the trials?' he says. 'What if they abandon it? What if you can't get the treatment again?'

He waves a hand helplessly. I look down at the letter in my hand. It takes me a while to focus on the squiggles. 'I have an appointment in two weeks. They're expecting someone to come with me and drive me home. They're expecting you to look after me.'

He drinks deeply from his wine and places it heavily on the marble coaster; slightly too heavily, as though he's trying to break the glass and cause a distraction.

'I can't do that. I don't want you to do it. I can't see you get something only to see it snatched away again.'

'But I want to do this. It's my body, and I want to do it.'

'I can't in all conscience allow you to do it.'

I can't believe what he's saying. 'So you don't want to help me.'

'I didn't say that,' he says softly.

'You didn't have to.' My scraps of patience were gone. 'Thank you for that vote of confidence.'

He casts his eyes to the heavens and sighs. 'You're not thinking straight.'

That stings. *There is one thing you don't do. Don't suggest I've lost my mind. My mind is the only thing I have left.*

'I'm not thinking straight?'

He knows he's crossed a line but, being a man, he has no choice but to plough on. 'The pain makes you try things that you really shouldn't try. Remember that American doctor who claimed he could shock the body into feeling less pain by causing you *more* pain? Remember that woman who put those bloody crystals on your body? We've been here so many times before. We've had so many false dawns . . . '

'I'm not talking about false dawns. I want you to explain why you think I'm not thinking straight.'

'Monica . . . '

'I suppose you consider yourself the benchmark of sanity in this house?'

Dominic's fork is twirling testily in his hand. 'OK, fine. If you want to put it like that, then so be it. Yes, I do.'

I laugh at him, a cruel laugh designed to provoke, and his voice becomes clipped and cold. 'Given that you're the one who takes four different kinds of mind-altering drugs, and who rattles like a pill bottle when she walks, do you not agree that it's a good chance that I'm the one who has a firmer grip on what is sane and insane? Is that a not unreasonable assumption to make?'

I start to speak but he holds up his hand. His knife and fork clatter on his plate. 'Yes or no?'

'If you put it—'

'Yes or no???'

'Fine, yes,' I glower. 'It is not an unreasonable assumption to make. I applaud you for your elegant summary of the facts. I suppose I also wasn't thinking straight when I imagined someone pushing me down those car park steps.'

He looks surprised. 'Well, if we're bringing that up ...'

'Someone did push me down those steps. I told you.'

'Three months *after* the accident, when you *also* told me that you thought the jackdaws in the garden were spying on you ...'

'That was the drugs.'

'You also told me you were Joan of Arc in a previous life.'

'I said that was the drugs.'

He raises his eyebrows and holds his hands up. 'And in conclusion, your honour ...'

'You cunt,' I say. I tip my chilli con carne on the floor. Then I run to the kitchen and slam the door. Then I go to the draining board and smash the dessert bowl on the floor.

The kitchen door opens behind me.

'You didn't have to do that.'

'I never want to see you again.'

'That's the pain talking.'

'Every time I say anything you don't like, that's the pain talking.'

'Well it is, isn't it?'

'Maybe I don't want to see you again. Maybe this is just me talking. Me!'

He goes to me and circles my body with his arms, holding me in a cage. This is the technique he has perfected; I can't break out of it without hurting myself. I can't cope with any more pain. I hold my arms into my body, like a boxer clinging to his opponent, holding on until the bell goes.

'Look,' he says. 'Look at me.'

'No.' I keep my eyes fixed on the floor, staring at shards of glass and little yellow globs of crème brûlée.

'You've ruined my crème brûlée.'

'I don't care.'

'No. You don't, do you?'

He stiffens, rage rising. He backs away, and leans on the draining board, looking at the night, or his own shadowy reflection in the darkened window. 'Well I care. Because I made it. I did everything. But because I sighed, because I ... damn well ... *sighed* ... you have to ruin it!'

'Dominic—'

He slams his fist on the draining board. 'Of course you don't care. You won't have to clear it up. You don't have to get out a dustpan and brush, and get down on your hands and knees and bend down and clean it up, or pick up that piece of paper, or carry that suitcase, or empty the bins, oh no, you don't have to do any of those things. That's why you don't care what you throw on the floor, because you don't have to do anything—'

'I'm – in – *pain*!'

'Change the record, Monica, I'm just worn out.'

'How do you think I feel?'

That was what I try to say, but the tears in my eyes and the rage in my throat just vomit out a stream of vowels, devoid of sense.

I stand in the middle of the kitchen, surrounded by broken glass and yellow blobs.

Dominic still leans on the draining board, breathing heavily, calming down. 'I just want to say something,' he says at last. 'I care about you. And if this treatment looked like a credible way to end your pain once and for all, then believe me, I'd be the first in line to support you.'

I break away, sniffing and snorting and burbling like a coffee percolator, and lean on the kitchen surface. He follows me, ready to catch me if I faint.

'Fine. Whatever,' I say.

'OK, good, so let's—'

'And what about my accident?'

'What about it?'

'The *accident*, Dominic. *The accident!* Do you think I'm mad? Do you think it was just an accident and the drugs are making me mad?'

He breathes out heavily, through his nose this time, and I can hear a faint whistle. He's irritated. He wishes this conversation wasn't happening.

'Look, if you think that's how it happened, then I believe you. But the police didn't.'

I stopped, sniffing, snivelling, wiping my nose. 'What?'

'We've been here. We've done this. They couldn't find anything. No evidence of anyone up there when you were. And there were no cameras up there to prove accident or otherwise.'

'I don't remember.'

'If we'd made a complaint at the time ... but as we made it months later there was only so much they could do ...'

'I don't *remember any of this ...*'

'I know. I'm sorry you can't remember all this, and I am seriously sorry I have to explain it again. And again.'

He went to the fridge and looked inside.

'How about a Mars Bar for dessert?'

'Lovely.'

110

I struggle to the bathroom to clean my face, take my drugs, and when I come back down he's in the living room, his finger on the TV remote, ready to order a movie. He's picked something mindless and stupid to take our minds off what's happened, because he knows the drill.

I feel chilled to the bone, even though the central heating is on maximum – that's what happens sometimes; my Angry Friend siphons off my body heat and I end up shivering while Dominic's walking around in a T-shirt – so Dominic makes me three hot water bottles, and I snuggle under a throw until the movie finishes, and we watch television on the sofa until there is no more television left to watch.

He makes love to me that night. When we go to bed he has already dimmed the lights, and he'd bought candles that smelt of lavender and rose.

I know he planned to, and he wanted to, but I also know it wasn't a good night for this, but I crave normality, so I acquiesce.

He tries long and hard, but I can't orgasm. Someone is laughing at me, dragging my attention from achieving a climax. Finally I just look up into his eyes and say, 'Dominic, please. I love you. It doesn't matter.'

His shoulders sag in grim acceptance, then he raises himself up, accelerates, and I nibble his ear, which always excites him, and soon he's coming, surging noisily into me with a cry of defeat. He flops onto the pillow next to mine, breathing deeply. I can already feel the warmth and wetness on my thigh.

'That was lovely,' I said.

He doesn't answer.

'Hold my hand.'

He takes my hand.

'It's always lovely. To be close to you. That's all I need. That's all I want.'

111

He keeps holding my hand. I'm very tired. I'm nodding off.

And then there is silence, as he leaves me alone with my Angry Friend, but that night he doesn't keep me awake. He takes me on a trip.

Dominic

Sometimes Dominic listened to Monica's breathing into the night, and most of the time he could hear that her breath wasn't quite slow enough, and he knew that she was still awake, desperately trying to push her head under, like a nervous child playing dare in the swimming baths, trying and failing and always bobbing back to the surface. But now he could definitely hear the tell-tale pshhhh-pshhhh of deep sleep; the slow rhythmic rush of air in and out of her nose.

Silently, so very very quietly, he got up and shuffled his feet into his silly tiger slippers. He went downstairs and into the study. He sat at the keyboard and switched on the computer.

He went to the JPEGs on the other side of the screen and clicked on the scans of the information leaflets of the drugs Monica took every day. Dominic was very organised and kept them all together; after all, he was living with a person not quite in her right mind – he needed to know what might be around the next corner.

He knew he was in a bad place, but he could never remember how he got from *there* to *here*.

Possible side effects
Brain and central nervous system: dizziness, tiredness or sleepiness, weakness, headache, difficulty concentrating,

confusion, difficulty sleeping, nightmares, slight hyperactivity, exaggerated behaviour, delusions, seeing things that are not there, anxiety, excitement, disorientation (not knowing where you are), restlessness, pins and needles, lack of co-ordination, shaky movements, tremor fits ...

His eyes slid off the list and onto the next one.

Common side effects
- Dizziness, tiredness
- Increased appetite
- Feeling of elation, confusion, disorientation, changes in sexual interest, irritability
- Loss of appetite, low blood sugar
- Change in perception of self, restlessness, depression, agitation, mood swings, difficulty finding words, loss of memory, hallucinations, abnormal dreams

The list went on and on, with every symptom known to medical science, from the prosaic (kidney failure) to the poetic (inappropriate behaviour) but as far as Dominic was concerned, there was only one that filled his waking thoughts.

loss of memory

Every day he thanked the Lord for the side effects; the exquisite double-edged sword that caused her to forget those things that happened. The bad things she made him do. It wasn't his fault; he *had* to do those things.

But now all that looked like changing, and now he had to do the bad things again.

'Why?' he muttered under his breath.

But there was no answer.

Monica

I'm back on the roof of the car park.

I'm not alone; there's my mum and dad, standing smiling. There are Dominic's parents, and they're smiling too. They're all smiling and all dressed in the clothes they wore at our wedding.

I look around for Dominic, but he isn't here.

I look down at myself. I'm not wearing my wedding dress; I'm wearing the filthy sweat-stained T-shirt I wore in the first year of the accident, the one with the happy bunny rabbits bouncing on it. The one I never stopped wearing because I couldn't dress myself and I couldn't bear to be touched. The T-shirt is long, but it's not long enough. I tug it down, pulling it over my thighs, stretching the middle bunny rabbit's cheeky smile into a slack-jawed yawn, covering the soiled knickers I woke up wearing, day after day after day.

But I know this is a wedding and I have to walk to the semi-circle of smiles waiting for me; they are standing there waiting for me, standing too near the edge. I walk to them, holding my shirt down as I go.

And there is Niall, there, by the top of the steps, in his lycra shorts, and he is jogging on the spot. 'You're not walking straight!' he shouts angrily. 'Stand up straight! This is your big day!'

And I try to straighten up, but the T-shirt isn't long enough, and then I am suddenly bare from the waist down, and I don't want to show my mother and my future in-laws my nakedness. I know I stink, because my mind tells me I haven't had a bath in a long time.

Niall gets very angry. 'Posture!' he screams. 'Posture!'

I scuttle to the edge of the roof, to the relatives. 'Please,' I say. 'We're not quite ready yet. Dominic's got lazy sperm.' But they just smile at me. They aren't standing on the roof, they are over the edge, hovering above the ground without a care in the world.

I look down at their shoes, and down and down and down, and I can see the entrance to the hospital, and I can see a tiny blue and yellow Mini driving around below, trundling round in circles like a drowsy wasp. It's Jesse's car, the first one she bought when she left college. The one she ploughed into a tree on her twenty-first birthday.

'Jesse!' I scream down. 'Jesse!'

But the little car shows no sign of stopping. It just potters aimlessly around the entrance, but there are no parking spaces. Eventually it gives up and drives out. I am so high up I can see it moving along the main road, getting smaller and smaller, until buildings and trees swallow it up.

I look back at the entrance, and notice that there's someone else watching Jesse's car, a figure dressed in black with a luminous bib, like a car park attendant. He looks up at me, and even though I'm hundreds of feet above the ground and he's standing by the entrance I can see his face like I'm nose to nose with him. It's a round, young face with thinning blond hair and a feeble ginger moustache, which is narrow and barely formed.

'Is that everything, Monica?' he says. 'Is there anything else you want to tell me?'

I think I'm nodding.

'Are you sure?'

He looks disappointed in me, and I feel very guilty and look away, and everyone is gone, the parents, Niall . . . I look back down and the man with the feeble moustache has gone too.

I'm aware I'm cold, and I'm too near the edge, but my body won't let me walk back to the centre. My mind is screaming at me to get to safety, but my feet stay put.

There's a crunch of gravel, a shape at the top of the stairwell, and a figure appears, out of focus. Pixelated. I stare hard, because I know this is the one who pushed me. I just know it. I strain my eyes to see who it is, but the person remains a cloud on the horizon.

Intangible, like smoke.

I hear a scuffle behind me and I whirl around, and I'm nose to nose with the cloud. It envelops me like a morning mist, and I'm feeling very, very cold.

The cloud forms into a giant hand, with long pointed black fingernails. It shoves me with all its might, and I fall, and I fall, and I fall.

Down and down and down.

I'm thinking: *This is a dream, I know it's a dream but if I hit the bottom in my dream then I will die I know I will that's what they say that's what they say that's what*

When I wake up, I'm drowning in sweat and clawing at the darkness. I lie in the matted remains of the bedcovers, snatching air into my lungs with big whooping gasps. My arm flails across to Dominic's side and finds . . .

Nothing. He's not there.

I struggle up and stare sightlessly into the darkness. 'Dom?' I say quietly. 'Dominic, are you there?'

I struggle out of bed, slowly, waves of pain pushing me down, telling me to stay where I am, but I want to know. I inch downstairs and hobble from room to room, until I see a glow from under the study door.

Then the door opens and I'm blinded by the light, and Dominic is in the doorway.

'Monica!' he says. 'What are you doing up?'

'I woke up and you weren't there.'

'I couldn't sleep. I remembered I had an email to send.' He grabs my elbow gently. 'Let's get you back to bed.'

'Dominic,' I blurt. 'I'm sorry about the argument.'

I stumble, and he can see I'm in trouble. He leads me back to my bed, and I stare at the ceiling while he sits in a chair, reading a couple of chapters from the dumb thriller he's got on his bedside table. Any distraction is good.

He reads the thriller to me until three o'clock, until his voice is hoarse, and the book is over, and then he reads me *The Velveteen Rabbit*, which is one of my childhood favourites, and then his voice gives up and he kisses me goodnight. Then he goes into the spare room. He can see I'm in a bad way, so he doesn't even ask to share the bed.

He is such a good man.

I am so lucky to have him.

I lie in bed, still awake, still listening to the chuckle of my Angry Friend, thinking about my life, and even in my pit of pain, I laugh. My memory has folded in on itself, like a well-thumbed suicide note.

Folded so often you can see the cracks.

Monica

I wake up . . .

. . . And the pain hits me, like I've driven at full speed into a wall.

My Angry Friend is going to make me (**pay you bitch**) for the car park steps, the argument with Niall, the fight with Dominic, the child on my lap. *Especially* the child on my lap. My Angry Friend is a bit of a (**bastard**) like that.

I'm not going anywhere today.

My Angry Friend has locked me inside my house, inside my bedroom, inside my bed, inside my body, inside my head, and hidden the key for the foreseeable future.

My eyes follow patterns in the ceiling, the swirls of plaster, the stem of the lamp; sometimes the swirls are foam bubbles in a coffee cup, sometimes they are wind-blown clouds. Once, when I was very bad, they used to move, undulating and surging like the tide on a beach.

My eyes flick to the dressing table mirror to catch a glimpse of myself. It's difficult to see where Monica ends and the rest of the world begins. I'm halfway to heaven; pillow, pyjamas, face, duvet. All is white.

I listlessly flick the channels with the remote, hopping from property show, to antique show, and back to property show again. Nothing that could hold my attention for more than a few seconds, let alone distract me from the (**fucking**) pain.

I switch on the DVD player with the other remote, and a couple being shown around a cottage disappears from the screen and is replaced by a menu page; Marlon Brando wandering around an orchard.

Dominic remembered. He's put The Godfather *in the machine.*

I click 'play', and I reacquaint myself with what used to be my favourite film. I get past the severed horse's head, the man shot in the throat, but when James Caan dances with agony while bullets pepper his car, I have to turn it off. Even watching this violence; this tiny, decades-old violence trapped in a little screen inside a television inside a cupboard, it makes my pain levels rise in sympathy.

It occurs to me that perhaps my brain told me to forget about *The Godfather* because it knew it was bad for me. It also occurs to me – the other thing I've forgotten about, the suicide attempt . . .

Perhaps I've forgotten all the other violent memories too.

I squeeze the remote, switch off the DVD player, and it's replaced by daytime television. Too loud. My thumb scrambles to the volume button.

My eyes are captivated by the moving images. People talking on sofas without pain. People sitting behind desks without pain. People dancing and singing without pain. The whole world is a party to which I'm not invited. The people sitting on sofas wave goodbye and smile, and dissolve to adverts. The adverts are even louder than the programmes, and my ears scream along with my body.

The adverts. At least they have people in pain. People falling off ladders and getting whiplash from a seatbelt. Granted, after making a phone call they're happy again, but for those few brief seconds

and there's Niall.

It's happening again.

Oh God,

it's happening again. Just like in the study.

Not again . . .

He's jogging through a park, muscles swelling and deflating with the vigorous movement of his arms. And then he's collapsing on a park bench and he's clutching his stomach, and sandwiches and peanuts are dancing around him. And now he's necking a glutinous pink drink, and then he's smiling at me in relief.

A person without pain.

The hallucination happened once before; I think I might have been thinking about him. That time he grinned impishly at me when he was cleaning a filthy kitchen with a wondrous liquid, holding it up so I could read the label. Taunting me. Housework? In this condition? *Fuck off.*

I must stop thinking about him.

But it's like when someone asks you not to think of something, and you immediately think of it. What's that called? *Irony, I guess.*

Stop thinking about Niall. I must stop—

The letter box clatters.

A letter.

Second post.

Another letter.

I'm irrationally excited. My life seems to be shaped by the discovery of important letters these days. The suicide letter, the letter from the hospital . . .

Perhaps it's another one from the hospital. Perhaps it's new information. Perhaps after lots and lots of trials they've suddenly realised the capsaicin cure is permanent and I can convince Dominic that it's worth the risk.

Can I get downstairs? I decide against it. But lying there, I cannot get the image out of my head, a beige rectangular shape, sitting there on the mat.

I flop out of bed like a landed salmon and squirm my way to the door, and slowly, slowly, out into the hall.

The view down the stairs looks dizzying, vertiginous; and the dream floods back into my addled brain. *I could have been climbing off a ledge of a tall building.* By bracing myself against the banisters, I find I can inch down the steps without jarring myself.

There it is, but it doesn't look like it's from the hospital. It's large and red; so red that it's blended in with the colour of the carpet. A large coffin-shaped envelope with my name and address on the front, handwritten in an exquisite stretched-out copperplate style. I can scarcely believe what I'm seeing. I wonder if I'm still in the dream, and that the letter is an invitation to fall off the top of the car park in my underwear again.

I open it, and the card is also coffin shaped, but this is in a shiny black. I can see my shadowy reflection in it, my eyes obscured in pools of darkness cast by my brow.

This is what it says on the card:

An invitation to the works of

Angelina Symcox

At The Art of Darkness Gallery

33 Lionsgate Way
Westbourne Grove
W11 2RX

Thursday 3rd July 3 pm–6 pm

Drinks and Nibbles Provided

It smells exquisite. A wonderful, familiar, chemical smell.

It's in one week's time, I think. *I want to go to this. I so want to go to this. I need to go to this.*

I crawl back to bed, clutching my prize, and I settle back down. Body and mind are inextricably linked, but it's only people who go through what I've gone through who really appreciate what that means.

I have hope in my hand, and my Angry Friend is already retreating, snarling into a corner. I close my eyes . . .

. . . And then I'm waking up.

And below me, the back gate bangs shut.

It can't be Agnieszka. It's not her day. It's not Agnieszka. She wouldn't come in the back gate anyway. It leads to a narrow passage that connects the other gardens on the street, and some empty garages. No one comes in that way.

I struggle upright but I can't move. My expedition downstairs has created more problems.

I try to push the duvet off my body *Jesus, I can't even do that* so I half crawl, half slide to the edge of the bed, and look down at the floor. It's a hell of a long way down. But I have to know who's out there.

I roll myself off the bed.

My cry, as I impact with the carpet, is loud and raw, and frightens me when I hear it.

Sometimes, I have to do this, because my screams are the only way of my brain letting my body know that it's in serious trouble. *Knives are in my back. My arms and legs are embedded with cutlery. I'm in a splatter movie with no 'splat'. There should be blood,* I think. *There should be blood. Why is there no blood? It's not fair that there's no blood. I have all this feeling and nothing to show for it, no proof. I'm just a woman lying on the floor with her hands pointing to the air in submission and fingers curled into talons, like I'm hiding under an invisible plank of wood. If there was blood, I would get a proper scream of horror, not some sympathetic sigh from my husband, or maternal cry from my cleaner. I want to hear a scream. I want to hear a scream from someone once in a while. If only from me.*

Rolling and moaning, rolling and moaning, and slowly, slowly, on my belly, with elbows in the air, and hands pushing my body along, lizard-like, to the window, then grab the legs of the, go on (**grab the chair!**) Now hold it, hold the chair, drag yourself up, elbows on the seat, arms on the seat, QUICKLY now! I'm tired, I'm so tired (**no time to be tired**). You have to get up there, get up there, got to see who's there. Find out. You have to find out. (**Come on, you bitch, don't wimp out like this!**) And I put a spurt on, up, bum on the seat, another scream, I'm twisting my spine, I have to bring my legs round until I'm sitting parallel to the window, and my shoulders and hips are facing the same way, and there's the ledge, an inch above my head, and I try to reach it but my arms can't move up, they can't do it, so I hold on to the curtain sash and move the hands up the rope, and I'm screaming again, glorious and loud, as there's no one about, and when they're far enough up the rope – I'm ready.

I'm ready.

I'm . . . ready.

Ready.

(**Go on, what are you waiting for? Stand up**)

I can't. I need to . . .

(**Stand up, you bitch!**)

All right, keep your hair on, you fucking cow! I just need to do this . . . my way.

(**Then fucking hurry up, bitch!**)

Anger. I need anger.

I need to think of things to make me angry. The Godfather. *The old man and his dog. The Atos 'doctor' with his sick-brown cheap suit with the stains and the briefcase with the dirty plastic tube. My dad's car and my pet bunny rabbit. The spade on his shoulder, still with blood on it. How could you be so stupid, Adrian?*

And Dominic.

Dominic with his world-weary sigh and his 'you're not thinking straight' comment.

And in conclusion, your honour . . .

'FUCCKKK! FUUUUUUUCCCCKKKKKKKKK!' I allow the explosion of rage and frustration to propel myself up until I am standing upright, and I collapse on the window sill, whimpering, with tears of relief, hugging the coolness of the painted wood. And I look out of the window.

And then I realise my glasses are still on my bedside table.

The tears turn to hysterical laughter as I look out and see two small green blobs (the lawn) and one long grey blob (the path) and a brown blob (the gate and shed and fence), and by the brown blob there is a small dark blue blob with a white blob on it.

Concentrate. You can make sense of what you see.

There's a big blue blob; moving around, man in a suit. And he's by the bins. He's looking in the bins. No. He's looking under the bins.

(**What the fuck is he**) my body quivers with a sudden surge of panic, and it shoots up my spine. And there's that familiar feeling. There's that rush of heat, like someone's opened the door to hell . . .

Here we go again

Alice falls down into the rabbit hole . . .

Dominic

It felt crazy to dig in broad daylight but luckily they had high walls around the garden, so Dominic felt reasonably confident that he wouldn't be overseen.

It was far more risky to dig in darkness, by his reckoning. Monica rarely slept, there was always that danger she would hear the telltale sounds; the click of the back door, the crunch of gravel, the scrape of the bin, and the sound of metal on stone as he started to break the earth. And if anyone saw him digging, then a man with a shovel in the garden during the day would be much more easy to explain than a man with a shovel in the garden at three in the morning.

When Dominic found the bag, it had completely perished, crumpled and compacted in the earth. Brown slime slipped out of the leather seams. He looped the straps around the end of the spade and placed it gently down on the edge of the rockery. He pulled on a gardening glove and wiped off the worst of the mud, excavating with his fingers until he found the zip, and tugged until the bag grew a huge flapping maw.

Nothing inside.

Dominic's mouth gaped open like the bag.

Where had it gone?

Where had the gun gone?

Where?

His mind flapped in all directions, like a plastic bag caught in the wind. Then he thought of Larry, and fury clouded his thoughts. He knew Larry had taken it. It was just like him.

Then he looked up, and saw Monica in the window.

Monica

I wake up ...

... Huge black slugs are swimming across my eyes. There is pain, and there is carpet ...

And I am a stupid, stupid woman. Why did I even try to do that? What did I achieve?

... and there are footsteps downstairs, heavy, clumping footsteps.

He's in the house now.

I try to call out 'hello', but my face is flattened, I'm drooling on the carpet because my cheeks are pushed together, and my lips can't move. What emerges from my throat is a tiny dry croak, devoid of consonants.

'Harrar? Harrar? Whovair? Whooivair?'

Clomp clomp clomp. Clomp.

They don't sound like Dominic's tatty desert boots. They don't sound like anyone I know. Moaning and rolling, moaning and rolling, back to the bed I go, slowly, slowly. Below me, the *clomp clomp* of boots becomes *thud thud* as the footsteps encounter carpet, and whoever-it-is is coming up the stairs.

Three thuds.

Six thuds.

Nine thuds.

Whoever it is, he or she is in no hurry.

I flail an arm, trying to grab the telephone cord, and it jerks to the edge of the table. Thankfully it misses me as it descends, but the receiver lands above my head and my arms can't move; one is trapped under my body and the other can't stretch above my shoulder. I am waggling my extremities like a seal on pack ice, trying to escape the men wielding their clubs.

And the door opens, and the footsteps come into the room.

'Hurrruh,' I say. *I'm sure 'hello' is a stupid thing to say to a knife-wielding burglar, but if I'm polite and I look helpless then perhaps whoever-it-is won't hurt me or worse . . .*

'Oh heck!' screams Dominic. His knees fall to the carpet, in my line of vision, and his face swims close to mine.

'What are you doing on the floor?'

'Tryn' t' ge' huk!'

His hands slide under me, and I moan with fear, as I know what's going to happen next.

'Nhhhhhh! Oh God! Oh God!'

'Come on, darling . . . ' he says through gritted teeth. He is straining very hard. 'Back to bed we go . . . '

He rolls me back on the bed, and I'm staring at the ceiling again. 'Ooh!' I gasp. 'Are we going to bed now?'

Dominic is gasping too. The effort to pick me up has nearly crippled him. He sits down heavily on the stool by the dressing table. 'What . . . just . . . What . . . were you doing down there? Damn, you scared me!'

'I scared you? You scared me! What are you doing clumping around downstairs? I got out of bed to see what the noise was.'

'That was stupid.'

I don't answer. I know it's stupid. I crane my head up and he scurries to put a pillow behind me. I look at his clothes and, sure enough, he's wearing his garden boots. 'You're in your boots. Your filthy gardening boots.'

He looks down and frowns, as if noticing for the first time. 'Sorry.'

In my life, there are lots of 'sorry's, like raindrops. One or two, and you feel them. If they fall on you in the thousands, they wash you like a shower, you just have to ignore them and walk on.

'Were you gardening?'

'No.' His hand crosses his forehead wearily and I realise he's very tired. He stayed up far too late, watching me, reading to me, looking after me. He's tired, and he's trying not to make me feel guilty. 'I did take a bag of rubbish out, about half an hour ago.'

'I heard a big clatter. Like someone was fooling around with the bin.'

'Yes,' he says without missing a beat. 'I was. The wind had blown it over again. Bloody bins. I miss the old metal ones; they were a lot sturdier than those plastic things.'

'Yes,' I say.

There doesn't seem to be anything else to say. I know what I saw, but what I saw was a lot of multicoloured blobs having a dance. I thought I saw someone pulling something out from under the bin, not in it, but it could easily have been Dominic sorting out the bin and making it more secure.

It's too hard to think. There's too much of my Angry Friend in my head, and he stretches out like an annoying passenger in a crowded train carriage, elbowing out everything else. I can't find words to say, and Dominic takes this as some form of disapproval, some suppressed anger.

At last he says: 'I hope you understand what I said last night. About the treatment.'

I say nothing.

'It's not that I don't want you to get better. I just . . . I don't want to see you hurt again. If I was certain . . . If we were absolutely certain that the effects would work for ever . . .'

I still say nothing.

'I know how disappointment affects you. And it does, mentally and physically. You know that.'

There are so many things I can say at this point. Too many.

(**Who gives a shit if I'm hurt again? What's that got to do with you, you fat STUPID little man? How dare you tell me the limits of how I can feel?**)

But I feel the coffin-shaped invitation in my hand, under the covers.

I must keep calm. I can't get angry. I can't get him angry. Last night I wandered into a full-blown argument, and it's going to put me in bed for days. I can't risk a flare-up. I want to go to Angelina's show. Please, Mr Angry Friend, let me go to Angelina's show.

Instead I say: 'I suppose you're right. I suppose I wouldn't know how I could cope if I lost the pain and it returned.'

'Exactly.'

'I'll cancel the appointment.'

'Good.' He moves to the door and then hangs there, sensing unfinished business, looking for something else to say.

'You do know I love you,' he says at last.

'I know.'

'I do hope you understand.'

'I understand.'

'OK. Good. Bye.'

'Bye.'

He's still at the door.

'Love you lots?'

'No, love *you* lots.'

'You hang up.'

130

'No *you* hang up.'
'No *you* hang up.'
'No you—'
'Brrrrrrrrr.'

I ring up and confirm the appointment.

Monica

I wake up . . .

. . . Not too bad today.

There's always that split second before I realise how things are.

When I was sixteen I had my first love, Nigel Cope. I really thought that he was The One, and that we would be together until we both died of old age, dribbling and incontinent, sitting in our wheelchairs.

When Nigel dumped me for Charlotte Redding three months later, I thought my world had ended, and my subconscious mind refused to accept it. I dreamed endlessly that we were still together. When I woke up there was that split second of believing that he was still with me, before reality flooded in, and I cried again.

It's the same now. That split second of the body fooling you that everything is normal, that there's no pain, before the reality floods into every nerve ending.

But really, not too bad today.

I realise I am in our bed, and that I am alone. Dominic has let me sleep. He has left a Post-it note on his pillow with the words 'No YOU hang up!'

Fuck you, I think.

I sink back into the pillows. I'm lying there, and I'm thinking of that tiny moment before reality floods in, and my thoughts turn to what I can do while I'm alone.

My hands fiddle with the elastic of my pyjamas. They sneak under it, like prisoners of war under barbed wire, and creep bellow my belly button.

I think of my husband making love to me, but the sight of him just makes me angry. Around him, flickering in and out, unbidden, like ghosts, are others. Nigel Cope, Martin Hemsworth from my RADA course, Stephano who I met during that time InterRailing to Venice and, yes, there is Niall Stewart.

That's the other tiny moment when the pain disappears. Endorphins flood my body, they drown out the nerve pain, and for those glorious seconds, those few glorious glorious seconds, I am a normal woman again, a woman who does not feel pain, only pleasure, only the orgasm, and then I am lying back and the only ripples I experience are ripples of joy, and I am a woman, and I lie back and there I am, experiencing a beautiful beautiful womanly thing.

And then reality floods in.

I get dressed and I'm at the computer now, it's been nearly a week since I got out of bed and I can feel the muscles and shoulders fusing together like ice cubes. I have to see Niall. I remember the fleeting vision of Niall as I fought my way to a climax, and I feel guilty. *I'm sorry, darling Dominic, but at the moment this is all I have left to pin my fantasies on.*

I've wasted enough time in bed. I have to get back to work. I have some phone calls to make. My email inbox has given me some exciting news.

The phone rings once before it's answered and I hear noise, laughing, shouting, the distant roar of a music system as it belts out Robbie Williams. I'm ringing 50 per cent of my clientele; the one who isn't the stunt-granny.

'Morning, Sunflower , how are you, my darling?'

'Hello, Larry.'

'Just a mo, I'm going into the kitchen. We're getting ready for a bit of a family barbecue before the afternoon match. The final.' He doesn't elaborate on which match it is, what league, what final, even what sport. He knows better than to think I would be interested, or patronise me by explaining stuff I don't want to know.

Larry's voice is deep and rough, coated with malt whisky and nicotine. I'm one of the very few people who know that he had cancer a few years ago, and that's what made him decide to stretch himself as an actor, and not just bump along the bottom playing thugs and hoodlums in soaps.

'Larry. I am going to make your day.'

'Every time you ring me it makes my day, Sunflower.'

'You silver-tongued devil.'

There is a rattling cough and a 'Huh-huh-huh' laugh. The man has the laugh of a pantomime giant. 'Don't let Jill hear you say that, she'll snap me like a twig.'

Jill is Larry's wife, one of the tiniest women I've ever met, as diminutive as a garden gnome. By complete contrast, Larry is one of the biggest men I've ever met, built like a wall. When he comes to visit I'm amazed he can force his way through my doors. When I see them together it is impossible not to imagine how they might have sex.

Hold on to your hat, Larry . . . '

'No . . . '

'Yes. Sir Peter Stiles says yes.'

I've been lobbying for years to get Larry into the National, and now one of the most respected directors in the country, and one currently residing at the National Theatre, has finally agreed to have Larry in his production.

There is a pause from the other end of the phone. All I can

hear is Larry's stentorian breathing. Then he finally says, 'Wow.'

He shouts across the room. 'Jill! JILL! JILL! JILL! Monica's got Sir Peter Stiles to say yes.'

'That's nice, Pumpkin. Good for you!' squeaks a tiny voice in the distance.

Then there's a 'huh-huh-huh' close to the receiver again. 'She doesn't know Sir Peter Stiles from Peter Andre, but she'll be dead chuffed when I explain who he is. Really? He said OK? Seriously?'

'Absolutely. He was very impressed with your audition.'

'You mean my interview.'

'Thank you, Larry. He was very impressed with your "interview". Hideous term.'

Another big chuckle rolls out of the phone towards me.

'Anyway, he's always been interested in you. Big fan of your telly work. And the "interview" clinched it.'

'Oh wow. Me getting to play the National ... When Jill realises what this means ... God, she'll just wet herself.'

'Bring her along. Get in as many of your mates as you can. Get them in the front row, and get them to laugh like drains.'

'At *Twelfth Night*? You don't know my mates.'

'You'll be surprised.'

'Well ... I dunno ...'

'You're just playing a pissed-up man larking about with his chums and playing tricks on some posho whoopsie. I'm sure they'll find something about it to laugh at.'

There goes that 'huh-huh-huh' again. 'I s'pose you're right. *Sir* Peter Stiles. Thanks, Sunflower, this is amazing. Top work. I'll do something for you one day.'

My 'sunflower' nickname goes back a long way. Back many years when I had my office in Soho, and he came to me for representation. I was wearing sunflower earrings and he noticed them almost immediately and commented on how lovely they were.

I was taken aback; I'd worn them for the first time that morning, and even Dominic never registered I was wearing them; even when he provided me with a quickie in the kitchen before he left for work.

When I took him on, he sent me a bunch of sunflowers that I put proudly in my little window overlooking Greek Street. When I got him his first job, and every job after that, whether I got it for him or he found it himself, he sent me sunflowers. He doesn't send them any more, because I work from home. But I know in the unlikely event I drag my wounded carcass to his first night, he'll be there with a bouquet for me, embedded tightly in his huge fist.

Larry told me later he always notices jewellery first when he meets new people, and my mind instantly made the connection to his murky and extremely not-very-legal past growing up in Catford. I immediately felt guilty about thinking it. Like many men of his age, Larry is a true gentlemen; when arriving at any premiere or first night he is always first to the bar with a fifty in his hand, and when leaving he is always first to drape your coat over your shoulders. I imagine little Jill must feel like a princess.

Of course he noticed the jewellery, just like he notices a woman without an umbrella, or a drink in her hand.

'Cheers, Sunflower. You're a miracle worker.'

With a final 'huh-huh-huh' he is gone.

I'm sure it was his innate chivalry that prompted him to return to me when I came back to the business. No one like Larry would leave a lady in distress.

My computer screen has long since gone dark, and when I push on the mouse it lights up. It has gone back to the little icons that denote my side of computer (a little picture of a sunflower), and Dominic's side (a little photo of a tiger).

I go straight to my icon and when I try to click on it, I get another bloody spasm. My hand jerks and the cursor jumps onto Dominic's photo. I've clicked on him by accident. Up comes the empty box where his password is supposed to go.

Now I remember.

Peck peck peck peck.

Four pecks.

When Dominic accessed his side of the computer to read the article on capsaicin he did four little pecks on the keyboard. Not six. He didn't type in 'Monica'. M-O-N-I-C-A. Six pecks. *We always use each other's names for our passwords*; that way we can easily access each other's stuff in emergencies.

I wonder why there weren't six pecks.

(Go on, try it)

No.

(You're afraid. You coward)

No.

(Hiding. That's all you do. Hiding from people. Hiding from the truth. That's all you do. I'm ashamed to call myself you. Just do it)

For once in your life . . .

I type in the word 'Monica'.

The little box shakes. Nope.

Stupidly, I type in the word 'Dominic', even though I heard four pecks.

Nope.

Peck peck peck peck.

It's our surname. That's what he's used. Just another name. Peck peck peck peck. Surname instead of first name.

I type in the word 'Wood'.

Nope.

The box shakes again, like my hands as they hover over the keyboard.

His father's name. Even though he's always been 'David' it could be ...

'Dave'?

Nope.

I type 'Name'.

Nope.

I type 'Pass'.

Nope.

I type 'Word'.

Nope.

I type 'Note'.

Nope.

I'm shocked that I can't get it after a dozen attempts. *This is our own personal computer in our own house,* I think it through, *so there's no reason to pick an obscure password.*

(Why the change?)

I mean, we have no secrets from each other.

(Have we?)

Don't be stupid. The drugs make you paranoid.

Just forget about it.

I don't know why I'm doing this. He's my husband. He stands by me. He's always stood by me. He researched my condition. He found out all the things I deserved: my allowance as a disabled person; his allowances as a carer. He found out about the new drugs.

He loves me.

I move the cursor up to the box, and my fingers hover over the keys.

I type in the street where we live 'Webb'.

The little box shakes. Nope.

I type in Dominic's mother's name. 'Jane'.

The little box shakes. Nope.

I give up and leave. Or I try to. A wave of nausea overcomes me, and I sink back down in the swivel chair, which lurches and nearly sends me crashing back down on the carpet.

Can I move without fainting? Not really. Not now. *Don't take the risk. Remember Angelina's exhibition. Don't take risks now.*

I decide to wait it out. I put my head on the desk and stare at the empty password box, working up the energy to walk.

Then I have a nasty feeling.

I think of a possible word. I try to frame it in my mind. It's only four letters long, but I have to concentrate on the correct spelling.

My hand reaches out. I press 'P'.

Do I really want to do this? I ask myself.

I press 'A'.

Is this just going to open every can of worms in the fishing shop?

I press 'I'.

If he used this word, it would tell me beyond a shadow of a doubt that Dominic is trying to keep things from me. He knows that I would shy away from it. Using that word is like using it as weapon against me.

I press 'N', and I press return.

Nothing. Computer says 'no'.

I sigh with relief, and then I realise I've knocked the caps lock on.

I put the word in, in lower case, and the computer screen turns blue, and up swims Dominic's screen wallpaper, a picture of Alec Guinness from *The Ladykillers*.

Oh, Dominic. Why? You used that word to hide from me. You just betrayed me.

The tension of the moment encourages my body to stab me in the leg, pain swims into my vision, and I put my head on the table until the ripples subside. Five minutes later, and I'm ready to carry on.

All right, Dominic, why? Why the password? Are you hiding something from me?

My fingers dance across the keyboard, looking in Word files, PDFs, JPEGs. I find Christmas card lists, abandoned novels, old letters to parents, but nothing that he could want to possibly keep from me.

'Meeses Moaneeka?'

Agnieszka is in the house. She must have let herself in.

'Meeses Moaneeka?'

'I'm here. In the office.'

She pops her head around the door, and her lilac smell fills the tiny office. 'Hello. I am here. I do usual?'

'Yes, usual.'

'Bedsheets today?'

'No, not this week.'

'OK. I start polish floor in kitchen.'

I watch her through the open door as she gets the hoover out and it erupts with noise.

She realises that I'm staring at her. She switches off the hoover and smiles. 'You want for me to make cup of tea for you?'

'No thanks,' I say. 'I fine for moment.'

Could I carry on looking through Dominic's files? Will she notice? Of course she won't realise what I'm doing. Anyway, she's at the far end of the kitchen now. She's finished with the hoover, and now she's uncoiling the cable of the floor polisher. Soon a throaty whine fills the air.

Reassured, I go back to the computer and I look at his wallpaper; there are things saved on the home screen.

I open one up and it fills the screen, it's a picture of a white blur. I see it's a film, because there are play and pause signs under the picture.

I press play.

It's an ugly bedroom containing a pine bed, and there is a fat naked woman on it, on her knees, being taken energetically from behind by a man. Her loose, low-hanging breasts slap together, rippling and pulsating. After a few minutes, another man appears, forcing himself into her mouth. She gives out a shrieking moan, and I realise that I have the sound on far too loud.

'Moaneeka? Are you OK?'

I scramble for the keyboard to pause it, and spirit the picture into the toolbar.

'I'm fine.'

'I heard scream?'

'Yes, just a stab of pain in my back.'

'Oh yes.' She nods furiously and her pretty dark ponytail bounces around her neck. 'Do you need me?'

'No, Agnieszka, I am fine.'

She returns to the floor polisher and I return to my computer, flipping up the screen again.

I watch, hypnotised, as the men push into her. They move around her body with their hands, attending to every corner like they're tucking in the bedsheets.

It's porn, I think, almost swooning with relief. *Of course it is. No wonder he doesn't want me to stumble across this. No wonder he keeps his password secret.*

We talked about it years ago, when things were difficult, physically, between us. I even remember me making the ultimate sacrifice, asking him to find a lover, if he ever needed to, and get his needs elsewhere. I remember the expression on his face, his jaw set firmly. 'Never,' he said. 'I would never do that to you.'

He wanted to hold me, I could see that. The scene we played out needed that moment, but we couldn't do that, of course, so his pledge came out as a bit flat and empty. So he bent down and

141

touched my hand. 'We'll be fine,' he said meaninglessly. 'We'll be fine.'

And then we never talked about it again.

So I shouldn't be surprised; I should be relieved that he's chosen pornography and not sought out a prostitute, or a lover. Oh well. Mystery solved. Let him keep his secret.

Perhaps that's what he's hiding under the dustbin! I think with a smile. *His collection of pornographic DVDs.*

I am not naive. In my experience I know that most men have their little hiding places. My father's was in the locked glovebox of his car. I will never forget driving with him in the country-side to see an aunt, and while we were traversing a particularly troublesome cattle grid the lock popped open, showering my lap with video cassettes with strange names scrawled on them. In my mind's eye I can still remember *Big Ones 12* falling on my little red shoes with the buckles on them, bouncing, finally coming to rest on my left ankle sock.

Daddy stopped the car, walked around to my side, asked me to stand on the verge while he tidied up his tapes and put them in the boot. He didn't say a word while he did it, but once we were moving he gave me a tight, embarrassed smile and said softly, 'Sorry about that.'

The next (and last) time he apologised to me was when he was walking back from the garden with his red-stained shovel.

I click on the little red 'x', in the corner and the film vanishes. I can see now that it is clustered on the left-hand side, with other files with interesting, suggestive names.

Apart from one. It's a file called MONICA.

I click on it and photos fill the screen.

The photos are of me.

Dozens of pictures. Hundreds of pictures. Pictures of me shopping. Pictures of me sitting in cafés. I scroll down. More and more. Judging by the length of my hair (and the grey roots showing), most of them seemed to have been taken three or four years ago, when the drugs had started to banish some of the pain and I was poking my head outside the house for the first time.

My vision starts to swim again. I clutch the edges of the desk to stay upright.

More and more pictures. All secretly taken. Pictures of me going into the hospital, walking with my stick. Pictures of me sitting on park benches, my face the colour of ashes. Pictures of me turning round, as if to say, 'Was that a click? I have a feeling I'm being watched . . .'

He's been following me. Or he's got someone to follow me. One or the other. Oh Dominic. What have you done?

Monica

I wake up . . .

. . . Not too bad today.

I have spent twenty-four hours trying not to think about what was on Dominic's side of the computer, or his patronising 'Father knows best' attitude over my capsaicin treatment.

I train myself to forget about such things, because I know if I allow myself the luxury of anger, if I let those thoughts in – just a crack – then tension will tie my body up in knots, and the pain levels will rise, and the dream of going to Angelina's will be just that, just a dream.

I have focused on good thoughts, fragments of happiness. Our rain-soaked wedding. Our giggly honeymoon. Laughing over the bad violinist. I don't know if my memories are real or just an illusion, a placebo to cover up the yawning chasms in my mind, but quite frankly, it doesn't matter.

Real memories or not, the effect is the same, and the big day has finally arrived, and the pain levels are low, and I'm pitifully grateful to my Angry Friend for giving me permission to leave the house.

Dominic has arranged a taxi for me. He seems pleased that I'm going; pleased that I'm happy, and probably pleased that I'm out of the house. Blessed peace for him. He tells me not to hurry back; just enjoy myself. 'Have fun,' he says. The words are strange to me. The whole concept is strange.

I slip into her shop, The Art of Darkness. It's already busy with guests, and I wander around the darker corners, hoping to creep up and surprise her.

Angelina has stowed away all the pictures of other artists and turned it into a shrine dedicated to her own work 'because I bloody can'. Not that her stuff doesn't deserve showing; it's magnificent and disturbing in equal measure. It has to be seen to be believed; wrought iron skeletons erupting from the walls; screaming trees; blackened horses running through fire. She has had her larger sculptures moved over from her studio in Ladbroke Grove; I'm in my scarlet three-quarter-length coat, and I feel like Little Red Riding Hood, picking my way through a dark forest.

There is an odour about the place; chemical. I suppose I've always smelt it, but as I've said, my senses are more acute now. I've smelled something similar recently. *It must have been the invitation.* I breathe it in and I feel light-headed; woozy, like when things start moving and monsters appear.

One side of the wall is dominated by a huge gaping mouth containing a tongue shaped like a drowning person, both made out of blackened copper. I stare at it for an age, not knowing if it's real or just part of my addled imagination. I stand and dare it to swallow me up.

There is a shriek of joy behind me.

'Mon!'

Angelina is there, stunningly dressed in a purple velvet off-the-shoulder dress, long silk black gloves and huge intimidating knee-length stiletto boots. Her hair is piled up on her head and she's gripping a cigarette holder (holding something which looks suspiciously like a spliff) in her right hand, and a flute of something sparkly in her left. She is ecstatic to see me, her red slash of a mouth pulled into a wide grin.

'Mon ... You came!'

She casts her glass to one side, stubs out her holder into a very expensive pot, holds her arms out, rushes forward, realises she daren't touch me, and flaps her hands with delight.

'You're here! You're here! Come and let me introduce you to everyone I know.'

She drags me from black-clad art lover to black-clad art lover (who all shake my hand in a polite, bemused manner), resting finally on a large scruffy man in the corner, devouring canapés. He is all blond highlights and earrings, designer stubble and dark tanned skin, and rather attractive; the only thing that spoils the effect is his rather unfortunate ponytail. It's too short, so it sticks out at a right-angle from the back of his head.

'This is my man, Clyde. I told you he's an artist, didn't I? But don't hold that against him. Clyde, this is Monica, one of my oldest and bestest friends. Be nice to her.'

Then she dives back into the crowd.

The man scrutinises me. 'You have great bone structure.'

'Thanks,' I say.

'Are you Monica? Monica, the one who had the accident?'

My stomach turns into a knot. *How many of her friends has she discussed me with?*

'I think so.'

'That's amazing. You look good. You wouldn't know it.'

'Thanks.'

'You're very beautiful.'

'Thanks again.'

I get a lot of young guys chatting me up, hoping to bag what they see as a MILF, even though I've never had kids. I know he's coming onto me. I move the subject away from how beautiful I look.

'So, Clyde ... What do you paint?'

'Imperfection.'

'Sorry?'

'I find beauty in the imperfect; I specialise in women who've been marked. I did an amputee last week. She had beautiful stumps. I find physical deformity very beautiful. Don't you?'

'Well. It depends. It can show strength of character, if you're a soldier, or a fireman ...'

'I suppose ...' Clyde doesn't seem interested in the concept.

'Have you known Angelina long?'

'A few years, professionally, but we've only been dating a short while. I've been enjoying getting under her skin, unpeeling the layers, finding the depths within. I find her fascinating.'

'Even though she's not scarred.'

Angelina takes this opportunity to give out a bizarre tinkling laugh.

Clyde smiles. 'As I say, I'm enjoying getting under her skin.' He waves at Angelina, who pulls a silly cross-eyed face at us both. 'She once told me she had a murky secret, some dark pact she has made with the devil, and she won't tell me what it is.'

He puts a cigarette in his teeth and lights up.

'I don't think Angelina would give her secrets up for anybody,' I say.

He doesn't seem interested in my opinion. 'I would like to paint you.'

My smile is transforming into a panicked grin. 'Well, I'm sorry to say that I'm perfect in every way.'

'Yeah, but you're not, are you? You have scars. I would like to paint your pain.'

'I don't think so.'

'Think about it. I would pay you. If you ever come off your drugs any time in the future, let me know. Because I would like to paint that.'

He blows a smoke ring. 'Actually, if you have any of your drugs spare, I'd like to try them. They sound fucking amazing. You must be on the most incredible buzz.'

'Not really.'

Clyde spies a small man in an ugly waistcoat and gives a double-take. 'Shit, that's Dylan Preece from *The Telegraph*, see you around.' And he vanishes after his prey.

Angelina extricates herself from a gaggle of overpainted women and charges towards me.

'What do you think of Clyde?'

'Seriously? You want to know?'

'Seriously?'

'I think he's hideous.'

'Oh.'

'Why did you tell him about me?'

'Why? Of course I told him about you, sweetie, you're my best friend.'

'I mean, about my accident.'

'Well ... It's not a secret, is it?'

'No.'

'You didn't say it was a secret.'

I sigh. 'No ...'

'I thought you might meet him sometime. I told him in the context of warning him not to hug you or do anything stupid like that. He can be very tactile when he's on speed.'

'Oh, OK.'

'Why? Have I done something wrong?'

'He said he wanted to paint my pain.'

'He said what?'

'He wanted me to come off my drugs, and to paint my pain.'

'You're fucking joking.'

'Oh, and he quite fancied trying my drugs if I had some to spare.'

'The little shitbag ... Right, he's had this coming for weeks ...'

She dives back into the crowd, steers a protesting Clyde away from the man from *The Telegraph*, and takes him to one side. There is a lot of shouting from Angelina as she sticks a varnished finger into his shoulder and prods his jacket. Another finger points to the door. Dylan Preece oozes quietly away, like a multicoloured film of petrol on a puddle.

Over Angelina's shoulder, Clyde glares at me. I hear fragments of the argument, mainly from him, because his voice is higher and shriller than Angelina's. 'Not such a big deal ... Don't get uptight about it ... I would have paid her ... I don't see what the deal is ...'

Five minutes later he's on the pavement outside, with his coat puddled around his ankles.

He picks it up and tries to muster up some dignity.

The guests of Art of Darkness stare on with bovine curiosity, like the row is some art installation performed for their benefit.

Angelina switches on her smile and returns to the throng. I carry on looking at Clyde. He leans on his sports car – I hope it's *his* sports car – with studied nonchalance. He looks like he's going nowhere. I watch his petulant face with a queasy fascination.

I poke my head out of the door.

'Hey,' I say.

He looks at me with disdain, chewing his lip.

'You don't look very happy.'

He ignores me. He makes a point of not looking at me, suddenly finding a shop that makes home-made baby clothes across the street incredibly fascinating.

'Listen,' I continue, 'if you're really hurting about breaking up with Angelina, well, just call me ...'

His focuses on me at last, and a smile trickles onto his face.

'. . . because I'd really love to paint your pain,' I say.

I close the door.

(**Fuck**) *that felt good*, I thought. *I'm such a bitch.*

The event continues and Clyde stays where he is. He's obviously waiting to sweet-talk his way back into Angelina's bed after everyone else has gone. The crowd is thinning, there's a bare half-dozen left. Finally, Angelina rolls her eyes, excuses herself, and hurries upstairs.

Thirty seconds later, Clyde is suddenly joined by easels, paints, brushes, jars of water that smash spectacularly around him. Angelina has decided to clear out the studio he inhabits rent-free above the shop. As he dives for cover, down come the paintings. Canvases of amputees, paraplegics, mangled war veterans and rescued lab animals rain down around him, crashing and splintering and becoming even more mutilated than their subjects. One lands on his car and embeds itself in the soft-top, and he screams, shouting obscenities up at the unseen Angelina.

He now decides to collect his stuff with the utmost haste. From the streams of water running down the front window, I'm guessing Angelina has filled a watering can and is threatening to drench his work as it lies on the pavement. He puts down the soft-top, rescues as much as he can, and roars off in an angry cloud of exhaust fumes.

Angelina comes down, dusting her gloved hands. 'Right, that's got rid of him,' she says to me, ignoring everyone else. 'It's ten past six. What say we lock up here and go back to my flat for vino?'

'Um . . . OK.'

'No "um" about it, sister. As of today, I'm single and I'm celebrating.'

Monica

We're back at Angelina's little flat, built above her studio in Ladbroke Grove. I don't know where she gets the money from but I recall her father was something big in biscuits.

The flat is what you might call 'designer bohemian'. OKA furniture is everywhere; tables and boxes scrubbed with lime. And huge velvet curtains from Scruples. There are delightful little pots and knick-knacks everywhere plucked from delightful little shops in Ladbroke Grove and the Continent, but none of her own work. I asked why once. 'I couldn't look at that stuff all day,' she said. 'It just bloody depresses me.'

We're on the second bottle of wine when I say, 'So that was the end of Clyde.'

'God, yes. He's been annoying me for a while. What a mistake he was. So glad I got your second opinion, otherwise I would never have had the courage to end it before the weekend.'

'You said it was a long-term relationship.'

'Well, he'd discovered where the washing machine lived, so yeah, I guess you could call it long-term.'

'I looked him up on my phone while I was waiting for you to lock up.'

'Yeah?'

'He's famous.'

'A famous tosser.'

'He's a hot British artist, so says Wikipedia.'

'He's a talented little boy, but there are lots of talented little boys. And at the end of the day, a wanker is a wanker is a wanker. And life's too short to spend your time dealing with wankers.'

I wave my glass in a toast. 'He'll be disappointed. He was so looking forward to finding out your dark secret.'

Angelina snorts. 'Oh, he mentioned that, did he?'

'Yes. Your pact with the devil.'

'The only pact I made with the devil, sister, is in return for being gorgeous and talented, Satan gets to torment me with losers with ugly ponytails.'

She laughs and tosses her head back, and her red hair ripples like the glass of wine in her hand. She turns away from me, looks out of the window and laughs again, but I can see her face in the mirror above the fireplace.

Her eyes are cold. *Perhaps she is thinking about Clyde. Or perhaps she is thinking about her pact with the devil.*

I wonder what it is.

'Anyway,' I say at last. 'Don't worry about him.'

She grins a dazzling grin, but her eyes take a while to catch up with her smile. They are still troubled. 'Don't worry, I won't. Tomorrow night, I'll find another selfish artist who thinks he's the next Picasso, but tonight belongs to us.'

'Well, that's a nice thought. But I'd better phone for a taxi.'

'Stay,' she says, putting her hand on my knee. 'Stay over. We'll get drunk and slag off everyone younger and thinner until the dawn pokes her rosy nose through the window.'

'I can't. Don't ask me.'

'You're forty-three, darling. You're old enough for sleep-overs.'

'I *can't.*'

'Why not?'

'Lots of reasons.'

'Name them.'

'Angelina . . . You know most of them.'

'Name them.'

'Well . . . I haven't got my pills.'

'Ah-ha!' She produces a bunch of silver foil packets from a

152

rustic pot and fans them out like a set of playing cards. I can see what they are, but she makes a big show of reading the names on the packets. 'Uppers, downers ... all the greats. These could really get a party jumping ...'

I narrow my eyes. 'Those are my pills.'

'*Quelle surprise.*'

'Where did you get those?'

'I had a little chat with Dominic, ages ago. I picked his brains and your medicine cabinet, in the case of such an eventuality ...'

'I *thought* there were some missing! When did you do this?'

'I told you. Ages ago. Let's not get bogged down by little details. Now you said you had reasons? Reason two?'

'My mouth guard. I have to have my mouth guard. When I'm sleeping, the pain makes me grind my teeth together. If I don't wear my mouth guard at night, I would grind my teeth to a fine powder within a month.'

'Gosh. What ... you mean something like this?'

She's standing by a chest of drawers, and she opens the top one, producing a familiar orange plastic box, about the size and shape of a powder compact. She opens it and shows me and, sure enough, there's a semicircle of plastic and metal, like a dental brace.

'Now where did you get that? I don't even have a spare. They cost a fortune.'

'Dominic went to your dentist and got a copy made.'

'When did he find the time to do that?'

'Does it matter? Now, any more excuses? Reason three?'

'Well I can't sleep on the sofa ...'

'I have a bed.'

'I can't take yours.'

'I have a second bed.'

'I don't want to be rude, but it would just cripple me if I tried to sleep on a saggy old bed. Or even any kind of bed that's not well sprung. Sorry, but that's the way my body works now.'

'I *said* I have a bed. Follow me to the boudoir.'

She takes me upstairs, and throws open the door of her spare room. On the bed is a shiny, plastic-wrapped mattress. 'One orthopaedic mattress. One careful owner. Which happens to be you.'

'You bought this for me?'

'Yep.'

'Angelina! I've got one of these. It cost us a thousand pounds, and that was years ago. How much did this set you back?'

'Mon, I spend thousands of pounds on useless crap every month. At least I've spent my money on something *useful* for a change.'

It's several seconds before I realise I'm weeping, and I just can't stop. Her kindness has reduced me to a blubbering heap. Angelina takes hold of me, her arms looping under my armpits, and she gives me a gentle squeeze. I bury myself into her bony chest.

'Please stay,' she whispers in my ear.

I nod into her bosom.

'Good girl, you know it makes sense. Now extract yourself at once; you're making my minuscule tits wet, and I don't want them to shrink.'

I ring Dominic. I put it off until the last minute; until I'm sure he's about to go to bed. I even call his mobile rather than using the land-line, because I know it's more likely to go to voice-mail and I can avoid speaking to him direct. The truth is, I don't know how I'm going to react if I hear his voice. Whether I'm going to cry with love at his thoughtfulness, or scream at him for spying on me.

Surprise! He picks up. I stammer, and eventually say: 'Hello, darling, it's me.'

'Hello. Where are you?'

'Angelina's. I've decided to stay over tonight.'

'Oh, OK.'

'Is that all right?'

'It's fine. Absolutely fine. More than fine, it's great. You have fun.'

'I will.'

'Are you sure?'

'Quite sure.'

'You'll be OK?'

'Oh yes, Angelina's going to take good care of me. She's got all the things you gave her; the pills, the mouth guard ... It was sweet of you.'

'It was her idea. And her money.'

'It was sweet of both of you.'

'Well, I'm glad you're having a girlic night. I'll just go to bed and rent myself a horror movie.'

'You do that.'

'OK, night then.'

'Night night.'

'Love you lots.'

'No, love *you* lots.'

'You hang up.'

'No *you* hang up.'

'No *you* hang up.'

'No you—'

'Brrrrrrrrr.'

And then he hangs up for real.

Dominic

Fifteen minutes after Monica left, Dominic was downstairs at the keyboard, looking up his favourites.

Fifteen seconds after that he was staring at the crude blocky website of ED'S SHEDS.

The website was dark green, with ugly old-fashioned writing, like it had been vomited out by Pac-Man. And it displayed really ugly-looking sheds at ridiculous prices. No one in their right mind would think of buying a shed from it. Which was precisely the point.

He entered the chatroom, headed GARDEN FURNITURE, and saw with a thrill of recognition that Arnie Terminator was there, waiting. He was the only other person in the chatroom.

Dominic typed:

Hi

Then almost immediately came the response:

Hi
   Howzit goin bud?
   Fine
   I'm looking to get some garden furniture. Like we
talked about on facebook?

There was a pause, probably no more than fifteen, twenty seconds, but Dominic's heart was pounding so much it caused his hand to jump and move the cursor across the screen.

More letters spilled out across the screen.

> Theere is no faccbook page bud u must be mistakn
> happy to sell you some weedkiller and a sprayer if
> that wld help u bud

Dominic rested his fingers on the keys and, with an extreme effort of will, started to type.

> That's just what I need. How can I get this stuff?
> Can you send it to me via the post?

Another pause. Then:

> No mate there a bit too big for amazon!!! Need to
> put them in my car. There is a pub we can meet???
> In Woolwwich.

Dominic typed a word.

> Today?

A name and a postcode flashed up. Dominic googled it and printed up a map.

He wondered if Monica would go through with the treatment. He knew by the way she glared at him from the bed that she would try and go through with it, whatever he said. There was the look of the old Monica in those eyes. Even though her head was embedded deep in the pillow, they seemed to glow with that old fire, that single-minded determination.

Dominic got in his car and off he went. The moment he got there, to Woolwich, he thought he had made a mistake. The car looked horribly conspicuous, parked alongside the carcasses of ruined shops with fly-posters on their boarded-up windows, like pennies on the eyes of the dead. He got out and made sure it was locked, clicking his keyfob off and on several times, making absolutely sure he saw the yellow flash from the lights. Even so, he looked back at it, as if sure he'd never see it again.

The pub was tucked behind a DIY warehouse, completely dwarfed by it. The only thing that could be seen out of the filthy windows was a sheer wall of corrugated metal and a gigantic logo of a criss-crossed hammer and spanner. The inside of the pub was tiny, crammed full of chipped furniture, faded chairs and tables, a darkened jukebox and a fruit machine that caught the light. He could see it was smeared with a thousand thumbprints.

The whole place was utterly filthy and he walked in like the worst kind of tourist, clutching his bag in both hands and hunching his shoulders, trying not to come into contact with any part of the insides. The only clean thing was the huge television on the wall which was showing American football. The television was very loud, swallowing up all the conversations. He went up to the bar, where an old fat woman stared at him with dead eyes.

'Pint of . . .' Dominic surveyed the brands, and he couldn't find any he liked. 'Lager, please.'

The woman got him a pint of something, pulling the pump low so she bent over and showed him a wizened cleavage, no bra. Ashamed, Dominic averted his eyes. She put his pint in front of him and he gave her a fiver and got his change. The whole transaction was conducted without a word.

'Mr Wood?'

There was a man behind him. He was quite smartly dressed, in a full suit, white shirt and a pencil-thin tie. The only evidence that he belonged here, and not in the city, was a pair of muddy Doc Martens and a wispy beard that clung for dear life under his chin.

'Hello?' Dominic must have sounded taken aback, because the man looked uncertain.

'Mr Wood. Yeah, It must be you, yeah. It's you. It is you, guy. Yeah!' He was persuading himself that Dominic was his contact, and by the end of his sentence he had convinced himself.

'Nice to meet you in the flesh, Mr Wood. Drink?'

From the way he nodded to the bar, it was obvious the man was asking for one, not offering to buy one. Dominic got him a drink and they sat in the darkest corner, next to the dead fireplace.

'Um … Nice to meet you too … Um …'

'Arnie, Mr Wood.'

'Arnie. As in Arnie Terminator.'

'That's it.'

'I thought it was just a name you used. Your web name.'

'Of course it is.' He shook his head, like Dominic was an idiot. 'I like to keep it simple. You carry on calling me Arnie and it stays nice and simple, don't it?'

'Fine.'

'So. To business.'

'Just to say, when I wrote all that stuff about gardening equipment, I didn't mean garden equipment.'

'Geddaway.' Arnie's sarcasm was thick and theatrical. 'You were shitting me all along. I've got two sheds and a wheelbarrow in my boot, all ready to go.'

'You know what I want to buy.'

His head bobbed low. 'I *know* that, guy, I did get it. Fair play to you for finding my Yankee buddy on Facebook.'

'Yes. Well I have connections. People who know stuff.'

'Bully for you, guy, knowing stuff is very important. Well, he's allowed to sell as much … garden furniture … he can lay his hands on. Lucky Yankees. Any Brit who enquires, he sends my way.'

Arnie's eyes flicked from right to left and back again.

'Now this is what we do, Mr Wood. I leave in five minutes, and you count slowly to twenty in your head – you can do that, right? And then you leave, and you take a left, a right, and a right, and you go to the red car with the Snoopy stuck to the car window. That's my trademark, cos Snoopy looks out for the snoopers. Right? OK, we clear?'

He tried to get up to leave, but Dominic put his hand firmly on his shrunken fist.

'Wait. I have to tell you why I need the gun.'

'I don't want to know, guy.'

'I need to talk about it.'

'Too much information.'

'I have to tell someone. If I can't tell anyone, then I'll fall apart. If I fall apart then I won't need the gun. Do you understand?'

'OK, OK …' Arnie shrugged and sat down again, glancing at his watch. 'The meter is running. Tell me why you need the gun, professor.'

'It's my wife.'

Arnie raised his eyebrows as if to say 'and?'

The words tumbled out of Dominic's mouth, strange and alien. He couldn't believe them even as he was saying them. 'I can't cope with her. She's in a lot of pain, and she's impossible to live with, and I thought I could cope with it but I can't. And I know I shouldn't hate her, but I do.'

'Yeah, well, women, eh? Can't live with 'em …'

'The thing is, she's not going to get any better. And I have to think of myself. I have to think of the life I want to lead. I've done everything I can for her. Everything. And I've got no hope left. I tried so hard. I searched so hard for a treatment to make things better.'

'Right. OK. If it makes you feel better, we can call this a treatment, right, prof? You are just buying a "treatment" off me, and when you apply that "treatment" …'

Arnie aimed a finger at his head and cocked his thumb.

'... she's not going to feel any pain no more. So, good on you, mate. You're doing the right thing. This is for her, right? For her own good.'

Dominic didn't answer. Partly because he had tears in his eyes and his Adam's apple had got wedged in his throat. 'Huh,' he sobbed at last. 'This is how lonely I am. I'm confiding in my own arms dealer ...'

'Shh!' Arnie waved his finger in front of his mouth, fanning spittle across the table. 'Don't be so facking obvious!'

Dominic pouted. 'You're the one who just put a finger to his head.'

'Yeah, well, that's different.' Arnie didn't explain how it was different. He crossed his arms and hunched over the table, eyes flicking to the television.

'I sympathise, I do. I take my hat off to you, man, I really do, but ... Look ... I know I'm cutting my own throat by saying this ... I mean, far be it from me to give a smart guy like you some advice, prof, but there are better ways to do shit like this ... Guns can be messy ... You know, you could ... make it look like, y'know, a suicide ...'

Dominic shook his head. 'I can't do that. There's an insurance policy. A big one. She commits suicide and I won't get a penny.'

'Oh yeah, I get you. Now you're making sense. But if some burglar was to break in and get surprised, and he got a bit trigger-happy ...'

'I can see you're way ahead of me.'

'Man, I was way ahead of you the moment you said "It's my wife".'

'I have to think of myself. Of my life and my future, long term. It's just sometimes we have to do things that – on their own – seem unpleasant, but you have to do them, for the bigger picture.'

Arnie fell silent, and for a moment Dominic thought he was thinking about what he said, but Arnie was just waiting for him to stop.

'So. You feeling better now? You got everything off your chest? Because I got other people to see besides you. I got a couple of beardies in Streatham who need a few bags of fertiliser and some pruning shears, if you catch my drift.'

Dominic nodded.

'Good. Now let's do this.'

'OK.'

'Remember. I leave, you count to twenty.'

Arnie left. Dominic counted to twenty.

They got in Arnie Terminator's car, a dirty, aged Mondeo. Before Dominic got in, he had to pick up half a dozen magazines from the passenger seat, and when he did some cans of Coke decorated with Arabic writing rolled over his feet. Arnie picked one up and waved it in his direction.

'Do you want a Coke?' he said. 'My mate's a lorry driver. He gets one free with every asylum seeker he brings through the Chunnel.' He pulled the tab and drank. 'Joke,' he added unnecessarily.

Dominic shook his head.

The car puttered off and Arnie squinted through the windscreen, holding his steering wheel like an orang-utan clutching a tyre.

'Now I'm only mentioning this in passing,' he said, casually, 'but you don't have to put yourself out. If you catch my drift.'

'I don't. What do you mean?'

'You could get someone to do it for you. I know some blokes. Won't cost you too much. You're gonna be the obvious suspect, after all, and hiring someone makes it easy for you to put some distance between you and the dirty deed. Make it easy for you to get yourself an alibi, if you catch my drift.'

'I'm catching your drift,' Dominic said.

'And they wouldn't be that expensive. After all, I hardly think doing your missus would be a challenge. Would it? From what you said, she's a bit of a sitting target.'

Dominic closed his eyes wearily. 'I suppose not. But it's personal, you know. We've been through a lot together. I wouldn't want anyone to do it but me.'

Arnie shrugged, the car did a little wobble.

'Suit yourself,' he said. 'It's your funeral.'

They drove along narrow little roads framed with shops and houses, all equally broken and neglected. Arnie seemed to take right and left turns at random and the longer the journey took, the more nervous Dominic got. He wondered if the whole thing was an elaborate joke and he was being taken somewhere quiet to relieve him of his life and the fat money-engorged envelope sitting in his jacket pocket. Dominic found himself fiddling with the door catch, flapping it gently with the edge of his fingers, as if his left hand had already decided to plan a daring escape from the moving vehicle.

Finally, they drove into a car park, a barren piece of land surrounded by aged tower blocks. The car trundled up to one of the garages. Parked outside one was an old blue Transit van; rusting and ugly.

Arnie unlocked the back of the van, opening the doors up to reveal nothing but a black canvas bag. He clambered inside, clicked on a mechanic's lamp hanging from the roof of the van and pulled the bag out. He dropped it at Dominic's feet.

Arnie unzipped the bag and held up a handgun, holding it delicately between three fingers and pointing it to the ceiling.

163

Dominic was expecting him to rattle off a list of statistics about the gun, the serial number, range, how many bullets per second it could fire, how many millimetres the barrel was, with decimal points, but Arnie wasn't into any of that.

'There,' he said. 'Point and pull the trigger. You put the bullets in there. If you want any more then find them somewhere else.'

Dominic produced the envelope. 'OK. Here's the money. What we agreed.'

'Pleasure doing business with you, professor.' He held his hand out but Dominic held the envelope even more tightly.

'Just a second,' he said. 'How do I know it works?'

Arnie's expression froze. 'What?'

Dominic realised things had suddenly taken a wrong turn, that he had said something wrong. He thought of a lie to smooth the situation over. 'Look, I tried to do this once before, but it turned out there was no gun.'

'What?'

'I tried to buy one before, years ago, but I got cheated. They took my money and it was just a pipe wrapped in a towel.'

'What?'

'So ... I just ... want to, you know ...'

Arnie Terminator stared at Dominic with wide eyes, mouth open. 'What – the – FUCK?' He slammed a fist into the van. 'What did you just say? What did you – just – SAY?'

Dominic took a step back. 'Arnie ...'

'You just said I was cheating you, you ... fuck!'

'I didn't say that.'

'You FUCK!'

Dominic

'Arnie' was working himself into a frenzy. Dominic felt his legs tremble, telling him to run. He didn't know why he didn't run. He felt he *couldn't*. It all felt dreamlike, like he was floating above himself, watching this poor, flabby middle-class fool clutching his money and meeting his ridiculous death in a deserted car park.

Anyway, he was in advertising, and the one thing he knew about was the right of the consumer not to be sold a product under false pretences. He was the customer, and the customer was always right. By pure instinct and bloody-mindedness, Dominic stood his ground.

'Well, it might not be real. I don't know you, do I?'

'You want to know if it's real, do you? Do you, professor? Do you?'

He fired the gun at the ground; it was fitted with a silencer. It didn't sound like the movies; more of a loud metallic click than a 'pff'. Dominic jumped back, arm over his face, as slivers of concrete spewed out of the ground.

'That's how real it is, professor! That's how real! Motherfucker!'

Arnie fired again, and Dominic screamed.

'Now give me the money, professor. GIVE IT TO ME! NOW, YOU FUCKER!'

Dumbly, he handed Arnie the envelope, and he tried to tear it open with one hand. It was quite a tricky stunt and his eyes kept bobbing down from Dominic's face to look at what he was doing.

Dominic realised that Arnie had had this scenario in his mind the whole time, or at least was entertaining the idea of taking his money and keeping the gun, as a possible outcome. He just needed a trigger – no pun intended – to justify waving the gun in Dominic's face. The realisation hit Dominic like a hot wave, and he felt rage bubbling up inside his brain.

Arnie was still standing directly behind his van, and when he glanced down again Dominic – without even knowing what he was doing – slammed the doors onto him. Arnie fell back into the van, trapped by his knees. Dominic pushed with all his might, ignoring Arnie's howls and his threats, and then his pleadings.

Arnie must have kept hold of the gun because there went the 'click' again and the high window of the van shattered. Dominic screamed, this time because there was a sharp pain by his ear. The world started whistling a tune with one high note and Dominic shouted at it to stop but he couldn't hear his own voice. He crouched down and watched with detached amusement as holes appeared in the doors. He imagined they must have gone *thunk*, *thunk*, *thunk*, but he couldn't hear; the whole world had a silencer now.

Something, a distant voice from deep inside the whistle, told Dominic that if he didn't do something quickly the holes would start appearing in his chest. He grabbed hold of one of Arnie's feet, still protruding from the bottom of the van. He twisted the ankle and Arnie screamed and struggled, wriggling to follow his foot as it revolved, but he was still pinned by Dominic's weight on the door. Dominic twisted until Arnie's screams reached a pitch, and he heard a satisfying 'crack' that came from between his hands.

Then he grabbed the other one.

This time he took his weight off the door, just slightly, and allowed Arnie to twist frantically over to avoid another 'crack'. Once Arnie had struggled onto his belly Dominic launched into the van and allowed his weight to descend on the smaller man.

'Yrr fkkrr. Fkkrrrr!' was all Arnie could say, as his face got pushed into the metal floor of the van. Dominic twisted the gun out of Arnie's hand, and Arnie gave another muffled scream.

Dominic could have made a million smart-alec comments, like 'hasta la vista' or something like that, but in the end he just said:

'Fuck you, Arnie.'

He felt liberated, as if all the frustration and fury he had been bottling up for years had been released.

'Frrrrrkrrrr!' said Arnie.

Dominic stuffed his money back in his jacket, grabbed Arnie's hair, pulled his head up and shoved it against the floor.

Then he shut the van doors, and ran. And ran. And ran.

And then he was on a high street, trying to stay calm and composed, trying to keep his walk slow and steady, trying not to run. Trying not to be conspicuous. Then he caught sight of his face in a shop window.

How ridiculous I look, he thought. *Trying not to look conspicuous when my ear is hanging off and there's blood down my face.*

I can't go back home like this. I can't. I can't explain this.

He ducked out of the high street and lumbered along the side streets like Frankenstein's monster, taking left and right turns at random, until he saw a grim sign above a terraced house. WILLOWTREE LODGE.

A bed and breakfast. One that doesn't look that choosy about its guests.

Dominic staggered into a faded, threadbare hallway. There was an old grey woman, small and curved. She was vacuuming the carpet, and she dropped the hoover when she saw him.

'Oh goodness! What's happened?'

'Car accident . . .'

Her hand twitched over to the telephone, which was sitting quaintly on an occasional table under the kitchen hatch.

'No . . . it's fine.' Dominic waved his hands to calm her. His bloodstained hands. 'I've rung the police. They'll be here soon. I just need a room to freshen up.'

'Oh, yes ... Of course.'

She scuttled to a desk and he loomed over her, slamming the envelope on the surface. The envelope was dark, stained with blood. It was also split, and the money inside could clearly be seen.

'I need a room for a few nights,' he said. 'While I recover. And get my car repaired.'

She knew something was up. 'Oh – of course. Where's your car? We do have numbers of garages ...'

'No need.'

'But if there was an accident ...'

She was confused. Nothing Dominic was saying made any sense. 'It wasn't ... Not exactly an accident ...' His mind was racing. He was aware that the gun was dragging against his pocket and the handle was starting to peep out from his jacket. He straightened up and turned his back on her, feigning embarrassment, and tucked it back inside.

'I was in the car with someone who wasn't ... was not my wife. She got mad at me, something I said, and she wrenched the steering wheel and crashed us into a lamp-post.'

The old lady started to speak but he held up his hand. 'She was fine. Airbag. She ran off, but I've got to get myself and the car sorted out before my wife finds out.'

That made more sense to her. Not complete sense, but her eyes were flicking to the blood-stained envelope. Taking his cue, Dominic peeled it open and started dealing twenty pound notes on the table. One, two, three ...

'I just need a few days to sort the car. Get my ear fixed, and mum's the word. I'd be very grateful ...'

Her eyes danced to Dominic's face, to the growing pile of money, and then back to his face.

Sold.

Ten minutes later Dominic was in a tiny room. He lay on the bed and it sagged wearily. *Oh no, not another body to sleep on me,* the springs groaned.

His eyes traced the cracks up the wall, past the chipped dressing table and up into the ceiling, where it converged with many other cracks around the light fitting, like a threadbare spider's web.

How did I get here? How did this happen?

That was when his mobile rang. It was Monica, thanking him for being wonderful. She was going to stay the night at Angelina's.

He sat up, put his head in his hands, and pointed his eyes to the floor, watching the vague swirls of the denuded carpet through his fingers. He could feel the ragged remains of his ear with his thumb.

Thou shalt not bear false witness.

He remembered the sermons of Father Jerome in his dingy lime-green presbytery, the place where the radiator gurgled like the devil himself was coming up through the plumbing, where they stored the unblessed wafers and the garments and the unchipped crosses for the feast days; where the Father wrote the commandments out on a squealing blackboard and asked the boys about the lies they told in the last week, banging the board with the eraser and demanding examples. *'Don't think about it! Just say them out loud!'* It forced him to rack his brains for lies that weren't too shameful. He thought about the stories, the lies, all mounting up around him, and he cried; for Monica, for himself, for both of them, and he did not stop crying until the room was dark.

Monica

With her long delicate fingers, Angelina pulls a couple of Rizla papers out of the packet, licks the edges and fastens them together. Then she takes a small cellophane-wrapped chunk from her bedside drawer, unpicks the wrapping and crumbles a bit of brown onto the paper, patting it into a thin line. Finally, she pulls a handful of tobacco from a tin, scatters it over the crumbs and rolls it up, jamming it into her mouth, lighting it and pulling a long grateful toke, eyes bulging and cheeks deflating.

She holds it in her mouth for five seconds before exhaling a thin stream of smoke, and she falls back on her beanbag. I've been given the ornate high-backed wooden chair, as beanbags and me don't mix.

'That is good shit,' she chokes. 'I knew I stayed with Clyde for a reason. I'd better make this last . . . '

She proffers the joint to me, but I shake my head.

'No thanks.'

'Sure?'

'I'll stay on the vino.'

'Did you ever try this stuff for the pain?' she says, waving her joint. 'I seem to recall you did, didn't you?'

I'm drinking when she says this, so I nod, drain my glass, plonk it down and say, 'Yes, I did try for a while.'

'No good then?'

'Not really. Well, I'm not sure if it did anything or it didn't. I couldn't smoke enough of it, because of my asthma.'

'How bitterly ironic. But I'm thinking of that super-dope. Those tablets you got on prescription. I was so jealous.'

'Nabilone. I was utterly zonked, off my tits, unable to function as a human being.'

'You lucky bitch.'

I laugh. 'Problem was, the super-dope gave me super-munchies, and I would hobble to the shop on my sticks, stock up on chocolate, eat it on the way back home, and turn around and go back again. It wasn't really the life I'd planned for myself. That's the problem; that's what I found very quickly after my accident. There are no drugs they've developed that actually deal with pain.'

Angelina is not a woman who leaps in and utters stupid things. Unlike Jesse, she leaves the crushingly obvious unsaid, because she knows saying the crushingly obvious is a waste of everyone's time. I'm so grateful to her for that, because questions are so often the things that drain my energy.

I still see the frown flicker on her forehead, the unspoken question on her face, but this time I'm glad to talk about it.

'Oh sure, there's your headache pills, and your Beechams Powders, your paracetamol, but nothing for chronic neuropathic pain. Most drugs just try to switch bits of your brain off, which isn't much use to me, really.

'It's funny, these chemicals, how completely they change you when you put them in your body, how your personality completely transforms. And the pain changes who you are too. I was just saying to a – friend – the other day, what with the mind-altering drugs and the pain screwing with my head, I have no idea how to work out which Monica is me any more . . . '

Angelina waves her glass expansively in the air. The red wine sloshes alarmingly near the lip of the glass.

'Monica, you're a sweetheart. You're a sweetheart now, and you always have been.'

'Thank you, darling. So are you.'

I raise my empty glass in a mock toast, and she scrambles out of her beanbag. 'Fuck, we're out of booze. I've got another bottle somewhere. Can't go dry, tonight of all nights.'

She stumbles off to the kitchen and I sit, and I feel the warm buzz of the wine numbing my senses, and I listen to the clatters and the 'fucks' as Angelina wrestles with a bottle opener.

She's at the door, new bottle in hand, when I ask, 'Angelina ... what was I like, before?'

She chucks wine into my glass. 'Before what?'

'Before the accident. I'm sure I must have been different. It stands to reason.'

'Not really.'

'But I feel like I've changed. My life is upside down, my relationship with Dominic has changed, everything has changed, and it's all changed because of one thing; I changed first. The accident changed me, and I changed everything else.'

'You're getting a bit bloody deep for my blood, darling. The only philosophies I read are the fortune cookies I get delivered with my dim sum.'

'It's not deep at all. It's just a fact. An empirical, observable fact. How have I changed? Go on, think.'

'You haven't really. Well ...'

'Ah! I knew there would be a "well".'

'I think you were much ... harder.'

'Really? That's interesting. Harder? How so?'

'Well, a lot of it was your job, you know, the flinty ball-busting agent, but you were certainly a bit more ...'

'Aggressive?'

'I was going to say a bit more of a fucking bitch, but yeah ...'

I giggled.

'So I was a bit of a cow then?'

'No, darling, not a cow. A bitch. You were my friend, and I do not have cows as friends. But you were less patient with people; with your clients, with Dominic, you didn't suffer fools gladly is, I believe, the cliché ...'

'Oho, when I hear that old phrase, the alarm bells do go.'

She pointed her glass at me. 'Now I want to be very clear about this. You were not a cunt. You were – and still are – a warm, clever, funny and adorable human. But then, you utterly chopped the bollocks off the slow-witted and the prematurely stupid. So, to sum up, you were a bit more like me.'

'I like the sound of that.'

'Once you got an idea in your head. A goal. You went for it, and to hell with the consequences. In fact . . .'

She stops, frowning. She looks almost disappointed in herself for saying too much.

'In fact what?'

'Nothing.'

'You were going to say something.'

'Nope. It's completely gone. I've completely lost my train of thought. I probably need more wine to oil the pistons.'

'You said I was less patient with Dominic? Did I chop his bollocks off too? I mean, we worked well together? We were happy, right?'

'Darling, you talk like you remember *nothing* from before the accident. I'm sure that's not the case.'

'I remember lots of things. Events. Sensations. But sometimes they're all disconnected, because *I've* changed. I . . . Sometimes I miss the *meaning* of what's happened. Do you understand?'

'I think so.'

'I remember arguments. Angry voices. Dominic's angry face. I remember a lot of tears.'

We fall silent.

'I'm not saying everything was rosy in Chez Wood . . .' Angelina spoke slowly, picking her words carefully. 'You were quite dismissive about him at times. Dominic Wood; the only guy in advertising who avoids work where he actually has to lie. You did get frustrated with him, from time to time.'

173

'I see.'

'It was sometimes stressful. You were a success, he was always on the verge of losing his job. That always creates friction. That's why I never go out with struggling artists; they always get bitter, and they always want to know why I'm displaying other people's work and not theirs. It's like in their eyes I'm having an affair.'

In their eyes I'm having an affair. Yes. You can see it in their eyes.

(**In his eyes**)

Yes.

I allow her to take a good long swig before I say, 'Was I the kind of person to hurt him?'

'You don't mean physically?'

'God no. Just . . . did I ever hurt him?'

She looks at me steadily. 'By which you mean, "Did I have an affair, and have I just forgotten?"'

'I suppose so, yes.'

'How could you forget that, darling?'

'I don't know!' I snap, suddenly impatient.

She looks at me, unflinching, holding her beatific smile, and I'm suddenly very ashamed.

'Sorry, Lena . . . Look . . . Like I said . . . There's memories in my head, lots of them, but they're like tube trains, coming through the tunnel when you're standing on a platform. They arrive all right, but you can't see where they've come from and you can't see where they're going to . . . ' I wave my hand in desperation.

Angelina's mouth twitches. 'Hmm. Not that I know of. To my knowledge, you never allowed anybody's tube train to enter your metaphorical tunnel. You were an outrageous flirt sometimes, but again, that's being an agent. You knew it was an important part of the job to tickle the testicles of actors, directors, casting agents, but they were always metaphorical testicles, not literal ones. You never seemed to go in for that kind of thing.'

'And Dominic knew that, right?'

'Oh yeah, I mean, I assume he did. I've never known him that well, but the way you talked about him, yes, I think he did.'

I don't respond.

'Monica, you're taking me on a very mysterious journey here, and it would help me if you gave me a travel guide. Why are we talking like this?'

'Dominic doesn't want me to have this treatment.'

'What treatment?'

'It's a new thing they have. They try to burn out the nerve endings under the skin.'

Angelina shudders. 'Jesus. I don't blame him.'

'But it's had some success, people have had it done, and they've had a lot of pain relief, and it's hardly worse than all the gruesome stuff they put me through in the early days. He didn't mind, then.'

She cocks an eyebrow.

'Monica, darling, one thing that has *never* changed about you is your ability to never ask a question to which you already have an answer. So what's your theory in all this?'

'I think he's frightened of me getting better, and me leaving him.'

'What makes you say that?'

'The way he acts, the way he looks so *scared* when we talk about the treatment. But not for me. For himself.'

Angelina knows there's more to come. 'And?'

'And ... Well.'

'And?' She makes a little twirling motion with her hand.

'And ... I found photos on Dominic's side of the computer.'

'Photos? Of what?'

I know from the tone of her voice she's expecting me to say 'rude photos'. *Men are so predictable.* So I am almost gratified at the comical look of surprise on her face when I say,

175

'Photos of me . . .'

'Well, you're a gorgeous creature, darling, it's only natural—'

'No, look . . .'

I grope for my bag under my seat, put it on my lap and pull out a plastic sleeve. I toss out some of the photos I'd printed up. They land on the floor at Angelina's feet. Twenty, thirty, forty . . . *Lots* of photos of me. Photos taken of me hobbling around after my accident, me on the street, trying to go to the shops, eating pasta in a café . . .

'And there's more. A lot more. And they're all taken without my knowledge. It's like he got a detective to follow me around in case I . . . did something.'

Angelina barely glances down at the photos at her feet. She's icy calm. She doesn't even remove the glass from her lips. 'And did you . . . do something?'

'*Of course not!* I was barely able to stand without crying! Do you think I was in any fit state to have an affair?'

'Then forget everything. Forget these photos. Tear them up. Forget them.'

I scoop the photos back towards me with my foot. 'I can't forget it.'

'Why the hell not?'

'Suppose Dominic thinks I'm having an affair? Suppose he does something?'

At this comment, Angelina finally puts her drink down. 'Believe me, he wouldn't.'

'But how do you know?'

'Because he's bloody *Dominic*!' she explodes, suddenly angry. She calms herself. 'Sorry, Mon, but the whole idea is so *ridiculous*. Dominic? I mean, *Dominic*? It's Dominic. Dear little God-bothery Dom, who believes in the sanctity of life, who goes to church every Sunday . . . I mean, come *on* . . .'

176

'Of course,' I say. 'You're right. You have to remember. It's the pain. It makes me think mad unthinkable things.'

'Darling, I completely understand.' She lunges forward and touches my knee, very gently. 'God, who knows what's going through *anyone's* head? I've killed Clyde in so many exquisite ways in my head this evening, but I have no intention of doing so ... Not tonight, anyway.' She grins savagely. 'When the hangover comes tomorrow ... who knows what I'm capable of?'

'So you're saying that having a lot of pain would make you want to commit murder? Perhaps it's Dominic that's in danger ... From me.'

She raises her almost empty glass and toasts me. 'Touché, Mon,' she drawls. 'Touché. Personally, I can murder another bottle. How about you?'

Monica

I wake up . . .

. . . And my body screams for release.

My Angry Friend is punishing me for last night. I put on a brave face for Angelina. I haven't the heart to tell her how I feel, not after all she's done. But pills and mattresses can only do so much.

My Angry Friend will have his pound of flesh.

She takes me for breakfast at the Eat Me café (scrambled eggs on sourdough toast), and after much hugs *oh, the pain* and promises to keep in touch, I leave her and sink into a taxi. It's only after the front door closes that I'm free to fall on the floor and cry.

Then my phone goes. It's Dominic. Still lying in the hallway, I press the phone to my ear.

'Hi, Mon. You have fun at the art thing? And at Angelina's?'

Keep the tremor out of your voice, Monica.

'Glorious fun. Thank you so much.'

'Great.'

'You two are the best. And you . . . are the bestest of them all.'

'I know.'

'Good. I'm glad you know.'

'Listen, darling, you remember that job interview I went for?'

'No.'

'The Gamble thing?'

I still don't know what he's talking about, so I just say 'yes'. It's easier.

'Well, there's good news.'

'You got a new job?'

'Not quite. Things are never that simple. They want me to go to a series of interviews over the weekend. In Swindon, would you believe.'

'Swindon? Is there *anything* in Swindon?'

'Some conference centre. A big zit by a motorway. They've got this fetish for *Apprentice*-style meetings and tasks and knock-out rounds. That kind of nonsense.'

'How horrible. Don't do it, darling. Don't humiliate yourself.'

'Yeah ... But I want this. I'm just ringing to say I'll be up there for a couple of days. At least until Monday. Perhaps even longer. I'll stay over.'

'OK ... No problem ...'

'You'll be OK on your own? I've not been away for, gosh, it seems like ages. How's the pain?'

'It's fine,' I lie. 'The pain's fine. If I get a flare-up Agnieszka can look after me, or I'll call Jesse. Or even Angelina.'

'Angelina? I'd love to see her bedside manner.'

'I bet you would.'

We were both aware that the conversation was starting to take an odd turn, so we made moves to end the call.

'Well, good luck and everything.'

'Thanks. Here's hoping.'

'Drive safely.'

'OK. Love you lots.'

'No, love *you* lots.'

'You hang up.'

'No *you* hang up.'

'No *you* hang up.'

'No you—'

Brrrrrrrr.

Monica

I am partly in shock, but partly exhilarated.

I am on my own.

Truth to tell, ever since Dominic tried to squash the notion of going through with the treatment, scenarios have been whipping through my brain. Scenarios where I would show him. Where I would take my life in my own hands, and have this treatment without him.

So I can go and get the treatment now? What if he sees a difference in me?

So what? I can lie. I do it all the time, I tell myself. *I lie when I don't talk about my pain. I lie when he asks me if I'm all right, and I say 'fine'. This is just another version of that.*

What he doesn't know won't hurt him.

So the moment the phone call ends I fight through the fog of pain. I have to get the treatment; Dominic or no Dominic. The first thing I need to find is

you must have someone to take you home.

180

I can't risk turning up alone.

I can't risk them refusing me the treatment. I have to find someone to take me.

Monica

The phone rings and rings, and keeps on ringing. Angelina isn't there. *Did she say she was going off for the weekend?* Has she just upped and gone on one of her 'working holidays' in France? I try her mobile.

Straight to voicemail.

'Hey, Lena, it's Mon. I really need your help. It's quite urgent. If you're back in London before Monday, give me a call.'

A day passes and no word from Angelina. I leave more messages, one on Friday evening, and two more on the Saturday.

Time is running out.

Monica

Larry's kitchen is Jill's domain, and it shows. It's filled with chintz, with fussy dressers covered in plates and knick-knacks. There is a faint smell of cat food, and a lot of the decorations have a cat motif; little china moggies sit grinning on pine shelves. A cat-themed clock grins from the wall. Photos of beaming children are plastered over the fridge and stuffed inside a corkboard.

I was a fool to come here. But I'm getting desperate. I stand awkwardly by the kitchen door, unable to sit.

Larry French lumbers in, barely fitting in through the doors. He is big, all curves, like he's drawn with circles. His big round head is fringed with a brown fuzz, and his big round nose is pushed randomly between two big round cheeks.

He comes up to me and I realise he's nervous. He's happier in the shed, in the living room, anywhere but here, but here seems the right place for him to entertain a woman. Where he can talk and look after me at the same time.

His fat fingers drum on the work surface. 'Now. Can I get you anything. Tea? Coffee?'

'Oh yes. Coffee would be lovely.'

He walks to the corner of the kitchen and stops. He does his big huh-huh laugh: 'Sod it. Jill's not here and I can't work the machine. In fact, I can't work any of this stuff. I can just about warm my dinner in the microwave without setting fire to the house. Instant do?'

'How about tea?'

'You got it. Sugar?'

'No thanks.'

'I'll get some biscuits out. Jill got an assortment from the milk-man. You can get all sorts from the milkman these days. We can get boxes of veg nowadays.'

'Fancy,' I say. 'I suppose they have to make a living. Dominic gets our milk from the supermarket.'

'Jill has a couple of pints on order, and a four-pinter for when Nathan comes back from uni.'

And Larry makes me a cup of tea. The mug has a cat on it (of course) and the words 'A purr-fect cuppa!!' I can barely lift it.

'So right, let's get this straight. I'm not quite sure what you're asking me, darling. So, right, there's this treatment . . .'

'Yes, it's experimental but it's proved to be quite effective against pain.'

'That's brilliant news, Sunflower. Fair play to you, you deserve a break. You want me to pay for it?'

'No.'

'Cos I've just had a windfall. An old mate just gave me a lot of money . . .' His brow wrinkles, trying to remember how normal, law-abiding people suddenly get hold of huge amounts of cash. 'In his will.'

'Thanks, but it's all on the NHS. These trials are, anyway. But Dominic doesn't want me to have it done. He thinks I shouldn't get my hopes up. It's only proved to give temporary relief.'

'What's wrong with temporary, that's what I say.'

'Exactly. I could live a normal life for a few months, come off the painkillers. Maybe even have a holiday.'

He nods, thinking hard. 'I see. So what do you need from me, flower?'

'Dominic won't help me. But look . . .' I flap the letter under his nose. 'It's a major treatment, and I'll be in no condition to make it home alone. They need me to bring a chaperone, or they won't treat me.'

'Oh, I get you now.'

He takes the letter and his huge meaty brow creases as his eyes dart from right to left. 'But the thing is, I'm starting rehearsals next week. I'll be in the National doing my thesping. I won't be available anytime during the day.'

'Oh. Of course you are. Stupid of me. I should know that. I am your agent, after all. I'm so sorry to bother you. So sorry.'

The pain is clouding my brain. I should have realised. Stupid stupid stupid.

(You need to get out of here now)

'Look, I got a lot of mates who owe me a favour. They could go with you, if you like.'

'No, really. It's fine. I'll make other arrangements.' A thought occurs to me. 'There's my sister. She'll be happy to help.'

'Whatever you say, Sunflower. But if she can't help, just say the word and I'll be there.'

He is so kind to me, and I can't even remember he's working on the biggest job of his life. *Acting job. Not bank job. I have no idea of the biggest bank job he's ever done.* I almost giggle at the strange thoughts in my head. I feel stupid, and humiliated, and the pain is edging me down the rabbit hole.

I really have to get out of there.

I somehow make it to the door. Larry escorts me. He is all smiles and big chuckles, but his eyes are not happy. He keeps looking at the cat clock, watching the tail moving like a metronome and the eyes bobbing from side to side.

Monica

'Hello?'

'Hi, Jesse, it's Monica.'

'Monica, I was just about to phone you——'

'——on Wednesday. I know you were. You phone me the same time every week. Just like you phoned Nana the same time every week when she was dying.'

'Well, there's no need to be like that . . . I do *care* you know . . .'

'Sorry. Look . . . I need a favour.'

'What kind of favour?'

'I need someone to drive me to the hospital. I'm having a treatment.'

'What kind of treatment?'

'It's a new kind of treatment.'

'I bet it's the one I just read about in the *Daily Mail*. I'll snip it out and send it to you.'

Oh great.

'Oh, great, but I need someone to take me there, tomorrow, and wait for me, and to look after me. It's going to be a pretty traumatic experience.'

'Tomorrow? What time?'

'The appointment's pretty early, nine o'clock, but I'll need you for the whole day.'

'Nine o'clock in the morning? I can't do that. I've got kids to take to school.'

'Can't Graeme do that for you?'

'He's tired in the mornings. He works all night.'

'He can get out of bed just this once.'

'Well, why can't Dominic look after you?'

'He's busy.'

'Well, so's Graeme.'

'Sleeping.'

She can hear the sarcasm in my voice. 'Fine that's it. You're out of line.'

'Jesse—'

'It's no excuse for bad manners. Graeme closes that restaurant at one, and leaves it at two o'clock at the earliest. There's no way I'm waking him after five hours' sleep. And if you'd stop to think about it, you'd know damn well I wouldn't.'

'Jesse, this is important.'

'Everything you've ever done in your life is important, Monica.

Every opening night, every school play you were in, it was always the most important thing in the world. It was important you had to talk about your latest boyfriend all night when I was trying to get to sleep.'

'Yes. Yes . . . '

'It was important to cut the hair off my dolly because you had a burning ambition to be a hairdresser.'

'I get it.'

'An ambition, I might add, that didn't last until the afternoon.'

'I said I get it. But this is important.'

'Not important enough for your husband to cancel whatever he's doing, so not important enough to wake Graeme,' she said firmly.

'What about Sam?'

'Sam? He's at university.'

'No he's not, Jesse, it's bloody July. He's on holiday.'

'OK, he's here, but if you think he's going to get out of bed for nine o'clock, then . . . '

'I'll be willing to pay him, Jesse. Fifty quid for a day's work. It could be half a day. Fifty quid for a couple of hours. Guaranteed.'

There is a long silence from Jesse. I can hear the faint gurgle of the dishwasher in her kitchen.

'OK, I'll ask him, but I doubt he'll want to, even for money. He's an idle so-and-so at the moment.'

'Brilliant. Thank you.'

'I'll post you the *Daily Mail* article.'

Must you?

'Thanks. I appreciate it.'

Monica

It's a lonely drive to the hospital.

I'm not in the mood for conversation. He senses this, and he asks if he can put the radio on. I say yes but I can't cope with the chatter and adverts, and after ten minutes I apologise and ask him to turn it off.

The raindrops slap the windows, and the *bwump bwump bwump* of the windscreen wipers is like an ominous drumbeat.

'I'll just park the car,' he says. 'I won't be long.'

I stand on the kerb and watch him drive down the street. For the short time I was inside the car it felt like a sanctuary, and now I am in the chill of the morning I feel incredibly exposed. I look around, suddenly nervous, like a young woman hovering at the doorway of an abortion clinic.

Inside, a bored receptionist tells me to follow the signs, but the woman who meets me at the doors of the pain clinic looks anything but bored. She is all smiles. 'Hello, Monica,' she chirps. 'You get here OK? No traffic problems? It is awkward this time of day.'

I'm a shell-shocked toddler on my first day in nursery. I shake my head dumbly. 'It was fine. My husband's parking the car.'

'Oh good. Just down here, we've got a bed all ready. Just call me Sue. We don't stand on ceremony here.'

She's being extremely nice, trying to calm me down, but it has the opposite effect. I've done enough of these to know that the nicer the nursing staff, the nastier and more painful the treatment. By the time I'm lying on the bed my hands are shaking so much I can barely switch my mobile off.

Call-Me-Sue then starts to strip my identity away from me,

piece by piece; first my belongings, then my clothes, and now I'm just an almost-naked woman shuffling around in paper slippers. I pad back and forth along the ward, looking at people, wondering what's wrong with them, wondering if they feel any of the pain I feel. They're probably thinking exactly the same thing about me.

'Anyone at home?'

There's a fruity disembodied voice. I think it's talking to me.

'Are you decent?'

'I'm not sure. I'd say "no", but then I'm not used to wearing a shower curtain with my bottom hanging out.'

There's a chuckle, the curtain is pulled back, and a man introduces himself as Dr Martin. 'Like the boot,' he says, pre-empting any feeble gag on my part. 'Just want to check a few things. You've not had this treatment before, have you?'

'No.'

'Well, with any luck you'll be in and out in no time. You've got someone to take you home?'

'Yes. My husband . . .'

I had a long debate with myself whether to say 'husband' or 'son'. *He looks so young.* In the end, I had no choice. Their records show I don't have children. *Say 'husband', I think. It might raise eyebrows, but not suspicions. I hope.*

'He's not in the building at the moment. He's just parking the car. It's very busy at the moment. Everyone's trying to get into central London.'

Too much information, Monica.

The doctor is barely listening. 'Good good good. We're doing eight people today, and you're the first. So I won't hang about. I'll be bright and awake for you, at least. Have you read the guidelines we sent you?'

'Yes.'

'Just to warn you, we'll all be looking pretty scary in theatre; masks, goggles, the works. That's not because we're trying to scare you, or we're scared of you, it's just that capsaicin is really potent stuff; that's why if you look at the guidelines, we ask you, please please please, don't try to apply any creams or lotions to the area; contamination is a big problem. And if it gets in anyone's eyes it can be very nasty. It just needs to transfer from your fingernails, to my hand, and we'll have to close down the theatre. Do you understand?'

'Definitely.'

'Now, can you lie on the bed?'

I lie on the bed and expose my buttocks to the world. At this point Call-Me-Sue pops in and says: 'I just got your husband a cup of tea ... My, he's a bit of a hunk, isn't he? Lovely twinkly eyes he's got. You are a lucky girl.'

'Don't let him hear you say that. He can't drive me home if his head won't fit in the car.'

Dr Martin and Call-Me-Sue laugh as one, and not for the first time I wryly observe the unspoken doctor–patient contract: they want you to be in good humour, and you oblige by *being* in good humour, and they show you they're inordinately happy to witness you being in good humour, and so, no matter how you feel, you end up working as a stand-up comedian for a willing audience of doctors, surgeons and consultants.

I'm conscious that my bottom is being prodded. The doctor has a fat marker in his hand and he asks me to draw the area where the pain originates with my finger.

'That's difficult,' I say. 'It goes everywhere. I can draw where the injury happened, if you like.'

'Sounds like a plan, Monica.'

I do so, and he uncaps the marker pen. 'This is to help me

find the best area,' he explains, drawing over where my finger went, making a big square shape near my right buttock.

'You're not going to eat me?'

Dr Martin and Call-Me-Sue have both probably heard that said many times before, but their laughter sounds genuine. 'Just call me Dr Shylock. This is a guide for me, so we know where to put the patch.'

I look at Call-Me-Sue. 'Can you give my husband a message?'

'Of course I can. You try and stop me talking to him,' and Call-Me-Sue makes a little 'reow' noise of pure lust.

'If I don't survive this, I'll leave you him in my will.'

She's not sure she should laugh at this, and she just smiles. 'What shall I tell him, luv?'

'Just tell him I really appreciate him doing this, and I know it was inconvenient, with his ... work ... and everything, but I'm really glad he's here.'

'I'm sure it's his pleasure.'

'I'm sure it is. I just want him to know, that's all.'

'Of course.' She pops out and is back relatively quickly. 'He's just nipped out for a paper,' she says. 'I'm sure he'll be back in a minute.'

I imagine my incredibly young 'husband', in the waiting area, poking through copies of *Vanity Fair* and *The Lady* for something to read.

'Am I to get an anaesthetic?'

'No ...'

'What?' I'm instantly alarmed. 'The letter said there was to be a local anaesthetic.'

'Ah, the letter is a little out of date, Monica. We found that when applying local anaesthetic it made the patch a bit slippery and difficult to secure. It didn't make much difference anyway. Don't worry, my dear, you're in very good hands.'

She's not budging, so I just have to accept her reassurances. When they wheel me into the operating room, my hands are so tightly bunched into fists I know there'll be nail-marks in my palms.

They prefer me conscious. People with masks cluster round me, blotting out the lights. I notice that Dr Martin has hairy cheeks. Great grey tufts are sprouting in clumps, like he's growing cress from his own tears.

The capsaicin is square and white, like a big tea bag. Dr Martin handles it with great care. Dr Kumar told me that the stuff was hellishly expensive, and they are treating it like spun gold, making sure that nothing is wasted. They cut out a circle, put it on my buttock, and for a while I'm thinking this isn't so bad. It's just a warm feeling.

'OK, so you just need to keep that patch on for another fifty minutes ...'

They roll me into the waiting room. I can see other patients reading magazines and books. It's not bothering them much.

They've been exaggerating, the poor wimps. They obviously aren't used to the levels of pain endured by yours truly.

The heat is starting to grow. It feels like a hot water bottle.

A HOT water bottle.

And then the warm becomes hot and the hot becomes a searing nightmare.

There is pain, more pain on top of pain; my buttock feels as if it's being held over a Bunsen burner.

I would try to count to thirty to take my mind off the pain, but the pain has sent me mad, and I have no concept of numbers, or even time.

Fifty minutes pass. Then they take off the patch but, if anything, the pain *intensifies*.

There is nothing in my head except the pain ... and something even worse.

I try and call for the doctor, for Call-Me-Sue, but they're already focusing on the next patient.

But I'm not focusing on anything, I'm just thinking

Is this what it's like to have a baby?

and I'm thinking it all the time, even as my soul curls up and cowers whimpering in the furthest corner of my psyche, even as I start to pass out, my mind keeps hold of that thought and clutches it even as the dark waters of oblivion close over my head.

Is this what it's like to have a baby?

I drift in and out of consciousness, and there's lots of shouting. And I feel weight on my chest.

'Monica!'

Someone's shouting in my face.

'Hello, Monica,' yells Call-Me-Sue. 'How are you feeling?'

'Christ.' It's all I manage to say.

'Good to see you back with us.'

'Good to be here. Bloody hell ...'

'It'll probably smart a bit for a few days.'

'Few ... days,' I murmur, through clenched teeth.

Christ, this is unbearable.

'We were very worried about you,' she says. 'You passed out, and we couldn't revive you. We thought we weren't going to get you back.'

'No ... kidding ...' I gasp.

My mind is crazed with the pain, gibbering and twitching inside my head. *Invisible flames are licking around my body.*

I've sinned, and this must be my punishment.

I've borne false witness against my husband, and this is what I've reaped. Not only have I enraged his God, I've helped Him by doing his work for Him; I've walked into the NHS and kindly obliged Him by allowing myself to get dipped into the fires of hell.

'I'm ... sorry, s-sorry ... Dominic ... Please ... Please forgive me ...'

Call-Me-Sue has probably heard a lot of crazy nonsense from patients who've had this treatment. She ignores my whimperings. 'Just keep pressing ice packs on the area, Monica, and the feeling will go away. Really. I promise you that. I'll just let your husband know you're out of theatre.'

'OK,' I croak. All of a sudden I'm praying and hoping that my 'husband' is still waiting, that his promise to be there for me wasn't just empty words.

'Dr Martin would like to keep you in for a few days for observation, if that's all right, Monica. We're just going to wheel you into the other part of the hospital.'

My fuddled brain picks out her words, comprehends them, and I buck in alarm. 'N-no. I have to leave. I have to leave. I have to leave now!'

'Monica, you had a really bad reaction to the capsaicin. Your body went into shock. Your heart stopped for a while. We have to see—'

'No. I ... I have to leave ... Now! Now!'

She reluctantly disappears to fetch my 'husband', and slowly and painfully I lever myself upright, grope for my clothes, and clumsily get dressed. I find if I take the cold patch off my buttock for a second, the heat becomes instantly unbearable, like a case of sunburn from the pits of hell.

'Your husband is all ready and waiting for you.'

'Good,' I say. 'I'm glad he hasn't left me.'

This she detects as a joke. 'No, I haven't run off with him yet, more's the pity.'

And soon she is wheeling me to the reception, imploring me to stay, but I won't have it. My right hand is pressed against my buttock, where the pack is doing no good at all.

Jesus.

What have I done to myself? Out of the frying pan and literally — into the fire.

What's Dominic going to say? He can't see me like this.

And we turn the corner, and there he is. My 'husband' puts down his newspaper and leaps up in concern.

'Are you all right, darling?' Niall asks.

Dominic

Dominic's bleeding had stopped. It had bled like a stuck pig for most of the first day, but by cramming toilet paper to his ear and strapping it in place with one of Mrs Henderson's tea towels, he was able to slowly staunch the flow.

He stayed in his room for three days, watching daytime shows, looking like an exiled Arab sheik. The ear still looked terrible, crusty and red. The bottom half was flapping.

Perhaps he could think up some excuse. *Something happened in Swindon, Monica. An accident. One of those things. Actually, it was a team-building exercise that went wrong. I got a paintball behind the ear. Would you believe it?*

Dominic had driven to the hospital that morning; not because of his ear, but because in his pocket – next to the gun – was a piece of paper, telling him that Monica's appointment for the capsaicin treatment was today.

He was waiting for her.

He had to know if she'd decided to go through with it. In his heart he knew she hadn't cancelled that appointment, but he had to know for sure.

It was well past ten o'clock now, and he'd seen no sign of her, coming in or out. Incredibly, it looked like she wasn't coming. She'd actually listened to him, taken his advice and given the treatment a miss.

He was starting to relax.

He would throw the gun away in the nearest litter bin. Forget about it.

He was sitting there, preparing an amusing story about a savage Chihuahua who jumped up off a woman's lap and grabbed his ear, when he saw his wife. She was leaving the hospital, not arriving. Surprise hit him in the stomach and caused a knot to form in his gut. She must have arrived early. He must have missed her arrival.

A man was holding her, a man he didn't recognise. *She would have found someone else.* He knew that. *If he wouldn't help she would have found someone else.*

She was hanging on to the man for dear life, her knuckles were white on his arm, and the other one clutched a ... *what? A patch? A bandage?* On her hip. An ice pack. The world stopped and numbness enveloped Dominic; he couldn't feel his arms, his legs, everything was made of rubber.

He suddenly felt squeezed, as if he was being stuffed inside his own ear. The dull ache on the side of his head was the only sensation that he was aware of. The high-pitched whining sound in his head returned, liquefying his brain.

The man and his wife had been detained by a jolly nurse. His wife (even though she was sweating and shaking and her eyes were rolling back in her head) was being forced to fill in a form.

The man looked on, concerned, questioning why she needed to do it at this moment. Couldn't they see she was in difficulty? The man was doing what Dominic would have done. Trying to be the Man in the situation. Trying to look authoritative and caring.

Dominic got up and staggered to the exit.

Now he was sitting in his car, staring at the windscreen. He was wondering what to do next. *Run away, and pretend he didn't see.* That was it. Hide in the bed and breakfast for another week, and stroll into the house and pretend he didn't know. And hope for the best.

But he had the gun. In case his worst fears came to pass, he had to hide the gun first, and he had to hide it within easy reach. In the house.

He turned the ignition and roared off towards home.

Monica

'Take the second turning on the right.'

'Niall, could you turn off the satnav, please?'

'Sorry.'

'Take the left hand lane for three hundred yards.'

'I can't cope with the noise. Not at the moment.'

'No worries. I'll turn it down.'

He turns it down.

'Take the roundabout and take the third exit on the left.'

'I'm sorry, it's the voice. I can't cope with it. I'm sorry.'

'OK, sorry.'

He pulls into a siding and prods the dashboard. The woman's voice disappears and he drives on, glancing at the screen, making sure he doesn't miss an exit.

'I'm so grateful for this.'

'It's no problem really. It's not a problem.'

'But I am really grateful.'

The journey home is quite different. I need to talk to take my mind off the pain. I'm sprawled in the back seat, clutching my side. We stopped at a garage to buy ice, and when they didn't have any, Niall bought all the bottled water in the refrigerator. I'm pressing all of them, one by one, against me, and the cool feeling on my buttock, even though very short-lived, is delicious.

'I hated bothering you.'

'It's no bother.'

'But I am bothering you. You had to cancel appointments.'

'They can wait. You can't.'

Niall accelerates and negotiates his car carefully around a particularly huge lorry. The noise from the lorry's engine is terrifying. From my odd angle lying and staring up, I can see the lorry driver, chewing on something, glancing down at me with detached fascination through his cab window as he glides slowly behind us, like a turtle in an aquarium bumping at the glass to look at the visitors.

I'm reminded of the time I was ill as a child and my father swathed me in blankets and lay me in the back of his car. I remember feeling cut off, as the suspension jogged my head, and all I could do was focus on the seams on the car's roof, the little square light and the plastic handle.

It's been a strange day. From the moment the sun came through the crack in the curtains and hit my already-open eyes, it felt like an unnatural sort of day. I remembered walking down to the bottom of my road, taking a couple of left and right turns, and along to the phone box for my prearranged rendezvous with Niall. It felt like that school trip to the Lake District I was forced to go on when I was nine. The bus picked me up from the bus stop I usually waited at for going to school, but this time it took me another way, down another road, away from the familiar and deep into unknown territory.

'Are you still all right?' says Niall. After uttering his fiftieth 'Are you all right?' he has acknowledged he is sounding repetitive and has added a 'still'.

'Fine. I'm ... fine. The sooner I'm in bed the better.'

An unfortunate turn of phrase from me, considering I'm in the back of a strange man's car, but the situation feels too crazy for either of us to dwell on it. 'We're just coming up to Kensington Church Street,' he says. 'Not far to go now.' He allows a quick split-second glance back to me. 'Quite a treatment.'

'Yes.'

'I've heard of this stuff before, of course, you have to know in my line of work, but not on this level. They've actually been using this stuff for muscle and joint pain since the nineties.'

'I know.'

'They've had amazing results in helping osteoarthritis and rheumatoid arthritis. Eighty per cent found some pain relief.'

'Fascinating.'

'Here's hoping.'

'Yes. Here's hoping.'

DI Geoff Marks

It was a long journey. It was always a long bloody journey. The digital milometer on DI Geoff Marks's dashboard flickered playfully between five and six miles an hour. The traffic on Putney Bridge inched along like snails in formation, and he watched the taxis and buses zoom past in their special lanes. He fantasised about sticking a siren on and charging through the traffic.

Fat raindrops exploded on his windshield and refused to be dislodged by his windscreen wipers, which squeaked and swished impotently back and forth. He should get them looked at but when had he got time to go to a garage these days? Anyway, he'd feel stupid, wouldn't he? Putting his car in for a squeaky wiper. It was one step up from putting it in the shop when the air freshener ran out.

Not the best day to come back from a holiday. It was rush hour – hell, it was *always* rush hour in west London, cars were permanently buggering each other over Hammersmith bridge and he could see some lucky bastards heading the other way, making a break for it, dashing with relief for the M4, like swimmers breaking the surface of the water and gasping for air.

Dad once told him: 'Geoff, don't buy a house out in Roehampton. You don't have to be near me, son. Get yourself a bijou bachelor pad in town. Take it easy on yourself. Live a little,' and Geoff replied, 'A flat in London? At those prices? You're having a bloody joke, Dad. I could buy a castle in Scotland for that kind of money.' And they both laughed at exactly the same time, because they realised they'd swapped roles – he was saying all the things he said to his dad after he got divorced, and his dad was saying all the things he used to say to Geoff, about the price of this and that, about buying a castle in Scotland for the price of a BMW.

He was right, of course. Dad was in a home now, and Geoff was stuck out in the sticks on his own, trying to drive into work and trundling along the road like some toddler in his pedal car.

Some idiot was right up his arse, practically kissing his back bumper, and for the twentieth time that hour Geoff wished he was in a squad car. That would make the bastard think twice about tailgating him.

He flicked his eyes into his mirror, mentally taking the twat's number and feeding his details into the 'most wanted' list, and realised how red and angry his forehead looked. There was a big faded shape around his eyes where his sunglasses had been. He looked like the world's crappiest superhero. Christ! That'll teach him. He can't win with this complexion.

He was going to get all the jokes when he got back to the station.

The traffic shuddered to a halt and he could see brake lights shining all the way from Holland Park to Notting Hill.

Scrub that. *If* he got back to the station.

DS Mike Fennel was there, at his desk, when Geoff got in, and he put his hands up in pre-emptive surrender. 'Yes, Mike, I know. I'm a beetroot. I'm a steamed lobster. I'm a sun-ripened tomato. You could use my face to cordon off traffic incidents on the M4. I'm redder than that telly comedian's arse when we busted Doris the dominatrix. Come on. Do your worst. I can take it.'

Mike looked at him with genuine surprise. 'I wasn't going to say any of that.'

'No, of course not.'

'No. Seriously. I wasn't . . .' His fingers pattered along the edge of his desk, feeling for his notepad, and he stared into space. 'You see, I've gone completely blind . . .'

'Oh ho ho ho.'

'They warned me never to stare directly at your forehead . . .'

'Guffaw.'

' . . . not without tinted glass. But I wouldn't listen.'

'Very good.'

Still doing the blind act, he held a note up under Geoff's nose, close enough to stuff it up his left nostril.

'Trevor – that is DCI Bradbury to you – wants to see you in his office.'

He did try to stop it but a sigh escaped Geoff's lips. Mike caught it and savoured it, inhaling it. 'Now, now, Geoff, you'll love it. Chance for you two to catch up, to reminisce about old times.'

'Oh joy of joys.'

'I'm sure it'll throw up all sorts of memories.'

Four years ago, Trevor Bradbury was just another copper. He was Geoff's puppy for a time; Trevor wasn't a bad lad, but he was one of those fast-track types who got promoted at an incredible rate. It was rumoured he was on his way to ACPO, but it was difficult for Geoff to have any kind of respect for a man who vomited over his good shoes when he saw his first dead body.

He trudged up the stairs, through the open-plan offices and across to Trevor Bradbury's glass-fronted office. The door was ajar, but Geoff tapped on it anyway.

'You wanted me, sir?'

DCI Bradbury looked just as young as he'd been when he'd emptied his insides over Geoff's best DMs and wiped the flecks of vomit off his chin. There was a clear inch-wide gap between his shirt collar and his scrawny neck. His bony fingers hovered mid-tap over his keyboard. 'Geoff, great – I heard you were back. Come in, come in. Sit sit sit.'

Geoff sat, awkwardly, in a low padded chair, and Trevor perched on his desk. He seemed to have dropped the big chief act. He looked almost excited. He was acting like he was still a baby copper.

'I've got something to show you. I thought it might mean something to you.'

He danced around his desk and pulled his laptop around to face Geoff. 'I don't know if you remember but when we were out on the beat together ...'

He never brought up those days. Not if he could help it. Old times meant nothing to him. This must be something special.

'Well, remember when we followed up ...' He shook his head. 'No. I think it's best that I show you. This is footage from a car park in Woolwich. There was a bit of a disturbance there a few nights back. Someone found some bullet casings on the floor and rang us, we checked a CCTV from a nearby garage, and *voilà*, the whole incident was recorded.'

He pressed 'play', and sure enough, Geoff saw a shitty-looking car park. He saw two light-grey blobs facing up to each other. 'IC1 males,' he said automatically. 'They look like they're having quite a disagreement.'

'They do, don't they? Keep watching.'

One grey blob shoved the other inside a van and slammed one of the doors on the other blob's legs, and then he was flinching; there was no sound but it was obvious that shots were being fired from inside the van. The grey blob outside the van twisted the legs around and leapt inside.

'Wait a couple more seconds,' Trevor said, staring at the screen. 'Just a couple – more – seconds ...'

Geoff watched as the bigger grey blob leapt out of the van,

holding a gun, and then ran helter-skelter towards them, right by the camera. DCI Bradbury jabbed hastily at the pause button, just as the grey blob was filling the screen. 'There,' he said. 'Who's that?'

Geoff shrugged. 'I don't know. Who is it?'

Bradbury was outraged his stunt hadn't provoked more of a reaction. 'It's him! It's that bloke who we thought was trying to kill his wife.'

'Him? I can't see it, sir.'

'It is him! You know! The wife who was flat on her back with the pain.'

Geoff knew who he was talking about. Of course he did. Trouble was, he couldn't see it. To him, it was just another tubby IC1 male.

'It's definitely him,' said Bradbury. 'I'll swear to it by all the gods. I'm very good with faces. Derek. No ... Dominic Wood. The guy with the crippled wife. I'd know him anywhere. Definitely,' he said, with undisguised triumph. 'Looks like he's up to his old tricks again.'

Geoff leaned in. 'I suppose there's a passing similarity.'

'Similarity nothing. It's him. I've got the eyes of a bus driver and I know who that is. And he's buying a gun. He's serious about it this time.'

'We thought he was serious about it last time, sir, but you know what happened.'

'His wife wouldn't put him on the hook, yes. But here we are, back here again. More evidence. Perhaps in the last four years she might have realised that he was serious about it too.'

'If she's still alive.'

'That's not a good thought.' He tapped his expensive gold pen against his lips.

Bradbury liked the man's wife; they both did. She seemed so vulnerable, lying stretched out there on the floor, obviously in mountains of pain. After they left the house and got in the car they didn't speak for a while; not until that afternoon.

Then, Bradbury started talking about his own sister, who got MS one day and her husband packed his bags within the year. Geoff listened, thinking about his dad, who had popped into his own mind after their visit to Mrs Wood. Geoff's dad, who moved away from Roehampton when he forgot Mum's name and started walking along the high street in his pyjamas, and during his more rational moments asked Geoff to do something that he wasn't prepared to do. Scrub that; that he didn't have the *courage* to do.

'Why don't you give her a call?' said the DCI.

'On what grounds?'

'On what grounds? It's *him*, Geoff.'

He was 'Geoff' again. It seemed for DCI Bradbury the years had been peeled away. It was all he could do to stop calling him sir.

Geoff spread his hands wide, helplessly. 'What do I say? Has your husband bought a gun recently? Can you check your bank statement?'

Bradbury dropped his pen petulantly. 'Look, just give her a ring. Make something up. See if she's OK. Then, if she isn't OK, talk to her some more, see if she's changed her mind about pressing charges.'

'And if she hasn't?'

'We've got enough evidence to bring him in on something, whether she wants to press charges or not. Suspected possession of a firearm, conspiracy to murder, we should put him on the PNC. Let's give him a fright. Let him know that we're aware he's up to his old tricks.'

Geoff didn't feel there was any evidence at all. One copper thinking a man on a blurry screen was the same man they sort of suspected of trying to kill his wife four years ago? If it wasn't a DCI getting excited about it . . .

But it *was* a DCI getting excited about it, and there is a long list of things you don't say to your guvnor. And 'you're completely bonkers, sir' is right near the top.

Geoff went to the door. 'I'll get on it, sir.'

Dominic

Dominic roared through the back streets of Kensington, using every shortcut he knew, easing his foot off the pedal only slightly when he went past the primary schools. His phone rang, large and loud, and his thumb nudged 'accept' on the steering wheel.

'Hello?'

'Dominic, mate. How are you?'

'Who is this?'

'It's your old mate Larry French.'

Dominic's hands gripped tighter on the steering wheel, trying to tie it into a knot. 'You're not my mate.'

'Well I'm your wife's mate. I'm her guardian angel. You know that.'

'What do you want, Larry?'

'I was just taking time out from a bit of a poncy workshop. Not a proper workshop with tools, mark you. We're fleshing out our characters today. Me, I just want to learn the words and get on stage, but there you go. But I digress. I was just wondering how your missus was doing, Dominic. I hear she's going for some sort of miracle treatment.'

'Is that a fact?'

'She came to see me. She said you weren't going to help her get this treatment.'

'That's my business.'

'I hope you're not thinking of doing anything stupid. Not like last time.'

'What last time?'

'You know what. PC Plod and his ilk have got enough on their plates without running after the likes of you.'

'Did you take my gun?'

'It's for your own good.'

'Don't threaten me, Larry.'

'I'm not threatening you, mate. I'm asking you. Your missus is a diamond. Don't try this stupid thing again. If you ever loved her you'll—'

Dominic terminated the call.

He left the car in the street, round the corner from the house. He thudded along the tarmac, dived in the back alley, and tried to open their back gate.

Locked, of course.

He struggled onto the wall and craned across to slide the bolt. And then he found himself lying on his back, staring at the white sky, heaving and sucking at the air. He had leaned too far, fallen over the gate into the garden, and winded himself. He struggled to his feet, controlling his breathing, and thanking his lucky stars he'd landed on the path and not impaled himself on a fork.

What was the combination of the shed padlock? What was it? Don't panic – just calm down and ... oh yes. That was it. The year of his birth. The lock clicked free, he stuffed it in his pocket and the door creaked open. The spade was leaning within easy reach and soon he was attacking the soft soil, spraying huge gobbets of mud onto his trousers, onto his shirt ... A piece of mud hit him behind the ear and the world lurched on its axis, and the single high-pitched note sounded in his head again.

Slower now, don't panic. Soon the bag was visible. He pulled it out, hearing the comforting rattle of the wire clippers inside knocking against the baseball bat. Pulling the carrier bag from his pocket he unwrapped the gun, just to look at it again, because he still didn't quite believe it when he saw it, wrapped it in the balaclava and the gloves, put it in the bag, and put the bag in the hole.

He was bending down to pick up the spade when he realised he couldn't leave the bag here. Larry would just take the gun again, or worse, Monica might become curious about him digging in the garden. If there was just a chance ... He had to put the bag somewhere else. He spun around, looking for options. Perhaps the shed? Monica didn't go anywhere near the shed any more. He could hide it in one of those plastic bin things they once bought to make their own manure. Cover it with old sacks.

Yes, that would do for the moment.

From somewhere inside the house, the telephone rang.

DI Geoff Marks

Geoff Marks discovered there was no file; just an incident report, with a transcript of the interview with Dominic Wood. He remembered it as if it was just that morning. They didn't like the husband one little bit, so they insisted on going through the procedure at a glacial rate, and he cooperated fully, but all the while he was shaking his head and saying it was all a waste of time, that if they just rang his wife at home, she would confirm it.

'It's just a game we play,' he said, grinning.

'A game?' Geoff said, with a suitable note of sarcastic incredulity. 'Right, can I get this straight? You go out and ask people to kill your wife as a game? Have you ever thought of Monopoly? Cluedo? At least that one's got a murder in it.'

'It's role play,' he said. 'For kicks. You know. Kinky stuff.'

'Kinky stuff. Right. Cos that's what I do every Valentine's Day for my missus. It beats chocolates any day.' Bradbury had added his voice to the interview, trying out his technique. Geoff knew he'd be a good copper, one day.

'So she wanted you to pretend to kill her.'

'Yes. Well done you. Got it in one.'

'Whatever turns you on, right?'

'Yep. Exactly. I go out and pretend to try and kill her. I go to the roughest, grimmest places I know and ask scar-faced thugs to do her in, and then I make my excuses and leave, and when

I get home I tell her I what I've done, and it ... turns her on.'

Geoff remembered the sight of his wife lying spark out on the floor, her face shiny, her hair sopping with sweat, and he thought that Mrs Wood didn't look like she was able to get 'turned on' by anything. Ever.

But she backed up her husband's story. And they took him home in a panda car, him grinning and looking out of the back window like they were escorting him, like he was the fucking queen on a tour of the Commonwealth.

Geoff still remembered looking down at her, just as he left, saying, 'Is that everything, Monica? Is there anything else you want to tell me?'

But she told him there wasn't, and they left, and as they drove away he was looking out of the window, still grinning, and then the curtains were drawn back, and Geoff remembered saying to Trevor:

'Well that's the last we'll see of her. One way or the other.'

Geoff rang the number in the report and, thankfully, it still worked. He heard the voice of that smug git telling him to leave a message. He mentioned it was the residence of Mr and Mrs Wood, so she was still alive.

Unless he'd done her in and remarried, of course ...

In spite of Geoff's scepticism, he was intrigued.

He left a suitably enigmatic message. 'Hello. This is Detective Inspector Geoff Marks for Mrs Monica Wood. Something of yours has just been handed into the station. Could you give me a ring?'

He gave the number of the station and ended the call.

Monica

I'm fading, not keeping up my end of the conversation, so it dries up, and the car goes silent. I start to recognise the tops of the taller buildings. Then he suddenly says:

'Do you have a key to your house?'

'Why ... uh ... do you want a key to my house?'

'So we can get in.'

'Oh yes. Of course.'

I have a key somewhere, but I can't bear to think of looking for it now. And I don't want Niall wriggling his hands inside my pockets. 'Uhh ... There's a key in the lamp by the door ...'

I listen to his footsteps, a rattle, and more footsteps coming back to me.

'No there isn't. There's no key.'

I flounder. 'But there should ... No. Dominic moved it, because he was worried it was too vulnerable ... There's a barbecue in the shed, with a ... cover on it. Dominic hides the ... the spare key inside. The combination is one, nine, six, nine ...'

So we're at my house. It looks different somehow, strange. It's still the same little Victorian end-of-terrace that it's always been, same as all the houses in the area; the same little gate with the squeaky hinge, the little path leading up to the white wooden door. The path used to be gravel, and then some doctor scared the life out of us by telling us I would be wheelchair-bound within a year, so Dominic had flagstones put down.

Dominic. Oh, Dominic.

What have I done?

There's the struggling agapanthus poking out of the big blue pot, the faded 'welcome' mat, the rusty lamp with the dusty glass panes. Everything is the same. *Why does it feel so different?*

But I realise it's me that's different. *It's me that feels strange.*

Dominic

There were footsteps outside, coming down the path. Dominic gave an almost comical gasp and looked around the shed for a place to hide. He dived behind a pile of logs and threw some potato sacks over his head. Why he had potato sacks, he couldn't fathom. He had never grown anything larger than a tomato. The rough, woven material rubbed against his ruined ear and made him wince.

Someone was at the door of the shed, probably expecting to jemmy open a padlock that wasn't there. He could imagine the burglar/mugger/psycho shrugging and thinking: *Great, some idiot's left the shed unlocked.* The door squealed open and a man came in. The man who took his wife to the hospital.

It wasn't good enough that this man pretended to be him in the hospital. He had come into his shed to do some gardening in his garden, picking up his pots and looking at his tools. Dominic could see the Man Who Was Now Him, through the gauze. The Man Who Was Now Him was young and fit and toned and he had dark hair. Lots of it, and none of it was grey.

He watched as the new Dominic slid up the barbecue lid, and for a moment the old Dominic thought the new Dominic was going to start a barbecue. *Good time of year for it.* The old Dominic approved. And then, when he saw the new Dominic was only after the key to the house, it all made complete sense. Perhaps it was for the best. The new Dominic was going to move in, and make Monica happy in every way he couldn't, and they would live happily ever after, and he, the old Dominic, would live here in the shed, and they would bring his meals out here, and he would eat them on the Black and Decker Workmate.

Dominic found that he was in serious danger of giving away his location to the new Dominic; his potato sacks were shuddering because he was giggling uncontrollably, and he couldn't stop.

Thankfully, the new Dominic found the sparc key to the house and left, and the old Dominic was free to fill the inside of the shed with hysterical laughter. After he finally calmed himself, the old Dominic wrestled free from the potato sacks and left too.

Monica

Niall has retrieved the key and is escorting me up the path. His eyes are flicking around the outside of the house, taking in details, and he looks like a burglar gauging the wealth of the residents, judging possible points of access.

I've finished with the water bottles and replaced them with the lukewarm remains of the ice patch the hospital gave me. I hold it onto my side and lean weakly against the brickwork while he fumbles for the keys.

It seems like minutes before the door falls open, but I'm no judge of time – or anything – at the moment. He looks at me expectantly, offering an arm for me to hold on to, but I shake my head, perhaps a little too violently.

'The alarm,' I gasp. 'You have to deactivate the alarm.'

He notices the beeping coming from inside and looks startled. The same nightmare scenarios are flicking through his mind, too.

'Just inside the kitchen door. Open the panel. Key in three-four-one-oh, and press the hash key.'

'Right. Three-four-one-oh. Hash key. Three-four-one-oh. Hash key.'

He disappears inside, and I wait, but the beeping doesn't stop.

'Monica!' he shouts. 'It's not working! Three-four-one-oh, hash, it's not stopping!'

The beeping is accelerating and is joined by another beep a semitone lower. In my pain-addled state, my imagination conjures up a tiny French police car driving through the house.

He appears again, his eyes wide. 'Can you hear it? I've put the numbers in twice now. What am I doing wrong?'

'I don't know.'

'Is this the right number?'

He holds my shoulders. I know he's resisting the urge to shake me. '*Is it the right number?*'

'Yes! I put it in every day!'

'Jesus fuck! I can't believe this!'

The beeping is scraping my brain of thoughts. 'I'm sorry, I can't concentrate.'

'You have to concentrate. We could be standing here with the police!'

'You're not helping!'

'That's it. I'm done! I'm done with this!'

He's jogging back to his car, leaving me, when I shout. 'DISARM! After the hash key you have to press disarm!'

He pivots on his heels and dashes back into the house. After a few seconds the beeping stops with a chirp, and the silence it leaves behind is the most wonderful thing in the world.

He emerges with a relieved (and sheepish) grin. 'Well done,' he says. 'Panic over. Bit of a brown-trousers moment, but we got there in the end.'

He offers his arm again, but I don't take it. I must have made a face because he asks, 'What's the matter?'

'You ran. You were going to run.'

'No I wasn't.'

'You were running for your car.'

'My phone is in the car. I was going to phone the number on the alarm and tell the police not to worry, that we'd screwed up the combination and it was just a false alarm. That's what you're supposed to do, isn't it?'

He's right. And if it wasn't the truth, then he was awfully smooth and quick with a lie.

Just stay on your guard, Monica Wood.

I allow him to support me and together we stagger to the open door. We're just about to go in when I sag and pull back.

'What's up?'

'Nothing. It just feels weird.'

'The patch?'

'No. That just feels bloody awful. This feels weird. Doing this. Like I'm breaking into my own house.'

Niall grins his dazzling grin. 'Yes, I can imagine.'

'It doesn't feel right. I feel like ... I feel like I don't know how I feel, and that's the strangest feeling of all. At the moment I feel most like a cow being led into an abattoir. I don't think that makes much sense.'

'Not really.'

'After I walk through that door I know that things ... Things will ... probably never be the same again.'

'OK, let's try this.' He grabs me around the waist. 'Hold onto your cold patch.'

'Why?'

His arms encircle me and suddenly my feet are up in the air and he's holding me in his arms; my arms automatically reach up and encircle his neck.

'There,' he says. 'Now you're not walking at all.'

He carries me over the threshold. And I thought things felt weird before.

I am coming into the house afresh, seeing all the things I'd not

215

registered for years. The little shelf with his 'n' hers wellingtons on them; fitted at a time when we'd decided to take long walks in the countryside. They are still here, six years later, the black boots shiny and unused, poking out of their cubbyholes like the noses of Labradors sulking in their kennels.

Talking of dogs, there is the extra hook next to the coats, the one labelled 'Benjy', that used to carry a long brown leather leash, which dangled into the umbrella stand. It was preparation for a dog that never arrived, a possible substitute for a baby if the fertility treatment didn't work; so we could look at it as we came in the door and it would tell us that 'there are always alternatives'. We even gave the dog a name, and it is still there, a ghost of something that never arrived, just like the pots of blue and pink paint hiding in the shed. *There are always alternatives.* How funny. Now there are no alternatives. No dog, no baby. I would struggle to look after a goldfish, now.

Niall wobbles up the stairs, slowly, ponderously, one foot, and then the other foot. *He's very strong.* He doesn't look like he's straining at all.

Unbidden, my mind swims back to my sweating, gasping husband who struggled to even lift me onto my bed a week or so ago. Then I try not to think about him at all. *This is not the ideal time to compare the men in my life.*

I give him directions to my bedroom and we struggle inside. I uncouple myself from his arm and collapse on the bed with an audible *flumph*, curling my body into a fetal position.

'Do you want help to get undressed?'

'No ... jeez ... No, I'm not a cripple, my arse is on fire. That's all ... God ... This patch is already warm, and it's the ... last one they gave me ...'

My teeth are jammed together. I can't open my mouth because of the pain. My left hand is curved like a talon, and my right is gripping the cold patch onto my bum like my life depends on it, like I've cut a major artery and it's holding the blood inside my body.

'Just ... do me a favour ... OK?'

'Anything.'

'Go downstairs, go to the fridge ... ahhah ... get the wine cooler from the freezer box ...'

'Wine cooler ...'

'Like a padded green sleeve with Fortnum and Mason written on it ... You can't miss it ... Wrap it in a clean cloth ... And it has to be clean ... Make sure of that ... Get a fresh tea towel from the airing cupboard ... top of the stairs, use one of those ... And bring it here.'

He nods furiously. 'Will do.' He yomps out of the bedroom, leaving the door open, and hurtles down the stairs.

I'm alone, helpless ... and there's a strange man in my house.

A man who looks like the wolf, and he didn't have to huff and puff. I just let him in.

I listen to the bang of the kitchen door. *I haven't much time.*

I peel my clothes off as fast as I can, hurling my blouse and skirt under the bed (leaving the knickers on to keep the patch in place), and then pull my pyjamas from under my pillow. It's very tricky, but the fear of being discovered by Niall in a state of undress forces me to work precisely and quickly, whipping my pyjama bottoms on in one swift motion.

I listen to Niall's footsteps as they come upstairs. The tread is heavier than my husband's, but more vigorous; four or five *thuds* and he's up on the landing.

When he comes in I'm tucked up in bed, covers up to my neck and welded under my chin.

'Here.' He hands me the wine cooler and my arm snakes out from under the duvet to snatch it. I put it on my bottom and it's a wondrous feeling. I bring out the old patch – which is now practically boiling – and hold it out to him.

'Can you put this in the freezer box? I'm going to alternate them.'

'OK.'

He takes the warm patch, but his eyes are not on it. He's watching my arm, and the pyjama cuff, and I know exactly what's in his head. *She's not naked under there*, he's thinking.

'Thanks.'

'How are you feeling right now?'

'Like a lobster in a saucepan.'

He perches on the end of my bed. I feel a sudden pressure near my toes. He stares at me, and I don't know what it means. Concern? What do I look like? I must look a mess.

(**What big eyes you have**)

'Do you want anything else from downstairs?'

'No, thank you.'

'Food? You should eat some food.'

'No thanks.'

'A drink then?'

I'm absolutely parched. 'Perhaps some iced water.'

'Your wish is my command.'

He disappears again and is soon back carrying a glass stuffed with ice cubes. The feel of the cool glass on my fingers is heaven, and I down it in one.

'You should eat some food.'

My thirst is lifted like a stone, and underneath it I realise there's hunger. I'm very hungry.

'You've not eaten much, have you? I bet they offered you next to nothing at the hospital.'

I nod my head.

'You have to eat now.'

'Well . . .'

'Shall I make you something?'

'OK. I'm sure I can cope with scrambled eggs.'

'I hope I can.' He smiles.

(**What big teeth you have**)

'Joke. I'm actually quite a good cook. Scrambled eggs will be no problem.'

Off he goes again. I reach out for my phone on the bedside table, and bring it under the covers. I leave it on my belly, so I can snatch it up in seconds; I don't know why. Yes I do. I'm nervous. I don't *know* this man. Granted he was my client, but I didn't take the time and trouble to know all of my clients; most of them were just a photo, a CV and a showreel. I know he likes extreme sports, and Peter O'Toole, and Sting, and I know he's got a frightening ex-wife, and has a child called Peter, and he can make scrambled eggs ...

But I don't *know* him.

He comes back about twenty minutes later, with a yellow eggy mountain on a plate, and he sets the tray very very gently down on my lap. *Cutting off access to the phone.*

(**That was obvious. You should have expected that**)

'Is that OK? Not too heavy?'

'No.'

Then he, very very gently, takes a pillow from Dominic (**my husband**)'s side of the bed and beckons me to lean forward, so he can prop me up.

'How's that?'

'Great.'

The tray is full; he's put on salt and pepper pots, and another glass of iced water. Just what I need. I start eating and it's delicious and creamy.

I'm so intent on the taste that I barely notice him leave and return with his own plate of scrambled egg. I have an irrational, indignant feeling (**how dare he make his own lunch**) until I calm myself down.

He's done all this for you, Monica. He's driven you to the hospital, looked after you, driven you back, helped you in a massive deception; the least you can give him is some lunch.

It's my house, so he's the guest. Like a good girl, I try to be a good host, and attempt to spark some polite conversation.

'Peter's really cute.'

He stares at me for a second; he doesn't know what I'm talking about, then he makes the connection. 'Oh ... yeah, yes he is.'

'Do you mind me talking about him?'

He looks at me for a few moments and then decides. 'No. I don't mind.'

'Good.'

'Well, we're friends, and as I am in your house ... '

I shift in my bed.

'Well, he's very cute. He has your hair and your eyes.'

'Ha. Yes, I thought that. I often thought ... if it pisses Lorraine off, you know, giving her unconditional love to someone who looks like a mini version of me.'

'I suppose it's difficult for you, not seeing him all the time. I would guess that's the worst part of being divorced.'

'Well ... ' He fiddles with the salt pot on the tray, twirling it round. 'To tell you the truth he was kind of the reason we split – not that I would ever say it to Peter,' he adds hastily. 'I never felt ready to have kids, and she was pushing so hard, and once I sort of said OK and then, when it didn't happen straight away and things started to get complicated, it wasn't so simple. There were the fertility tests, the *in vitro*, and so then I had to pretend really hard to doctors and everyone that I really wanted a child, and she was sitting by my side listening to this act I was putting on, and she was believing what I was saying, and I felt I was getting further and further away from what I wanted ... I felt ... I felt I was looking down on my own life, like in a dream, while it was being shaped around me. Do you get what I'm saying?'

'Oh definitely,' I say. 'The one thing about my life, actually I'd say the main thing, yes, the main thing about my life, about how I live, the pain and everything, is that feeling. Everything happens around me. My life is not my own.'

'Exactly,' he shouts, suddenly animated. 'I didn't want kids. End of story.'

'Oh, I wanted kids,' I say. 'That is to say, Dominic and me, we wanted kids, we did all the *in vitro*, and the tests, because I wanted them more than anything else I could think of. I wanted kids so much it hurt. When I got pregnant it was like heaven had singled us out for a miracle. Sometimes I think it's just as well that I have so much pain now, because it overshadows that other pain … Just about. And Dominic … He sat there with me, talked to the doctors and nurses, and he said he wanted them so much, because he saw how much pain I was in without them, and because he loved me, and wanted me to be happy, he wanted them too. So he meant it. He really really meant it.'

Niall stares at me.

He's realised he's said something wrong. He's realised he's taken a wrong turn and even though simply by being here he's won round one, he's lost round two to my husband. Even though it's only slight, he can feel that disapproval hanging in the air.

He's going to do that thing that men do. That wolves do. His sheep's clothing has slipped, and he's going to try to put the costume back on. To modify what he just said. Sure enough …

'Well, when I say I didn't want kids, I probably meant that, deep down, subconsciously, I didn't want kids with Lorraine. Perhaps there were problems with us before, and I didn't want to face up to them …'

He gets up, stretches his arms so hard that his little shirt rides up and shows a belly button garlanded with a tangle of thick black hair.

'You see, I'm sure I would want kids if I found the right woman … Someone *really* special …'

'Is that an offer?'

'Could be. I was about, you know. At the time. On your books, so to speak.'

He flashes me a dazzling smile.

'Thanks for your gracious offer, Niall, but I would have kept trying with my husband, thank you very much.'

'But you haven't, have you? You're not trying any more.'

He picks up a photo from the dressing table. Another smiling wedding photo. He inspects Dominic with a casual, appraising gaze, and puts it down. My husband has been summarily dismissed.

'I mean you're not, are you?'

Why is he asking this?

'Are you? You can tell me if you are, but I get the sense you're not.'

(**What a big nose you have**)

'We can't.'

My body is burning like a furnace, but my voice is cold.

'I thought you of all people would understand.'

'I . . . what?'

'My body is swilling with drugs. Do you think I'd want to carry a life inside me for nine months with all the stuff I take? The baby would be born a junkie, it could have two heads . . .'

'Oh.'

'. . . and I can't go without the drugs for nine months. I couldn't go without them for nine seconds. I just can't do it. My whole system would shut down. I thought you would get that.'

He slumps against the dressing table. 'I'm sorry.'

'And adoption would be impossible too. Skim my medical notes and you'll think I'm part cripple, part junkie, part suicide risk. I couldn't look more inappropriate as a candidate if I was in an iron lung and smoked fifty a day.'

He knows this conversation is another dead end. He's stumbled down another path which puts him at a disadvantage against Dominic.

'Of course,' I say. 'If this treatment works, if it works permanently ... I could ...'

He's not interested. He looks out of the window and leans on the sill, tapping the vase with his little finger.

'So ... your husband doesn't know you've done this?' He keeps looking out the window, looking at nothing, as if what he just said is a casual observation. (**But it's not**)

'No,' I say.

'So ... are you going to tell him?'

'Maybe. If it works.'

'But he didn't want you to do it because he was afraid it would give you false hope. That's what you said. He thought, even if it worked, it could only be temporary.'

'OK, so no. I'm not going to tell him.'

He nods approvingly.

'Do you think he doesn't want you to get better?'

Exactly what I said to Angelina.

'Of course not.'

'But he doesn't want to give you false hope.'

'That's what he says.'

He's working up to something.

He circles the bed and perches himself on my dressing room table. 'Who are you now, Monica?' he says, smiling.

'What?'

'You told me you were lots of Monicas. The pain made you into different Monicas. I just wondered which one you are now. The Monica I met didn't want to keep any secrets from her husband. This is obviously a different Monica.'

'This is a Monica who loves her husband very much, but won't be told what to do. Not about this.'

He sniffs, says nothing.

'Why, you think I should tell him?'

He shrugs. *Up to you.*

The silence lengthens.

'I couldn't run the risk of him trying to stop me. Even though he loves me, and we're a team, at the end of the day it's my body, I don't think he should have a say in what I do with my body.'

He makes a 'hmm!' noise, very quietly.

'You don't think that.'

'Oh I do, it just, well … It kind of makes my point, doesn't it?'

I'm tired, and I'm hurting. 'Sorry, did you have a point, Niall?'

'Yes,' he says, suddenly energised. 'Yes. About kids. It was my body and she was just telling me what to do with it. "Put it in now, I'm ovulating", "Wake up, get inside now." She was forcing my body to create life, against my will.'

'I don't think that's quite the same at all,' I snap. 'I think you should go.'

'I was just—'

'Thank you for your help, but I think you should go.'

'No way.'

'Please.'

'You need looking after.'

'My husband can do that. He's been doing it for years.'

'How will he do that, when he doesn't even know you've had the treatment?'

'I'm a woman in pain, lying in bed. He knows the rest. Cups of tea and breakfast in bed. That's all I need.'

'You're fooling yourself.'

Get him out of here.

'Thank you very much, but I think you should leave now.'

'I don't think so.'

DI Geoff Marks

Geoff had his lunch in the Pret down the road, and when he got back there was a flurry of activity in the station. There were coppers running around, leaping in and out of squad cars. He could smell the starch of freshly ironed CID shirts.

'Bradbury wants to see you,' said Mike. 'Twice in one day, you lucky bugger.'

When he went back to Bradbury's office and knocked on the door Bradbury leapt up, startled. 'DI Marks,' he said. 'Glad you're back.'

So it's back to formalities, Geoff thought. *Something's up.*

'Everything all right, sir?'

'You haven't, by any chance, set the wheels in motion regarding our mutual friend Mr Wood?'

'I rang Wood's wife just before lunch. Answering machine implied she was still alive and kicking – well, probably not kicking, judging by the last time we met her. I'm planning to go round there this afternoon . . .'

Trevor had gone as pale as his ill-fitting shirt. 'Sod it,' he said. 'You do know Derek Cooper's here?'

The new golden boy from CID. Shit.

'Oh.'

'He's seen the tape, and he's as sure as eggs is eggs that the mystery man in our footage is some Russian gangster operating out of Crouch End. They're going over there mob-handed right now, to make an arrest.'

He threw a black and white photo down on the desk. The man in the photo did look a lot like the man on the CCTV footage.

'He reckons this is the piece of evidence that will finally help him get the bastard off the streets.'

Trevor never came naturally to swearing. 'Bastard' came out like a posh kid experimenting with dirty words.

'So it would be good if you could follow up your phone call with an apology to Mr and Mrs Wood. Sorry to bother them, and all that. You know what IPCC are like these days . . . '

An hour ago Geoff was annoyed that Bradbury had sent him off on a wild hunch. Now he was annoyed that Bradbury was telling him to back off. Call him a contrary old copper, but he was a big believer in a copper's gut instinct, and to see Bradbury wither like this . . . it ever so slightly got on Geoff's tits.

'Seriously?'

Bradbury looked at Geoff with his steely 'I'm the boss' gaze. 'Yes, seriously.'

'I mean, it does look like his IC1, granted, but it also looks like Wood, too. Shouldn't we just follow it up on the off chance? We have a duty of care to Mrs Wood . . . '

DCI Trevor Bradbury looked like Geoff had asked him for a snog.

'A duty of care, DI Marks? On the off chance? Are you completely mad?'

'I mean, we don't know for certain that he *is* this Russian low-life Cooper's been after . . . '

'You mean, cast doubt on Detective Superintendent Cooper's key piece of evidence? Would you like to tell Derek you're going to scupper his case? Tell him, "Oh don't bother, Detective Superintendent Cooper. Don't bother with your . . . Vlad the Impaler sort . . . that you've been after for two years, because we actually think the man in the footage is an advertising executive from Kensington who plays sex games with his sick wife"? Would you like to have a word with him now, Geoff? He's in a car screaming towards Crouch End, but I'm sure he's OK to pull over for a chat . . . '

Of course Geoff didn't want a word with DSu Cooper. DSu

Cooper was only slightly less thuggish than the crims he collared.

'No, sir.'

'No, sir. Good, sir. Well done, sir. Now get on the phone and make nice with the public. There's a good chap.'

Geoff left the office with his tail between his legs, seething. That was that, he thought. Leave it to Derek to sort out. Perhaps Golden Boy was right. There were a lot of pale, pudgy guys in the world.

Perhaps Trevor *had* let his imagination run riot. Geoff knew why he did. The incident with Dominic and his wife disturbed him. Disturbed them both. Subconsciously, Trevor just wanted closure.

Geoff rang the number again, and left another message. 'Hello. This is Detective Inspector Geoff Marks for Mrs Monica Wood again. Sorry to bother you, but the object in question has been identified as belonging to another person. Once again, sorry to bother you. Many apologies. Bye.'

Monica

Somewhere in the house, the phone rings. And rings. And then cuts off. Neither of us mention it. Niall does not break his gaze.

His eyes are scorching me, burning me as badly as the capsaicin. I feel stabs of pain in my arms and legs. The tension (**fear**) is making my body react.

'I appreciate what you've done for me . . .' I start to say.

'You need looking after. If your husband won't do it, I could. I will.'

227

'You have no right to put this pressure on me. I've not led you on. I made things quite clear.'

The *ker-chunk* of the front door breaks the spell.

'Meeses Moaneeka? You are here?'

'Jesus! It's Monday! What is she doing here?'

(**You stupid idiot. Don't you remember? You got her in today, to change the sheets, because you knew you'd be having the treatment**)

Don't call me an idiot. This is the cleverest thing I've ever done.

'Get out!' I hiss. 'Get out of here!'

'How?' he says, stupidly.

'Through the door!'

'But she's—'

'The *back* door!'

Niall runs around like an idiot in a farce before leaping into the bathroom – just as Agnieszka enters.

'Meeses Moaneeka?' she whispers. Her voice is so powerful, when she lowers it to a whisper it trembles, like a caged monster striking the bars. 'You OK?'

'Yes, I OK.'

'I change sheets now? You get up?'

She walks cautiously into the room, one foot. Two feet. In the pebbled glass of the en-suite bathroom, I can see the dark fuzzy shape of Niall behind it.

My Angry Friend.

'Can you do it in a moment? I need to … to get something … Before you change sheets.'

'You want something? I can get you.'

'Hmmm …'

I so rarely ask for anything that she pounces on my 'hmmm'.

'Anything you want? I get you, no problem, Moaneeka. You say, I get.'

'Well ... I would give away my fortune for a bar of chocolate. I don't think there's any in the house.'

'You want chocolate?'

'I've been craving the big creamy bars, the organic ones by ...' My brain fails me. 'It's a pair of names. Two names, like Holland and Barrett, or Bradford and Bingley, Simon and Garfunkel ...'

She nods with recognition, the understanding nod of one chocaholic talking to another. 'I know eet. I get from shop op the road? No bother.'

'Oh, could you? Take the money from the tin by the kettle?'

'I will be no time. Fifteen minute. Then I back.'

And she hurries out of the bedroom.

No sooner has the door clicked shut than there's soft footfall in the bathroom.

Niall appears. He stares at me dispassionately, for too long. Suddenly terror squeezes my heart. I realise that he knows exactly how long he's got before Agnieszka comes back. Fifteen minutes.

(**My Angry Friend**)

'I said leave.'

'Not before I explain myself.'

He's obviously not moving so I jut my chin out and raise an eyebrow as if to say 'well?'

'I asked you which Monica you are now, and I did it for a reason. I think you sometimes forget. I knew you before that accident. *I knew you.* I remember you had a real spark, a ... a determination, to get anything you wanted, and a ruthlessness to get rid of people who held you back.'

'You don't say.'

'Even with the pain, you have a real fire in your eyes. What I'm trying to say is, it's not the pain that's changed you, not some ... accident. That didn't change you. It's the drugs. It's the drugs that ... they've made you meek. And I'm not sure Dominic thinks he can cope with that sparky woman coming back. All I can say is, I think I can. Cope with it. That's all.'

'I think you're deluded,' I snap. 'Utterly deluded. Just like that bullshit about being trapped into having a baby. No one trapped you. No one gets trapped by people who love them.'

'No?' and he looks pointedly at me.

'Fuck off out of my house!' I shout.

'That's her,' he grins. 'There's that Monica right there.'

And, satisfied with his final riposte, he leaves.

Niall

Damn!

Niall's trainers thumped angrily down the stairs.

Damn damn damn!

He forced himself to be calm. *Remember, she has pain. She doesn't know what she's saying half the time.*

Be that man, Niall. Be the strong, wise, gentle man that she needs. That's why you have transformed yourself.

That is why you have brought yourself into being.

For her.

It occurred to him with a shock that he had driven her back home without even asking her address. He wasn't supposed to know where she lived! How did he have her address in his satnav? That was a problem. *Think, Niall!*

That was it. He saw her details on her hospital form, while she was getting her treatment. It would be on there. *Yes, that was extremely plausible.*

He had to admit, he was a very clever man. More suited to her than the man she'd married. It was obvious her husband couldn't cope with her. He was slowly disintegrating, melting like a snowman in the sun, and it was just a matter of time before Niall replaced him.

Niall noticed the telephone by the door. A blinking light with a '2' in red neon. He remembered that the phone had rung and then stopped. It was a message from her husband, no doubt, desperately trying to glue the shreds of his marriage together. Well, Mr Monica Wood would get no help from him.

He jabbed 'erase' and the messages disappeared.

Monica

The days go by and I'm left alone to dwell on what Niall said. Fortunately the searing heat carries on raging through my body like a forest fire, and crowds out any unwelcome thoughts.

The heat slowly disappears, which is a great relief. Crawling up and down the stairs and retrieving ice packs is not fun. One morning, I realise something important has happened. I get out of bed, and with a surge of excitement I realise that the pain caused by the burning patch is the *only* pain.

And now it's dying down.

It was that simple. I was expecting something more dramatic. Perhaps I imagined I'd rise from my bed with a shower of sparks like Frankenstein's monster ... But no, the only thing that accompanied my epiphany is birdsong, the faint hiss of the dishwasher and the truculent burble of Radio 4 in the kitchen.

I need to say something; I have to say something. I have to give this momentous event some kind of fanfare.

'It's gone.'

And, louder:

'The pain has gone.'

I say it many times, alone, in the house, using different

permutations of the same sentence (the pain has *gone*, the pain *has* gone, the *pain* has gone . . .) as if saying the words might help me to make some sense of what has happened.

'My Angry Friend has fucked off.'

I stare at the tiniest parts of myself; my (ridged) fingernails, the (grey) hairs on my wrists, the tiny (arthritic) whorls on my knuckles. It's as if I can't make sense of what happened, not all at once, so I have to start small.

My knuckles. There's no pain in my knuckles.

My fingers. There's no pain in my fingers.

I work thoroughly around every part of my body. Legs, buttocks, breasts and thighs. I find myself holding my hands in front of my face, and staring at my arms and legs in disbelief.

I've gone for so long knowing nothing but pain, my own body feels like that of a stranger. It feels like being drunk in reverse, where my fuzzy, unfocused world has given way to a sharper, stranger reality.

I drive into town. I don't use a disabled space. In fact, I make it a point not to use a disabled space. In fact, I walk over to the disabled space and *dance* on it. I *stamp* on it! I *jump* on it! I flick rude gestures on it. An old woman walks past and looks at me, and I know what she's thinking, and I don't care.

The pain; it's not gone away, not completely, but I'm finding that I can bring my daily intake of painkillers down without becoming a dribbling puddle of misery. I can move without my Angry Friend treading in my footsteps and kicking at my heels. I can speak and think without him jabbing his finger in my ear.

Oh God.

It's worked.

Now to tell Dominic the truth.

Monica

On the third day, Dominic comes home from Swindon. I hear the door go, the huff-scuff on the mat, and I run to him. I actually *run* to him.

'Hello, you,' he says.

'Hello, you.'

'Sorry it took longer than I expected. I feel like I've been gone years.'

'Yes, I feel that too.'

He looks at me, up and down. Appraising. His eyes are narrow. 'Are you OK?'

'Really good. Great, in fact.'

'I'm glad. I was worried about you.'

Is it my imagination, or is there an edge in Dominic's voice?

'Don't worry about me. I can look after myself.'

'Of course you can.'

'How was the *Apprentice* audition?'

'What?' He struggles to work out what I'm getting at. Then the penny drops and he waves his hand. 'Oh. The job went to some blonde from Guildford with legs up to her armpits.'

'I'm sorry.'

'I'm not. The whole procedure was so hideous, I just kept thinking "do I really want to work with these people?", so I think it was a lucky escape for me.'

'If you'd only realised earlier, you'd never have had to go to Swindon for a whole week.'

'That's true.'

He bends down and kisses me on the cheek. I see a huge jagged blur on the edge of my vision.

'What's happened to your ear?'

He moves away and frowns. 'What do you mean?'

'Your ear. It's all ragged at the bottom. It looks like you've had stitches.'

He feels the side of his face. 'I know . . .'

'So what happened?'

'Don't you remember?'

I'm confused. 'Remember . . . What?'

'You did this. Don't you remember?'

'I did?'

'The evening I cooked for you?'

'What about it?'

'You were being my sous-chef, and you had a spasm. You brought your arm up fast while you were doing the carrots and nearly sliced my ear off.'

'Jesus!'

He winces.

'I mean . . . my G— Blimey. I'm sorry.'

'That's OK. The blood gave the chilli con carne some extra pep.'

'You bled?'

'All over the place. These things happen.'

'But they shouldn't. I'm so sorry.'

'It's *fine* . . . It was just a few stitches. That's all . . .'

'Didn't we make love afterwards? I don't remember any blood. I must have nibbled your ear. I always nibble your ear . . .'

'It was painful. I stayed above you with my arms straight. Don't you remember?'

'I . . . think I do . . . I'm sorry about that.'

'You said. It's fine.'

'Let me make it up to you. Let me show you something amazing.'

Monica

'Have I told you about my new drugs?'

'No. No you didn't.'

'Dr Kumar put me on a new combination of drugs.'

'Right. I wasn't told about this.'

'It was at our last appointment. Dr Kumar added a new one into the mix and, well ...'

(**It's easy to lie**)

'I don't want to give you false hope ... But I feel it's really having some kind of positive effect.'

'Oh great. Really great. What's the name of the new drug?'

Stupid. I should have thought of that.

'Oh ... oxy-gabba-something. I've got the box in the car. Would you like to see it?'

'Show me later.'

As you've probably guessed I've decided not to tell him about the capsaicin.

I can't let anything spoil this.

This joyous wonderful feeling.

'Just watch me.'

I touch my toes and run up the stairs and back down again. His eyes follow me with bug-eyed disbelief.

'See?'

'That's incredible. I've not seen you do that since before the accident.'

'I've always had good days and bad days. You know that.'

'But ...' He doesn't ask questions. Perhaps doesn't dare, or perhaps the spell will be broken. But his mouth manages to form a 'how..?', before he realises it's a stupid question to ask. He's already been told 'how'.

He doesn't take his eyes from my face for a second and finally says: 'But how long have you, has this … ?'

'About three days. I didn't ring you on the first day because, you know, but on the second day, I thought "this is really holding", and it's the third day now, and I'm still feeling really good.'

He stares at me and says, 'On the third day He rose again …'

'Dominic. Don't go all Jesus on me. I'm not Jesus.'

He's not listening. 'I don't believe it,' he mutters.

'Let me prove it to you,' I say. 'Last one upstairs is a rotten egg!' And I charge upstairs, and it's my turn for my feet to go *thud thud thud*.

The moment we get into the bedroom we fall upon each other, tearing at each other's clothes. I push him back on the bed and straddle him, something I haven't done in five years. We mash our bodies together, treating each other like pieces of meat, and I wonder if my moans are reaching the neighbours. I don't care if they do.

This is my body.

I want to show him I'm better, I think, *but I also want to show him that I love him, and I'm not going to run off with another man, not Niall, or any other type of man, just because I'm able to walk to the car without screaming or passing out. I am Dominic's wife and always will be.*

There is nothing for him to worry about.

And then, as the sunshine slowly drains from the sky, we fall asleep.

Monica

I would have thought, now I had lowered my dose of painkillers, the dream would go. But it doesn't go anywhere. If anything, it looks more vivid. It's as if an old painting has been restored, and the layers of dirt and dust have come off, revealing vivid blues and reds and purples.

I'm back on the top level of the car park, on the roof, high above everything else, and now I can see the tops of the houses, the little green squares of garden, a school with children milling about and fighting on the climbing frames. I see them as clearly as if I'm awake. I can see men inside the cranes, high above the skyline, their hands pumping the controls and moving their huge machines back and forth. I realise they're trying to fix London, but it's a never-ending task. There's always something more to be done.

Niall is there, clearer and closer and more intense. He shouts, 'Posture, Monica! You have a backbone!'

'I've got a backbone!' I shout back. 'I've been fighting for five years!'

'You don't get it, do you? I'm your only way out of this! Use me! You have to show him you have what it takes! You have to show him you have a spine!'

He stares at me, and then his face folds in disgust.

'Oh what's the use,' he says. 'Watch me.'

And he pitches off the edge of the building. Dumbfounded, I run to the edge and look down. There's Jesse's car, and it's still circling, looking for a parking space, but I can see the car park attendant below, the round-faced man with the thin blond hair and the undernourished ginger moustache. He's standing there again, looking up at me, in his black uniform with his luminous tabard, but now I can see it much more clearly.

He's not a car park attendant. He's a policeman.

'Is that everything, Monica?' he says. 'Is there anything else you want to tell me?'

This time I do more than nod. I say: 'No, officer. Nothing.'

'Are you sure?'

'I'm quite sure. I don't know what you want me to say.'

Disappointed, he turns and walks into the hospital.

I turn, and the cloud is resolving itself; thin arms, slender legs.

'Hi, Mon. This will hurt me more than it'll hurt you, yeah?'

Angelina strides towards me, elegantly turned out in her long black winter coat. She stretches out black fingernails, and her hand presses my chest.

'Bye-bye, kitten . . . '

And she shoves me, and I'm staggering backwards, and I'm falling over the rail, and down, and down, and I can see the cars parked in the lower levels as I fall past them.

And then I'm on the floor, in the road, and I can't move, and Niall is bending over me.

'Shit. Are you all right?'

But I can't answer him, because I'm dead.

Monica

Dominic is flickering in and out of consciousness; my shout of terror has pulled him out of sleep, and his body hasn't decided whether to go back under or not.

'Wha, hmmm, huh?'

I stay very still and very quiet, and soon his breathing becomes low and regular. In ... out. In ... out. I pull on my dressing gown and go downstairs, staggering, moving too fast, like I'm on the moon. I'm automatically moving like the pain is weighing me down, and I'm constantly surprised at how light everything feels.

I go to the study. Now my mind is freed from battling with the pain, it's hungry and restless. I'm insane for knowledge. I want to look at Dominic's computer again, to see what else he's hiding in there.

I press on and the computer erupts with a chime. *Too loud!* Our bedroom is right above the study. I turn down the volume, in case I'm caught out by more lustful moans from Dominic's secret library.

Up comes Dominic's tiger, and I key in the dreaded word: 'pain'.

The box shakes: no.

I worry I've got the caps lock on, but no. I put the caps lock on and try again. No. Then turned the cap lock off, and try again; all those futile things you do on computers when you know the problem is somewhere else.

But the box carries on shaking its head. *Nothing.*

There's only one explanation. Dominic's changed his password. *Why would he do that?* The answer is in my head before I even manage to ask the question.

Because someone told him I've been looking at his computer.

Angelina told him. It's the only explanation.

She wouldn't, would she? Break a confidence? Was this what the dream meant? Some metaphor? Some weird message telling something ... What? Don't trust my friends? Don't trust my Angelina?

It's not the only explanation. I'm getting angry with myself now. *Don't be so hysterical. Dominic could have just changed his password. He might have felt guilty for using the 'p' word, and just ... changed it.*

Or:

I could have done something when I was on his computer, erased something by accident. He might check his browsing history every morning, or the printer log, or something like that. He might have realised I'd been on his side of the computer and changed the password.

Either way, what can I do? Confront Dominic?

I can't. Not now. I've lied to him now. Suppose I accuse him of taking photos of me? It would seem so pathetic after what I've just done. He would say he'd been absolutely bloody right to be suspicious.

Be sensible, girl. I'd just sound mad and paranoid.

But I AM mad and paranoid. I know that. The drugs and the pain make me like this. I know my brain is physically different. It just happens to be a medical fact. Just like the shape of my jaw has been changed from the nights trying to grind my teeth, and there are ridges on my fingernails, and chalk-white hairs at my temple where there were none before, my brain has been transformed, it is as different now from before the accident as a cabbage is to a cauliflower. The question is, how mad and paranoid have I become?

Just my normal mad and paranoid, or extra mad and paranoid?

Evidence. There's only one way to sort this out. Facts that tell me what's happening.

Monica

Of all the things I dreamt I would do with myself when the pain was gone, this is not what I imagined.

The moon is big, covering the garden in a soft white glow. The wet grass sparkles like the lights of a fairy village, but where I stand, I am dipped in darkness. Good.

At last I get to wear my 'hers' wellingtons.

I grapple with the bin, push it aside and grasp the shovel. I dig for a long time. My arms hurt like hell, but it is not the scream of my Angry Friend, it is the groan of long neglected muscles.

I hold the spade high, and the damp soil on the edge catches the silvery light, and looks a dark red. A fragment of memory. My mind flashes to another time. A child screams. It is me. My father's hand on my shoulder. His blood-spattered spade. My mother's shout.

'How could you have been so stupid, Adrian?'

I will myself to think about other things. Now is not the time to be bothered about shadows of the past.

While I dig, I pass the time by imagining what I will find in the ground. *More photos of me, perhaps, or sophisticated bugging equipment. A computer tracking my car . . . Perhaps even a plastic wrapped file detailing my assignations with a long-forgotten lover?*

There is . . . nothing.

I find nothing. There is nothing here. I must have imagined it. *'How could you have been so stupid, Monica?'*

Dominic must have just been putting the bin upright, like he said. Not digging. Not hiding something in the ground.

(**But you can't be sure**)

I'm just mad and paranoid.

(**But you can't be sure**)

I entertain the notion that Dominic might have removed something, rather than hiding it, but I have already spent too long chasing this rabbit down a hole. I need to know what's in my head.

It crosses my mind – only fleetingly – that I should come completely off the drugs. See what happens. See if all the blocked memories flood back into me. I don't think of it long, because the thought of what I might feel – without painkillers, even with the pain diminished – makes me feel nauseous. It feels too drastic.

The dream, Monica. Remember the man in the dream.

Who was that man at the end? The one with the unfortunate moustache?

'Is that everything, Monica?' he said. 'Is there anything else you want to tell me?'

'No officer. Nothing.'

'Are you sure?'

Not a car park attendant. A policeman.

Monica

It's a week later, and Niall's texts are coming thick and fast. U OK? Nx, ANY BETTER? Nxx, CU SOON? Nxx

... and so on and so on. The texts are all practically identical, but it's funny how some come across as pleading, some angry, some tetchy, some pathetic. Perhaps each XXX from Niall is a Rorschach test opening different windows on my own state of mind.

I don't reply to any of them. The moment in the bedroom felt dangerous. Out of kilter. I want to forget it. I want to forget *him*. Perhaps another reason why I want to forget him is a reason I don't want to admit to myself. He reminds me of that time before, when I had pain.

Here's someone else I don't want to see. I have an appointment with Dr Kumar, a post-treatment consultation to see how I'm doing.

Let's put a brave face on it. I think it's time for celebration, for both of us, and I decide to skip into his surgery to demonstrate how good I'm feeling. I plonk myself in the chair, lean back as if I don't have a care in the world, and stretch my legs ostentatiously under his desk. Then I realise I'm acting and moving like a slut, and I sit normally, but the grin stays plastered on my face. I'm waiting for praise from teacher.

Dr Kumar is fiddling with his pen. *Click click click*. He looks less than delighted to see me, which is odd. He *always* looks delighted to see people; without fail. Being delighted to see people is part of his character; it's imprinted in his DNA. I would have thought he would be *even more* delighted to see me, given the context of my successful treatment. Perhaps his personality just works in a weird topsy-turvy way.

'Good day to you, Monica, and how did you find the capsaicin treatment? Not the pleasantest of experiences, yes?'

'Well, it wasn't pleasant. You were right about that. But as you can see ... I'm feeling a lot better.'

'Oh good. I am very glad. How would you gauge your pain levels? How much percentage?'

'Probably ... about forty per cent less. Yes, forty per cent. I would say that. And I think that's a conservative estimate.'

'How encouraging. That is very encouraging indeed.'

He asks more questions, making notes as I talk and then, about half an hour later he says, 'Well I am so glad you've had relief for this time. This is very encouraging. I hope this has been a rewarding experience for you.'

'Well ... It has been. Definitely.'

And we sit there, awkwardly, for a few seconds.

'So what happens now? Do I make an appointment with you now, for another treatment, or do they contact me?'

Dr Kumar takes a deep breath. 'I am afraid that the process led to the discovery that you are suffering from atherosclerosis ...'

'I know, they told me. They want me in for tests. More bloody tests.'

'Until we can diagnose the severity of the condition, and due to the adverse effect on your heart, they do not feel they can treat you again at this moment in time. For the foreseeable future.'

'How long will that take?'

Dr Kumar smiles, embarrassed. 'There is no way of knowing. It is another new discovery we have to work with. It has probably come about due to the stress you have been feeling these past few years ...'

'Due to the pain.'

Dr Kumar just smiles. 'I am glad that the treatment had a beneficial effect on you, but this discovery, your condition, at this moment, it makes you too much of a risk.'

'I can take it.'

'The point is, Monica, you cannot. You nearly died. You went into cardiac arrest. They do not want to risk your life by doing this to you again.'

'Suppose I *want* to risk my life?'

He smiles, weakly. Now I know why he didn't look happy. I should have guessed. My super-sense is never wrong.

Anger is starting to grow inside me.

'This is irony, isn't it?' I say at last, coldly. 'My heart is fucked due to the stress because of the pain, and I bet the drugs haven't helped. They won't have helped, I guess?'

'I wouldn't like to say that. I wouldn't like to say that definitely ...'

'And now my body isn't strong enough to cope with the only treatment that works. How fucking ironic.' I'm thinking furiously. 'Look. It's fine. I'm fine with it. I'll sign a piece of paper. I don't care. I'll take the risk.'

'Killing you during a medical trial is not a positive outcome for anyone, especially you.'

'You're condemning me to a life with unending pain. Do you know that?'

'Your adverse reaction makes you a dangerous risk. I'm sorry.'

'How can you decide what's worth my life? What about *my* quality of life? Suppose my quality of life matters more to me than having a life? Who are you to put such a high price on my worthless fucking life!'

'Your adverse reaction means you are too much of a risk.'

I'm furious now, and this time there's no pain to hold me back. 'You're repeating yourself now. Coming out with pre-prepared phrases like the fucking Atos man. At the end of the day, it's all just an exercise in arse-covering. I get to have my arse covered in magic chillies, and because it didn't work out how everyone hoped, you get to cover your arse with some ... fucking box-ticking form, some red tape, some health and safety bollocks ...'

'Monica, please listen. Perhaps in the future the procedure can be refined but until then ... This is not just about you, this is about all the others that this could help. If someone dies on the trial they could cut funding, or even close it down completely.'

'No. This *is* all about me! This is all about me! Me and my pain! There is no one else, because that's how pain works, and you should fucking know that by now! I thought you were on my side!'

'I am on your side, Monica. If you wish you can try the new morphine tablets. The results are very encouraging. We can see if they are efficacious in your case ...'

'Fuck you and your efficacious! You don't get to use me as a fucking beagle and chuck me back in the kennel the minute I get smoker's cough!'

I don't remember leaving Dr Kumar's office. I don't even remember taking the morphine tablets with me. I stuff them in the glove compartment. The next thing I know, I'm back in the car, sobbing and banging my head as hard as I can on the steering wheel. Why not? If my Angry Friend is coming back, best to prepare the way with a fat headache.

I should never have told him the percentage of pain loss. You should never tell them the percentage.

Thud. Thud thud. THUD.

I'm know I'm trying to make the airbag go off, so it can engulf me like the cloud in my dream. It's not happening. Even without pain, my weakened body ... I don't even have the strength to do that. I fight to regain my composure.

Perhaps the pain won't come back.

(**You know it will. Don't be a silly bitch**)

What do I do?

(**You know what to do**)

I don't. I don't know anything.

(**Just live. Live your life, and live your life hard. Make love to your husband. Work some of that weight off. Travel with him. Drink with him. Laugh with him. Use this time, because it will be over soon**)

But I'm still angry. 'This is Keats! This is just like Keats! I'm Keats!' I yell to the inside of the car. 'They make it easy on everyone else. Let's just keep the pain relief back from me, in case there's a tiny chance of me killing myself.'

And then, after the tears are gone, I decide what to do next.

Monica

'Let's go away,' I say.

Dominic looks slightly taken aback.

'Like where?'

'A holiday. A romantic holiday.'

He smiles. 'That's a nice idea.'

Surely he knows that I will never leave him now. Crippled or healthy, I will always be at his side.

'OK ...' he continues. 'It's been a while. A long while. We could take a train up to see my dad. Maybe get a little hotel in the Highlands.'

'No, let's really go away. Let's go to Rome. I know you've always wanted to go to the Vatican, kiss the Pope's ring and all that jazz. I'd quite like to see where John Keats died. God and poetry, the perfect combination.'

He stares at me, searching my face for signals. I know what he's thinking. *Is she joking? Has she become unhinged by the medication?*

'Really?'

'Yes. Let's go.'

'There are steps in Rome. Lots and lots of steps.'

'So I read on the internet. The Keats-Shelley memorial house is actually at the bottom of the Spanish Steps. I'm ready for it.'

'Will we be going on the Eurostar?'

'No, a plane will be quicker.'

'Seriously?'

'No, on a magic carpet. Of course I mean a plane.'

Dominic knows that flying is not good for my condition. It's not just the stress of getting to the airport, the humping of bags on and off machines and carousels, all that can be avoided with a bit of forethought and cooperation from the airline; and it's not the sitting in a cramped seat for hours at a time – if I'm clever I can keep moving, and find places to move about.

There's one thing I can't get around; the take-off, the part of the flight where you are required to sit down. No excuses. The plane moves up at a 45-degree angle, accelerating at a terrific rate, and you can feel it pushing you back in your seat. What's happening is that the acceleration is placing g-force on your spine and compressing it together. It's something you wouldn't particularly notice. But if you happen to have chronic nerve pain that's derived from an injury based in the small of the back . . .

The first time we tried to fly after my injury we did something unambitious; a short package trip to Spain. I was completely unprepared for how it affected me. I ended up with a huge flare-up, and I spent the following week lying down in a darkened room in the hotel. I might as well have drawn the curtains in my own bedroom and listened to flamenco music on my iPod.

He sums this all up by saying: 'You know what happened last time.'

'I'm feeling really good at the moment. Look.' I give a little dance. 'Let's go to Rome. Let's have a second honeymoon.'

'OK. Fine.'

And he backs away from me, almost afraid. *He's so worried I'm going to leave him.*

He's halfway up the stairs, and I call to him.

'Dominic?'

'Yes?'

'I do love you.'

Monica

So we're off to Rome. It's taken six weeks for Dominic to get time off work, and I still feel OK. No sign of the pain. I wake up every morning and wait for reality to fall in on me, but it doesn't happen.

Now our cases are packed and weighed, and there's a taxi coming to take us to Heathrow. Dominic is still watching me, bug-eyed. He can't get used to me moving around fairly normally. He is obviously expecting me to shatter into a thousand pieces at any moment. He asks me how I am every ten minutes. Sometimes he even asks me how my memory is; if I can remember moments from that first year, after the accident.

I shake my head and he nods, thinking. I expect him to look more disappointed, somehow.

Monica

Our flight is gloriously uneventful. Dominic is still staring at me, wide-eyed, I think he's waiting for something to happen, but I pat his hand and say, 'Read your book, I'm fine. Really.'

He sits there in his seat, not reading his book, and I sit there in mine, coping with being fine. I look out of my window, unable to tear my eyes away. It's the first time in ages I've not looked out of a plane through a fog of agony, and I'm captivated by the sights below. My mind is frantically throwing out images and metaphors.

I need to write a poem about this. If I can. I have to see if I can read my handwriting now . . .

The suicide letter again. In my head.

How did I write it?

Forget about the bloody letter, Monica. You're on holiday.

At the moment England is shapeless and murky, as if it is lying at the bottom of deep water. The clouds drifting by our wing are like lumps of pack ice drifting on a frozen lake, and not too much later the weather clears, and I am staring down at the Alps, white and green and speckled, gouged out of the earth, like someone had attacked a tub of mint-choc ice cream.

My perceptions feel different. I feel different. I wonder what it would be like when my own murk clears, and the pin-sharp pictures finally arrive in my mind.

We emerge, blinking in the wobbly nicotine-stiffened air of Rome. Scarcely able to believe what we're doing, we take a taxi to the hotel. Our big black Mercedes noses into the fast-moving stream of Fiats and Toyotas, causing howls and hoots from the drivers, and soon we are bumping and jerking along terrifying, narrow roads as our driver makes gestures to everyone he sees. A girl on a moped zips past us wearing nothing but a crash helmet, a light summer dress and a pair of trainers. Her dress flaps in the humid heat revealing long brown legs.

Even though we're being thrown about inside the car, I still feel nothing; no pain.

Nothing.

When we reach the main street, we are besieged. Traders circle and jostle us, waving fake Gucci handbags, bottles of water and, mystifyingly, statuettes of the leaning Tower of Pisa. Dominic looks in my direction, concerned, but I'm smiling like an idiot. I feel nothing. There is a beggar lying across the pavement, tapping his stick rhythmically on the kerb. *Tap tap tap.* We have to skip round him and onto the road to get to the hotel. I wonder if, at the end of the day, he would dust himself off and saunter away, but then I feel guilty. That's just what people think about me when I park in those disabled spaces.

I hurry back and put five euros in his hat. He gives me a broken grin and keeps on tapping.

Tap. Tap. Tap. Tap.

And I'm reminded of the password. The photos Dominic took of me. How Dominic changed his password to stop me snooping. Fleetingly I wonder if he has got over his paranoia. I hope so, because for now, everything is all right.

Everything is perfect.

Forget about it.

As soon as we enter the hotel room we hold each other tightly and fall onto the bed, casting our clothes off and dropping them on the floor. He pulls me onto my knees, and I wonder if he wants me to assume a doggy pose like one of his pornographic films; but he wriggles under me, happy to lie back and let me sit astride him, again. I'm happy to oblige as I'm enjoying my new freedom, but it's not the first time that I think it wasn't quite like it was before. I'm sure when we had an active love life, Dominic was at least, well . . . *active.* I hold him by his shoulders and roll, until we change places and he's on top of me. I remember the old thrill of watching his chest above me, moving back and forth.

He lasts about twenty seconds before his arms give out and he collapses on top of me.

I wake early. Far too early. The noises of the morning are only just beginning; just a solitary barking dog. Dominic is still flat on his stomach, snoring slightly.

I can't wait. Time is too precious. I have to go. I can't control my body but this time it's in a good way. I throw on some clothes, leave a note for Dominic, leave the hotel, and find myself walking to the Spanish Steps. Tiptoeing over the traders setting out their wares on the pavements.

I get to the Keats-Shelley House, only to find that it's closed. Not open until the afternoon. I sit outside the heavy door and read my book about the poets, enjoying my freshly found level of concentration, devouring the pages. I read about how Keats died, in terrible pain, but surrounded by his friends. How sad they burnt all his furniture because they were afraid of the tuberculosis!

I look up at the windows and fantasise about being in the room where he breathed his last, being one of his friends. I read a little about Byron, and am strangely moved by his last words: 'I think I shall go to sleep now.'

It's restful in the square, and I feel at one with it all; I feel at one with Keats. I read 'Ode to a Nightingale', and decide I have to write my own 'Ode to Keats'.

I brace myself and walk to the top. It's been a long time since I've had the courage to go up this many steps; it would be frightening if it wasn't so tiring. I sit in a café and I write a poem on the back of the napkin that comes with my coffee, about pain and sharing.

> *If I could place a curtain round these steps*
> *Plant a beech bush for a nightingale's nest*
> *Would you and I fall finally to our rest?*
> *Could we find peace and sweet release from pain*
> *To live a life of love and love again,*
> *Feel joyful lungs, lips, limbs; sweet health's refrain*
> *Sing soulful satiating poetry?*
> *If that could be my ode, at your behest*
> *I think I now could fly these Spanish Steps.*
> *Away, away, my burdon clings to me,*
> *So weightless, acheless, I shall fly to thee.*

The handwriting is almost normal; almost mine. Like the handwriting on that suicide letter I couldn't have written.

Ever since the agony and ecstasy of the treatment I'd tried not to think about the suicide letter. I'd chosen not to think about it, because I so wanted everything to get back to normal. And now my poem has forced the thought back into my mind.

My Angry Friend has been banished, but he is still there, hiding somewhere, jumping up and throwing the fragments of the letter in my face and screaming (**Look! Look at it! Look there you silly bitch! They're lying to you! They're all lying to you!**)

'No, leave me alone!' I say it out loud, startling a man near me, taking photos with his phone. 'I don't want to listen to you any more!'

(**Look! Look at what you wrote!**)

I can't. The suicide letter is long gone.

(**Not the suicide note, you daft cow! The poem! Look at the poem!**)

Then I realise I've spelled the word 'burden' incorrectly, and I feel a shudder of what is coming for me. *Please God, keep him away for a little while longer.*

I stand at the top of the steps and look down. They fall away to the ground quite steeply, and I feel dizzy just looking. Very dizzy. I have more memories of steps. More steps.

Car park steps.

Hospital car park steps.

The memory is sharper now, and it's too much.

It's making me feel nauseous.

And there's a hand at my back, and I scream. Very loudly. And I almost pitch myself off the steps and fall.

'Are you all right?'

Dominic is there. It's him. It is his hand on my back.

'My God! What were you trying to do?'

Dominic flinches. 'Do? I wasn't trying to do anything. I was just meeting you. I got your note. I followed you here.'

'Why did you say that? Why did you just say "Are you all right?"?'

'Because you looked like you'd just had a heart attack when I touched you!'

'You scared me! Why didn't you say something?'

'I did! I called to you! I guess you weren't listening.' He looks at his watch. 'Come on. We've got to head off. I want to see the Vatican.'

'But I've only just got here!'

'Monica, it's nearly eleven!'

'But they open the house at one o clock.'

'Oh no! No way are we waiting here for two more hours. We're on a schedule here. Time is precious. You're not being fair, Monica. This is our holiday and you just take off the first chance you get?' He shakes his head in disappointment. 'We're heading to the Vatican, before it gets too hot to walk.'

'But I want to see Keats—'

'He's dead. He's not going anywhere. Come on. The Vatican. We'd said we'd do that on day one. You promised.'

(**Time is precious**)

So, reluctantly, I surrender, and we go to the Vatican. We go over a huge bridge, the Ponte Vittorio Emanuele II. It's lined with bits of statue; huge grey people with missing arms and heads.

This place is full of broken bodies. I think I fit right in. In fact the whole city is like me. An ageing lady who's still beautiful, but who's had a few knocks too many in her long, eventful life. And it shows.

When we get to the Vatican, it's a circus. We're jostled in the square, jostled in the huge queue to get into the place. Dominic is in awe, looking at everything, devouring every painting, every fresco. But he always keeps one eye on me. When I suddenly shiver at the sight of a tortured statue of a luckless saint, he's at my side.

255

'Are you all right? Did the shock on the top of the steps – did it jar you?'

'I'm fine.'

'How's the pain?'

'It's fine. I'm fine.'

'But you shuddered. I saw you.'

'It's *fine*, Dominic. I just had someone walk over my grave.'

Dominic grins. 'This is Rome. We're probably walking over everyone's grave. Come on. Let's go and get something to eat.'

The day darkens, and we go back to the hotel, ring down and reserve a table. Giddy with the idea of a romantic meal, I put on a sheer green silk dress slashed to the thigh (I bought it during a mad month when I decided I was going to compete with Angelina) and shoes so vertiginous my toes start screaming the moment I take them out of the suitcase.

Dominic throws on a jacket. 'Ready?'

My eyes flick up and down his body. His jeans, his open-neck golf shirt and crumpled corduroy jacket. 'You ... are not going downstairs like that.'

'Why not?'

'Jesus, Dominic. Do I have to spell it out? This is our first proper meal together since I've felt better. I've not been able to wear these shoes for five years. Have a sense of *occasion*, for God's sake.'

He looks at me. He doesn't know what to say. Something that looks a lot like recognition spreads slowly across his face, and with some effort his shoulders descend, his hands unclench, and he relaxes and smiles as if to say 'no bother'.

He raises his arms in mock surrender and goes to find the suit that I know he has forgotten to pack. He eventually emerges with a tie, (**the one I hate**), and I can see he couldn't manage to do the top button up on his shirt, his (**fat**) neck is exposed beneath the knot.

The moment I enter the restaurant I feel incredibly overdressed. No one is wearing a tie. One man is even wearing shorts. Dominic doesn't seem to notice, and follows the maître d' with obvious hunger. We are given a table near the kitchen, as we booked too late. All the other diners allow their gaze to wander around the room, and I know they're only doing that so their eyes can rest on us for a few seconds. I can hear their thoughts.

What is that tart wearing?

God. Desperate for attention or what?

I wish my wife had the courage to show her boobs like that.

We order, and the meals arrive very quickly. Too quickly. Like they've been sitting on a hot shelf – identikit meals, like fast food burgers, sliding down a chute ready to put in a box with paper napkins, plastic cutlery and a toy for the kids.

Dominic notices my expression.

'It's all right, isn't it? The meal?'

(**No, actually**), I think (**it's not**). I'm looking down at my plate, and I'm looking at something inadequate; underprepared, over-cooked pre-packaged slop for the masses.

This is what we have to do. This is what we can afford. We have no money left. Remember that, Monica. Be nice to him. He loves you.

I've just taken a mouthful, so I just nod my head vigorously. 'Absolutely,' I eventually say. 'It's absolutely perfect.'

'It's very convenient, eating here, at the hotel. That's my thinking. We don't have to walk back from anywhere.'

I keep eating, pushing the indifferent lasagne around my mouth, moving my jaw furiously. Trying to swallow.

'You pulled an odd face. Are you sure you're OK?'

'Yes, Dominic,' I say in a very low voice. 'It is very convenient. We don't have to walk back from anywhere. But I want to eat in different places. In case you haven't noticed, I'm feeling better

257

now. I can do things now. I can walk out of a hotel and get a cab and eat somewhere nice.'

'I know that. But we have to be careful . . .'

'And I know there's no money. But the restaurants here are cheap. Cheaper than the hotel. But you'd rather not go out. Once you've seen the things you want to see, you're happy to stop there . . .'

'Monica . . .'

'So you don't have to pretend you're not doing all those things because you're being thoughtful to me. Seriously. It insults me and it insults you.'

There's an expression on Dominic's face; or rather a collection of expressions, a Picasso portrait where all the different aspects can be seen at the same time. The recognition from the hotel room, mixed with resentment, confusion, and above all, fear.

Fear.

He's afraid.

My mind spins back to another hotel, another time.

'Why did you have to do this?'

'It's a four-star hotel. It said so on the website.'

'In these countries, Dominic, five star is four star, four star is three star, and three star is a slum. Have you ever seen a three-star hotel advertised on the continent? It's like haggling. They say five star assuming you know it's nothing of the sort. Have you learnt nothing from your time with me?'

'Are you all right?'

'What?'

'You were miles away. Staring into space.'

'Just thinking.'

'About what?'

'About Egypt.'

'What about Egypt?'

'Another hotel meal. Another restaurant.'

'What can you remember?'

His voice is suddenly urgent; his eyes are fixed on mine with an intensity that borders on the fanatical.

'What can you remember?' He says it again, low, almost menacing. 'Tell me what you can remember.'

I have a sudden flash, *of plates crashing, people's heads turning. A waiter rushing over to our table as I stand up and walk out of the restaurant. I am walking strongly, briskly, without pain, one arm stiff by my side, another clutching my purse, and I can see myself in many mirrored walls, stunning in my silk green dress, and behind me I can see waitresses rushing to pick up the mess I've made, and Dominic flapping like a startled chicken, throwing money on the table, trying to make things right,* and I feel suddenly cautious about talking to Dominic. Suddenly there is something else, an undercurrent. Something that has always been there, that I had not truly appreciated until this second. My eyes focus on my left hand holding my fork, the tablecloth decorated with bulging tomatoes and dancing wine bottles.

Perhaps he's not scared of me running away.

He doesn't want me to get better. But there's another reason. Another, completely different reason.

'What can you remember?' A third time. He's holding his serviette in his hand, so very tightly, like he's about to perform a magic trick. Like he's about to pour the jug of water into it.

'I . . . nothing.'

'What?'

'I think a waiter dropped a plate. Did a waiter drop a plate?'

'Yes, that's right. He dropped a plate.'

His voice is now relaxed but his eyes are still fixed on me, searching my face.

(What big eyes you have)

DI Geoff Marks

Time went by, and Mrs Monica Wood slipped DI Geoff Marks's mind. He assumed DSu Cooper was still conducting his *Sweeney*-style investigations in Crouch End and his 'vital piece of evidence' was on the money. Good luck to him. Then one evening, just as he was clocking off, Mike Fennel waved a piece of paper under his nose.

'Oh, I forgot. Someone came in for you a while back. A woman. Asked for you specially.'

'OK.'

'Actually, she didn't know your name. She just had a description of you. The usual. Ginger. Face like a boiled swede . . . '

'Right . . . '

Geoff tensed. Citizens who come in with a description of an officer, rather than a name, have usually seen a copper doing something naughty and want to make a report.

Mike knew what he was thinking. 'No, it was nothing like that. She wasn't a "concerned citizen". She said you helped her a few years ago. Wanted your help again.'

'Did she say how many years?'

'Must have been at least two. She mentioned you had a shitty 'tache. That pubic monstrosity that used to fester under your nose.'

'Oh. She mentioned the 'tache, did she? That means it was a while back. I was shamed into shaving it off at least three years ago.'

'Yes. And she still wanted to see you. She'd tried three of the local nicks before she came here. You might want to put a bit of cream on your forehead, Geoff. She looked a bit of all right. Long dark hair. Nice eyes. Nice everything, in fact.'

'That's lovely, Mike, as ever. They should name the sexual misconduct forms after you.'

'Just telling you what I saw, Geoff. Nothing wrong in appreciating the female form. That's how we all got here, after all.'

'That's how *I* got here, Mike. They found *you* under a rock.' He looked at the note. 'Any idea what she wanted?'

'That's all she said. She just left a name and a mobile number.'

He looked at the paper – 'Monica Wood' . . .

And felt like the air had been pushed out of him.

'You all right, mate?' Mike sounded concerned. 'What is it?'

'When did this come in?'

'Ooh . . . ' He pulled a face. 'About a week ago?'

'A *week*? A whole week? You're kidding!'

'Keep your ginger wig on, Geoff. She said it wasn't urgent. She just said to ring her when you had a moment. Why? Who is she? Not an old flame, is she?'

'Oh nobody,' Geoff said, pouring on the sarcasm. 'Just nobody. Just a potential murder victim.'

He looked at the piece of paper, the numbers dancing in front of his eyes. It was her. After all these years. Right now. Coincidence? It couldn't be. He glanced at his watch – it was a shade before ten p.m. Was it too late to call?

He couldn't resist.

Monica

It's evening, but it's still hot, and we have the hotel windows and the shutters open, the curtains are billowing inwards like ghosts from the past.

We are making love again; me on top, again, bouncing furiously and energetically, him once again below, a helpless passenger. I hold on to him fiercely, as if trying to pull his whole body inside me. I'm clinging to him like a drowning woman holding on to a piece of reassuring driftwood.

After we finish, it's only a few seconds before we untangle from each other's arms and Dominic's breathing comes slow and even.

My eyelids flutter and close.

'I'm so sorry.'

(**Christ, was that it?**)

Silence.

(**That receptionist looked a nice boy – perhaps I should ring for room service?**)

I shake my head. *It's you, isn't it? My Angry Friend, sticking these mad thoughts in my head. Go away. Go away and shut up and leave me alone. I adore my husband. I know I do. I can feel it. I have always adored him. Even though I never suffered fools gladly, I love him.*

He starts to snore.

There is a dull buzz and my phone flashes and scurries across the bedside table. It threatens to leap off and escape. I dive for it, and answer it.

'Hello?' I whisper.

'Mrs Wood?' says a voice, well spoken.

'Speaking.'

'I'm Detective Inspector Geoff Marks. I got your message. Is this too late for you?'

I glance at the bedside clock. Our evening is over, and it's still only eleven o'clock.

'No, not too late.'

'I'm sorry I didn't get back to you earlier. I gather you've been asking for me.'

'I have.'

A long pause.

'I ... think I know what you want to see me about?'

'Right.'

'I think we'd better meet, don't you?'

'That's a bit difficult. I'm actually in Rome.'

'Right. I thought the line was a bit echoey.'

'I'm on holiday.'

'With your husband?'

What an odd question.

'Yes, I'm with my husband.'

'Is your husband there? In the room with you?'

'Um ... yes. He's asleep.'

'O ... K ...' There is a note of caution in his voice.

'I don't want to disturb him. I'll go through into the bathroom, if you want.'

I dance around the bed, picking up my pyjamas from where they'd landed, keeping half an eye on Dominic's slumbering form. I bend down to retrieve my slippers and my face is level with his. And his eyes are open, staring into mine.

'Dominic?' I hiss quietly.

But he doesn't respond. He is still asleep. He's sleeping with his eyes open. We share a bed so rarely these days, I forget he does that sometimes.

I open the door, so very gently, there is only a dry click from the lock, and I stand on the other side, allowing my bottom to guide it shut with another faint click. I plonk myself down on the toilet.

'OK ...' I whisper.

'I wondered if I'd ever hear from you again. I hoped I would.'

'Right ...'

'How are you now? How's your back? You were in pretty bad shape when we last met.'

'So you know me? We've met before.'

'Sure we have.'

'I think I should explain something before we talk. I don't remember you at all. In fact, the only reason I managed to track you down is because I kept seeing you in a dream.'

'A dream.'

'Yes. You've been inside my head, for years, in my dreams, only I thought you were a car park attendant. Then I saw you were a policeman.'

'I see.'

'That sounds a bit mad.'

'Well, you said it.'

'Sorry about that.'

'So you can't remember how we met.'

'Not in the slightest. It's the drugs that made me forget. And the pain too. I have to spend so much of my mind focusing on the pain I can't retain anything. I've forgotten whole chunks of my life from years back; mostly from the first year of my accident. It's like the body's own way of protecting itself.'

Silence. I can hear his breathing.

'Hello? Geoff?'

Then I hear a noise from the other room. A squeak of bed-springs. The scrabble of fingers on a bedside table as someone retrieves spectacles. Dominic is up and lumbering to the bathroom. I can hear his heavy tread. His shape is in the glass of the door. The door handle squeaks up and down, but he doesn't say anything. He doesn't even knock at the door.

He's groggy. He doesn't even realise I'm not still in bed. He can't work out why the door won't open.

'Look . . .' Geoff starts to speak at last.

'I'm a bit busy now, Geoff,' I snap. 'Something's come up. Can you ring me tomorrow? Would that be convenient for you?'

'Monica?' Dominic has staggered back to bed and realised it's empty. 'Are you in there?'

Geoff is pondering, thinking. 'I understand,' he says. 'How about I phone you at midday tomorrow?'

'Monica?'

I snap the phone shut. 'In here.'

'You OK?'

'I'm fine. Just a spot of . . . You know . . . The usual.'

'Oh.'

'It was never going to be perfect, Dominic. We knew painkillers were never going to be the answer.'

A black shape appears at the top of the glass, about the size of a football. He's resting his head against the door.

'No. Painkillers were never going to be the answer.'

Monica

We've nearly finished breakfast when Dominic says, 'You've been glancing at your phone a lot. Are you expecting a call?'

I realise what I've been doing: pressing the button to illuminate the screen, checking the battery power, looking at the tiny phone icon to see if there are any missed calls.

'I suppose I am,' I say. 'I'm waiting for a call from Angelina. She said she'd keep me posted if she sold anything after her viewing party.'

'Good for her,' he says, neutrally. I'm not sure he believes a word of it.

The morning bleeds away, so slowly, and we go sightseeing. I still want to go back to see the Keats-Shelley memorial house, but Dominic insists on his timetable. So we go to the Pantheon. I sigh, and give up the fight. It's nearer, after all.

The Pantheon is, of course, another place of worship. Originally constructed by Marcus Agrippa, it fell, rose again under Hadrian, and the Roman Catholic church moved in hundreds of years later, occupying the site like a godly hermit crab. Now it's a big cool building full of pews and statues. Dominic makes a beeline to a pew and kneels to pray, while I wander around looking at the statues.

Monica

Of course I'm drawn to the cross; Jesus hanging limply, fastened to his wooden prison, body twisted in an ugly V shape, hips hanging to the left.

His head lolls down at me, staring past me.

'That night,' I whisper. 'In the garden of Gethsemane. You were waiting for something dreadful to happen. You were waiting for all your friends to betray you, one by one. And you were

266

waiting for the pain to start. Pain and betrayal. You knew there was going to be both, sometime soon, and all you could do was just . . . wait for it. Was that hard?'

Jesus doesn't answer.

'Because I'm not coping well. You can talk to me because, seriously, I do feel your pain. I do. I know how you feel. Seriously. I get it in the hands and feet too. All the time. I think about you sometimes when I get those pains. Did you get that thing with the pain? It stops you thinking, but it can't stop you thinking.'

Jesus doesn't answer.

'Could you think about the future, when you were up there? All those people who would talk about you in years to come? How your friends and your mother would cope without you? I bet you couldn't. I can't. Pain keeps you in the present tense. Past and future are too much effort, am I right?'

I'm babbling now. My voice is increasing in volume too. I know it, but I can't stop.

'I know what you were thinking up there on that cross. Exactly the same thing that crosses my mind eight times a day. Life is just one long hilarious irony after another, right? That's all we need to know. We're two of a kind. Look at me. Falls down hospital steps while trying to have a baby, and now so full of pain and drugs it's a kindness to the world I don't have one. And look at you. Born a carpenter, and you die on a huge wooden shelf. We're a right pair, aren't we?'

Monica

An old woman in black, in the process of crossing herself, shoots me a look of pure venom, but I ignore her. This is my time. I'm talking to the Son of God. I think, after the last five years, I've earned it. I let my voice climb in volume.

'Tell me, Jesus. I often wondered, well, you probably know I'm going to ask this. When you came back, you know, when you resurrected ... was the pain still there? It's just my doctor told me about this ... phenomenon. It's really fascinating. You can feel pain in a limb, and even if you lose it, you carry on feeling the pain. Does that apply to the whole body? Was it agony, even when you lost your body?'

The old woman decides it's time for an intervention. '*Silenzio, per favore. Questo è un luogo santo ...*' Then she goes 'shhh' at me.

'Are you shushing me?' I snap. 'I'm talking to him, not you. This happens to be a private conversation.'

I advance towards her and she scuttles away, tutting.

'You know nothing about that man up there,' I cry, pointing a quivering finger at Jesus. 'You might think you do, but you don't! At least I have some idea of how he felt ...' I wave my hands in the air. 'There are stigmata in here, you know! Right in here! But just because no one sees them, then it doesn't matter!'

An arm grabs me. It's Dominic. 'What are you doing?'

'Talking to Jesus. What of it?'

'Let's talk to him outside.'

He steers me, quite roughly, out of the church. *It's amazing how quickly he got used to me not being in pain,* I think. *If he did that to me two months ago, I'd have screamed the place down.*

'Take your hand off my arm. You're hurting me.'

'You were causing a scene.'

'She shushed me!'

'She had a right to. It's a holy place.'

I can see he's angry. *That's you. The big man. Willing to face up to mumbling Atos inspectors and feeble old geezers, but when it comes to God I know whose side you're on.*

I say nothing, but something, probably force of habit, makes him assume that I filled the silence with an apology. 'That's all right. No harm done.' He smiles. 'Let's go and find lunch. I want some proper pizza.'

(Of course you do)

'It's still morning,' I snap. 'It's not even lunchtime.'

'It's twelve o'clock.'

I know it's twelve o'clock. *Any minute now Geoff is going to call. Any minute now . . .*

Dominic is still talking. 'By the time we get to a pizza restaurant it will be lunchtime.'

'Dominic, I could throw a stone into the air and hit a restaurant. We're not five minutes away from one wherever we are.'

'I want to go and sit. And talk.'

'And eat.'

'What's that supposed to mean?'

'Oh, do I have to spell it out?'

'I think you should. I think you should come with me to a restaurant and spell it out.'

'I'm not ready to sit. I feel fine. I want to go back and see the Keats-Shelley House.'

'Well I don't.'

'If it hasn't got a fucking cross above the door and a dying man hanging inside you don't want to know.'

This hurts him. He looks enraged, but he calms down with a huge effort, but I feel like goading him some more. I tell myself I don't know why, but I do.

'You know what? Forget the poets. Let's go to the Colosseum. Come on, Mr God-botherer. I dare you. The Colosseum. Don't worry, it's fine for Christians now. They got rid of the lions years ago.'

'I want to go somewhere so you can calm down.'

'I'm already calm.'

'No you're not.'

'Stop watching out for me, Dominic. I'm not you, and you're not Jesus.'

And, much to my own surprise, I stride off.

I realise – with great surprise – that I don't have to walk. I don't have to wait for him to come and grab my arm, and tell me to grow up, or tell me to get a grip, like he usually does.

I start to run. It is a strangely exhilarating experience, running through the tiny streets, watching trattorias and ristorantes flash by, knowing that I can run, and run fast, and realising, given the excess weight Dominic's acquired over the last couple of years, that I can outrun my own husband.

I take left turns and right turns at random, down winding cobbled streets. I half expect to hear Dominic's wheezing behind me, and feel his hot breath on my ear as he gains on me, but there's nothing. I wonder if he even started to run after me.

When I'm satisfied I'm alone, I sit on a bench and catch my breath, giggling slightly. I'm already feeling guilty. I decide to go to the Colosseum; partly because I said the words and it was a point of principle that I should go, and partly because I hoped Dominic would try to intercept me.

It's 12.47, and Geoff still hasn't rung. I'm beginning to think the policeman was just part of my deranged imagination.

I wander around and through the Arch of Constantine, taking snaps, and soon I'm in another queue, and heading into the huge amphitheatre. Huge smudges of shadow hit me as I skip around the perimeter and through the cells and cages; light, dark, light, dark, like I'm a running figure in a Kinetoscope.

This is more like it. I think. *This is much better than a church. It's open, I can see the sky. The sense of claustrophobia is gone.*

And there's Dominic. Looking around in a desultory fashion, mooching and shading his eyes against the sun. He has forgotten his sunglasses, of course. He would be lost without me.

I decide to skirt round the amphitheatre and surprise him. If I jump out and say 'boo!' or something I can laugh off what just happened as a joke; a game; an irrational giddiness brought on by the lack of pain.

I'm halfway round and I've lost sight of him. Surely I should have met up with him by now? Is he going round clockwise too, and we're following each other?

Oh, there he is. I can see his back. His shirt is decorated with rings of sweat.

I start to stalk him, and am just about to creep up on him, when my phone goes.

Of course, I realise. *Twelve o'clock in England is one o'clock in Rome. I should have thought of that.* I retreat into the shadows and take the call.

'It's me again,' Geoff says.

'So it is.'

'So you don't remember anything about me, or how we met?'

'No,' I say, and I start to laugh. And cry. I'm not sure which is weirder. It takes me a while to stop – too long – and by the time I regain my composure, I wonder if he's disconnected the call. He hasn't.

'No. I told you. I just saw your face in a dream. Just your voice saying "Is there anything else you want to tell me?"'

'Right,' he says thoughtfully. 'Well I certainly said that to you, as I left your house. Are you sure you can't remember anything else?'

271

'No. What did you mean by that?'

'Ah . . . Now it's my turn to say "It's a long story". Are you sure you want to know about this?'

'More than anything.'

'I met you when I came to your house. I had come to your house to arrest your husband for attempting to murder you.'

Then there is a stabbing pain in the small of my back.

'Mrs Wood? Hello?'

It is deep. And angry.

(Et tu, Brutus)

My Angry Friend has returned.

Monica

Then Dominic walks through. I click the phone shut without another word.

He's not looking that hard, thank God. His head is bobbing left and right, searching for me. He's squinting, and he's not peering too intently into the shadows.

Then my phone goes again. It must be Geoff, wondering why we just got cut off. I fumble with the phone, kill it, but it's too late.

He must have heard my ringtone. But he seems not to hear, and he lumbers on through the arches, and the darkness swallows him up.

I stay there, unmoving, in the shadows. I don't know how long I stay, but I know it is longer than I should. The cold stone is sooth-ing on my back after the knife. The pain is solitary, a single blade lancing into my back, but I know that there's more to come. The phone vibrates again. This time, DI Geoff Marks doesn't even say hello. He says, 'Are you OK?' and his voice is heavy with concern.

'I just dropped the phone.'

'Right.'

I say nothing. It's up to him to talk.

'I'm sure this might be a shock for you, if, as you say, you've lost your memory.'

'How did he try to kill me?'

Geoff Marks is suddenly coy. 'Allegedly. We didn't prosecute.'

'OK. How did he allegedly try to kill me?'

'We had a tip-off that this bloke was pestering the regulars in a pub. It turned out it was your husband. One of the regulars confirmed that your husband was intending to hire him to kill you. So we went to your house and arrested him. That's when I first met you. You were lying on the floor with cold cups of tea and dirty plates around you. Your husband informed me you were in extreme pain from an accident, which tallied with what our witness said; the witness claimed that your husband told him that he couldn't take any more, and that you were too much of a burden to him.'

Burden. That word again.

'Mrs Wood . . .'

'Do go on,' I say. 'It's absolutely fascinating.'

'We took him in for questioning and he said it was a joke.'

'A joke?'

'That's right. And you confirmed that it was a joke, and that was that, really. There wasn't really a crime.'

'I see. Right.'

I don't know how a woman like me, who's experienced so much pain, can feel so numb. But I do feel numb. Tears are struggling their way onto my face.

My husband has been so loyal to me. He's stood by me, through everything.

Everything I ever knew was wrong.

'And I don't know if it's a coincidence, but your name came up last month. We got CCTV footage of two men having a fight in a car park. One of them looked like he was buying a gun. It looked a lot like your husband.'

'Oh.'

'I'm sure it might be a lot to take in. I'm sure you might not believe me, but I can show you the original incident report. Can we talk when you get back to the UK?'

'My holiday finishes in six days . . .'

'OK, I'll see you in—'

'But I'm getting the next flight out today. I'll see you tomorrow.'

Monica

The corridor to the hotel room goes on for ever, and I feel very exposed as I pad along it. My sandals make *sh-lip sh-lop* noises on the lino and they sound incredibly loud.

This is crazy.

Dominic?

My Dominic?

I must be mad. That's the only explanation. The other explanation is that I am sane, and the rest of the world has gone mad.

Once outside my door I listen intently for signs of Dominic moving about. Nothing. He's not inside. Probably still looking for me at the Colosseum, panting away as he trots round and round like an overfed hamster in a wheel.

As I cling to the wall, a memory flashes into my head:

'You got arrested trying to kill me? Why, Dominic, why?'

'Guess,' he shouts. 'Just take a wild guess!'

Was it a real memory or just imaginary? An image created by what the policeman just told me?

I am. I'm going mad. It's the only logical explanation.

Once I get in the room I dash about like a mad thing, pulling dresses out of the wardrobe, scooping underwear from the edge of the bath, and throwing them in the direction of the bed, a shower of pants, stockings and knickers forming a puddle inside the yawning mouth of my suitcase.

Soon I'm packed and ready. And then I realise that our passports are in the room safe, and Dominic set the combination. *Fucking bollocks.* Just be calm. *This shouldn't be too hard,* I think. *He can't have been trying to be too clever. Not like with the computer password.*

I try his date of birth, day and month. No luck. Then I try mine. Nothing. Finally, with a twinge of regret, I put in 2005 (the year we got married) and sigh as I hear a whirr, a clunk, and feel the door vibrate in my hand. It swings open and I grope inside, feeling the comforting shape of the passports on my fingertips. I take my passport, tuck it into my coat, and wheel my suitcase to the door. Then I have a thought. I go back and take Dominic's passport as well.

Then I'm out of the hotel and hailing a taxi. As I watch the car veer across the lanes and head towards me, I tip Dominic's passport into one of the litter bins near the main entrance; and then I force it down, down, down, as far it will go, embedding it like a fossil deep in the crust of the Earth.

That should slow down his return.

I'm lucky. The smiling lady at the check-in desk tells me there are seats available on the first flight back to London, and I'm in the air within the hour. As the great metal beast climbs into the clouds I feel two more twinges in my back; deep lances of agony. The pain of that flight to Spain floods into me.

He's coming back, I think. *My Angry Friend is waking up, and he'll be stronger, because I'm not going to take any painkillers to stop him this time. I want to know if my whole life has been a lie.*

I want to remember everything.

(**Everything**)

Dominic

Dominic mooched around the Colosseum, looking for Monica. Stupid. He felt such a fool.

He handled it so badly. Obviously God didn't want him to talk to his wife. *Perhaps that's it*, he thought. *My punishment.*

Perhaps it was a test, like challenging Moses to kill his only son. Perhaps that was it.

He should have persevered.

It was only as he went back to the hotel, and found the door resting on the lock, Monica's missing suitcase, his missing passport, and the empty safe, door yawning open like the cave of Golgotha, that he realised what the test was, and that he had already failed it.

Monica

DI Geoff Marks and I decide to meet in a place that's mutually convenient for both of us, which turns out to be a rather nice coffee shop in Kensington High Street, not far from the hospital car park. I get a sudden urge to go up there again, look out on the skyline.

Not today.

I've come straight from the airport, I've parked my little wheeled suitcase in the corner, and I'm nervously drinking a cappuccino and shredding sugar sachets into tiny strips. Fantasies flash through my mind with lightning speed; weekly coffees with Geoff, regular assignations in Kensington discussing cases. Me being his guru, my detective brilliance combining with his flat-footed copper's instinct to become an unstoppable crime duo.

It's about ten minutes before he turns up. He sits down, shaking his umbrella and unwinding a scarf from his neck, and I can't help staring at him. Despite the lack of moustache, he is literally the man of my dreams.

'Sorry I'm a bit late. Been knocking on doors all day, trying to find witnesses to a homicide, and it took me a bit off my patch.'

'That's OK.'

He smiles at me, an unthreatening grin. He gets straight to the point. 'As I said, we brought in your husband about four years ago.' He pushes a folder towards me. 'Here's the incident report. Everything.'

I flip it open and stare at the squiggles on the pages, but that's all they are. Squiggles.

'There's the witness statement in there. And three others. All the same. "Make it look like an accident," he said. "Like some robber was going to break in and get startled, and shoot my wife." He was very specific.' He paused, looking at my face, then continued, slower, trying to ration the flow of information into my ears. 'He said his wife was a cripple, and he was tired of looking after her. He said it wasn't much fun living with a cripple.'

'He said that. You're certain he said that.'

He nods.

'So what happened …' My voice comes out as a dull, fuzzy rasp, so I try again. 'So when you arrested him, he told you it was a joke?'

'That's what he said. Some kind of weird in-joke between you. Like a sex game.'

I giggle, and I keep giggling. I can't stop. My laugh takes on a life of its own. Geoff Marks looks around him, nervous, at the other customers, who are all flicking their eyes in our direction. But I still can't stop.

He offers me his paper napkin, to try and staunch the tears of hilarity pouring down my face – and hopefully staunch the bubbles of laughter coming out of my nose and mouth. But still I just can't stop.

This is what I forgot, I think. *This is what the drugs repressed. They didn't make me forget my husband was going to kill me. They made me forget that the pain had driven me insane.*

My giggles finally subside, and all that's left is an occasional honk from my nostrils.

'Sorry,' I say. 'It's the thought of Dominic playing sex games.'

'And we rang you up from the station to confirm this, and you did.' He leans forward. 'But this is all news to you.'

'The only thing I remember is you. Your sceptical face in the doorway, you saying that line …'

' "Is there anything else you want to tell me?" ' He smiles. He sips his coffee and flashes a sympathetic smile. 'So … *is* there anything else you want to tell me?'

I shake my head. 'I don't know. I have to think.'

'OK.'

'I don't remember any of this. I just remember pain, and hopelessness. Events are just a blur.'

'I see.' He looks disappointed.

'Dominic ... He could be telling the truth,' I say at last.

'Would you like to see the CCTV footage?'

I don't want to, but he's already pulling his laptop out of his bag.

The footage is silent, and black and white, and I watch a man who looks exactly like Dominic having an argument with a smaller man. The man who looks exactly like Dominic has a gun pulled on him, and fights off the smaller man. Even as I watch it, I get tense, rooting for my husband. *Come on, Dominic!* I'm thinking. *Get out of there! He's dangerous!*

'It's him, isn't it?' says Geoff. 'That's definitely your husband.'

'I don't know. I really can't be a hundred per cent sure ...' I lie. 'It's all so confusing ... If I could remember what happened before ... I promise, if anything comes back ...' I tap my head. 'Leave it with me. I've got a plan to help me remember ...'

And the plan is, I come off the drugs and plunge myself into an inferno of agony.

'... and if it works, I'll let you know.'

'OK ...'

He can feel I'm getting cold feet. *He's probably seen it with a thousand rape victims, a million battered women who've had time to sleep on it. Is this all real? they ask themselves. Am I just making trouble for the sake of it? Has there really been a crime here, and even if there has, isn't it somehow my fault anyway?*

'You have a life insurance policy, don't you?'

I'm still thinking about the CCTV footage, so it's a few seconds before I respond.

'Yes.'

'Pretty big life insurance, I must say.'

'Yes. My dad took it out for me; when he got diagnosed with cancer, he got a bit obsessed by the idea of protecting his family. So, because he was dying, and of course the insurance companies wouldn't touch him, he took out policies for the whole family instead; Mum, Jesse and me. When Mum died my sister and I got huge payouts; she was able to open up a restaurant – which went under during the crash – and I was able to set up my own agency. Which doesn't exist any more. A bit of a waste of money all round. I've been adding to the policy every year, in case . . . '

'I know. If you die, he gets almost half a million.'

I don't contradict, or pretend to resent the inference. He reaches out to hold my hand. I don't take it away.

'Just look after yourself,' he says at last. 'I'm going to make enquiries.'

'I'd rather you didn't.'

'You don't have any choice. I have enough evidence to bear out a reasonable suspicion that your husband is planning your murder.' He pats his laptop. 'When he returns from Rome I'll want to interview him to find out his whereabouts when this incident took place.'

'OK.'

'And I don't want you putting yourself in harm's way. No trying to contact him, or talk to him. Not until I've interviewed him.'

'OK.'

'Promise?'

'Promise.'

'Good,' he says, but his face shows he doesn't believe me for a second. Neither do I.

'I'd better go,' I say.

Monica

The pain is coming back.

I can feel it growing inside me, like a malignant child waiting to be born. It's been building since Rome, and the flight back to England nudged it awake.

But no painkillers; even though my body is screaming at me to put my dose back up to what it was before. Not this time.

The amitriptyline is the hardest to give up; it helps me sleep.

It's tough, but ...

I want to remember. I want to know.

I'm back, standing outside our house. The house has changed again. This time, it's not my house. It's a relic, an empty house, like the Keats-Shelley House. The photos and pictures and objects inside are exhibits of a life that's long over, that's coughed and wheezed to a grisly end in a backstreet in Rome.

No more tears. Please. Not now.

I know I don't have a lot of time, because it's not just the pain that's returning. It won't take long for Dominic to get a new passport. I need to get some more clothes. I need credit cards and my driver's licence. I need that box of morphine tablets in the kitchen drawer that Dr Kumar prescribed for me. I need to lie down.

So much pain.

I feel for the keys to the front door. They're not in my jacket, not in my trousers, and I'm about to excavate the contents of my suitcase on the front door when an image pops up in my head. I can (**see the keys on my bedside table in the hotel room**) and I left them there because my subconscious mind took the fact I was returning from my holiday with my husband as read. (**Idiot**)

Don't panic. There are keys in the shed. I put them back. I smuggled them off the kitchen worktop where Niall left them. (**Idiot**) And put them back where they belonged. They're in the barbecue. I just have to go around the back, get in the shed, and *oh, God so much left to do.*

I twist the lock to 1969 and it snaps open, and I'm standing in half darkness; the light from the gaps in the wooden walls casts glowing beams across the floor. There is a thick smell of wood varnish that suddenly makes me dizzy.

My Angry Friend is so powerful now. More powerful than he's been for years.

My vision clouds, there's roaring in my ears, and I'm scrabbling at the air for a handhold, and I know it, I bloody know it, here I go, I know damn well I'm going down

(**the**)

(**rabbit hole**)

And there's a musky smell, a prickly coarseness on my face, and something hard is pressed into my cheek. I'm finding it hard to breathe. I don't know where I am. But I can't move my body to find out.

Through a slow process of easing my face to one side, I realise I've fainted head first into one of those plastic bins Dominic bought. Once, when he was really depressed about his job, he had a manic phase of going self-sufficient; making his own manure and growing his own food. Now the plastic bins are just used to store any old rubbish.

Slowly, I lift my head to avoid the hard thing sticking into my cheek, and fumble under the potato sacks. My hand closes on something cold, heavy and metallic. The shape feels very distinctive. My fingers close around it, take it out, and I can see what it is, and I'm pointing a gun into my own face.

But at that moment I don't care about why, or how. I can barely register shock. There is just agony. I can see the light beams are now slicing me into tiny bits. I fall off the plastic bin and land into a fetal position so the beams don't hit my body.

Somehow, I get the key and get back into the house, holding the gun in the crook of my arm, like a baby. I gather some odds and ends into a bag, and then I sag and lie on the carpet, staring at the ceiling, the gun resting on my chest.

The fear and tension is letting my Angry Friend in.

Faster and faster.

I used to look at this ceiling for so long. I used to tell myself I was lucky. *Lucky!*

After all, there are people in the world who don't have ceilings at all . . .

'Hello? Meeses Moaneeka?'

It's Wednesday. I didn't hear the door go for the roaring in my ears. Agnieszka's here. And I am helpless, stranded like a beetle on its back.

'Meeses Moaneeka? You here? You back from holiday?'

I can see the table moving its legs in a slow jig, and I can see Agnieszka, holding her coat against her hip, heading for the study, looking for me. I shake my head, gasping, trying to control my breathing. *She can't see me holding a bloody gun!* I thrust the gun in the cabinet under the television, thrusting it behind the DVD box sets.

And then she's here.

'Meeses Moaneeka? You OK?'

'Yes, Agnieszka. I fine.'

'You on floor. Is not fine.'

'I'm just doing my exercises. The doctor, he say to do them.'

'Exercise. OK . . . I leave. I am here if you need . . . '

Up I get. Bit by bit. On the sofa. Then sitting on it. Then sitting on the arm, then up on my feet. Pick up the bag. I move one foot, then, the other, slowly, slooooowwwlly. Left. Right. Left. Hold onto the door. Left. Right. To the front door. The front door.

The front door.

Door.

Everything is a shimmering swirl, a dust cloud. The car is in front of me, on the drive, but it might as well be ten miles away. Left. Right. One leg into the well of the driver's side.

Slide across.

Slowly.

Grab the other leg. Pull it into the car.

The pain from the exertion is overwhelming.

Almost.

Now is not the time to go down the rabbit hole. Keep going. I snatch at the car door and try and pull it closed. It bounces off my dangling seat belt. I scramble to drag it inside, like I'm pulling in the ropes and getting ready to leave in my hot air balloon.

'Meeses Moaneeka!'

She's behind me. Wondering where the hell I could be going in my condition. I'm wondering too.

'You not well! Very sick. Please to come inside. Meeses Moaneeka!'

Moaneeka. Moan. Eeek. Ah. Three sounds of pain.

She taunts me every time she says my name. No more. I can't stand it. I buzz the window down.

'Stop saying my name like that, you bitch! Get away!'

I stupidly add: 'You're fired!'

I trundle out of the drive. In the rear-view mirror, Agnieszka looks at me in the doorway, not upset, more confused and concerned.

Monica

I watch as Angelina locks the art gallery, whistling as she pulls the shutters. Thank God she's shutting early.

I can't wait any longer. The unseasonal cold is eating into my bones, and the edges of my vision are rippling like everything is a mirage.

This is a dream. I know it is. I can't do any of this in real life.

I open my car door and say, 'Angelina.'

Angelina spins round, and in a twinkling of an eye there's a dainty can of mace in her hand, pointing right between my eyebrows. Her eyes. Wide.

'Where the fuck have you been?' I shout. 'I've been calling you for months.'

Then she lowers her arm and clutches where she thinks her heart should be in her ribcage. She's wrong. 'Jesus! Mon! What the fuck?'

'Sorry. Are you all right?'

'Holy bollocks, Mon,' she gasps. 'I think I've just done a Piero Manzoni in my knickers.'

'Can I come in?'

'Make yourself at home.'

I lock up my car and we enter the gallery. The lights are off save for spotlights illuminating the faces of the sculptures. We're being inspected by a hundred eyes.

'I'm sorry I startled you.'

'Startled me? I nearly ended up like Cedric here.' She jerks a thumb at a mangled skeleton sinking in the floor.

'Where have you been?' I ask again. 'It's been months. I've been calling. The shop's been closed . . .'

'Sorry darling, but it was a whirlwind romance. Two days after

I had my little art show, Howard came back into the shop, asked if I'd really split up with Clyde and threw himself and some Eurostar tickets at my feet.'

'Howard?'

'You remember Howard?

I shake my head.

'Oh, you'd remember Howard. He owns most of the coastline of France. He invited me over for the summer to refurbish his new villa. I decorated his interior, and he decorated mine.'

I have no time for Angelina's provocative statements. 'I waited for the customers to leave. I needed to talk to you alone.'

'Darling, if you wanted to talk to me alone, I'd kick the tasteless bastards out on the spot. You didn't need to wait on the street.' She slumps into a very expensive, very tatty chair. 'So what can I do for you?'

'I need to stay with you for a while.'

She blinks. 'What?'

'Just for a night. Two nights at the most. I just need to get my head together.'

'Is everything all right between you and Dominic?'

'Not really.'

'Oh no . . .' A long hand painted with black nail varnish snakes out and gropes at the trolley laden with spirits. 'I really hoped you weren't going to say that. What happened?'

'I discovered something. About Dominic.'

'Not crotchless panties. *Always* with the crotchless panties.'

'Angelina, be serious for once!' I snap. She stops mid-pour and looks at me, surprised.

'OK, hon,' she says levelly. 'Talk to me.'

'I worked out what is going on.'

Angelina twirls her fingers impatiently, beckoning an explanation from me.

I take a breath. 'Dominic's been trying to kill me.'

'What? Mon, he loves you! He's been standing by you for years. You're making no sense. It's the drugs. You said yourself they make you paranoid.'

'I have proof ...'

'You're joking with me.'

'I *saw* the police incident report, he showed me a copy. Dominic went into the pub and tried to have me killed. They have witnesses. He said he wanted to kill me. I was a burden.'

'Mon, be serious. Your mind is ...'

'My mind is what, Lena? Are you going to say I'm mad?'

The next thing I know, I'm waking up, and Angelina is standing over me, concerned. I can see the tiny fuzz of hair on her top lip, the hairs coated with make-up.

'Are you all right, darling?'

I shake my head very slowly, and struggle to stand. 'I'm ... not good, Lena.'

The room goes dark and I'm suddenly in her arms, halfway to the floor.

'Jesus, Mon. What just happened? You keeled over like a felled tree!'

'It's a long story, but I stopped taking my drugs.'

'What? No wonder you look like shit! Why the hell did you do that?'

She doesn't wait for an answer. She half carries me out of the shop and folds me into the car, and I can feel the car moving as it drives to her home. I can hear myself moan on every step up to her flat above the studio. I can hear the clatter of her platform shoes as she races into the kitchen to find the drugs she was given by Dominic.

My husband. My loving husband who did that wonderful, little thing for me. Who stood by me in those dark, dark times. Who researched all the treatments, all the drugs ...

288

I know life has been difficult . . . But murder . . . ?

She's back and some tiny pills are pressed into my hand. 'Are these the right ones?'

I push them away, with difficulty. 'I don't want them.'

'What? Darling . . .'

'No pills. Not yet.'

'What the hell are you doing? You told me . . .'

'It's not as bad as it seems. Not quite. I had that treatment.'

'The one Dominic didn't want you to have?'

'Yes.'

She gasps, realising. 'And it worked? The pain's gone.'

'Sort of. The pain did go but now it's coming back. It's coming back fast. God . . . It's coming back very fast . . .'

She picks up the packet and kneels before me. 'Then take the bloody pills, darling!'

'Not yet.'

'Jesus, Mon! *Why?*'

'Because I'm not finished remembering. I reduced the dosage, and then I started to remember things . . . Listen, just . . . listen.' I breathe deeply. I have to focus. Focus on beating back my Angry Friend. *I need to concentrate.*

'Dominic got arrested by this policeman, and when they took him to the station, he told them to ring me and confirm that it was a sex game we play with each other . . .'

Lena cocks an eyebrow.

'I confirmed that Dominic was telling the truth.'

'Well then. Panic over. What's the problem?'

Christ. My Angry Friend is sitting on my body, pressing me down. I'm drowning.

'But I don't remember. Do you remember us playing a game like that?'

Angelina flaps her arms and twists her lips. She looks quite comical. 'Well ... How would I know? What you guys did inside your marriage is no concern of mine ...'

'It doesn't sound right. It doesn't sound like me.'

'You said yourself: you don't know what sounds like you sometimes. You don't know what you were like. You've asked me if you'd had an affair, for God's sake. And Dominic trying to kill you? Dominic? Does that sound right?'

'I found a gun.'

'A gun? A what? A gun? Where?'

'In the house. In the shed.'

'Show me.'

'I left it ... Stupid ... I wasn't thinking straight ...'

'Well, if it was in the shed ... It was probably there to shoot rats or mice or something. Lots of gamekeepers have guns. My auntie Victoria's man had a massive great—'

'Angelina ... you're being very sweet defending him ... but I'm not going back home ... Not until this is sorted out. Not until I completely remember what happened ... If you don't believe me, then I'm sorry. I'll just find someone who does. I'll go to my sister's in Surrey.'

Angelina stalks back and forth, over to the window, then back again. She throws herself into her chair. 'Fine.' She gets up again and stands, legs apart, her face a jumbled mix of concern and fury. 'Fine, darling, if that's the way you want it ...'

She disappears into her bedroom. Noises float from behind the door; scuffling, cupboard doors banging. I hear a zipping noise. I wonder what she's doing and the tension building in my body makes the room spin.

Five minutes later, Angelina comes in and drops her suitcase in front of me. 'There. I'm packed. If you want to do this, then let's do this.'

I look at her, dumbfounded.

'Darling! You're not thinking straight . . .'

'That much is true.'

'You don't think when Dominic finds you missing, that my place is the *first* place he'll look? And you don't think your sister's will be the *second* place? We'll spend the night here, and we'll go to a hotel in the morning, yeah? I know a scrummy little one in Knightsbridge which is very discreet.'

She's putting on a big strong macho front, but tears are making her eyes glisten. She jabs a varnished finger in my direction. 'But the moment that bloody stubborn little brain of yours unlocks the truth, then you're knocking back those bloody pills like a rock star at the end of a forty-date tour. I will personally provide the funnel.'

And then she falls to her knees again, and hugs me, very delicately, encircling my body so very very gently with her long arms.

Her bracelets brush against my arm, and the world wobbles again, but I keep it together.

'I don't want you to go.'

And we both cry, for me, for both of us. For a lost past, and a lost future.

Monica

I can't sleep, of course.

The bed is comfy, but my Angry Friend is all conquering. Without the drugs to sedate him, he's roaming around my body with a bicycle chain and a can of paraffin.

The sounds of traffic are louder here. There's also a party going on – not near – but I can hear it very faintly. I can hear the fuzzy echoes of 'Crocodile Rock', and 'Rebel Rebel' and 'Waterloo' – I'm guessing a middle-aged birthday party.

I've forgotten all of the lyrics, and I'm driving myself crazy, trying to remember what Suzie and Elton got up to.

I pull my eyes over to the clock. Eleven thirty. I've been staring into the blackness of the room and the darkness under my eyelids for an hour. Perhaps I should get up and get a milky drink.

There's soft footfall outside my door. That clinches it. Angelina's up, and I'm in the mood for a late-night chat. It will take my mind off the rats gnawing at my arms and legs.

I open the door and look around; the kitchen light isn't on. Her bedside light *is* on, but there's no one there. The bed is gaping and empty.

I breathe deeply. The chemical smells from her unfinished paintings downstairs are very strong here. Perhaps Lena needs them to go to sleep. They are very relaxing.

Without the drugs, my mind is starting to make connections. More and more connections. I suddenly realise why the chemical smell is so familiar.

It's the same smell as my suicide note.

The oils. Painter's oils.

What?

How is that possib—

A noise.

A woman's voice downstairs.

I grip the guardrail and look down the stairwell, and there's Angelina sitting on the bottom step, huddled against the banister. I can see two Chinese dragons on her kimono, snarling, claws out, fighting for space along her narrow back.

I almost call out, but something stops me.

'It's me. She's here.'

I freeze.

'She's OK,' Angelina whispers into her phone. 'But she's starting to remember things. She's already gone to the police.'

She pauses, and then: 'She's fine. I don't know ... She's just ... fine. Yes ... No, not everything ... She's talked to the policeman. Yes, that one ... I don't know ... Well you tell me!'

She rests her head against the wall and sighs, a long sigh, listening to the jabbering from the other end of the phone. 'OK ... Just ... listen to me ... No, stop ... I'm not covering for you ... This is what you are going to do, Dominic ... You've just got to get here now. Whatever happens ... Yes! You've got to ...'

I try to lift my hands but they seem to be welded to the guardrail. I lift up one finger at a time until they're free, and then bunch them into fists. I hold them down by my side, trying to keep my arms rigid, but they are shaking so much I'm punching my own thighs.

I hold them out in front of me, and they are a blur in front of my eyes.

I have to pack, and I have to pack quickly and quietly.

I'm back in 'my' bedroom, rooting through the cupboards.

I empty my bag of everything I don't need, and fill it full of everything I do. Clothes. Toothbrush. The mouth guard that my 'friend' has thoughtfully had made for me.

Slippered footsteps pass outside my door. I shove the bag under the bed and quietly slip underneath the covers, close my eyes and wait for the door to open, for someone to come.

I watch the handle turn. It moves slowly, down, down ... And then it rises again. She's changed her mind, and the light under the door flickers as the slippers move away.

Time to *Jesus I hurt* go.

I daren't switch the light on, so I grope for my clothes in the darkness, feeling for knickers and jeans, shirt and jacket. *I can't find my scarf* (**leave the scarf**) *I need the scarf* (**forget the bloody scarf**) *I can buy one when I get on the road to* . . . Where?

Down the narrow stairs. They're fashionably minimalist; narrow polished wood, no stair carpet, so I half walk, half slide, careful not to overbalance. The bag is too heavy.

Far too heavy.

I unlatch the door and the world collapses in on me. My head explodes, and I yell in shock, but I can't hear myself.

(**You stupid woman. Of course there will be an alarm. Of course there will**)

It is a hellish sound, a computerised *whup-whup-whup* that's designed to make burglars pray for the good old days of jangling klaxons. It wakes my pain as it would a sleeping child, and my Angry Friend screams out at the top of his lungs.

He screams in triumph.

The street is empty, but that won't be for long. Already squares of light are appearing in upstairs windows. I have to go. I scrabble at the latch and run out, staggering under the weight of the bag and my pain.

Do I have time to get to my car? Let's try, I need it. I can't do public transport like this.

I'm running, but I can't.

I think the bag is snagged on something. I look back and Angelina is holding the strap.

'Mon, wait!'

'Get away from me!'

'You can't leave!'

'Oh I know that! You rang my husband, you bitch traitor!'

'Please!'

'You wrote my note! My suicide note! You want to kill me!'

'It's not like that! You need to listen!'

'I don't need to do anything, let *go* of me! Get off me!'

There's a tug of war over the bag, and I'm in no condition to fight with her, not in ideal conditions, but Angelina is wearing a tiny kimono, and one of her hands is clutching the hem, trying to keep herself decent in front of the people peeping out of their front doors.

I give the bag strap a yank. I succeed in making her stagger over the kerb, losing a slipper in the process. I also succeed in pulling the bag free, and it sails over my head, landing untidily in the road and spilling my bits and pieces out of its guts.

I'm almost on my knees now, but I somehow manage to crawl to the bag and pick it up. I grab at it, but my spatial awareness is shot to ribbons, and I'm snatching at empty air. I'm a blind woman, groping forward until my fingers connect with the strap.

The bag is so heavy. So very heavy. My fingers feel like they're being broken, but *my God oh my God oh my God* I manage to scoop up the bag, but there's no time to stuff everything back; my car keys are left lying in the gutter.

Cars are coming, transfixing me with their headlights, and I can see out of the corner of my eye that Angelina is recovering her slipper and pulling out her phone.

'Monica! Mon! Please! You need to understand!' she is shouting as she dials. Then her words become noises as I put distance between us. I don't have any time left, no chance to run back for the car, so I'm forced to blunder away, into the night. I just hope there's enough pills left inside the bag to keep me going.

Where am I going?

I don't know.

I need to go to my sister's. I need to go to Surrey. If I tell her what's happened she can hide me, tell all callers that she's not seen me. She won't let me down. I can stay there, and remember. Maybe call the police.

A cab comes right past me. I wave at it, and tell the driver to take me to Waterloo.

'Are you OK, darlin'?'

The cab has poor suspension, and as it roars into central London I'm tossed around inside.

I manage to brace my left leg against the door, and I have a tight hold on the roof straps, but I can't help it; a groan escapes my lips every time it discovers another pothole.

'You all right, gel?'

'I'm fine,' I say, and I whimper as the cab lurches again.

'You're pissed, aren't you?' says the cabbie.

'I'm not, I'm really not,' I mumble. 'I've just got a condition.'

'Bollocks. That's what they all say. You look like shit, darling. Sorry about this, but I got a rule. No one pukes in my cab.'

The cab thunders to a halt and he leaps out, opening my door.

'Out you come.'

'Where am I?' I groan.

'Nearly at Waterloo,' he grunts, not unkindly. 'Don't worry about the fare, darling, have this one on me.'

He places my bag at my feet, and before I realise it I'm staring at the taxi's retreating rear. I can barely focus, everywhere there are lights and noise, a collage of neon, and shouting and car engines. I'm plunging, falling into the darkest of holes. My body a black smear of pain, I look around the streets and I don't know where I am. Then I realise. I didn't know *who* I am. Or even why I have come here.

I sink slowly to the ground and throw my arms over my head. The clatter of boots and shoes continues around me. No one stops. I'm just a beggar, or a drunk. I'm not their problem.

Focus. I need to focus. I think I remember something; a flash of my plimsolls as they pointed at the direction of an old-fashioned television. *When I was little.* When I was little, I think I stayed up late, and I saw a film about a man who just kept getting smaller and smaller. Eventually he got so small that he could barely get across the house without being attacked by spiders the size of elephants, climbing chairs like mountains. I was getting smaller too, the pavements stretching on for miles, the buildings hanging over me like sheer mountains. I glimpse up, and all I can see are the nostrils of people as they pass by over my head.

The lights and noises are searing my senses. There's too much to cope with here. I cower against the world and stagger into an alleyway, and practically fall down the steps until I hear the sounds of the river.

Amidst the myriad screams of my body, yelling at my brain, demanding my attention, I can hear a tiny voice say: *The river. That's the Thames. I think he dropped me at the Strand, and now I'm near the Embankment.*

If I can just get to Charing Cross station, get across the river, then I'll be at Waterloo. Then I can get a train to . . .

Who? Jerry? Jenny? Who do I need to get to?

I press myself against a wall and drop my bag by a drain. The whole world is rippling, shimmering like a mirage. The buildings are dancing, and the world is contorting with agony. I need to get somewhere, or I need to die. It doesn't matter which; whichever comes first.

And there he is, in front of me.

My Angry Friend.

He has come to face me, at last.

There he is, as I imagined him. Black jeans, black leather jacket. Unshaven.

'Please,' I cry. Every word I have to push out of my throat. 'Help me.'

297

'Sorry, love. Busy.'

'Please. I don't know who I am.'

He walks up to me, looks long and hard.

'What's up with you? Are you pissed?'

'Help ...'

He looks down at my trousers. 'You've wet yourself, you filthy bitch.'

Then he looks around. He pulls a knife and holds it to my face.

'Scream and you're dead.'

All I have to do is scream, and he will kill me. It seems like the perfect plan, with no drawbacks. I try to say 'It's a deal', but there's nothing left inside me, just a moan. He realises I can't do anything, just press myself against the wall and hope it might devour me.

'Don't worry, love, this won't hurt a bit.'

He starts groping inside my pockets, extracting my wallet. He flips through it with professional aplomb and pulls out my debit cards.

'There's a cashpoint up on the Strand. We're going to go up there, like a nice happy couple, to make a little withdrawal, and then ...' He thinks about it. 'Then I'll think of something else.'

The fear and the tension sends the pain spiralling into the stratosphere, and my eyeballs roll upwards in my sockets, looking to heaven, leaving my consciousness behind.

I can't remember my address, my sister's name, or why I'm here. I don't think I can remember my cashpoint number. *He's going to kill me.*

But Monica, says that tiny voice. *There's a drawback.*

I'm startled. I thought the voice was my Angry Friend, but it's not. It's me. Another voice. Another me. The voice knows the man will kill me when he's finished, because I have seen his face.

(**You can't die here**). I should not die like a broken doll, not here on the rain-soaked steps of the Embankment; (**you have things to do**) you shouldn't die here, not now. *But what do I have to do? Why can't I die here?*

(**OK**) says the voice. (**If you insist, I'll tell you**)

The body is not mine. Endorphins flood my body, and for a brief moment, just a very brief moment, the pain subsides and I can think of something else.

I wish I had that gun. Why did I leave it behind? Stupid. But no good to me anyway. Probably wouldn't have had the strength to squeeze the trigger. (**But you could have used it to threaten him. Think about that when you're bleeding to death in the shadows**)

(**Stupid stupid stupid**)

While he frisks me, my arms fall around his waist, like we're two lovers canoodling in an alleyway . . .

. . . and I can feel his knife. It's in his back pocket. I grab the handle and slide it out; not smoothly enough, because he feels the movement and grabs both my wrists, wrenching them to my chest, crushing them hard.

'Now that's mine, love, you can't have that. Give it back, now, or Daddy will have to take it from you.'

He thinks he's hurting me. He thinks I'm a helpless, insensible, dead-eyed doll.

The fear. The endorphins. Everything kicks in.

I remember.

I can remember!

The memories hit me like punches, one knocking me one way, then the other. Shock after shock. I remember what Dominic did, why there's a gun in my house, what he said after he got arrested by the police, and I am suddenly consumed with rage at what he did.

(**How dare he**)

(**Damn you, Dominic. Damn you**)

I focus everything I have, all the pain, all the frustration. I focus on the pity from my ex-friends, the misjudged comments from acquaintances, the ignorance of my sister, the disapproving looks from the OAPS, the smiling idiocy from Atos, and most of all, the terrible betrayal from Dominic and Angelina, and this final stupid humiliation from this black-booted scumbag, and my fury becomes white hot.

(**Enough**)

(**No more**)

I lash out with my knee. I catch him neatly in his balls, and he howls, and he falls, dragging me down with him. He smacks his head against the huge dustbins, practically knocking himself cold.

I grind my foot deep into his crotch. His hands flail impotently at me. (**You can't free yourself, because you can't think, because you can't think about anything but the pain. That's the tiny one per cent of the pain I feel. Now you can have some more**)

I grip his knife firmly, with both hands, and drive it deep into his leg, severing his femoral artery. He is thrashing, jerking, screaming, and I enjoy his pain.

There is a huge dark stain spreading across his crotch as he gushes like an oil well.

(**You've wet yourself, you filthy bitch**)

He rolls me off him and staggers away to the river, flailing, looking for help, screaming for assistance.

(**I should leave**)

And as I stand there, clutching his knife to my chest like a baby, I realise the terrible truth. Everything makes sense.

The suicide letter. The gun.

All of it.

I struggle, and I slide, like a fawn learning to walk, trying to stand up for the first time, but I manage it, and then I am picking up my bag, feeling the weight of it, and I am looking at the river, the direction where my Angry Friend ran away to lick his wounds.

(**Thank you**) I say. (**I've been waiting to do that to you for so long.**)

Hello?
Is there anybody in there?

ROGER WATERS/DAVID GILMOUR

Monica

I wake up ...

Monica

This is the first day of the rest of my life, and I'm leaning on a squishy chair in the corner of Angelina's gallery.

The door of Art of Darkness bleeped when I came in, so it's only a matter of time before Angelina comes out to see who's here.

I ease myself into the chair, slowly, slowly. Morphine is coursing through my veins. The pain is still very very present (**God it's present**) but I'm rationing myself to the absolute minimum. Just enough to stay conscious and move about. Nothing more. It's difficult.

Angelina comes out of the back room, sees me, and staggers backwards, like I've just lunged out and slapped her. I can tell she's looking into my eyes, and she recognises who I am. Monica. The old Monica. Before the pain came.

She falls to her knees; not easy in the pencil skirt that hugs her legs.

'Mon?'

I speak. My voice isn't different, but there's a different emphasis, a different colour to the words. It feels strange in my throat. 'Hello, Angelina.'

'Mon . . . I . . .'

Angelina also sounds strange. I have heard her drunk, angry, stupid, disparaging . . .

But never afraid.

'I've had a bit of a journey since I last saw you. I know, Angelina. I know everything. I can *remember* everything . . . '

A tear trickles down her face. 'I'm sorry. I'm so sorry.'

'You wrote my note. My suicide note.'

'Yes.'

'Good,' I say with some relief. 'That's what I remember. I'm glad that's true. I was worried my brain was telling me a load of nonsense. It does that a lot. So, still cosy with my husband?'

She doesn't answer.

'I thought you were my friend. You let me down.'

'Please . . . '

'Didn't you? You let me down, and stabbed me in the back.'

'Mon . . . ' A tear rolls down her cheek. 'I don't want to go to prison.'

'You won't go to prison.'

'Mon . . . '

'I promise.'

'Mon . . . '

'I promise you're not going to go to prison. Do you believe me?'

She wipes her noise with the back of her hand. She looks about twelve years old. 'Yes.'

'Then do as I say. Stay out of my way. Don't talk to Dominic. I'm going away. There's a man I met.'

'A man? Who?'

'I'm too tired and in pain to go into detail. This will explain everything.'

There is a note tucked into my sleeve. It's a scrawled mess, but it's legible. It's all I could manage. I pull it out and hand it to her. Angelina reads it, and horror bleeds into her face.

'You can't leave us.'

'I can.'

'Give me one good reason why I should help you.'

'Because you're my friend.'

'That's fighting dirty.' She is crying very hard now. 'What about Dominic?'

'He will understand. You will make him understand, do you hear me? Because I want you to write me another letter. For him. The instructions are all in there. Did you pick up my car keys? I notice my car's not outside.'

She is thrown by my change of subject. 'Your car? It … It's round the corner. I put it in a disabled bay, and put your blue badge up, so it wouldn't get towed. Um … I put the keys here … Somewhere …'

She struggles to her feet. I struggle up too, out of the chair. She scrabbles in a drawer, hands me my keys. Then I hug her tight. She is still crying.

But I do not cry.

Monica

Now I'm sitting in a café with my phone in front of me. I am supposed to be making a call, but the morphine makes everything hard to do. It's a completely different type of 'hard' to do; not like with my normal painkillers.

The mind is fuzzy, distracted, unable to think about one thing at a time. My head feels like a balloon on a string, hovering above my shoulders.

I have to focus.

This is the second thing I have to do. I make a call. DI Geoff Marks is delighted to hear from me.

'You sound different,' he says.

'Yes, I do,' I say. I don't add anything.

Silence.

'I just called to tell you that you were right,' I say. 'Dominic has been trying to kill me for years.'

'Right.' He exhales. 'Thank God you came to your senses. What made you realise?'

'A lot of things. Have you talked to my husband?'

'Not yet. As far as we can ascertain, he got back from Rome but never returned home. We're looking for him.'

'I'm going to solve this my way.'

He's confused. 'I'm not following you, Monica.'

'Then don't. Follow me, I mean. I'm going.'

'Where?'

'Don't try and find me. I've got a friend who can help me. I don't know him that well, but I trust him. He's going to help me get away.'

'Monica, this is stupid. You have to make a statement.'

'I don't have to do anything.'

'Listen to me.'

'No. YOU listen to ME, Geoff. My husband might try to stop me leaving . . .'

'He'll probably do more than that. It would be far simpler if you just make a statement.'

'That's not my way, OK? Just forget about bloody statements. I'm not making one.'

Pain. Breathe. Control. I continue. 'You must stop my husband coming after me. Put him in a cell.'

'That's what I'm planning to do.'

309

'Good. Thank you, Geoff. Thank you for everything.'

I ring off before he can say anything else.

Monica

I'm walking up the path of a small flat, tucked on the ground floor of a semi-detached house.

The morphine is making my mind dance. When I look up at the darkening sky, I see limitless possibilities in the shapes of clouds, when I look down I see death. Cracked leaves from a dead bamboo plant are scattered underfoot. There is a carpet of corpses for me to tread on. I feel certain the old me would be weeping, by now.

I have to focus.

I try not to think about the old me, who was quite weak and rather self-pitying. Who took my condition as permission for inaction.

This is the new Monica who is also the old Monica, the one who, to coin Angelina's cliché, doesn't suffer fools gladly.

I have to focus now.

I negotiate my way over the mountains of tiny brown corpses, ring the bell, and watch through the opaque window. Soon I can see a shape, which gets large and darker as it moves towards me. I'm reminded of the black cloud of (**something**) in my dream, surging towards me, thrusting me over the edge of the car park to let me float into oblivion.

A lock rattles, the door opens.

'Monica?'

Niall is in his dressing gown. He looks a little more frayed at the edges since the last time I saw him. His tidy beard has crept up his cheeks. From his tousled damp hair I'm guessing it's not long since he's been in the shower.

'Hello, Niall.'

He allows his door, his mouth and his dressing gown to gape open. My presence on his doorstep does not quite compute. His eyes start to glisten. 'Oh my God! I'm so glad to see you … I hadn't heard anything from you for ages! You got my texts?'

I sigh. 'Yes, Niall, I got your texts.'

'I was so worried something had happened to you.'

'Nothing happened to me. I just didn't reply to them.'

'Yes. Sorry. Yes, we did talk about that. I remember. Sorry. Sorry. Of course. You did say—'

I get a feeling if I don't take the initiative, I'll be standing in the doorway until the morning. 'Can I come in?'

'Well, yes, sure, certainly.'

He opens the door wider. I can see wellingtons and shiny dumb-bells in the hall.

'Sorry about the mess. I wasn't expecting … well, come in. Do you want a coffee?'

'Decaff if you have it.'

'I have it. I actually have that special blend you like. The French roast. I got it in case you … '

He leaves the sentence hanging, shakes his head, smiles, and hefts piles of papers off the high-backed chair. He gestures me to sit down.

'Thanks.'

As I sit, he bends down and tries to ignite the gas fire, pressing the big button with a repetitive clunk. The gas fire ignites, spouting blue flames up into the alcove.

'That OK? Warm enough for you?'

'That's fine.'

He is naked under his dressing gown, as he flaps away to make the coffee I can see his thick brown thighs. I listen to the sound, the blub-blubblub of the kettle, the clatter of mugs and spoons. A few minutes later he emerges with a tray.

'So what's going on? Why are you here?'

'I need your help.'

'I thought you didn't want to see me again.'

'That was just a silly disagreement. Things have moved on.'

'OK.'

'I'm a different person now.'

'Different? How?' Then he remembers. 'The capsaicin patch? The ... treatment? How did it go? What happened? Did it work?'

'It worked better than anyone imagined. I felt much better.'

'Fantas—'

'I'm *completely* without pain.'

'What?'

'I am without pain. The capsaicin worked better than anyone imagined.'

'But ... Wasn't it supposed to just be temporary?'

'That's what they all said. Apparently I'm a walking miracle.'

'So you feel ... '

'I feel nothing,' I reply. And on this point I'm telling the truth.

'Nothing? Really?'

'Yes. Really.'

'I can barely believe it. This is amazing.'

'A miracle.'

'Exactly. That's what it is. A miracle.' He shakes his head. 'Please ... Walk across the room for me.'

'What?'

'Like when we first met.'

'I remember.'

'Show me you're better.'

I'm ready for this. I've had a week of long, deep-tissue massages, in a spa in the hotel I've been staying at. The last one was yesterday. So I stand up. And I walk.

I'm Superman. I'm Wonder Woman. I'm Batgirl. I'm all of them, and more besides.

The main problem, as I move, is I'm being distracted by the cobwebs behind the light fitting and the dust on the bookcase. I wonder fleetingly if the spiders come out at night and write their names in the dust. I walk there, to the bookcase, and back to Niall.

'There you go.'

'Well,' he says, eyes wide. 'That's amazing. You look a little stiff, but you're walking much better now.'

(**He sees what he wants to see**)

I have anticipated his next question too.

'Have you told Dominic?' he asks.

'No. I was going to tell him, but I decided I couldn't trust him.'

'What? You couldn't trust him?'

I reach out and hold the plunger of the cafetière. I push it down, hard and strong, like I'm detonating a mountain of dynamite.

'I discovered that my husband and my best friend were having an affair.'

Niall shakes his head. 'What?' he says again, unnecessarily. 'Your best friend?'

'The details don't matter.'

'That one you told me runs an art gallery? Was she and him . . . ? All the time?'

'Niall . . . What did I just say?'

'You just said your husband and your best friend were having—'

'No, I just said, and you can watch my lips this time, if you like. The – details – don't – matter. I'm not here to tell you my life

313

story. I'm just here to tell you that I'm leaving Dominic and I'm planning my future. A future without pain.'

I can see he is finally waking up. I can almost see the fantasy flickering inside his skull, like an old movie shining from a projector. *She's come here to me. We're going to be together, and live in my little flat and I will protect her . . .*

'I think I'd better get some clothes on,' he says at last.

'I think you'd better.'

He rushes to change, and this allows me to lie on the sofa for a few precious minutes. I'm thinking about all manner of crazy things, and I need to herd my thoughts together for the journey ahead.

I hear the *thud thud thud* of his feet as he returns, peel my head off the cushion and regain my position on the high-backed chair. Niall has thrown on some sweatpants and a T-shirt. He curls back on the sofa, opposite me, hugging his ankles and putting his chin on his knees. It's like we're having a sleepover.

'But the way you talk – you talked – about your husband . . . He loves you . . . '

(**The wolf wants to make sure**)

'That's not the person you described . . . He sounded devoted to you.'

(**He's testing the story**)

'He's a very good liar. But it doesn't matter. I don't want to talk about it. Let's focus on the future. Can you turn the fire down a little? It's a bit too much for me.'

'Of course.'

Niall gets up, his slippers flapping on the parquet flooring, and twists the knob. 'So what's the future?'

'I can't go home, can I?'

'No.'

'I'm leaving the country. Perhaps for ever.'

Monica

'You can't be serious.'

'I can't be more serious. My head is clearer than it's been for years.'

'It just seems a bit ... extreme. Look, you can stay here for a while, there's plenty of room. I could sleep on the sofa ...'

He throws his arm up to indicate the grubby flat. I shake my head.

'Sorry, Niall, this is not for me.' I lean over and touch his knee. 'You're right about what you said. What you said when you took me home. I didn't want to believe you, for Dominic's sake, but you were right. I remember now. I used to have a real fire in me. I didn't suffer fools gladly, I don't settle for second best, and ... I don't hide in damp corners like this.'

Niall looks quite crestfallen.

'I need you to drive me to Dover, so I can get a ferry to France.'

'France? Why France?'

'I have friends out there. A client of mine retired and went to live in the south of France. She owes me a lot, and I'm sure she'll put me up for ... however long it takes.'

'Until when?'

'Until I build my new life. I'm still pretty weak. There's been years of dealing with pain and that's had long-term effects on me. I still don't know the limits of my body. I need someone to drive my car. Are you going to help me or not?'

Niall rubs his stubbled cheek. The sound is terrifyingly loud in my ears. 'Give me twenty minutes to get ready.'

'Make it ten.'

'Yes, ma'am,' he grins, and leaps up, and I see the little boy inside the man.

I sit there, and I listen to him moving around, dragging out a large suitcase, opening and closing drawers. I hear his *thud thud thud* in the corridor and he explodes into the room, like a boy off to his first Scout camp.

'I'm ready.'

We get out and walk to my car. It was dusk when I arrived, now the streetlights are glowing.

He opens the passenger door for me, and I try not to whimper as I climb in. He slams the car door with too much force. He doesn't seem to notice; he's staring straight ahead, his fingers tapping on the roof of the car.

At last, he clears his throat. 'I know this isn't a good time to say this, but I'm glad you came to me.'

'I'm glad you agreed to help.'

He smiles and hauls his bags into the car.

'You're bringing a lot with you,' I say.

'Well . . .' He grins awkwardly. 'I don't know when I'll be coming back.'

He looks up and he holds my gaze. He doesn't have to say anything. The street lamp bathes his face in an intense, yellow glow. It makes him look even more determined.

'Thanks,' I say.

He gets in the driving side and, deep down, I sag with the effort of what I'm doing. I'm already tired, and I've only just started this journey. The car trundles away and I allow myself to slump against the door, my cheek against the window.

The streetlights are stretched in the reflection of the passenger-side window, and they glide across the glass like spaceships, like moonbeams flying in formation, heading for a safe place away from something terrible.

I just have to stay focused.

After we get on the main road I say, 'I'm glad too.'

'What about?'

'That you're here with me.'

This is the absolute truth.

His shoulders relax and he reaches out to touch me. He keeps his eyes on the road, so his fingers scuttle clumsily across the side of my face, on my neck, across my nose. He nearly lodges a pinkie in my nostril, but he manages to locate my cheek and cup it in his hand, tenderly, lovingly.

'Stop.'

His hand withdraws. 'Sorry.'

'Sorry. I didn't mean stop doing what you were doing. What you were doing was very comforting. I mean, stop the car before we hit the motorway.'

'OK.'

'I need to go home first.'

'What?'

'I can't go anywhere yet. I need to leave this letter for Dominic.'

'No way. We can't go back to your house. That's mad.'

'Don't call me mad, Niall. This is important. It's important to say goodbye to the past, and it's important to explain why I'm saying goodbye.'

'But he's made sure he's the past, Monica. So let go of him now. What's to explain? He had an affair, you're leaving him. Goodbye.'

I sigh. 'You just don't understand.'

That's the phrase that I know clinches it. *You just don't understand*. It puts him on the outside of my life. Just like the talk about having a baby, it's his lack of empathy that shows him up. But he's a clever boy. *He's learning.*

He taps the wheel with the tips of his fingers.

'No,' he says at last. 'You're right. I'm being insensitive. We'll park outside, and you can bung your letter through the letter box. How's that sound?'

Monica

My house is almost in darkness when we pull up outside; just a dim glow from one room.

'He must be out,' I say.

'He's at home. The lights are on.'

'The *kitchen* light is on,' I say, with all the patience I can muster. 'We always leave the kitchen light on when we go out.'

I push against the car door. *Jesus! It's heavy.*

He watches as I go up to the door with the envelope. He's waiting for me to pop the letter through the mouth of the door. I can picture his jaw falling open as I push the keys into the lock, twist, and go in.

Monica

I'm standing in the kitchen. The tension in my body rises and pain fights for control of my body. Breathe. Relax. Breathe. Relax.

(**It's all under control**)

I leave the envelope carefully on the table. Right in the middle. Then I head towards the living room, and the gun hidden behind on the low shelf. I'm praying that Agnieszka hasn't dusted behind it. *But then she's never done it before.* I'm praying that Dominic hasn't come back home and had a sudden craving for watching a series of *The West Wing.*

In the darkness of the living room I lie flat on the floor, lying on the prickly rug, and stretch my arm out. My fingers tickle the edge of something hard and cold that doesn't feel like a DVD box set. I have it in my hand but I can't get up. The blackness around me is shimmering. I need to get up, but I can't. I need to get up. *The gun is so heavy.*

I crawl up the wall, and hang on the wall light.

'What the hell do you think you're doing?' hisses a voice in my ear, and I nearly scream, because I think the voice belongs to Dominic. It sounds like Dominic. But it's just Niall.

I still have the gun in my hand. I pretend the gun is part of the wall light, which sounds ridiculous, but it's very dark and he's not looking at my hand. He's glaring straight into my face. All I can see is the silhouette of bristles on his cheeks, oscillating as he works his jaw.

'You said you'd just deliver the letter. You didn't say you'd come in the fucking house!'

'I'd forgotten something,' I breathe, slow and steady.

'You'd forgotten something?'

I have to keep control. 'It's all right. Dominic's not here.'

In the darkness, I can see the shape of Niall's head shaking. 'We didn't deactivate the alarm. It's not beeping. If he's not here why isn't it on?'

I am thinking that myself.

I'm thinking: perhaps my tame policeman hasn't caught up with Dominic yet.

But I just say: 'We don't always switch it on.'

'Have you found what you're looking for?'

'Yes.'

'Thank God,' he says, not bothering to ask what it was. He's too angry. 'Come on. We're done here. We're going now.'

And he leaves, expecting me to follow him, and I try, but I'm trying to hide the gun, and when I put it behind my back and try to tuck it into my knickers it unbalances me, and I collide with the frame of the kitchen door, jarring my whole body. I stagger, as I go into convulsions, and I sob as a fist closes over my body and

(**squeezes**)

very hard.

Instinctively, I sink down. As my knees hit the floor I already know I've made a mistake; the impact shudders through my body and I stifle a scream in my throat.

I can't get up. The floor is rippling under my knees and I claw at it, clinging on to the tiles, pulling at the kitchen table leg like I'm hauling myself up a mountain.

I clamber under the table and crawl into a fetal position, hugging the gun, praying for the waves of agony to subside.

The pain is what saves me.

I can see feet running *towards* the back door, but they are not Niall's feet. These have slippers on, slippers with smiling tiger faces. The tigers stop at the table, and I can hear someone above me, opening the envelope, reading the letter, and a stifled sob.

The tiger slippers move behind the stairwell, peering out from behind the umbrella stand, waiting to pounce on their unsuspecting prey.

I can't speak. I have no voice as my mouth is a maw, a hole sprouting from something that is not a face, but a ruin of molten wax.

Niall's realised I haven't followed him. His trainers walk slowly into the kitchen, slowly around the table, and I think I should tug at his trousers, to warn him, but it's too late.

The tigers attack.

The table shudders as Niall is shoved against it. A high-pitched 'fuck' escapes his lips.

'WHERE IS SHE?'

Dominic's voice.

'I'm not ... She ... she's not here.'

'You stupid—! WHERE IS SHE!!'

The table shudders again.

'Get off me.'

'Oh you silly, stupid little ...'

And then the tigers rock back on their paws. Niall has struck back, and he is strong, and in good shape. Another punch, and the table sags under a dead weight; Dominic is lying flat across it, his legs dangling, the tigers pushing their faces into my abdomen, as if trying to feed on my carcass.

He struggles to his feet but Niall is ready for him, and there is a 'fahh' sound, and then Dominic's falling, and his eyes are staring right into mine.

Monica

Can he see me?

He looks so out of it from the punch it's difficult to tell. His eyes are wide and sightless, just like when he's sleeping.

Yes, he can see me. A small thread of spittle slides out of his mouth and down to the floor, and his lips move apart, and his right hand twitches in my direction. He's watching me under the table, me hugging his gun tightly to my breast, instead of a baby.

I touch his fingers with mine, I can't help myself, but he is already floating away from me, his consciousness bobbing away like a balloon slipping from a toddler's careless fingers.

His eyes close.

There is heavy breathing; Niall is staggering around, but I can't reach him. I can barely move or speak.

The door does that scuffy-bang thing, and I can hear the crunch of gravel as his feet hit the tiny bit of garden by the back door, the muted *clump-clump* as they race over the flagstones down the path.

I wonder what he's going to do when I don't come out of the house. *Does he have the courage to come back for me?*

I grab hold of the underside of the table and lever myself up, scrabbling on the edges. I'm on the edge of a cliff, and if I drop . . .

The car lights wash the kitchen with yellow, and I stagger to the door.

'Monica!'

Niall is gunning the engine. He gets out of the car and pulls me inside, I'm shaking, shuddering, with the effort. *My clothes. I need to take my clothes off. They're hurting me. Oh God.* When can I die? (**I want to die**)

In amongst the pain raging in my ears, I can hear another voice screaming my name.

'Monica! Stop!'

My husband is screaming.

Niall says 'fuck' again, under his breath, and does a lightning three-point turn, crunching into the wall, and we roar away.

Dominic

Dominic's eyes opened and he saw blackness. Nothing but blackness. For one moment he thought he had gone blind. Then he thought he was in limbo, waiting for hell, but there was the red winking light of the fridge, which told him he was lying on the kitchen floor.

The letter was in his hand. She had gone. And she had taken that man with her.

He staggered to his feet with a groan.

After all that effort! All that *lying!*

He picked himself off the floor.

'MONICA! STOP!' he screamed. It was a scream of pure rage and helplessness.

He heard a car engine. One more chance. If they were still here, he could throw himself in front of the car. He could stop them.

Dominic ran, screaming, out of the house, only to see the rear of Monica's car leaving the end of the street. As it turned into the road, the two little red brake lights glowed at him, like the eyes of something of purest evil.

He kept running, out of the gate and down the pavement. His eyes were filled with more light. So much light it hurt. Blue lights. Dark shapes emerged in front of them, blocking out the blue lights. The dark shapes were so dark, they were wearing luminous vests.

'Dominic Wood?' said a voice.

'Yes.'

'Can you come with us, please, sir? We'd just like to ask you some questions about an incident.'

'No.'

'Just an hour of your time, sir. It's rather serious.'

'I'm busy. Can't you see I'm busy? My wife has left me.'

'I'm sorry about that, sir, but this can't wait ...'

'Leave me alone.'

'Fine. Dominic Wood, I am arresting you for purchasing and possession of an illegal firearm. You do not have to say anything. However, it may harm your defence if you do not mention when questioned something which you later rely on in court. Anything you do say may be given in evidence.'

Monica

We're in a motorway restaurant. Niall has gone off to Boots to buy some plasters for his hand. He's grazed his knuckles quite badly on Dominic's face.

I'm propping myself on a stiff plastic-covered chair and trying to unpeel a triangle of plastic-covered food.

My phone scuttles away from me; butting the napkins off the edge of the table. I look at it – it's reading 'unknown'.

Should I answer it? It could be Dominic. Well so what? He can't get me here.

I press answer and put it slowly to my ear. 'Hello.'

'Hello, Monica. I thought you wouldn't answer if my number came up, so I withheld it.'

'Clever.'

'I thought so.'

'It's good to hear from you, Geoff.'

'You too. I just thought I'd tell you; your husband is in custody.'

'Good. How long can you keep him there?'

'For trying to buy a firearm? At least fifteen hours. Now if we can find where he put it we could have him in for twenty-four.'

My mind flips to the bag under my seat.

'Don't worry. Fifteen hours is long enough. My friend and I will be long gone.'

'Monica ... Please. Don't go. This is not the answer.'

'But this is what I want to do. This is my way.'

'There's nothing I can say, is there?'

'Not really. How is he? How's Dominic?'

'I've not been in to see him yet. The arresting officer said he was upset. Angry. But a bit defeated ... Well no. Resigned. Yeah, that's the word he used. Resigned.'

I don't say anything more. I just ring off.

Niall

Niall stood in the doorway of Boots, between the sunglasses rack and the umbrella display.

He couldn't take his eyes off her.

Monica was eating a sandwich and talking on the phone to that friend of hers in France. He wondered how she would react when he said he was coming with her. No, he *knew* how she would react. She would throw her arms around him and burst into tears with relief.

He wondered how he would do it. He had his passport ready, in his pocket, and he could wave it in her face, and she could make the connection. He would love to see the expressions cross her face: confusion, puzzlement, and then, finally, joy.

He still felt whiplash from the events of the last three hours. The next stage had been reached with staggering speed. Monica's husband had forfeited his place by her side, and she had come to him *to him*! *To him!* to take her away to safety. And he was replacing Monica's husband, and he was rescuing her and he was doing it all.

For her.

To be honest, he felt slightly exhilarated that he had left Monica's husband a broken mess on the kitchen floor. It was good that the last she had seen of him was a screaming, incoherent, rage-filled apparition in the rear-view mirror. It was symbolic somehow, and symbols take on a weight in people's lives. He was sure Monica had seen their flight from her home as an important moment.

He was more and more convinced that pushing her down those steps was the right thing to do, for all concerned. A woman like Monica needed a push, sometimes, to get her life back on track. After all, if it hadn't happened, her husband wouldn't have shown himself for the weak, self-interested man he was.

A Monica without pain would have endured such a man, and their lives would have bled into the sand inside some sham of a marriage. But the Monica *he* had made, the stronger, wiser Monica, had turned her back on that man.

He thought about the letter Monica had written, and left on the table. He wondered if he should sit down here and write a letter to his son, and explain what he was doing and why he had to go.

He decided against it. Peter was too young to understand, and Lorraine would just tear up the envelope. Perhaps he would send a message in about twenty years, and Peter would come and visit him and Monica in their French villa and eat pastries and drink wine, and he would understand.

Everyone understands in the end, it's all just a matter of time. *Time is a great healer*, they'd say. *Just ask Niall and Monica. They understand.*

He had to remind himself sometimes. It was down to him, after all. He didn't mean to push her down those car park steps, it was just a surge of desperation when he saw her there, alone on the roof. He had to save her from herself.

It was *for her*.

Niall

From the moment Niall met Monica he loved her, deeply and unreservedly. Seven years ago he was just an amateur actor, doing little plays with his mates, doing them for the crack more than anything. From the split second he took that curtain call in that tiny pub theatre in Little Venice and peered out into the gloom, and saw that mysterious woman on the front table, with her legs, the coat, the gloves, the lipstick, he loved her.

He sensed, no, he *knew* that the woman would be waiting in the bar downstairs to buy him a drink, to tell him how good he was. She pulled off her gloves, put her naked hand on his and a ripple of excitement surged through his body. She put him on her client list and she got him auditions for parts (apparently the industry called them 'interviews' now, which didn't sound as exciting) for bad telly, cheap adverts, and he got all the roles he went up for. He got them all.

It was *for her*.

It was part of the arrangement; he would do those things and she would be happy with him and he and Monica would eventually end up together. That was the arrangement. Of course it was never said out loud, but it was *there*; you just had to watch for the signs. He recognised all the clues.

For her.

She'd tell him to shave, put on a tie and suit so he could be 'fat yobbo at nightclub', and he'd gladly do it. She'd tell him to grow a three-day stubble so he could sell drugs to little girls in *EastEnders* and he'd do it in a heartbeat. He even did *Heartbeat* in a heartbeat. He was a great evil poacher. He looked very sinister.

For her.

One day, she rang and asked him to come to central London.

Joy! She took him for lunch in a little Italian next door to the Soho Theatre in Dean Street, with grapes painted on the walls and bottles on the tables wearing little grass skirts.

She said it was about time to talk about the next stage. That was what he had been waiting for. The next stage of the arrangement. She ordered the food, and talked ambition, about bigger parts, bigger roles, perhaps theatre? *Educating Rita* was just getting under way for a regional tour. Perhaps he could try for Rita's slobby husband?

It didn't feel like the next stage. It sounded almost as if she was sending him away. He was confused. Then, when she was halfway through her mozzarella salad, she got a call. Her husband had forgotten his keys and was wondering how he could get back inside the house.

She erupted with rage, bringing the tiny restaurant to silence. She said he had interrupted a vital meeting with an important client. She meant him! He, *Niall Stewart*, was the *important* client! She said he was more *important* than her own husband. That was the first sign.

She said it was his own stupid fucking fault that he was locked out, and she wasn't in any fucking position to do anything about it. Perhaps he should try and get in round the back? Only he could hardly do that, could he? If he got off his fat flabby arse and went to the gym sometimes, perhaps he would fit in the bathroom window, but there was no chance in his current condition. He'd have to go to a coffee shop and wait until she got home, and she wasn't going to be home early. Next time, put a spare key in the lamp, or somewhere? Just try and *think*, Dominic, why don't you?

That was the second sign. *She despised her husband because he was overweight!* She only liked trim, toned men. Niall looked down at his own belly, making his T-shirt ooze over the belt of his jeans.

When the menus came round again, he skipped dessert, even though he had a hungry eye on the profiteroles.

He went to the gym the following day. Over the next twelve, tortured, sweat-stained weeks, he brought his weight down, tightened his gut, and started to develop muscle tone.

For her.

The interviews kept coming in, but he didn't get as many roles. And then he got no roles. He wasn't looking right any more. Not a 'type'. She kept putting him up for 'angry slob' roles, but the 'angry slob' roles went to actors who looked angrier and slobbier. He didn't mind, because that wasn't important. It was the next stage of their arrangement.

For her.

Then he got the phone call. She was slimming down the agency, because of personal reasons. Keeping things lean. He approved of her logic. He knew she liked things trim. After all, that's what he was working towards, wasn't he? To become what she wanted, so they could be together.

And then she continued talking. Things hadn't been working out as she'd hoped. She felt she could no longer represent him in a way that he deserved. These things happen. He shouldn't take it personally. Perhaps he could try someone else? She had a list of other agents she was sure would be a great fit for him. She wished him well in his future career. She was sure he was going to be very big.

It wasn't until a good minute after the phone call had been terminated that he realised he had been let go. She didn't want to be with him any more. She had ended the arrangement.

None of it made sense! He'd done all she'd asked for. *It didn't make sense!* He had to know what was going on.

Niall had an actor friend who was still on Monica's books, one of the lucky ones she'd kept on. She showed him the email she got from Monica the same day that he was let go.

Dear Clients

I am delighted to inform you that Dominic and I are expecting our first child in March. For this reason, I am welcoming Karen Willikins to the agency. She will help spread the workload at this crucial time, and she will be the agency's point of contact for interviews and contract negotiations. She will be contacting all of you over the course of the coming week. I'm sure you will make her feel welcome.

This is purely an administrative measure to make sure the agency doesn't lose track of you when I am not in the office. Rest assured, I will be keeping a close eye on you all. Manic Dynamic is a boutique agency that prides itself on being personally involved in the career of every actor on its list. I selected each and every one of you to be part of our little family, and I have no intention of changing the way this agency operates.

I have no plans on taking maternity leave, and I look forward to seeing all of you in your first nights, right up until the moment they hang my feet up in the stirrups!

With kind regards

Monica Wood

He was consumed by rage and confusion. He had been *betrayed*! After all his work! After everything he had done! She turned her back on him and decided to have a baby? With her *husband*, of all people? *None of it made any sense!* Then he forced himself to calm down. There had to be a rational explanation for this. Perhaps her husband had trapped her into having the baby? Perhaps he wanted her to look fat? Perhaps she had got pregnant by accident and her husband was forcing her to go through with it?

He had to know.

For her.

He spent his days finding out what had gone wrong. He followed her home in his car and found out where she lived. He watched her go to the hospital in Kensington, with her husband. Like he was escorting her. Like her husband was making sure that she would have the baby. Making sure she wouldn't run away.

He waited outside their house for days. Her husband was there all the time, it seemed. There was no chance to talk to her on her own. He got more and more agitated as the days passed, knowing there was a ticking time bomb inside her, ready to explode. On the ninth day, when Monica and hubby left together in their car, he just turned his ignition and followed them, without knowing what he was doing.

He knew where they were going. If they left together, Niall knew for certain. Sure enough, they went to the hospital. He followed them all the way in to the car park. He needed a chance to talk to her. He needed to do something.

For her.

He went up and up the multi-storey, round and round, round and round. Searching. At the top he saw her car, and parked his car next to it. And he waited.

For her.

Maybe it was the altitude. Maybe it was the round-and-round driving up the multi-storey; perhaps it made him dizzy. But when he saw her, alone, looking out onto the London skyline, coat fluttering in the wind, he didn't know what to say. Guys never know what to say. They would do everything they could to avoid words and, to be honest, after all the waiting and agonising . . . he didn't have a single coherent word in his head.

He didn't have a plan, and when people didn't have plans, they did things that they never really planned to do at the time.

It seemed to make sense in the moment. It seemed the obvious way to get rid of the baby. In his head, it sounded like the only way to free her.

So he went

... *for her.*

It all happened in complete silence. *She didn't even scream!* He guessed she was as surprised as him. She was on her back, lying in an ugly unnatural way, one leg touching the bottom step and the other leg tucked up awkwardly under her body, like a rag doll dropped from a pram. Her white coat was splayed out around her, and at that moment he thought she looked like an angel, dropped by a careless god from heaven.

'Shit. Are you all right?' Someone was saying those words. By a process of elimination it was probably him.

His arm – the one he'd used to push her down the steps – was still outstretched, rigid, straight out in front of him. His arm seemed to want to go and help her up, but his body didn't want to follow. His mind said: *There are lots of very good reasons why you should not help her. I can't think of them at this very second, but trust me on this; there will be. Important reasons.*

He moved, stiffly, awkwardly, back to his car, and sat there in the driver's seat. His mind told him not to move. *They'll check the CCTV* his mind told him. *There might not be cameras up here, but I'll be willing to bet there are some at the entrance.*

They'll watch for cars leaving at the time of the incident! They'll watch for cars leaving in a hurry!

He hunkered down in the back seat, threw a blanket over himself, and listened to the noises, the shouts of alarm, the heavy grinding on the gravel as an ambulance struggled up the multi-storey ramp. He waited for a long time until all the noises went away. Then he waited even longer, until it got dark. Then he drove away. There were no police around.

In the days that followed he cowered in his flat, terrified, waiting for a knock on the door, waiting for the police to come and stare at him and ask him loads of questions that he didn't have a hope of answering. He eventually had the courage to emerge, and drove past Monica's house but the curtains were closed and the house was dark. He checked the website of Manic Dynamic and found that Monica's contact email had been removed. There was just the email of her new assistant.

He killed her! He must have killed her! It was the only logical conclusion. *He had to go! He had to get out of the country!*

Niall

Niall got a job on a cruise liner. He wasn't able to get 'fat hippy' parts any more, but there was always a vacancy for a shipboard trainer to work off the pina coladas and five-course breakfasts.

From the moment Niall met Lorraine he loved her, deeply and unreservedly. From the split second he finished the morning step class, and peered out and saw her on the front row, with the legs, the leotard, the headband, the lipstick, he loved her. He sensed, no, he *knew* that the woman would be waiting in the bar afterwards to buy him a drink, to tell him how good he was.

Over a couple of mimosas, Lorraine told him her life story – well, the last three months of it. She worked for a publishing company (full of people shallower and more annoying than her), and she was (slumming it) on a (tacky holiday) cruise to get over Dennis (ratbag) who looked after non-fiction, and who, ironically, wouldn't know the truth if it kicked him in the bollocks (Dennis's non-fiction titles included 'lying tapeworm' 'lying slime bucket', and 'lying cheating bastard'). Siobhan (cow) had got an invitation to Glyndebourne (posh cow) and stood her up days before they set sail; so Lorraine came on her own (to find a man) as an act of defiance. She said a lot – a LOT – of other stuff, about scuba diving in coral reefs and swimming with dolphins and snowboarding and the types of (classy) holidays she usually went on when she was in a better frame of mind, but Niall didn't really pay attention. Mostly he drank cocktails and watched her delicious lips move.

Watching the shapes they made.

Trying to count her teeth.

They didn't see much of the Greek islands. They stayed in Lorraine's cabin for most of the voyage, exploring each other's inlets, and by the time the ship docked in Portsmouth, they'd decided to live together in her very expensive flat in Hampstead, and she'd designed wedding invitations and worked out a space for the cot before he'd managed to unpack his suitcase.

That was the start of the whirlwind; and what with the drama of constant sex, earning money from every acting job he could find, running around buying nappies, bibs, buggies, and oddly shaped plastic bottles, Monica's broken body seemed like an hallucination, a fever dream, a piece of flotsam from his imagination that had tried to convince him that it was real.

Nine months after Lorraine told him she was pregnant (over a lunch of asparagus tips and pomegranate juice) he had gone out into a hospital corridor because had a splitting headache, and he needed to take a break from Lorraine's shouts and pleadings for the bastard baby to leave her body.

He went to lean on the window sill and watch the ambulances park. At that precise moment, as his wife's screams reached a crescendo and Peter made his first tiny mewling cries on the planet, he saw Monica's husband drive into a space, open his boot, take out a couple of walking sticks, open the passenger side door and help Monica struggle out of the interior.

It was *her*.

She was alive!

He went back to the old routine, following Monica back and forth from the hospital, his car gliding back and forth down her road like a shark. He found out the names of her doctors, and rang up the clinic (putting on a rather good impression of Monica's husband though he did say so himself), and bit by bit found out what had happened, and then he focused his efforts on getting back into Monica's life. Lorraine and Peter all but evaporated from Niall's consciousness. Before Peter could walk, Niall was out of Lorraine's flat and living on his own.

And then he made himself a new role. He became 'Niall the osteopath'. He boned up on techniques, took a couple of classes in deep tissue massage and reflexology, and then soon it was time for opening night. When she lay on the bench in the gym, pinned there by her pain like a pretty butterfly to a board, that was the moment. It was time for lights, camera . . .

Action!

And now, as he watched her fiddle with a sandwich carton, he was mesmerised. He could scarcely believe he was back where he belonged, after all this time. The arrangement they had made, so long ago, was coming to pass. Over these past months he'd come to think that he'd done Monica a favour, pushing her down those steps. Because without that, without her pain, and her struggle, she wouldn't have known who was *really* there for her. *He* wasn't some fair-weather friend. All of Monica's fair-weather friends had gone, and—

No, when he thought about it, *really* thought about it, he had to admit it. Thanks to him, everything turned out for the best.

For her.

DI Geoff Marks

'How is he now?'

'He's had a bit of a hissy fit, but he's just sitting quietly now.'

'I'll be right there. Has he asked for a lawyer?'

'No. Which is odd. Someone complains that much, you'd expect them to want legal counsel the second they're asked. He's a weird chap, isn't he?'

'You've got that right. I'll be right over.'

Dominic had his head in his hands. Geoff heard him saying something under his fingers, he thought it was swearing, but after about the fourth time, he realised Dominic was saying 'Thou shalt not bear false witness', over and over again.

'Interview commencing at three thirty-six p.m. Present are Mr Dominic Wood, DI Marks ...'

'And DC Webb ...'

Geoff stretched over his chair and leaned onto the table.

'Can I remind you that you're under caution, Mr Wood?'

Dominic nodded, but didn't remove his hands from his head.

'Now ... Mr Wood. Remember me?'

He eased his face over his fingers. Geoff was finally seeing him close up and in the flesh after four years. It was definitely the same guy Geoff remembered. About two stone heavier, greyer, with a thinning crown, but he recognised him. That smug little 'I've got a secret' grin of his was unmistakable.

He crossed his arms and looked at Geoff, for a long long time. 'Yes, I remember you. You were there. You arrested me last time. You had that really bad moustache.'

Geoff's hand went to the empty space where his moustache used to be. 'If you want to take a trip down memory lane, Dominic, yes it was me who pulled you in. When you tried to get a bloke in a pub to kill your wife—'

'Yes, and my wife told you at the time—'

'—and you *persuaded* her to cover for you. You didn't fool me for a moment. And now you've been nicked for trying to do her in again.'

'I don't know what you're talking about.'

DC Sally Webb tried to have a go. *She's new, and keen*, Geoff thought. *She'll probably be giving me orders in a couple of years.* 'Dominic. Do you understand why you're here?'

He said nothing.

She continued. 'We have recovered footage from a CCTV in Woolwich.'

Still nothing.

'A man in a car park, buying a firearm. Have you ever been to Woolwich, Dominic?'

He looked at Geoff, smiled, and said: 'I'm not here because of some stupid footage from some stupid camera, am I? She got you to put me in here. My wife put me in here. Didn't she? She's put you up to this.'

'Let's talk about Woolwich, Dominic,' says Sally.

'Let's not.'

'Do you want to see the tape?'

'Not really.'

'Suit yourself. Can you tell us who it was who sold you the gun?'

He ignored Sally and looked at Geoff again. 'Monica's lovely, isn't she? She can wrap anybody round her little finger. Big strapping lad like you would be no bother.'

Geoff had had enough. *Time to cut to the chase.* 'I put it to you, Mr Wood, that you were buying an illegal firearm with the intention of doing harm to your wife.'

'You think you're saving her life.' He looked at Geoff with pity. 'I'm sure that's what you think. You're probably very taken with her. Probably even a bit in love with her. That's what happens when they all meet her. Everyone wants to protect her. Including you.'

He placed his hands on the table and pushed himself away; almost as if the cheeky bugger was getting ready to leave. 'I imagine that's what you think, isn't it? You think you've saved her life. Well, actually, you haven't.'

He actually gave a little laugh. 'Quite the opposite. By bringing me here you killed her. As surely as if you fired a gun in her face.'

Monica

We drive into the night.

Niall is not speaking. I'm wondering if he's still cross about me going into the house, but he's tapping nervously on the steering wheel. I think he's still shaken by his encounter with Dominic. He's not glancing across every two minutes. He's stopped trying to squeeze a conversation out of me.

My head is lolling across the back of my seat, the little red dots of the brake lights on the motorway are becoming fat and distorted, as my eyes close and their luminescence filters through my eyelashes.

I'm drowsy; I have so many memories now, and without the painkillers they look new and fresh, crisp to the touch, so I'm skipping through them, light as a feather. I can't help it. Perhaps it's the morphine. They flood into me; almost as overwhelming as the pain.

I can see myself dancing out of drama school having given the finger to Mr Favreau Of The Wandering Hands; setting up my agency in the tiny room on the first floor in Greek Street with the green door, the faulty buzzer and Germaine and her furtive clients on the second floor. There I am, standing in the rain, white silk plastered to my body, throwing my bouquet outside a church somewhere in Fife, then having a slurred argument with Dominic's parents over empty bottles of Krug and crumbs and dirty paper plates; something about sex before marriage.

Something like that.

I'm in a hospital room, watching my father's red-flecked eyes staring up at me; me looking dispassionately down at him; feeling nothing.

My mind frolics back to the day, that Christmas Day, the day I got Jumpy the rabbit. The same day he escaped and found his way under the wheel of Dad's car.

Squeak. Crunch. Silence.

We had had Christmas lunch, and we were leaving to see Granddad and Nanny in Devon, and Dad was going out to get petrol for the car; his caramel-coloured Morris Marina, which still smelled faintly of the milk that tipped over in the boot that summer; the car that disgorged its cargo of pornographic videos on my little red shoes.

I was in the garden on my trike when I heard the squeak; I rounded the corner and saw the car; the blood; the tiny quivering heap of fur on the drive. I screamed, and I didn't stop screaming when Mum charged out of the house and carried me into the house. She took me to my room and ran downstairs to get me

340

some warm milk, and in that minute I looked frantically out of the window and saw my dad go up to the shed and get a spade.

I had to go out and see, and I ran out.

I can see Dad again, walking away to the back of the garden. I can see the mark on the wrist where his watch used to be (he'd taken it off to time the turkey in the oven) and his shirt peeping out from the back of his trousers. I can see the still-twitching remains of my rabbit in one hand, his shovel in his other hand.

And then walking back with just the shovel.

'Sorry. It was for the best, trust me, little lady,' he said. His hand rests for two seconds on my shaking shoulders. 'He was in a lot of pain.'

And that was all he said about it. And that was all I said to the nurse when I left his hospital room. It seemed poetic to me, even though I was the only one who knew what it meant.

DI Geoff Marks

'Interview suspended at twenty-two twenty-eight. DS Webb, why don't you get us some tea.'

'Are you sure, guv?'

'We'll be fine. We'll both be just fine, won't we, Dominic?'

Sally flicked her eyes to Geoff, then to Dominic, and back again. 'OK . . .' she said slowly. 'I won't be long.'

The door closed, and the moment she left, Dominic spoke.

'Thou shalt not bear false witness,' he said. 'Do you know what that means?'

'It's about lying. Funny you should bring it up.'

'A bit more than that. It was originally about lying in a court of law. Hebrews took a very dim view of that. It was usually punishable by death. Nowadays we take it to mean any kind of lying ... I wonder if *you're* prepared to lie in a court of law, Detective Inspector? I wonder if it'll come to that?'

'You're trying to play games with me.'

'I wish I was. I've taught myself how to lie. I've said all sorts of nonsense, to get what I want. I'm good at it. I've lied to Monica, for years now.'

Dominic pressed his hands flat against his face, and Geoff realised he was crying. 'Such a terrible burden. Such a terrible exquisite burden ... '

Geoff slammed his fist on the table, making Dominic wobble like a jellyfish.

'It's a beautiful performance, Dominic,' he snarled. 'Really Oscar-winning stuff. But that's all it is, just a performance. We know you wanted to kill your wife. We've got evidence. Footage. Eyewitnesses ... '

'Evidence? You want evidence? Oh, you can have some more evidence if you like. Have more evidence. Check out my computer's browsing history. Check out Ed's Sheds. I'll give you my passwords. That's where I found my contact. The one who sold me the gun. I'm going to walk out of here, because I failed. It was just a big game, but it's over now, and I failed. None of this means anything now. It's all for nothing.'

'It's not a game, Dominic. It's very serious.'

Geoff pushed his face forward so he was nose to nose with Dominic, and Dominic pouted with an expression of injured innocence. Geoff felt that if he even blinked, his subconscious mind would strike, and he'd open his eyes to find Dominic lying at his feet with his head caved in by a chair.

'Just get to the fucking point,' he snarled. 'Tell me what you want to tell me. You obviously want to unburden yourself. So just tell me what you want to tell me, OK?'

'Is the camera on?'

'No, the interview has been suspended. You saw me turn it off.'

'I'll talk to you now. Just you. No witnesses. No camera.'

'No deal.'

'If you want me to make a proper confession afterwards, on tape, I will. I promise.' He grinned. 'But I don't think you will after you hear what I have to say.'

'I'll take you up on that bet.'

'I'm sure you will.'

'So . . . It's just us. So tell me.'

He shrugged. 'Why not?'

He raised his hands in surrender.

'Are you ready?'

DI Geoff Marks

'Tell me, Inspector. Have you ever had a loved one who just wants to die? Someone who just wanted to end it all?'

Even as the 'no' came out of Geoff's mouth, an image of his dad swam into his brain; brave old Dad, who never asked him for anything, except one thing, and Geoff couldn't give him that thing. And he walked out of the care home, and he felt his dad's eyes watch him as he left.

'I can't say I have,' he added.

'Well I had someone. My wife wanted to die.'

Geoff laughed. 'Oh, right. I get it. That's your defence, is it? Very cute.'

Dominic continued as if he hadn't even spoken. 'She made her mind up. She wanted to die.'

Geoff laughed. 'Most fairy stories start with "Once upon a time".'

'There's no reason to lie any more. She planned it, worked out the drugs she would overdose on, and she actually wrote herself a suicide letter ... well, she dictated it to a friend because she couldn't write any more; the pain wouldn't let her. All she could manage at the time was an undignified squiggle.'

He smiled. 'Her friend Angelina is an artist, a good one, and Monica confided in her, told Angelina exactly what she wanted. She got her to make a suicide note, a perfect forgery, very elegant, perfect spelling, all in Monica's handwriting, so she could leave it by her body. A proper goodbye.

'But when it came down to it, Angelina lost her nerve and told me what my wife was planning.'

Monica

My memories are pin-sharp now, like my dreams. I feel like I'm standing on the top of a very high building and I can look down on my life, spread out before me. The scaffolding and the cranes have gone, and all the memories have been constructed.

*

I can see the tops of the curtains, and the light streaming in from outside, catching the fragments of dust and making them shine.

I can see the shape of Dominic's nostrils as he looks down at me, flaring at me with disbelief. He is holding the pills I had prepared, safely out of my reach.

'How did you find out?'

'Angelina told me.'

'That skinny bitch. I thought she was my friend.'

'She is. That's why she told me. She wanted me to stop you killing yourself. She doesn't want you to die. I don't want you to die.'

'I want to do this. It's my body, and I want to do it.'

'You can't think that.'

'Why can't I think that? My pain censors what I can do with my body. Please don't censor my thoughts as well.'

'It's not you. It's the pain talking. The pain is making you think differently.'

I exhale wearily. 'Dominic, I *am* the pain. The pain is me. The body and the mind are inseparable, because the mind is connected to all the nerves and hormones and feelings. If I spent my whole life hungry, I'd be a different person. If I spent my whole life scared of being butchered in a backstreet in some horrible country, I'd be a different person. If I spent my whole life being tortured, I'd be a different person, and let's not kid ourselves, I am spending my whole life – being – tortured. Fuck, when I had my periods I was a different person, and that was just a couple of days a month . . .'

He opens his mouth, but I'm too quick for him.

'Sit down. On that chair.'

He sits.

'I want to end this,' I say. 'I've been doing this for a year now, and the doctors say it's not going to end. Even if something comes up, a treatment, it's not going to change. It's not going to change enough. I don't want to live like this any more.'

Dominic was getting angry. 'But what about me? Don't I have a say in this? I love you. I need you in my life.'

'Oh shut up! You stupid man! Don't be so selfish. Stop flapping your stupid mouth and engage your brain for once in your life!'

He shuts up. I know I'm being cruel. But that's who I am. I used to do it so I can get the results I want. I used to spend my life screaming at theatre producers, television directors, BBC accountants ... Now it's just Dominic. He gets the full force of my rage now, and it's not fair, it's really not fair, but that's the way it is, and I don't have the strength to change now.

Another wave of pain. My face crumples in agony. 'Why are you doing this? Why are you arguing with me? You're just making it worse.'

'Oh of course!' He pushes his cup and saucer off the table. 'Can't have a discussion, or I'll elevate your pain levels!'

'I'm doing this for you too. Don't you understand?'

Dominic has something in his eye. 'No you're not. You're just thinking of yourself.'

'No. I'm not going to be yoked to this useless body for the rest of my life, and neither will you. This way you get a chance to find another life.'

'This is *exactly* what Mum said to Dad.'

'What?'

He hesitates.

I say 'What?' again.

'I ... Look ... You thought my mum just died. Everyone thought she just passed away in her bed. Well that doesn't really happen with cancer. She asked Dad to kill her, and when he refused she took pills, tried to take her own life. She didn't succeed, so he gave her what she wanted. Let her take all the pills she wanted. Fed them to her when she got too drowsy.'

'That's terrible. Why didn't you tell me?'

'Because Dad didn't want anyone to know, because I only knew because he got drunk at the wake and told me. He was a devoted Catholic, and it tore him apart. The worst thing was, she was getting better. *She was getting better*, the doctors said, and if she just could hang in there ...'

He laughs, and snot bubbles inside his nose.

I let him compose himself and then I say, very softly, 'That's really sad, Dominic, but that was your mother's decision, and I'm sorry your dad found it so hard to abide with her wishes. But it was her life, and this is mine. The best you can do is prepare for life without me. Something your dad singularly failed to do.'

'Me? Hah! Me! Prepare for life without you? Me? Dominic Wood?' Dominic's mind is scrambling now. He's just saying words; any words.

'You'll be OK. You'll be fine.'

'Me? Look at me! I'm useless! I'm the worst advertising consultant in the world! I can barely pay the mortgage ... I need you ... I just ... need you.'

He stands up, swaying slightly. 'I'm going to get drunk. I don't care if it's ten in the morning, I'm going to open a can. And I'm going to watch you, and stop you.'

He goes into the kitchen and comes back with a can of beer, which he chugs defiantly in front of me.

'This is ridiculous.'

'So you say.'

'I thought you would be supportive.'

'I am. I'm helping you through this, so you can realise your mistake. There will be other treatments, other operations. You'll look back on today, and you'll laugh.'

'I don't want to do that.'

'Tough.'

'You're not being fair.'

'Neither are you.'

The room falls silent for a long, long time. All the ticking clocks have been removed from the house, because I can't bear listening to them, so there is no sound but the faint drone of cars outside and the swish of beer in Dominic's can.

But I can hear things. I can hear the sound of myself thinking; thoughts mashing together in my head.

And I can hear the sound of my Angry Friend breathing, close to my ear, like an animal. Laughing at me. Daring me to deal with him. Like I deal with all the others.

(**Give him an ultimatum**)

'You're right,' I say at last. 'I can't leave you like this. It's not fair ... '

His eyes glisten with hope. I feel so bad when I see that hope, but it's my life, and I have to go through with this.

' ... not when there's the life insurance policy.'

'What insurance ... Oh. You mean the one your dad took out on you, just before he died ... '

'That's right. I've kept it going all this time. It's massive, Dominic. If I die you get almost half a million pounds. If I die you will never have to worry about a thing. You can pay off the mortgage. Go round the world. You can look after yourself.'

'But I don't want to ... '

'But if I commit suicide you get nothing. Life insurance companies are a lot like your church, Dominic. Suicide doesn't count.'

A look of horror slowly floods his face.

'So you have to kill me. Break into the house and shoot me, or something. Make it look like I've been attacked by a random burglar. Then you'll get the money. Then you'll be all right.'

He rocks back on his chair, almost falls. He shakes his head like

348

a wet dog, as if I have poured something unpleasant on him from a great height. Which is true, I guess.

'That's sick. I won't do it. I refuse.'

'I'm not *arguing* with you, I'm *telling* you, as a courtesy. This is what's going to happen, whether you help to kill me or not, I can get someone else to do it.'

'Who?'

'I know people. I'll get someone else to help me,' I said at last. 'You won't stop me.'

'Who?' Dominic looks afraid, shattered. But I'm already working out the logistics in my mind.

Tears blur into my eyes but I blink them away, and the memories keep coming.

DI Geoff Marks

'She really loves – loved – me, you know, but she always thought me a bit weak. A bit pathetic. Advertising is a game played by sharks and she always thought me a bit of a dolphin, paddling about, grinning like an idiot.'

He stopped, and tapped his mouth, as if he was thinking. 'And she was right. I'm terrible at it. I've always done my best, but it's never been quite enough – or not nearly enough.'

'All right, fine.' Geoff wasn't interested in self-pity. 'So, let's say for the sake of argument, that she asked you to kill her.'

'That's what happened.'

'And you really refused. You really said no to her.'

'Of course I did.'

'Even though that's what she wanted, and you'd get half a million quid into the bargain? It sounds pretty tempting to me.'

'Of course I said no! Life is sacred. Hope is always with us, and life is a gift that shouldn't be thrown away lightly. Anyway, I love – loved – her with every fibre of my being and I couldn't bear to have her leave me. You understand.'

'So you kept on saying no.'

'Of course I did. But Monica being Monica, she never took no for an answer. If she put her mind to it, it was going to happen. No question.'

He looked up at the ceiling and gathered his thoughts.

'She contacted one of her clients. Larry French. I'm sure you know the name.'

'Oh yes, I know the name.'

Geoff knew of Larry French. Every man in the Met had a story, or knew someone who had a story about Larry French. And after they'd told you the story they'd tell you he got off bloody lightly.

'Larry met with her. He saw how bad she was, and he saw how sincere she was about dying, so he agreed to help her. It took some persuading, as he's not a fan of voluntary euthanasia.'

'Unless that voluntary euthanasia involves grassing him up to the police.'

Dominic barked with laughter. 'That's funny. I like you, Geoff.'

'So Larry agreed to help her die.'

'Yes. He did. But I know my wife. I'm wise to the way her mind works. I was recording all phone calls in and out of the house. Was that paranoid of me? Spying on my own wife?' Dominic didn't wait for an answer. 'I suppose it wasn't paranoid at all, as I did find out she was planning something. So what do you think I did when I found out what she was planning?'

Geoff exhaled. 'I don't know. Confront Larry?'

'That's one thing. He said he understood how I felt, really he did, but at the end of the day it was her business. He said "he owed her one". Guess again.'

'Call the police?'

'You know I didn't. And I couldn't have lived with myself if Larry got into trouble. Larry's a reformed character. He was – is – a good man.'

Geoff snorted with laughter. 'Good!'

'Whatever you think of him, he's been loyal to my wife. He could have gone to any one of the big talent agencies, but he stayed with Monica when all the others went. That's what Monica thought was the measure of a man; the one who stays on deck with you when the ship is sinking. So, what, I should put him back in jail for planning to do what my wife wanted him to do? Granting her wish, however appalling? No. I couldn't have lived with myself. Guess again.'

Geoff shrugged. 'Haven't a clue.'

'But you know very well what I did next, Detective Inspector. That's how you and I met.'

Monica

'We've been driving for ages,' I mumble. 'You can stop for a rest if you like.'

'It's only been twenty minutes,' Niall says. 'And I'll feel more comfortable when we get to Dover.' He flicks his eyes up to the mirror. 'We took a risk stopping once. I don't want to stop again ... I've seen those movies where they pull into gas stations and the owner has Wanted posters behind the counter and someone always recognises them, and it turns into a huge chase, and that's how they get caught. That's always the fugitive's fatal mistake ... dropping off for a breather in a sleepy roadside café.'

I give a sleepy giggle. 'I don't think they have Wanted posters in Costa Coffee.'

'All the same ... '

I lift my head wearily. 'I don't want to take the excitement out of our big adventure, but we're not actually Bonnie and Clyde.'

'I assaulted your husband.'

'He assaulted you first.'

'Monica ... '

'Trust me. We're consenting adults on our way to starting a new life together. And I want – no, I need – to walk around and move about.'

He digests what I just said. *Consenting adults.* The first indication that we are together, properly together. That I am with him, now, for the rest of my life.

What else can he do? He flicks the indicator lights and pulls into a car park surrounded by logos.

I lean my head on the table and listen to the sounds of the coffee shop, and I doze. I can taste blood and vomit in my mouth.

Down the rabbit hole.

Then I wake up, I am back in bed, cleaned up and in my pyjamas, and Dominic is watching me. He's sitting backwards on a chair like a detective preparing to interrogate a suspect.

I almost scream but I realise I'm half dozing, half waking, and the memories are so clear in my mind that, to all intents and purposes, until I wake up properly, they're real.

*

I'm on my own again, and then the doorbell rings.

I'm lying on the floor, my usual pose, and I stretch my arm out to click my specially rigged intercom.

'Hello?'

'Hello, is that Mrs Wood?'

'Yes.'

'It's Detective Inspector Geoff Marks and Police Constable Trevor Bradbury. Can we come in?'

'Is there something the matter?'

'Can we talk to your husband?'

'Dominic?' I said. 'Why do you want to talk to him?'

'Is he here?'

'No.'

'Will he be long? Can we come in and wait?'

I don't know what to say. 'Ahm . . . '

'Mrs Wood, we'd like to speak to your husband. Can you open the door?'

'No.'

'Are you refusing to open the door?'

'I'm not refusing anything. I'm sorry, but I can't move. I have this condition. Chronic pain. I can't get up off the floor.'

There's silence from the intercom, until one of them says: 'Mrs Wood, you must have visitors sometimes. There must be a way to let them in. If you can't let us in, then we'll just have to go and look for him at work.'

I hesitate, then say, 'There's a key in the lamp by the door.'

The door rattles, and there are two police officers peering down at me. The PC's baton is dangling over my face. He's tall and scared-looking. The other has a ginger moustache, but his face is not right for it.

'Are you all right, Mrs Wood?' says Ginger Moustache.

'I have chronic pain, everything hurts. Just moving my eyes in your direction hurts.'

'Your husband left you on your own like this?'

'He has to. He has to go to work.'

'When will he be home?'

'Soon. What's all this about?'

I don't know what happened, but I think I blacked out. The tall one is gently tapping my face.

'Mrs Wood? Are you OK?'

Then there's another rattle of the door. Dominic is staring at the two policemen in our front room.

'Is everything all right? What's happened? What's happened to my wife?'

The taller one looms over me. 'I think your wife just blacked out. Are you OK now, Mrs Wood?'

I nod.

Dominic is looking intently at them. 'What are you doing in my house?'

Ginger Moustache steps forward. 'Are you Mr Dominic Wood?'

'Er ... Yes.'

'We'd like to ask you a few questions, sir, if that's all right.'

An uncertain smile spreads across Dominic's face. 'I don't know. Is it? Can I ask what this is about?'

'It concerns a conversation heard in a pub.' The policeman's eyes flick from Dominic to me, and then back again.

My husband shrugs his shoulders. 'I don't know what you're talking about. I'm sorry, you're going to have to explain yourselves better than that.'

'Perhaps we can talk to you outside, sir? In private?'

'Dominic? What's wrong? What do they want?'

'Nothing.'

'We'd just like to have a few words with you, sir.'

'Fine. Ask me here.'

'I don't think you'd want us to do that.'

'Don't tell me what I want.'

I am getting angry now. 'Dominic! Tell me what they want!'

They ignore me, of course; Dominic and the detective practically stand over me while they go nose to nose. I might as well be dead.

'So you're refusing to come with us, sir.'

'Of course I am. I'm not going anywhere.'

Ginger Moustache deflates with a huge sigh, and then draws himself up to his full height. 'Fine. We're arresting you on suspicion of soliciting to murder. You do not have to say anything but it may harm your defence if you do not mention when questioned something which you later rely on in court. Anything you do say may be given in evidence.'

Dominic moves away and the taller policeman stands in front of him. 'You have to come with us, sir.'

'Can I at least give my wife something to eat before I go? I can't leave her on her own for hours and hours.'

'Fine.'

Dominic goes into the kitchen and makes a sandwich and a glass of milk for me.

'What's all this about? Dominic hasn't done anything.'

'I'm sure you're right, Mrs Wood. But we have to ask him some questions. It shouldn't take long.'

Dominic emerges from the kitchen, the tall policeman one pace behind him, and sets the tray down by my head.

'I won't be long, darling,' he says. 'Don't wait up.'

'Dominic!'

'Don't forget to eat. You need your strength.' And then

355

before I can even comprehend what is happening, he and the policeman are gone. I struggle to the window on my elbows, moaning and hissing through my teeth, feeling like a stiffening carcass that still retains the agony of its death throes. Somehow, I manage to wriggle my way up the sofa and look out of the window.

The tall one has just slammed the rear passenger-side door on my husband. Dominic looks at me with a grin, and gives me a cheery wave out of the window as the car pulls away.

I whimper back to the tray and find a tiny square of paper under the serviette. A note.

Hello darling. If you're reading this, it means the police have taken me away. I'm in trouble. They've got evidence that I'm trying to kill you. Like you asked me to, remember? I'm going to tell them it's all a joke, a private joke between us, a kinky game we play where I pretend to kill you for kicks, but they won't believe just me. So you have to tell them that it's all a joke OK? A joke between us.

Please help me. Dominic. xxxx

Two hours later and the policemen return, and they sit on the sofa, staring warily down at me.

'Mrs Wood ...'

'Yes?'

'Your husband has told us a story ...'

'About kinky games, yes.'

Ginger Moustache gives me a look.

'We do like playing games, actually. He pretends to kill me.'

'OK ...'

'Is that what this is about, officer?'

356

'So the fact he approached four people in a pub, in turn, and offered money for them to murder you ... '

What?

'Yes,' I say, my voice slurring in shock. 'That sounds about right.'

'That was all a bit of a joke between you, was it?'

'Yes ... Yes. That's what it was. It was all a joke. A game we like to play.'

Eventually they bring him back home. Both policemen hover in the doorway, trying to leave but not quite managing it.

'Well, I understand you may need distraction, Mrs Wood,' says Ginger Moustache. 'I can see you're obviously in a bit of trouble, with your pain and all, but can you stop playing these silly games?'

'I'm sorry,' I hear myself say. 'We'll try and control ourselves.'

The tall one starts to move, but Ginger Moustache is still by the front door.

'Is that everything, Monica?' he says. 'Is there anything else you want to tell me?'

'No, officer. Nothing.'

'Are you sure?'

'I'm quite sure. I don't know what you want me to say.'

Disappointed, he turns and walks down the path to his car.

Dominic doesn't talk to me. He has a shower, and when he emerges he hums an amorphous bright tune to himself. I listen as the tune wanders from 'Here Comes the Sun' to 'Yellow Submarine' and then finally meanders into the theme from 'The Addams Family'. I know it's his way of calming himself down, to tell himself and the world that everything is all right.

But everything is not all right.

Not all right at all. Fury consumes me.

'Dominic, talk to me!'

'Yes?'

His head pops around the door.

'Dominic, if you don't come and sit down here *right now*, and talk to me about what happened . . .'

'If?'

'Just bloody do it!'

He sat down.

'You went to a *pub*? A *pub*? And tried to *hire* someone to kill me?'

'Yes.'

'Why?'

Dominic shrugs.

'You went up to some people in a bar! You actually had money in your hand? Jesus!'

He flinches at the religious oath, and then he shrugs again. 'Yes. Do you want some tea?'

'Oh, of *course*! Fuck, yeah! Let's have some *bloody tea*! That makes everything seem better!'

'I'll go and make a pot,' he says brightly, and disappears off to the kitchen.

I'm incredibly angry. The tension is mashing my nerve endings together and tying them in knots. I fight to keep a clear head.

He returns with a big silver tray – a wedding present from my mum – and pours milk leisurely into a cup, acting like he'd just come in late due to signalling failures at Clapham Junction, rather than being driven home by coppers.

'Can you get up from there, or do you want to use a straw?'

I look at him with narrowed eyes.

'You got arrested trying to kill me? Why, Dominic, why?'

'Guess,' he shouts. 'Just take a wild guess!'

'No.'

'Go on!'

'No!'

'OK, I'll tell you,' he says with sudden anger. 'You're going to get someone to kill you, and you just expect me to go along with it? You're my wife, and I love you, and I don't want you to take the easy way out and leave me.'

'Can I—'

'The *coward's* way out, leaving me, and your family and your friends and me behind! In sickness and in health, that's what I signed up for! So did you!'

'I can't just live my life for you—'

'That's what people do! That's what we do! That's what my mum should have done for Dad!'

'I'm not your mum.'

'But I'm my dad. I'm helpless, just like my dad. You know that. That's why you think you have to leave me all this money. Because you have to look after me.' He jabs a finger at me. 'And *that's* why I got myself arrested.'

'I don't understand, why ...?' Then I realise. Of course. 'You wanted to get caught. You deliberately went out of your way to get caught.'

'Exactamundo. I was about as subtle as a half-brick. Even then, no one reported me. So in the event I had to ring up the police and grass myself up.' He stands up and points angrily at me. 'If anyone kills you, I will look guilty as hell, and I will go to prison for it.'

'That's not fair.'

'Tough. Your job as an agent is to give people offers they can't refuse. Which you did to me. My job as an advertising consultant is to present fiction as truth. Which I've done to you.'

He brings his head down low until he is almost whispering in my ear. 'If you get yourself killed, you will put me in prison. And I won't get any of the insurance money. If you love me, are you prepared to put me there? Think on that.'

'This isn't over,' I said. 'I'm not finished. Not by a long way.'

Dominic grins with genuine affection. 'Oh, Monica, my love. That's the idea. This is so over now.'

DI Geoff Marks

'So, just to be clear ... you're saying you asked that bloke in the pub to kill your wife. To make yourself into a suspect for her eventual murder?'

'Yes.'

'That's insane.'

'I told you that it was the only way.' He sounded very tired. 'If my darling wife died, no matter how she died, I would put myself in the frame for it. I figured the only thing that kept her on this earth was her love for me. And I was right. She stopped thinking about trying to get herself killed. For a while. So I was right to make that sacrifice for her,' he gave a sudden bark of laughter.

Geoff thought about this for a while. 'OK. So that happened, what, four years ago? What happened then? And why did you start up again? Why buy a gun from a low-life in Woolwich?'

'I'll tell you why.' He leaned forward, suddenly energised. 'Because I prayed every day for a means for Monica and me to stay together, and four years ago, a miracle happened.' He laughed. 'Of course, God being God, he never gives you what you have in mind. He loves irony. He didn't take away the pain. He took away her memory. She was put on a new combination of drugs that wiped out a year of her life. She forgot she wanted to die. She practically became a new person.'

Dominic could see the scepticism on Geoff's face. 'The mind is a very delicate thing, Geoff; most mass shootings in the US are down to psychoses brought on by prescription drugs: anti-depressants and steroids. I know this, because since Monica got struck down, I've done research into it; a LOT of research. Funnily enough, I discovered that one of our neighbours was put on steroids by her doctor a few years ago, just for a few days, mind, and it changed her personality completely. She used to be incredibly careful with money, and she suddenly started blowing all her savings on cars, drink and gambling; she became a hedonist, and when she came off them, when she detoxed, she hadn't a clue why she did what she did. She didn't know what had got into her.'

He tapped his forehead. 'People murder their kids, jump off buildings, or completely forget who they are under the influence of perfectly legal drugs prescribed by doctors. I *know* what they can do, and let me tell you, Inspector, there is NO drug on the market that doesn't involve side effects, and most of those side effects are to do with mood altering and mind altering. The mind has a way of protecting the body, Inspector. It shuts down the memory of pain, when it can. Not just physical pain. Emotional pain. Every argument Monica and I had about her trying to commit suicide was gone. She became a new person, with hope, energy for the future ... It was a miracle ...'

'I don't believe it.'

'That's quite all right. Neither did I. At first, I thought she was putting on an act. I was paranoid she'd wait until my back was turned, I'd let my guard down, and she'd just go ahead and do it. I hired a private detective to follow her everywhere, log her every move. Here ...'

He produced a card and flipped it at Geoff.

'Here's his number. You can call him. I gave him a reason he'd understand. I told him I was worried about my wife having an affair. He followed her around taking pictures, trying to catch her out, and I carried on hiring him as long as I could afford it, and then a bit longer than that. But by that time I finally believed that she no longer had the urge to end it all.'

He looked into Geoff's eyes. 'And of course, I'm sure you understand that there was no way in heaven that I would remind her that she once wanted to kill herself. Everything became as it was, and I've lived a lie ever since. I told her friends – Larry and Angelina – what had happened, and they were glad too, and relieved, because they didn't want to live without her, either. So we all decided to live a lie.'

Geoff was sitting now, reading the card. He thought he knew this detective. A former copper. It would be interesting to hear his story. He looked up. 'Then why start up again? Why buy the gun?'

'Because it was the painkillers that took the memories away! The *drugs* that kept her from remembering. And a couple of months ago she'd discovered this new treatment; capsaicin. I won't bore you with the details, but basically it's very effective for short-term relief.'

He looked at Geoff expectantly.

'Well?' he said. 'Don't you see what that meant?'

Geoff waved his hand sarcastically. 'No I don't, actually. Please continue.'

He glared at Geoff like he was the stupidest man on the planet. 'Short-term relief! She gets this treatment, and it works, just for a short time. So what happens? She comes off the drugs, and she *remembers what she wanted to do*. Then the pain returns and she wants to die again, *and the whole thing starts up again*.'

'I get it. So, you bought the gun because you wanted to look guilty again.'

'Absolutely. I also went home, to confession, and talked to my old priest about having these urges to kill Monica. I knew if she died in suspicious circumstances, and I claimed to have done it, he would find a way around the seal of the confessional and tell the police. Father Hancock's that kind of priest. He's flexible. Then, when the time was right, if Monica remembered, I'd tell her what I'd done. What I'd planned. I'd be ready for her this time.'

'But – you didn't *know* for sure that she would remember if she came off the drugs. You couldn't have been certain any of this would happen ...'

'Of course I didn't know for sure. I'm not stupid. This was all insurance. If she didn't remember, then life would go on like before. I'd say nothing, my priest wouldn't break the oath of the confessional ... Everything would just be ... As I say ... insurance. In case she tried to do it again. I tried to be clever about making myself into a suspect.'

'The gun wasn't very clever, Dominic. We found out about the gun. It's the reason why you're here.'

'The gun was a mistake. That was stupid, but it was out of my hands.' He shook his head, marvelling at his own stupidity. 'I did actually get hold of a gun, before. After you arrested me. I buried it in the garden ...'

Dominic noticed Geoff's expression. 'Ah! Didn't know that, did you, Inspector? I can be subtle too, you know. There are ways, even for a boring man like me. I buried it in the garden, as a possible discovery, more proof that I was a homicidal husband. So if Monica ... If she ... Well, I'd show it to her, to show how determined I was to take the rap for her death. But Larry took the gun away, so I panicked. I can't believe that little idiot drove me into a car park and attacked me – right next to a CCTV camera! I would have thought he would have known the camera was there. The damn fool!'

There was a gentle knock on the door.

'Hands full with tea things ...' said Sally. 'Little help?'

Geoff opened it a crack. 'Sorry. Can you give us a few more minutes, Sally?'

The expression on her face told Geoff she wasn't completely happy about giving him a few more minutes with Dominic, but she gave a nod and left them alone.

'It's a fantastic story,' Geoff said at last. 'And you tell it very well. I'm almost convinced ... ' He leaned on the table. 'But there's one problem. There are these little things called facts. Awkward little facts.'

He put up three fingers, and tapped one. 'Fact one: your wife told me not a few hours ago that she thought you were trying to kill her ... '

He tapped the second one. 'Fact two: she was, even as I was talking to her on the phone, attempting to get away from you, afraid for her life ... '

He tapped the third one. 'Fact three: and the most important fact of all. If, as you say, she'd given up the plan to kill herself *before* she lost her memory, then why are you running around car parks buying guns? None of these facts fit. They don't even suggest that you're telling the truth. In fact, they suggest the exact opposite.'

Dominic shook his head and rolled his eyes.

'I *didn't* say she'd given up on killing herself. I said she'd stopped *thinking* about it for a while. I just *told* you that Monica wasn't the type of woman to give up. She's a woman who carries on until she gets what she wants. I know her so well.'

He massaged his forehead with his fingers, as if trying to push the memories away. 'That's why she kept the suicide note, Geoff. I bet she hid it away from me so she could look at it every day and visualise her goal. It's her method to stay focused on a task, keep to the endgame. And it always works because, well, here we are. I can see you're still not getting it, Geoff, so let me put the last piece in. Just before she lost her memories, she thought up a way to outmanoeuvre me. A better plan.'

'A better plan.'

'She would force an alibi on me.'

'What alibi?'

He spreads his arms wide. And Geoff understood.

'This . . . is your alibi?'

'I'm pretty certain it is, don't you? Perfect alibi, don't you think, me stuck in here with you, with you staring at me? And then, just in case I try anything clever, like me claiming I hired someone to kill her, she arranged things in such a way that I would never ever, ever, claim responsibility for her murder.'

'And how would that work? What would stop you claiming responsibility?'

Dominic gave a sigh; a long sigh. 'OK. It's all too late now, so I'll show you. I'll show you what's happening right now. And before I walk out of here, you'll believe me.'

He brought a letter out of his pocket.

Monica

After a while, the orange electric night gives way to dawn, and we leave the roar of the motorway. The colours of the houses are brighter, and the sky looks cleaner.

It's as if we've emerged into a different, brighter world.

'Over there,' I say. 'That bed and breakfast. That's where we're staying.'

He parks and pulls our bags out of the boot, and arranges them carefully on the pavement; suitcases first, bags on top. Not for the first time, I marvel at how young he looks.

Such a child.

He looks like a little boy building a fort with sofa cushions. He finishes piling up the bags and looks doubtfully up at the bed and breakfast, at the grim fake-Georgian façade, encrusted with seagull shit. 'It's a bit grim.'

'We're going incognito. We are meant to be Bonnie and Clyde, remember.'

He grins. 'Which one of us is Bonnie, and which one's Clyde?'

'I'll let you know.'

'Can't wait.'

We enter the reception, and Niall is set on being the man, and checking in for both of us, but he is suddenly confused. 'What name shall I say?'

'We're booked under Mr and Mrs Wood.'

A number of thoughts cross Niall's face, but he accepts being 'Mr Wood' as a necessity, and checks us in. Soon we are in our room. It's tiny, the carpet is faded, the bedcovers are threadbare, and the curtains are practically rags, but it's clean and tidy. There's a single sunflower lying on the desk. I wonder who decided to put it there.

Niall puts the bags down on the chair and stands there, staring awkwardly around him, looking at the curtains, looking at the carpet, not looking at the bed.

'Nice,' he says. 'Bijou. Very cosy ... I guess I'm on the chair tonight.'

He tries to make it not sound like a challenge.

'I'm sorry,' I say. 'I need to get my clothes off and lie down.'

'OK,' he says, 'I'll just wait outside the—'

The word 'door' is swallowed by my mouth, as I spin him around and kiss him hard, on the lips. After a second he responds and his tongue slithers past my teeth. His mouth is hungry, sucking on my lips and then exploring my face.

His arms come up to encircle me. He holds me too hard and oh, the pain.

(**The glorious, glorious pain**)

My scarlet coat is removed, and his fingers curl under the straps of my dress.

'No,' I say.

He starts to move away, stung with rejection.

'I mean, no, not like this. Get your clothes off,' I say.

There is shock on his face, but only for a split second. He falls back on his haunches and pulls off his shirt, revealing that tidy physique of his. Hair wanders up from his pubic bone, up through his abdomen and spreads out across his chest, like a river becoming an estuary and meeting the ocean.

He moves nearer to me, and his body blots out the light from the dusty bulb.

'This OK?' he says.

Then, without letting his gaze fall from my eyes, he wriggles out of his trousers and underpants. He comes closer. I can feel something brushing, bumping against my thigh.

'OK,' I say, 'but not yet perfect.'

'Oh?'

'I want something more.'

'I'm glad.'

He doesn't expect what I say next.

'I want you to hurt me.'

'What?'

368

'I want you to hurt me. I want pain. I miss the pain.'

'You . . . miss the pain?'

'I've been thinking about the pain, ever since it went. The pain made me what I am. Now it's gone I can see it for what it is. A purifying thing. A purifying fire that's held me and burned everything away from me, everything except what's important.'

'So, what's important?'

I bulge my eyes at him and smile.

'You mean . . . me?'

'Of course I mean you. You appeared when I needed you.'

'I know. I feel that too.' He kisses me hungrily. I break away to speak.

'You were there, just like the pain. You made life complicated, but made it better in the end.'

'Yes,' he says, nuzzling my throat.

'You came to me, just like the pain, and turned my life into something real.'

His voice floats up from my right breast. 'That's right, I did. I came and then so did the pain, and we both . . . '

'. . . you both made me feel alive.'

'Exactly.'

'I want to feel alive with you. Not like I was with Dominic. Prove to me that I'm alive. Hit me. Hit me in the face.'

'What? No!' He looks up and recoils, but I keep the moment going. I grab his hand and force it into my cheek. It connects with a dry slapping sound.

'Hit me! Hit me, you bastard! Give me my pain back!'

He gives me a slap across the face, a half-hearted slap.

'What kind of man are you? Hit me! Hit me, you little coward.'

He gives me a hefty knock on the chin, and I can taste blood in my mouth.

I turn my back on him.

'Now push me down on the bed. Push me like you pushed me down those steps.'

He looks startled. 'I ... what? What steps? I don't know what you ...'

I turn with sudden energy and grip his wrists. 'Come on, Niall. Do you think I didn't know?'

'I ...'

'You following me around in your little car? Waiting outside my house? Looking for your moment?'

'You knew?'

'I knew you were there. I was waiting for you.'

'You were?'

'Of course I was. Wasn't it obvious? I was waiting for you to change my life. Why else would I stand there for you, all alone, on the edge? Think about it, Niall. Just think about it for a moment. Wasn't it obvious?'

Tears are sprouting from Niall's eyes. 'I didn't realise. Obvious ... Of course it was ... Obvious ... You wanted me to do it. Oh God. I ran. I wasted years ... I should have stayed ...'

'You should have stayed. But we're together now.' I turn again, back to him. 'So go on and push me! Like a man! Push me down on the bed. Push me hard and make me helpless, like I was with the pain.'

Niall pushes me in the small of my back, just like he had done five years ago. I pitch forward and the mattress swallows me up.

'Now do it quickly. Do it to me so quickly, like you're a hungry wolf, and you can't control yourself. Now! Quickly!'

He slides into me, deep and hard, and all of a sudden I'm screaming on the inside. My mind is raging with the pain, and it's all I can do not to howl. There's a strange man inside me; not Dominic. That's not happened since ... When? Since 1996?

Who was that with back then? I can't remember anything.

'Push me down. Tip me over the edge and let me fall. Make me helpless.'

'YES!' The wolf howls.

I can't think of anything now but the pain, and the relief.

It takes mere seconds. Niall accelerates, groans, and rears up on his hindquarters, and I feel a warmth inside me. His head flops on my shoulder, the inkwell beckons, and I threaten to fall down the rabbit hole.

My dress has stayed on. My breasts, belly and abdomen are still hidden from him.

'Shit,' he says.

'Now ask me if I'm all right,' I say.

'Are you all right?'

I say nothing.

'Are you all right?'

'No. Say it all together. Say: "Shit, are you all right?"'

'Shit. Are you all right?'

'It's perfect,' I say.

He falls off me, lands on the other side of bed, and it dips with his weight. I cling on to the mattress to stop myself rolling into him, and my thigh is damp.

'Was that OK?' he gasps, finally.

'As I said. Perfect,' I say. 'Just perfect.'

'So you didn't mind me . . .'

'How could I possibly mind?' I nibble his fingers. 'It can be our thing now. You can hurt me now. It can be our thing.'

'Yes.' His voice is tiny, like a child's, full of wonderment. 'It can be our thing.'

'Why don't you close the curtains? Give us a bit of privacy.'

'Of course,' he says brightly, and dances over to the window and stares, awestruck, out to the sea.

Dawn is coming up. One more dawn.

'So many seagulls,' he gasps. 'I'm sure there are much more of them now, than when I was a kid ... They're much bigger too, I swear it.'

'Niall, the curtains are still open! Show some modesty, for God's sake.'

I throw a pillow playfully at him, and he catches it. He dances around, going up to the window with his crotch covered by the pillow. He does a mock wave to non-existent bystanders below, and with a huge effort I laugh through the pain.

'Why don't you take a shower?' he says.

'No thank you. I just want to lie here and relax.'

'Do you mind if I take one?'

'No of course not.' He starts to the bathroom and I say, 'Oh. Before you get in ... We've no milk for tea. Can you slip on some clothes and grab us a pint from the shop?'

'Sure thing.' He puts his shirt on, extracts his jeans from the puddle of clothing on the floor, and slips those on too. He doesn't bother with his socks or underpants. And then he's at the door.

'Wait,' I say. 'Come here. A kiss before you go.'

Grinning, he trots back to the bed.

'No problem,' he smiles. And leans over, pushing his head next to mine.

This is when I go mad.

Monica

I fly at him, clawing and punching, grabbing at his face with my nails, channelling my pain into one furious onslaught.

He falls back, totally surprised. 'What the fuck? Monica, calm down!'

But I won't calm down. All my rage, all my fury, all the pain of the last five years bursts like a poisonous cyst and pours out of my face.

'Bastard!' I scream. 'Bastard bastard bastard! You fucking bastard! You fucking, cunting bastard! You fucking fucking *fucking* bastard!'

We both fall onto the thin carpet, and my spine jars on the floor, sending white hot knives into my pelvis.

He's on his back, his face already marked where my nails have drilled into his cheek. He is slapping my hands away from his face, trying to defend himself, but not too hard. He doesn't know what's going on. I know what's going through his mind.

(**I'm the mind reader this time**)

Is she mad? he's thinking. *Have the endless years of neuropathic pain sent her mad? Has she suddenly had an attack of guilt about leaving Dominic, and this is how she's dealing with it? Either way I'm in a hotel room with a screaming woman. I've got to calm things down or I'm in trouble.*

I know what he's going to do next, and I'm right. He grabs my wrists and rolls us both over so he's on top. He pins my wrists to the floor and sits astride me. The edges of the hotel room shiver and ripple around me, and I feel like I'm being held underwater. I struggle and shriek until my voice sounds like a scratched record. 'You did this to me! You did it! Bastard bastard bastard!'

He's strong. God, he's strong. He brings one knee forward to pin my right arm to the floor, freeing his left hand which he tries to clamp over my mouth.

'Monica, what's wrong? What's wrong with you? Do you need anything? Do you need your drugs? Have you taken something?'

I go limp; he relaxes, just a bit, then I bring my knee up into his bollocks, and my teeth sink deep into his hand. He howls and lashes out, punching me. The pain of his fist against my nose is the deepest, warmest most glorious pain I've ever experienced.

Niall says 'Jesus Christ', and the weight of him on my body is gone. I fall back to the floor. He is scrabbling to his feet, but he stops, stunned, mouth open.

The gun is already in my hand.

Niall says 'Jesus Christ' again.

Monica

Niall stares stupidly at the gun. I've wrapped the barrel in one of his socks. It looks quite comical.

'Jesus Christ,' is all he's managing to say.

The gun is so heavy; I can barely hold it. I scramble up into the chair and rest it on the arm. I am shaking so much and my teeth are chattering. I place both hands around the gun to keep it steady and keep it upright.

'So you pushed me down the steps. I just wanted to make sure.'

The wolf is cornered, he looks right and left. Left and right.

He speaks at last. 'Sorry . . . What? I don't know what you mean.'

'Of course you don't.'

'I pushed you . . . where?'

'Down those steps.'

'What steps?'

'Down the steps. The bloody steps! You know what I mean! The car park steps! You pushed me, and that is why I've spent the last five years in fucking agony!'

Finally he says: 'None of this is true, Monica.'

'What?'

He keeps his voice calm. 'I don't know what you just heard, but I didn't say I pushed anybody. Is this something to do with your accident?'

'Of course it is!'

'Then I'm afraid . . . It's the drugs, Monica, they're making you think things. You're creating a fictional world, which makes sense to you. You can't cope with your husband betraying you, so you're making me into the villain.'

The sock-covered handle of the gun feels slippery in my hand. Niall shimmers and blurs, as my eyes fill with water.

Is that true? I think. *Is what he just said true? Did he not just admit he pushed me down the steps?*

Did I just manufacture the last few minutes because I so want to find the person who pushed me?

Did I?

Because it's so important to my plan, and because I so need it to be Niall, that I just made up his confession in my head?

'I think you want someone to blame,' he says. 'And your subconscious mind seems to have settled on me.'

'Nice try,' I say at last. 'You know the inside of my head is scrambled. It's very tempting to exploit that.'

Niall still has a mock-puzzled look. 'But this is the first I've heard about any car park steps. I honestly don't know what you're talking about.'

'You're a very good actor, Niall. Of course you are. That's what I saw in you. I'm good at spotting acting talent, and that's why I took you on. But acting is just lying. Lies can be very effective for a short while, but you can only do one at a time. The problem is, when old lies pile up around your feet, it's harder to add new ones.'

'Listen, Monica, what I just said was true. We were just making love and you went *crazy*. Are you OK?'

I'm still imagining what's in his head. *OK, no sudden moves,* he's probably thinking. *This can be saved. I can turn this around.*

'As I said, too many lies, and people stop believing you. You are the original little boy who cried wolf, you know that? For example, I know you're not an osteopath.' I giggle. 'More like a psychopath. You're just an actor who does a bit of personal training on the side. You don't even work in that hotel. You hired a room, and you used the facilities as a paying guest, to feel me up. Clever of you.'

'I wasn't feeling you up. I just wanted to help you.'

Niall is slowly moving towards the bathroom. He's trying to put the wall between us.

'Stay where you are!' I scream.

He stops. 'I was just—'

'Shut up and listen to me. How could I have been so stupid? I even saw you in adverts on daytime telly, jogging and cleaning a kitchen, and I thought it was my fantasies about you coming to life! Fuck!'

The gun is so heavy. So very heavy.

'And there's something else you've forgotten, Niall. Five years ago. You said, "Shit, are you all right?" right after you left me broken on those steps. That's what you said. "Shit, are you all right?"'

'I told you, I didn't—'

'My memory is like Swiss cheese, but I definitely remember you saying that, because it was so important to me, deep down. It's stayed in my dreams. It's lain there, sitting like a key to a box. And once I started picturing you on that roof behind me, I was struck by your voice, how familiar the voice was, how those words sounded like you saying them. Of course I could have been making a false connection in my overheated brain, so I got you to say those words, just now. And it was you. It was you on that car park roof, Niall.'

'You're mistaken.'

'It was definitely you. I'm as certain of that fact as I am certain of anything.'

I wonder what's in his head now. I can't stop thinking about the cogs in his head. *Time to go into damage limitation mode.* That's what he's thinking.

There's no way she's not going to be persuaded that I didn't push her. She's not going to let me go. Even if I get out of here, she's going to call the police.

I don't want to talk to the police. That's what he's thinking.

Time to talk her around. Time to adjust the truth again.

Sure enough . . .

'OK, look,' he says, his eyes tearing up. 'I know I should have told you before. It was a stupid accident. I'm so sorry, but that's all it was. I saw you on the roof, and I went to greet you. I put my hand on your shoulder and I startled you . . .'

He covers his eyes, as if to hide tears.

'God, you don't think I haven't gone through that horrible moment a thousand times in my head? I mean, if only I'd *said something* to you before I put my hand on your shoulder, perhaps you wouldn't have jumped so badly, but it happened, and when it happened, I got scared, and I ran. I'm not proud of myself, but I ran away like a coward. I felt so *bad* at what happened, Monica, you have to believe me. When I saw you in the gym, it was so providential. Just ... a miracle, that you'd drawn yourself to me, just when I was in a position to help you.'

He runs his finger through his hair wearily. (**It's a brilliant performance**)

'Of *course* I told you I was an osteopath. You would hardly let me work on your body if I told you I was just some actor with a few basic massage skills, would you? And of course, I didn't let on I was there, during your fall. I think that would have been an impossible conversation to have, don't you?'

He smiles, (**the most genuine fake smile I've ever seen**).

'So look, that's the plain honest truth. I'm standing here asking for forgiveness. All I'm guilty of is trying to make amends, Monica. That's all I was trying to do. I couldn't undo what I'd done, so I was trying to atone, the best I can, for what had happened.'

'So it was a miracle, was it?' I say. 'Us meeting up in the gym?'

'I'm not a religious person,' he says. 'But it seems like a miracle to me.'

'I'm sorry, I didn't frame the question correctly. I'll try again. So it was just a coincidence, was it? Us meeting up in the gym?'

His eyes grow cold. *Where is she going with this? What have I said now?* That's what I can see in those eyes.

I stand up, holding the gun. I don't know how, but I do. I walk over to my suitcase, pull out a plastic wallet from it, and extract a sheaf of papers. I throw them carelessly up in the air, and they fall down around Niall's shoulders like fat snowflakes.

Niall looks down at the printed sheets, mystified.

'What are these?'

'Photos of me, Niall. Taken by a private detective.'

'O ... K ...'

'In the first year after the accident, my husband had me followed by a private detective.'

'What? He had you followed? Why?'

'It doesn't fucking matter why. That's not important now. Can you see, Niall? Can you see, in all those photos? What can you see?'

He's looking and he can see a car. He can see his car. It's parked not far from me when I'm walking down a road. He can see his car again, edging into the corner of another frame, parked near a café where I was sitting. And he can see himself in a park, sitting on a bench, looking at me on the next bench. Watching me weep and trying to feed the pigeons.

I sink back into the chair and wave my hand at the bits of paper. 'So there you are. And there you are, *and ooh*! There you are *again*! Funny that. My husband didn't even know you existed, but it was him who caught you, he did it for me, even though that's the very last thing he wanted. My life is one fat irony.'

I go and sit back in the chair. Some of the bits of paper have landed on it. I daren't turn away from Niall to brush them off, so they crinkle against my bottom as I lower myself down.

'So you were *never* an osteopath, and you *did* push me, and it *wasn't* just a chance encounter. I told you about lies piling up, Niall. Oh. And here's another one. I talked to Karen Willikins, my old assistant. Surprise surprise! I wasn't even your agent at the time, was I? I'm guessing ... correct me if I'm wrong, that I sacked you, and you got mad at being sacked, and when you saw me on the car park roof, alone and defenceless, you took your petty, small-minded revenge? Is that it? Is it as simple and as grubby as that?'

My goading is working. He draws himself up, angry now. He really is the big bad wolf, now. His nostrils are flaring; he is ready to huff and puff and blow my house down.

Here it comes now, I think. *Here comes the truth.*

'I love you! Don't you get it?' he yells. 'I loved you from the

379

start! I knew that I was the best thing for you! Better than that . . . husband of yours. I heard you shout at him on the phone! Calling him useless and everything else under the sun! He wasn't good enough for you, and I knew I was! I saw, with my own eyes, how much better I was for you.'

Back and forth he goes, pacing, growling, snapping at me.

I'm stunned by what he's saying. Is he saying that my injury is my fault? *Yes, he thinks that. He's convinced himself of it. Don't let him persuade you it's true. It's not your fault.*

'And you know it too, deep down! You've brought me here to trap me, but you didn't! If you're honest, really honest, deep down, you *know* you brought me here to free yourself!'

I flinch. *He's right. He sees it.*

'I know it! I can see it in your face! You *know* you've brought me here to replace him! You're using me so you can move on and leave it all behind!'

He's right again. I gasp with the awful realisation of what I'm doing.

'No . . .' I say.

'Yes! Yes you are! I mean, so what if you know the truth now? Nothing's really changed, has it? So what if I did follow you? I followed you because I *loved* you! So what if I did push you? I pushed you because I *loved* you! Because I saw you were getting trapped in a terrible marriage, trapped by having a child with . . . him!'

He's crying now – properly crying, not just pretend – and his nose is starting to run.

'Everything – *everything* – that's happened to you has been for the *best*! You said in the pub that the pain made you into a better Monica. And you just said, just now, when we were making love, that the pain came into your life, and I came into your life, to strip everything bad away, like a fire, and you might tell yourself that it was a lie to trap me, and you don't believe it, but you do believe it! Together, the pain and me, we have stripped away everything that's wrong about your life, your horrible job, your lousy friends, and yes, your fat husband too! He was wasting your life, leeching off you, failing you, and the only way you could see it was all wrong was by having the pain! By having *me*! I came into your life to show you what a supportive caring man could be! You hugged me. You cried. You accepted my help.' He's crying now, sobbing angrily. '*You need me!*'

I do need him. (**He knows**) I do need him.

'And now you're better, we can start a new life. We can move on and go to France and ...'

That snaps me back into focus.

'You idiot,' I say.

'Don't call me an idiot.'

'You fucking idiot.' I laugh.

'Don't laugh at me.'

He even moves towards me, before I twitch the gun in my hand.

'You see, Niall, I'm good at lies too. Do you really think I'm all right? Do you really think the pain has gone? Do you think the pain can be wished away just like that? I'm still up to my fucking neck in pain ...'

I stand up, flick off the straps of my dress, and show him my nakedness. I show him what's beneath. Big ugly patches, covering the front of my body; across my breasts, my belly, my abdomen.

'I'm drowning myself in morphine patches just to be here, Niall. I'm barely able to keep conscious fighting the pain, and *you didn't even notice*? I just pretended to be over the damn pain to lull a simple-minded fool like you into admitting you pushed me down those steps.'

I laugh again, my cruellest laugh. The one I used to use a lot. Before the pain.

'I've spent five years learning that lesson, that pain can't be wished away with a magic cure. I told you that before, and you didn't bother to listen. I just had to tell you I was cured and you believed it, because you just heard what you want to hear. Because that's how you go through life, just hearing what you want to hear.

'Well listen to this, Niall. And listen hard. I hate you. I hate you more than anyone else I've ever hated. More than the friends who left me, the Atos man, the stupid people who never understood, even the darkest moments when I despised my husband ... It is nothing, NOTHING to the concentrated, everlasting hate I feel for you now.' There is a new expression on Niall's face, but I'm too angry to care. 'You made me like this! Like a mad scientist makes a monster! You ran, and you left me in agony, and then you waited a while, and then you put your filthy hands on my body and relieved a tiny bit of that agony. You little shit. You plunged me into the fires of hell, and you sold me an electric fan.'

'You've still got the pain?'

'Yes, didn't you hear me? Aren't you listening?'

'I am.'

'Well hooray for that!'

'It's just,' he says slowly, 'if you do have your pain ... I would severely doubt you have enough strength to pull that trigger.'

(**Finally**)

He's thinking, *Perhaps it's simplest that I should kill her.*

But this is not the way I planned this. So I raise the gun, and shout: 'This is for Dominic!'

'Dominic' is my safe word.

He gives a bellow of pure frustrated rage, and rushes to take the gun.

Monica

Suddenly, the hotel room is a scene from bedlam.

The door bursts open and they both rush into the room. Someone runs forward and blocks my aim. All I can see is the word POLICE emblazoned on the pocket.

Someone else screams in Niall's face, 'Get out of here, you idiot! She's trying to kill you! Run! We'll deal with her! Get out!'

Niall's face is a picture. He starts to speak . . .

'Get out of here!' she screams again. 'Run as far from here as you can, and don't look back!'

. . . thinks better of it, and dashes out.

Monica

I am back on the bed. I am trying to imagine Niall running, terrified, from the bed and breakfast, past the bemused clerk, and into the street.

'Are you all right, Mon?' Angelina's voice is soft, a whisper.

The pain is screaming in my ears, but my spirits are fluttering high, high above me. Now I'm imagining Niall running along the street in his bare feet, with his shirt flapping behind him. I'm imagining the silent, circular eyes of the CCTV camera capturing his panicked little form as he runs, thinking his life is in mortal danger. Thinking how lucky the police were there to save him.

'Darling?' Angelina hisses. She takes off her police hat and runs towards me, her face knotted with concern, but I shake my head. 'Don't touch me, Lena. Evidence ...'

She understands, and backs off, looking me up and down.

'Jesus, Mon. Was this all worth it?'

I don't answer the question. 'You look very nice in a police uniform.'

'It has been said,' she says, but her eyes are sad.

Larry is there too. He looks comical, dressed as Dixon of Dock Green. I try to laugh, but my voice is going. The last vestige of morphine is draining from my system, and it's reminding me why I'm here. My system is shutting. Down.

His gloved hand is holding the pillow I threw at Niall. 'Are you sure you want this, Sunflower?'

Angelina bursts into tears.

'I'm sorry,' I croak. 'And I understand why you kept everything from me, when the drugs were in my head, and I couldn't remember. I understand. Truly I do. But this is the real me. And this is what the real me wants.'

I try to dial a number on my mobile, but I can't.

'Please, Lena ... Last number I called ... Just press redial.'

She does, and holds the phone to my ear.

'Hi,' I say, my voice barely a whisper.

'Monica,' says DI Geoff Marks on the end of the phone. 'Your husband's been telling me this story ...'

'I want to drop all charges against my husband.'

'Monica—'

'And I want to talk to him.'

'I can't—'

'Now.'

There is a brief pause, and my husband comes on the line. My beautiful, gentle, useless husband. Who I pity, love and adore in equal measure.

'Monica, don't do this.'

'Please.'

'I love you.'

'I know. And I love you. I forgive you. Please forgive me.'

'Monica . . .'

'No more words, Dominic. Just goodbye. That's all. Sorry about everything. And goodbye.'

'OK. Love you lots.'

'No . . . love *you* . . . lots.'

I am so suffused with pain that I can't speak any more. My voice is a ghost. Dominic provides the script for both of us.

'You hang up.'

Silence.

'No *you* hang up.'

Silence.

'No *you* hang up.'

Silence.

'No you.'

Silence.

'Brrrrrrrrr.'

Silence.

I press the button with the last of my strength. I hang up.

I lie back on the bed. Somewhere, from a million miles away, I can hear voices discussing things. Things not intended for my ears. Was it my mother? *How could you have been so stupid, Adrian?* Were they muttering about where to bury the rabbit? Where to put my capsaicin patch? No more. Not again. No more treatments. No more painkillers. No more false dawns.

No. They weren't talking about Jumpy the rabbit, or treatments. They were talking about me.

'I'll do it, Buttercup. You don't have to do this.'

'No, it's fine, Larry. She always wanted me to do it. I promised. I said I would. I owe this to her, yeah?'

'No, Buttercup. We'll do it together.'

And then I see a cloud. A lovely cloud held by two chubby hands along one corner, and slender hands along the other. I can see the ghost of black fingernails inside the surgical gloves. And there is something so soft and warm on my face.

So soft.

So warm.

'Goodnight, Mon. Goodnight, my lovely Monica.'

I think I'll go to sleep now.

EPILOGUE

DI Geoff Marks only saw Dominic twice more after that interview. The first time was during the trial, when Niall Stewart got convicted for Monica's murder.

Of course he got convicted; how could he not? His DNA was on the pillow that suffocated her, the gashes on her cheek, the marks on her arm, the semen inside her body, just everywhere. There was CCTV footage of Niall running from the bed and breakfast, and other bits of footage from motorway cameras showing their journey to Dover in Monica's car.

Things were discovered in Niall's flat. Souvenirs of Monica. Items of clothing. His wife was brought in as a hostile character witness and gave a scathing testimony about the oddness of his character. It all cemented the image in the jury's mind of Niall as a dangerous sociopath, who sweet-talked his way into Monica's life.

Niall's story, that Monica had been alive when he left her, and there were police who suddenly turned up out of the blue ... Well, it was logged and recorded, but without physical evidence or motive it sounded madly implausible. His barrister told him not to repeat the story during the trial. Particularly the bit about Monica holding a gun on him. It wouldn't come across well. It showed a lack of sympathy for the victim.

His barrister grasped a long straw, a theory that Monica's husband was behind the murder, and put Dominic on the stand. He was cross-examined about the incident four years ago, about the time he asked people in a pub to kill his wife. Dominic repeated his story – and this time Geoff supported his testimony – that it was just a kinky game between husband and wife.

Dominic cried a lot, but he recovered enough to quite reasonably point out that he had no idea where his wife was during her murder. Monica had fled the family home in a great hurry, with her new muscle-bound lover in tow. He was very angry at her betrayal, yes, but even if he wanted to do her any harm, he was languishing in police custody at the time.

Geoff was called to the stand and stood there, stiff and awkward in his full uniform, and explained that Mr Wood had been interviewed because he resembled a man who tried to buy a gun in Woolwich. It turned out to be mistaken identity, so Mr Wood was released without charge.

Dominic added one more thing to his testimony. Shortly before her death, his wife rang him on her mobile, to say sorry; about everything. She left him heartbroken, but he appreciated the final apology from her.

The jury took forty minutes to deliver their verdict: guilty.

DCI Geoff Marks saw Dominic just once more, a few years later, on a cold autumn day in North Kensington. He was driving in plain clothes, just after getting his promotion. He was not on duty, just looking for a decent beer garden and allowing the weak sunshine to find his face through the rooftops. He was enjoying thinking of moving to Cambridge, imagining himself driving around in a shiny vintage car, and arresting crusty old dons in their caps and gowns.

He saw a glimpse of someone he recognised, just a flash through the railings, and he stopped the car straight away.

He heard the squeals of the kids even before he rounded the greenery and saw the park. A lot different to his day, where you just had swings and slides, and if you fell off, you had hard tarmac to break your fall. There were huge multicoloured monstrosities, looming over the place like H.G. Wells's Martians.

Dominic was sitting on the bench with a woman, and they were both watching a little boy grapple with ropes on the far corner. Geoff watched the boy wrestle his way to the top of a huge cat's cradle and give a cheery mittened wave to them both.

Geoff felt the letter in his pocket, where he still kept it close. Monica's letter. Dominic gave it to him, after his police interview.

Dear Dominic

I am sorry I have to write this, but not as sorry as I feel that you have to read this.

I've found the man who pushed me, and it was thanks to you. I'm going to make him pay for murdering me five years ago, and for killing that future life we were trying to make together. Just like I said I would.

This is my choice, and if you love me you'll stay silent, and you will burn this, and let justice – true natural justice in the eyes of your God – take its course.

If you choose not to, then I will be dead, you will be poor, and he will go unpunished. I don't think that's what the Lord has planned for us all. Do you?

By the time you read this I will be dead. Do not grieve for me, for I am now without pain. When we meet again it will be wondrous for both of us.

Yours truly for ever,

Monica

Dominic told Geoff that he could do what he wanted with it. Burn it, show it as evidence, whatever. He was the law, after all. Dominic took the decision out of his hands and put it into Geoff's. *I suppose Monica was right; her husband was a bit weak.* Judging by the fact the letter was still in his pocket, Geoff was forced to admit that he was a bit weak too.

The woman turned to look at Dominic, and Geoff was struck by how like Monica she looked, the same dark hair, the same pale complexion. She was beautiful, and looked at him for just a second, and it was a look of love, sure it was, but it was also something else. Geoff had seen that look on coppers' faces loads of times.

Searching, investigating.

Then the boy took a tumble, crashing to earth with a jolt. He wailed, loudly and angrily, with a child's lack of shame, and the woman leapt up and ran to him, dragging him upright, dusting him down, inspecting his knee, kissing his tears and taking the pain away.

Dominic stayed on the bench, watching the scene with concern. Once he realised that everything was OK, and the boy hadn't broken any bones, he turned his head away, and his eyes fixed on Geoff's.

They stared at each other for a long time. Or it felt like a long time. It was probably just a few seconds. And then there was the tiniest ghost of a smile on Dominic's face, then he mouthed something.

Thou shalt not bear false witness.

Then he turned his face away and looked back at the boy, who was already climbing back up the climbing frame, and whooping on top of the world.

And then Geoff looked away too, and left.

AFTERWORD

Have no fear, gentle reader, Monica is still alive and kicking. Because there is another 'Monica' somewhere. Everywhere. There is probably a 'Monica' in your street. The odds make it likely.

There are hundreds and thousands of Monicas across the world, all types, all ages, all suffering from neuropathic pain, and most of them suffer in silence. What would be the point in suffering noisily? They'd just be irritating their family and friends.

The 'Monica' I came to know inspired this book. She had an accident and ended up in extreme pain. The facts of the accident aren't important. It doesn't really matter how and why it happened. She could have had a car accident, got struck down with cancer or found herself in a warzone – the point is she, like so many others, ended up in constant unremitting pain.

Somehow she carried on, because that seemed to be the best alternative. But not the only one. I'd be lying if she hadn't spent some of those long nights with a big pile of pills and a bottle of whisky, contemplating another path, but she's still here, with the help of family, friends and, yes, painkillers.

She was a willing guinea pig for the capsaicin treatment when it was in its experimental stages, and it did relieve some of the pain

391

for a short time. I'm glad to say that, thanks to her and others like her, capsaicin has been rolled out on the NHS for more sufferers of chronic pain.

Her Angry Friend never completely goes away, but 'Monica' lives in hope.

This book is for her, and for those brave enough to decide to live with pain.

And for those brave enough to decide not to.

N. J. Fountain
February 2015

ACKNOWLEDGEMENTS

Thanks to...

Nicola Bryant, for saying in 2007 'let's write a movie about a woman who has had an accident and who thinks someone tried to kill her'. Thanks to her for allowing this book to rise from those ashes, for her encouragement, her ideas and her proofreading, and Monica's poem. This book would not be here without Nicola, and *Painkiller* is as much hers as mine.

Piers Blofeld, for his faith in my work, and putting me out there, and all at Sheil Land for their efforts.

John Lawton, for his friendship and help.

Katharine Vile and Simon Trewin, for leading me to Piers.

Andrew McGrouther, who advised on matters of policing. Any procedural howlers can be fully attributed to me and not him.

Catherine Burke for seeing the potential. Thalia Proctor, Jo Wickham, Emma Williams and Liz Hatherell, and all at Little Brown for being 'Team Fountain'.

Tom Jamieson, for his support and creativity.